How long would it take before she felt completely Amish?

There must be a way to smother her past at the same time she built her future. *Then you could be the perfect Amish wife Isaac is looking for*, Rachel thought before she could halt it.

He considered her a *gut* candidate for his perfect wife, and she had to find a way to persuade him she wasn't. It'd be simple if she didn't want to protect their friendship.

She didn't want to dash his hopes as her own had been when she'd discovered her late husband's first love was his military career. She couldn't fault him. He'd never pretended to be something he wasn't.

As she was.

No! She was a plain *mamm* with two sweet daughters who wanted to help in the recovery of the flood-torn village. What she'd been in the past was in the past. What she was now was what she wanted to be in the future, but she was struggling to find her way each day.

Which made her the worst choice for Isaac to marry.

Jo Ann Brown has always loved stories with happily-ever-after endings. A former military officer, she is thrilled to have the chance to write stories about people falling in love. She is also a photographer and travels with her husband of more than thirty years to places where she can snap pictures. They have three children and live in Florida. Drop her a note at joannbrownbooks.com.

Carrie Lighte lives in Massachusetts next door to a Mennonite farming family, and she frequently spots deer, foxes, fisher cats, coyotes and turkeys in her backyard. Having enjoyed traveling to several Amish communities in the eastern United States, she looks forward to visiting settlements in the western states and in Canada. When she's not reading, writing or researching, Carrie likes to hike, kayak, bake and play word games.

JO ANN BROWN

An Amish Mother's Secret Past

&

CARRIE LIGHTE

Her Amish Suitor's Secret

LOVE INSPIRED
INSPIRATIONAL ROMANCE

Recycling programs
for this product may
not exist in your area.

LOVE INSPIRED®
INSPIRATIONAL ROMANCE

ISBN-13: 978-1-335-46292-3

An Amish Mother's Secret Past and Her Amish Suitor's Secret

Copyright © 2022 by Harlequin Enterprises ULC

An Amish Mother's Secret Past
First published in 2020. This edition published in 2022.
Copyright © 2020 by Jo Ann Ferguson

Her Amish Suitor's Secret
First published in 2020. This edition published in 2022.
Copyright © 2020 by Carrie Lighte

For questions and comments about the quality of this book, please contact us at CustomerService@Harlequin.com.

Harlequin Enterprises ULC
22 Adelaide St. West, 41st Floor
Toronto, Ontario M5H 4E3, Canada
www.LoveInspired.com

Printed in U.S.A.

CONTENTS

AN AMISH MOTHER'S
SECRET PAST

Jo Ann Brown

This is for you, Rachael. I can't wait for the day when you sign your first published book for me!

And they shall beat their swords into plowshares,
and their spears into pruninghooks:
nation shall not lift up sword against nation,
neither shall they learn war any more.
—*Isaiah* 2:4

Chapter One

The day couldn't get any worse, ain't so?

Rachel Yoder prayed the answer was "no" as she pushed the stroller with her two sick *kinder* along the sidewalk edging the village green. She was supposed to be helping at the day-care center today to offset the fees for her daughters' care, but instead was taking Loribeth and Eva to the *doktor* because both were running a low-grade fever.

The little girls had been fussy from the time they'd awakened an hour before dawn. Loribeth, who was almost three years old and had hair as black as Rachel's, had her thumb in her mouth, a habit she'd given up six months ago. Rachel hadn't said anything to the toddler, because she knew sucking her thumb was giving her some comfort while she was feeling lousy. Eva, a year younger and with eyes the same warm blue as her *mamm*'s, was hunched into a pitiful ball on her side of the stroller. The September morning wasn't chilly, but the two-year-old shivered as if it was the middle of January and clutched her stuffed bear close to her. She wrapped her finger in a string from her bright blue bonnet.

Looking at them, suffering and sick, broke Rachel's heart. The pace of her steps increased as she walked across the village green. She watched for holes in the grass so the stroller didn't bounce and make the girls feel worse.

"We're almost there," she said, though she doubted the girls were paying any attention to her. They were too lost in their misery.

A few cars moved along the steep street flanking the green. The trees cast long shadows toward the western mountains, and a few leaves crunched under her black sneakers. She tilted the stroller over the curb and hurried along the sidewalk toward the center of Evergreen Corners.

The *doktor*'s office was new, having opened in mid-August. It was staffed two days a week and was affiliated with the hospital in Rutland, which was more than an hour and a half north of Evergreen Corners. The office was sandwiched between the village's diner and an antique shop on the far side of the bridge spanning Washboard Brook. The brook, which had become a torrent during the hurricane last October, was now so low that only the flattest stones were covered with water.

Traffic was busier across the bridge, so she waited for the walk light before she crossed the route that ran north and south. Hearing a moan from the stroller, Rachel paused and bent to check on her girls. They were holding hands as if trying to comfort each other. Tears filled her eyes. Their family was a small one—her and the girls since her husband's death. The tragedy had changed their lives, though she doubted the toddlers were aware of the depth of their loss yet. They simply knew their *daed* wasn't at home.

After tucking the blanket around them, she straightened. Her eyes widened when she saw someone else crossing the road. He was tall—so tall she doubted her head would top his shoulder. He wore a straw hat atop his sun-streaked caramel hair that fluttered in the breeze. She knew his eyes were the dark brown of muddy soil, though she couldn't discern that because the brim of his hat shadowed his face.

He walked toward her with his purposeful stride. It always suggested he was in the midst of something important, and everyone should get out of his way.

Isaac Kauffman was the unofficial leader of the Amish volunteers in the village. He worked under the auspices of Amish Helping Hands, the group that coordinated with plain communities to assist at disaster sites, and he had found many of the volunteers himself. She'd heard some *Englisch* volunteers call him "Mr. It's Gotta," a shortened version of "Mr. It's Gotta Be Perfectly Square." Apparently *it's gotta be perfectly square* was a phrase he used often while laying out the forms for concrete cellars. Despite their teasing, it appeared the volunteers appreciated his dedication, and he inspired everyone to make their own work match his expert foundations.

He displayed an air of arrogance few Amish men did. Her *daed* had conveyed the same silent message of believing he was better than the people around him. For his older daughter, he'd made it clear she could never meet his expectations, no matter how hard she tried. She'd struggled year after year, desperate for his approval. She'd given up and run away several times. The last time she'd jumped the fence and moved into the *Englisch* world with a vengeance.

Now...

She didn't have time to complete the thought before Isaac's path intersected hers.

"Gute mariye." His deep voice resonated like the sound of heavy machinery.

She replied to his good-morning, but other words dried in her mouth. Isaac Kauffman intimidated her, though she'd long ago vowed she wouldn't let anyone daunt her. She'd made the pledge while surrounded by loud, powerful men and women. Isaac was not loud. In the four months since his younger sister, Abby, had introduced them after Rachel's arrival in Evergreen Corners, Rachel had never once heard him raise his voice. He didn't need to. When Isaac Kauffman had something to say, everyone paused to listen. He was a man who didn't demand respect, but he received it.

In that important way, he was unlike *Daed*. She wished she could stop comparing her *daed*, Manassas Yoder, to Isaac Kauffman. She couldn't, because the aura Isaac projected raised her hackles before he said a single word. Like a *mamm* hawk, she bristled at his approach, determined to protect her young daughters from what she'd endured for too many years. She wasn't being fair to him, but she didn't care. Loribeth and Eva were too precious to her to risk them being hurt, as she'd been.

So she continued to be tongue-tied whenever she was around him. She'd found ways to avoid him or would just say a few words in passing, because she could manage a greeting, but nothing more.

Why couldn't he be more like his sister, Abby? Abby was outgoing, approachable and open, though she was as dedicated to helping as her brother was. It was difficult sometimes to remember the two were siblings. Isaac was almost ten years older than his sister. That made him about five years younger than Rachel.

"Are you heading to the community center?" Isaac asked when she didn't say anything else.

"No."

His eyebrows lowered at her terse answer, but he recovered and gave her a cool smile. "I thought you could take a message to my sister for me, but if you're not headed that way, I can—"

Loribeth threw up, spewing in Isaac's direction.

"Oh, no!" Rachel cried.

She reached to turn Loribeth away from him, but Eva began to vomit, too. The *kinder* sobbed, and their faces twisted with pain. Pulling tissues from her purse she dabbed at their gray faces. She jumped, unable to halt herself, when another round of sickness erupted from the girls. She leaned both of her *kinder* back so their lolling heads rested against the supporting wall of the stroller.

"Are they all right?" Isaac asked from behind her.

"They woke up sick this morning." Why did his simple question make her feel inadequate? "We're going to the *doktor*'s office."

"Is there anything I can do?"

She gasped when she saw his boots were covered with what had been in her daughter's stomach. *God, why did You let her throw up on* Isaac Kauffman?

It'd been accidental, she reminded herself. Isaac was being gracious, though she wondered if he'd ever had to deal with such a thing before. She couldn't imagine him—even as a little boy—getting sick on someone else. He was too exacting, never seemed to make a mistake.

Or so she'd heard the other volunteers say when they came in for meals.

She shuddered as she recalled how strict her parents had been. Any mistake she'd made—even the simplest, most innocent one—had been deemed as dire as the most vile sin. Each was punished with lashings from a belt or by being denied meals, and each had led to her becoming more rebellious.

Don't question the reasons behind someone else's kindness, she warned herself. *Be grateful God sent help.*

Ja, that was how she must look at Isaac's unexpected assistance. As a gift from God at the moment she needed it most. Would Isaac have been solicitous if he'd known the truth about her *kinder*'s parents? How would he have reacted if he'd known that four years ago, Rachel and her late husband had been serving with the United States Army in Afghanistan?

* * *

Hearing Rachel's dismayed apology, Isaac looked at his splattered boots. "Don't worry. I can assure you they've been covered in worse."

He'd hoped Rachel would laugh at his jest, but she kept saying how sorry she was. Never before had he heard her string so many words together. Abby had assured him Rachel wasn't shy around everyone, and that she chattered like an eager squirrel while working in the community center where the volunteers took their meals. She'd always been quiet in his company.

He wanted to put his hands on her shoulders and urge her to calm herself. Her *bopplin* were screwing up their adorable, pudgy faces, and he didn't want three females crying in front of him. He knew too well how *kinder* could be, because he'd raised his younger brothers and sister after their *mamm* died and *Daed* had sought consolation in the bottom of a bottle he thought Isaac didn't know he kept hidden in the barn.

Isaac had met Rachel several times at the community center's kitchen. She had the blackest hair he'd ever seen, without a hint of silver, though she looked to be in her middle thirties, around his age. The color was as if the night sky had been stripped of its stars, but their glow had been left behind. When she glanced at him as she tried to clean her *kinder*, he realized her eyes were almost the same vivid blue as the sheen of September sunlight on the hair in front of her pleated, box-shaped *kapp*.

Her face, however, was almost as colorless as her *kinder*'s. Was she ill, too?

"Can I help?" he asked.

"No!" She sounded as appalled at the idea as she had when her little girl had thrown up on his boots. She squared her shoulders, then added, "*Danki*, Isaac, but that's not necessary. I know you're busy. Like I said, we're on our way to the *doktor*, and he'll give them something to settle their stomachs."

"I'll pray for quick healing for them."

"I'm sure it's some twenty-four-hour bug, but their fevers worry me. *Danki* for offering. Again, I'm sorry—"

"It's okay, Rachel." He bent toward the stroller to tuck in an end of the blanket covering the *kinder*.

He froze when he looked into eyes as deep a brown as his own. The words he'd been about to say, that he wished Rachel and her little ones well, disappeared when he saw the entreaty in the older girl's eyes. Why was the *kind* looking at him like that? She didn't know him.

Sorrow pinched him as he remembered hearing the *kinder*'s *daed* was dead, leaving his pretty widow with two *bopplin*. Did the little girl long for a man to comfort her when she was ill? Did the *kind* remember her *daed*?

He sighed. Though there had been many years when he'd wished his *daed* had been different, he wouldn't have traded a single day with him. *Daed* had remarried and given up drinking. The jovial man Isaac recalled from his youth was back. It was a treasured gift, one these little girls would never experience because their *daed* wouldn't return.

"Is there something else, Isaac?"

At Rachel's question, he realized he'd been lost too

long in his thoughts. Standing straighter, he said, "Let me walk with you to the *doktor*'s office."

"That's not necessary."

"If they start throwing up, you may need help."

When she hesitated, he couldn't help wondering if he'd done something to offend her.

Learn to do well; seek judgment, relieve the oppressed, judge the fatherless, plead for the widow. The verse from the first chapter of Isaiah rang through his mind. It was one he'd learned from his mentor, Clyde Felter, when he was a boy and had followed Clyde around while the wizened mason taught him how to work with stone and concrete. Clyde had liked to quote Scripture, and his favorite verses had to do with helping those who were in need.

If Clyde had been standing beside him, the old man would have insisted Isaac do what was right. What was right, Isaac knew, was overruling Rachel's polite refusal for his assistance.

Isaac took the stroller's handle and motioned for Rachel to lead the way to the *doktor*'s office. She didn't move for a long moment, then nodded. *Gut!* She could be sensible. He chided himself for his impatience. She was anxious about her *kinder*'s health. What a *gut mamm* she was!

The type of *mamm* he hoped to have for his *kinder* when he was able to purchase a farm and settle down with a wife and family. He pushed aside that thought. His family still needed his assistance at their farm in northeast Vermont. His youngest brother, Herman, should be taking over soon, and then Isaac could move ahead with his plans.

As they walked over the bridge, Isaac glanced at the buildings on either side of the street. Most near the brook had been damaged during the flood, but only the massive brick factory building remained closed. It was scheduled to open next month, almost a year after Hurricane Kevin had sent a wall of water crashing through the village. To the north, along a slow curve in Washboard Brook, he could see the half skeleton of the covered bridge. It wouldn't be rebuilt soon because the list of bridges needing repair or replacement in central Vermont was long. Fortunately, the highway bridge in the center of town had been repaired.

When Rachel paused by what once must have been a private home, which was set in the shadow of a huge Victorian with an antique store on the main floor, he saw the plaque announcing the small building housed the Evergreen Corners Medical Clinic. The white cottage had dark green shutters with silhouettes of pine trees cut into them. The front door was a welcoming red and had a wreath decorated with fake thermometers and tongue depressors hanging on it.

Putting her hand on the stroller and drawing it toward the door, Rachel said, "*Danki* for coming with us, Isaac. You've been kind."

"We help one another."

She flinched at his answer, and he realized it had been more curt than he intended. How often had his sister warned him he needed to be more aware of his tone when he spoke to others? Abby could discern his true feelings in spite of how his words sounded, but he'd been a part of her life since she was born.

He reached to open the door, and Rachel checked her daughters before she tipped the stroller over the threshold. She couldn't hide her amazement when he followed her into the office. Had she expected him to leave her with two sick *kinder*? When she looked away without saying anything, he guessed she'd come to accept that he intended to do as he said.

The *doktor*'s office appeared empty. No patients waited on the half-dozen plastic chairs arranged along the walls. Posters with health information decorated the light green walls. Opposite the front door, a half wall was topped by frosted glass.

A window in the glass wall slid open. "Can I help you?"

Isaac said, "Go ahead. I'll watch your girls."

Rachel hurried along a bright blue section of the tile floor to the half wall. Her voice was hushed as she spoke with the gray-haired woman who sat on the other side of the window.

Rocking the stroller as she had, he listened while Rachel gave her name as well as the *kinder*'s and explained why she was there.

"Oh, the poor dears," the woman said. "There's a nasty bug going around, and it seems to like the little ones the most. The doctor has just arrived from Rutland." She smiled. "He was delayed by the birth of triplets this morning. Please take a seat, and I'll call you in as soon as he's ready to see you."

Isaac chose a chair and watched as Rachel kneeled

next to the stroller. She drew some wet wipes from her black purse and dabbed them along the little girls' faces. They moaned, and he was glad he'd stayed. It had been the right thing to do.

He knew Glen Landis, the project manager overseeing the plain volunteers in Evergreen Corners, would understand why Isaac was late for their scheduled meeting. Glen would be leaving the town at the end of the year along with most of the aid organizations. A new project manager would be appointed, if necessary. Isaac had heard rumors he would be offered the job, but Glen hadn't mentioned anything to him.

If offered, would he take it? It didn't fit in with the plans he had for his life, but how could he walk away when so much remained to be done in Evergreen Corners?

A door to the right of the half wall opened, and a man stepped out. The *doktor*, who wore a red-and-white-striped shirt and blue jeans under his white medical coat, was a short, rotund man with a pair of gold-rimmed glasses perched on top of his bald head.

"Mrs. Yoder?" the *doktor* asked with a reassuring smile. "I hear the stomach bug has come to your house."

"Ja." She stood and faced him. "Are you ready for us?"

"Whenever you're ready. Let's see what we can do to make these two youngsters more comfortable." When she started toward the door, the *doktor* looked at Isaac. "Why don't you come in, too? It'll be simpler with two sick children to have both parents there."

"Isaac isn't their *daed*." A bright pink flashed up Rachel's cheeks. "He's a… He's a…"

"I'm a fellow volunteer in town," Isaac said quickly. "Isaac Kauffman."

"I see." The *doktor* hooked a thumb at the door. "If you don't mind volunteering right now, Isaac, it'll make the exam easier for everyone."

Standing, he nodded. The *doktor* walked through the doorway, and Rachel followed, pushing the stroller. She didn't turn her head in time for him to miss her expression. She wasn't happy about him coming into the examination room. He'd stuck his nose in where it didn't belong with no more excuse than her *kind* had thrown up on his boots. He'd have to find a way to apologize later.

The *doktor* was washing his hands when Isaac joined Rachel and her daughters in the examination room. Like the waiting room, the walls were covered with posters. A table topped by a paper sheet dominated the room, and three plastic chairs were set along the wall.

"I'm Dr. Kingsley." He dried his hands and walked to the examination table. "What's wrong with these cuties, Mom?"

"They're running a slight fever," Rachel replied. She pointed to each *kind* as she spoke their names. "Loribeth, the older one, had a temperature of one hundred point two, and Eva had ninety-nine point eight."

"Any other symptoms? Fussiness? Coughing? Vomiting?"

"All of them."

The *doktor* glanced at Isaac, his gaze slipping to Isaac's boots. "Ah, so I see."

"I wasn't quick enough to get out of the way," Isaac said, annoyed at the *doktor*'s jesting tone.

"No one can be fast enough to escape every time." Dr. Kingsley motioned for Rachel to put Loribeth on the exam table and for her to remove the *kinder*'s dress. Picking up his stethoscope, he said, "My oldest once stood at the top of the stairs and vomited. She hit every step. My wife and I were grateful we'd pulled out the old carpet days before." After warming the stethoscope between his palms, he cupped it so Loribeth could examine it.

The little girl ignored him, whining and holding up her arms to her *mamm* in a wordless request for comfort. Rachel soothed the little girl but glanced at the stroller as the other *kind* began crying. Raising her remarkable eyes, she shot Isaac a pleading glance.

Hoping he remembered the skills he'd learned when his siblings were tiny, he unlatched the straps holding the toddler in the stroller and scooped her up. She retched, and he steeled himself, but she didn't throw up. He cradled the *kind* until the *doktor* had finished examining her sister.

While Rachel held Loribeth, he put Eva on the table and stepped back to let Dr. Kingsley check her, as well. He was pleased to hear the *doktor* announce the *kinder* were fine except for the stomach bug. He prescribed something to ease their cramps and help them sleep.

"If they're feeling better tomorrow," Dr. Kingsley said, "and I suspect they will be, you can discontinue the medicine. However, they're contagious. You all are. You should go home and stay away from other people until at least tomorrow. If you don't have any symptoms by noon tomorrow, you shouldn't be able to pass along the germs any longer."

Isaac bit back his groan. He was supposed to be finishing the preparations for a new foundation today. "If I'm working outdoors, will being around other people be a problem?"

"It won't be a problem as long as you don't breathe around them or touch anything they touch." The *doktor* gave him a regretful smile. "I know it's difficult, but the best way to avoid this spreading is to stay away from others for twenty-four to thirty-six hours. I suspect we'll be seeing more children from the day-care center today and tomorrow."

Accepting the inevitable, Isaac stood to one side as Rachel dressed her *kinder*. She thanked the *doktor* and put the girls into the stroller with Isaac's help. As soon as they were on the street, she began to apologize again.

"It's not your fault, Rachel. God decided I need a day off. I'll spend the time doing the paperwork Glen has been after me to complete. It's better I skip a day than infect everyone else."

When he asked if she needed help getting the *kinder* home, she shook her head and thanked him as she walked away.

He watched her push the stroller along the sidewalk. Odd. He hadn't paid much attention to her until this morning. He'd noticed her, of course, because she was a lovely woman and a dedicated volunteer.

Maybe he should have looked more closely. He'd turned thirty-five and no longer had the obligations he'd had for the years when his *daed* had been impaired by alcohol. It was time to find the perfect wife. He wasn't seeking a great romance. His heart, he knew, was too practical.

He'd escorted plenty of girls home in his courting buggy when he was a teenager. Not once had he been interested—nor had they—in him taking them home a second time. As he grew older, the pool of available women had lessened in their district and the neighboring ones in Lancaster County before his family moved north. His hope he'd find his match waiting for him in northern Vermont hadn't worked out, either.

He knew what he wanted in a wife. An excellent cook. A *wunderbaar mamm* for their *kinder*. A hard worker who wouldn't hesitate to join him in making the farm he intended to buy a success. Someone who loved animals. A woman of deep faith.

As Rachel crossed the road, heading away from him, he smiled. He'd seen that she fit one of his criteria. She was a dedicated *mamm*. What about his other requirements for a perfect Amish wife? Did she meet them?

It could be, he decided, time for him to find out.

Chapter Two

Rachel sat on the edge of the low tub and watched her girls splashing in the warm water. As the *doktor* had assured her, the medicine had settled their stomachs since morning, and their temperatures were almost normal. Keeping an eye on them as they pushed an inflatable fish between them, she reached for another towel to drape across the floor where water puddled beside the tub. It was so *gut* to see her daughters feeling better she didn't mind the mess.

She leaned against the wall behind her. The trailer Rachel and her *kinder* called home was set on a knoll not far from the high school. The mobile home's owner had made the space available for volunteers, in gratitude for their help in repairing his *mamm*'s house soon after the flood. The few pieces of furniture in the cramped spaces were cast-offs, but some generous soul had found two small beds because her girls were too young to sleep in the bunks that had been in the bedroom. Those bunks had been sent to someone else to use. She could barely squeeze between the two beds, but her daughters were happy sharing a room.

In the kitchen, the dishes had chips and scrapes, but everything was usable. With most of their possessions in storage, the setup was perfect. Rachel had room to cook and not much to keep clean. The backyard, though it sloped toward the high school, was fenced so she could let the girls play outside while she watched them through one of the trailer's many windows.

When Glen had arranged for them to live in the mobile home, the project manager couldn't have known how much the place would remind her of her earliest days in family housing on various Army posts after she'd married Travis Gauthier. Simple, small rooms with white walls and well-used cabinetry.

Her lips tightened, and she stiffened as she did whenever she thought about the life she'd left behind after Travis died when his truck hit an improvised explosive device. Nobody must know the truth about her past. A long time ago, when she'd run away from home for the last time, so she could escape being forced to marry a young man she detested, she'd found what she thought was the place she was meant to be. She'd joined the Army, becoming a transportation officer and serving around the world. A small whisper in her mind had urged her to reconsider, but she'd muted that voice until after Travis's death.

As she searched for what she'd do as a widow with two young *kinder* and no ties anywhere, she hadn't been able to ignore the voice and the longing within her to be closer to God. She'd moved as far as possible from her former district in Ohio and been welcomed into another community in Maine. Her new neighbors had assumed she'd been baptized as Amish, and they'd accepted her as one of them. For the six months she'd lived among them, she'd made every effort not to say or do anything to make them question their assumption.

Yet, living among the *Leit* under false pretenses had gnawed at her, so when the chance came to help with rebuilding Evergreen Corners, she'd volunteered. In the small town, she was able to straddle the plain and *Englisch* worlds as she had for the past twenty years. She hoped while she worked alongside other volunteers, her prayers for guidance about the future would be answered. She could accept being ostracized from the plain community for her choices, but she didn't want her little girls to have to pay the price. There must be a way to do as God wanted and return to the Amish and be baptized. She had to wait for God to show her the path.

The doorbell rang, breaking into Rachel's thoughts. She looked at her girls as the bell sounded again.

If she grabbed towels and wrapped them around her daughters, she could carry one in each arm to the front door. It'd been a rainy afternoon, and she didn't want to risk them getting chilled while she answered the door.

Never taking her eyes off the girls, she stretched so she could shout down the hall. She used the voice she'd perfected in the motor pool when she had to get everyone's attention over the cacophony of tools and loud voices and parts hitting the concrete floor.

"*Komm* in!"

Eva got water in her eyes and began to cry. Rachel

distracted her with another inflatable fish, allowing her to dab away the teardrops. The little girl began to giggle.

"Is she all right?"

At the question from behind her, Rachel flinched so hard she nearly tumbled into the tub. A broad hand on her arm steadied her at the same time it sent warmth swirling along her skin.

She looked over her shoulder, though she didn't need to. The deep voice told her Isaac stood in her bathroom doorway.

What was *he* doing here?

Her fingers were patting her hair toward her *kapp* before she could halt herself. She didn't like the feeling that it was impossible for her to live up to his high standards. It'd be simpler if she wasn't trying to persuade everyone she was no different from any other Amish widow. She didn't want anyone asking questions about her past.

When he removed his black hat, his light brown hair was tousled. Rachel was surprised that it wasn't as perfectly trained as the rest of him. She silently scolded herself. She was being petty.

"They're fine," she said.

"So my boots are safe?" he asked.

"Ja." Embarrassment warmed her face, and her cheeks must have been scarlet. She couldn't remember the last time she'd blushed. "If you want to wait in the other room, I'll have them out of the tub soon."

"Let me help."

She was so astonished she blurted the first stupid thing that came into her head. "They're wet."

"The usual situation when a *kind* is in the bathtub."

Okay, she had to wonder why he wanted to talk to her when she'd acted ridiculous. Without further comment, she handed him a towel from the floor, one that wasn't as wet as the others. She picked up another and lifted Eva from the tub, wrapping her in soft plushness. She watched as Isaac did the same with Loribeth, who regarded him with big eyes.

"Don't wiggle," he said in *Deitsch*, the language he would assume the girls spoke. Most Amish *kinder*, especially those without older siblings, didn't learn to speak like *Englischers* until they started school when they were six years old.

"Who are you?" the little girl asked in the same language, and Rachel released a silent sigh of relief.

"My name is Isaac."

"I-zak?" Her nose wrinkled. "That's a funny name. My name is pretty. It's Loribeth."

"Did the bath make you feel better, Loribeth?"

"Pudding makes me feel *gut*." She regarded him with a serious expression. "Chocolate pudding."

"I think," he said with a wink at the little girl, "chocolate makes everyone feel *gut*."

"Choco!" Eva crowed, bouncing in Rachel's arms. "Yummy! Choco puddin'?"

"Not now," Rachel said. "You need to brush your teeth and go to bed."

"Choco puddin' for break-ist?"

"How about you and Loribeth help me make chocolate pudding tomorrow for supper?"

Both girls tried not to appear too disappointed as they nodded. When they looked at each other and giggled, she shook her head. They were young, but she suspected they'd already learned to work together to get what they wanted from their *mamm*.

Isaac held Eva, once Rachel had put on her diaper and nightgown, while Rachel got Loribeth ready for bed. The littler girl wore diapers at night. Rachel glanced in Isaac's direction to see if he'd taken note of the fact her younger daughter wasn't completely potty-trained, but his expression told her nothing. Hurrying made her fingers clumsy, and Loribeth complained when Rachel pulled her nightgown over her head backward.

Rachel twisted it around and buttoned the front. As Loribeth scrambled into her small bed, Rachel lifted Eva onto hers. She listened while the little girls said their heartfelt prayers and kissed them as she tucked them under the covers.

She turned to pick up the wet towels and was startled to discover Isaac already had. She hadn't noticed him leaving the room. Forcing her jaw to ease from its taut line, she was able to smile when Eva called her name.

"Med-y?" asked the toddler.

With a genuine smile, Rachel shook her head. "You don't need any more medicine. The *doktor* said once your tummies were okay, you didn't need to take any more. You and Loribeth are *gut*, so no more medicine."

"*Gut.*" Eva settled into her pillow, pulling her beloved *Boppli* Bear against her chest.

Rachel drew a blanket over her younger daughter, though Eva would kick it off. The little girl hated having anything on her when she was sleeping. Soon Rachel would have to open the boxes with the girls' winter clothing and find Loribeth's old pajamas for her younger sister.

After turning to make sure Loribeth was set for the night, she saw a puzzled expression on the little girl's face. "What is it, *liebling*?" she asked.

"I don't like that I-zak."

"You don't know him." She hadn't expected to have to defend the man who unsettled her, but her daughters must not do anything to draw attention to the fact they hadn't always lived plain. She guessed no Amish *kind* would speak so about an adult.

"Don't want to know him."

"Loribeth, that's not what God asks of us. We're supposed to be friends to everyone."

"Not *him*." She turned her back on Rachel, making it clear she didn't want to discuss Isaac any longer.

Rachel turned off the ceiling light, made sure the two night-lights were on and slipped out of the room, drawing the door almost closed. Was her daughter going to be as rebellious as Rachel had been as a teen?

She must find out why Isaac had come to the trailer and walked in as if he owned the place.

Because you told him to. She couldn't ignore the honest voice in her mind. She *had* asked Isaac to *komm* in, though she hadn't imagined he was the person knocking on her door.

Rachel paused at the end of the short hallway leading to the compact kitchen. Isaac stood in front of the sofa in the living room as if he couldn't imagine sitting without permission.

"Isaac, *danki*." She bit her lip. Isaac had been annoyed earlier when she'd thanked him over and over. "I appreciate your help in getting the girls out of the tub."

"They seem to be feeling better."

"They are. I've stopped the medicine because they were able to keep ginger ale and crackers down this evening."

He motioned toward a pot from a slow cooker sitting in the middle of the dining table. A dishcloth covered the top. "My sister sent some chicken soup over. She said you'd know when to give it to the *kinder*."

"I'm sure they'll appreciate it tomorrow."

"Not as much as *choco puddin'*, I would guess."

Was that a hint of a smile she saw on his face? Was he amused by the girls, or did he think her parenting skills were a joke?

"If Eva had her way, she'd have pudding for every meal every day." Hoping he wasn't wondering where her manners were, she added, "I made a cake before the girls got sick. I put it in the freezer, but I could warm it if you'd like a piece."

"Sure."

"You don't care what flavor it is?"

"I've never been offered a piece of cake I didn't like." He gave her another of his rare smiles as they went into the kitchen.

The owner had told her the appliances were a color called avocado-green, but if she had an avocado that dull, she would have tossed it, unsure if it was safe to eat. Walking to the stove, she asked, *"Kaffi?"*

"It's late, so I shouldn't." He started to say more, but halted when another knock came at her door.

Startled, because she couldn't remember the last time she'd had anyone drop by in the evening since her arrival in Evergreen Corners, let alone two visitors, Rachel hurried to the door. She opened it and gasped, "Abby! What are you doing here? Oh, that was rude!"

"Not at all." Abby's smile was easy.

Isaac's sister's hair was as blond as the streaks in his, but they were otherwise opposites in appearance. She was short while he was tall, and her eyes were a greenish-gray instead of the earth-brown of his. However, they were eager volunteers. From what Rachel had been told, Abby had come to the village within weeks of the flood and had remained in Evergreen Corners to oversee the kitchen in the community center, where the volunteers were fed three meals a day. In addition, she'd taken on working with the teenage volunteers in an effort to curtail bullying in the village. Her efforts, like her brother's, had been successful. However, unlike Isaac, Abby asked of others only what they could give.

"I'm the one who's being rude," Abby said as she stepped into the trailer. "I couldn't wait for Isaac to come home and tell me. How are the girls?"

"Asleep, I hope. I put them to bed after a warm bath."

"That's *gut*." She glanced toward the kitchen. "I hope Isaac isn't being too much of a bossy bother."

"No!" Rachel lowered her voice. "He's trying to help."

"He doesn't *try*. He does everything perfectly." She

smiled. "I love my brother, but I don't make excuses for him."

Rachel decided she'd be wise not to say anything in response. "*Danki* for sending over the soup."

"I'm glad I can help. I figured they'd be ready for real food soon." She chuckled. "Unlike the kids in the youth group, who are ready for food at any time and at any place."

Joining in with her soft laughter, Rachel's uncertainties were alleviated when Abby agreed to have some cake, too. Rachel went into the kitchen and hoped Abby's presence would ease the tension between herself and Isaac. It wasn't much of a defensive plan, but it was the best she had at the moment.

The morning sunshine sifted through the leaves on the tree outside the window of the apartment where Isaac lived with his sister when he was in southern Vermont. The apartment was over a garage belonging to the mayor of Evergreen Corners, Gladys Whittaker, and her husband. From the moment the space had been offered to Isaac and Abby, it had become his home away from home. Abby wouldn't be returning to live at the family farm in the Northeast Kingdom because she was going to marry, but he'd been traveling back and forth every couple of weeks. He'd ridden with other volunteers in the rented van so many times along the mountain roads he felt as if he could drive them blindfolded.

Not that he knew how to drive a car. When his friends, during their *rumspringa*, had gotten licenses, he hadn't. He'd intended to commit himself to an Amish life, and he hadn't needed a taste of everything that would be forbidden to him once he was baptized. Instead of a fast car, he'd spent his time listening to the radio he'd hidden in the hayloft, along with a few comic books that would have earned him a long lecture if *Daed* had discovered them. As his *daed* spent most of those years sneaking alcohol from his stash in the barn, Isaac had been extra careful to keep his contraband out of sight. He'd thought nobody had known about his stash until a few months ago, when Abby told him she'd found his comic books and had read them. She'd been delighted, as he had, by the outrageous stories of people who could fly and see through buildings and spent their lives fighting evil.

This morning, he wasn't reading about the adventures of a superhero. Instead, he was perusing the local newspaper as he finished his cold *kaffi*. *The Evergreen Corners Crier* was published weekly. Front-page news focused on events at the high school, and the inside pages were filled with birth announcements, obituaries and menus for the senior centers in the neighboring towns. The Evergreen Corners seniors had met at the community center before the flood and now shared the space with the volunteers, who depended on the kitchen for their meals.

He'd scanned those stories, but his attention had been riveted on the classified section. A single picture showed a fuzzy image of a weathered barn and a house. The photo had run in the paper each week for the past three months as part of a real-estate ad. The copy spoke of eighty acres, more than twenty wooded. The property had been a dairy farm.

Leaning back in his chair, Isaac looked around the apartment's kitchen, which was barely larger than the one in Rachel's trailer. What would the kitchen look like in the battered old house? It probably was large enough for a family and could be the heart of the home he hoped to share with a wife and their *kinder*.

"Gute mariye," Abby sang out as she came into the kitchen. Earlier, as she did each morning, she'd made a hearty breakfast for them before she went to the community center to do the same for whoever needed a meal before the day's work began.

Isaac's dream popped like a soap bubble, and he closed the newspaper, not wanting his sister to guess he was mooning over the farm outside of the village.

Too late, he realized, when Abby said, "You should go and look before someone else buys it."

"It's been for sale for a long time. I don't think anyone's interested in it."

"You are." She chuckled as she added more detergent to the water in the sink so she could finish the dishes.

"Our family lives almost three hours north of here. Why would I be looking at farms here?"

She shot a sugary smile in his direction. "Because your favorite sister lives here."

"My *only* sister."

"But your favorite, you've got to admit."

Part of him wanted to give in to Abby's silliness, but he had too much on his mind. The farm, the work ahead of him…two little girls and their *mamm*. God had brought them into his life. Why?

Abby scrubbed the pan she'd used to make them

pancakes. "It wouldn't hurt for you to contact the real-estate agent. She's right here in town. I'm sure she'd be glad to show you around the farm."

"I'm sure she would, but I don't want to waste her time when I'm not ready to buy."

"Why not? You know more about running a farm than anyone else in the family. Even *Daed* isn't as skilled a dairyman as you are!"

"A farmer needs more than himself to make the farm successful."

"You may be able to hire older teen boys to help with haying and harvest."

"Harvest comes at the same time as preseason football practice."

Her eyebrows rose. "Wow, you've given this some thought, haven't you?"

"A lot."

"So what's keeping you from seeing the farm?"

"I told you. I'm not ready."

She gave an unattractive snort. His sister never hid her opinions around him. "I know you, Isaac Kauffman! You hate wasting time, but yet you're acting like a boy dreaming of a new baseball glove. You should visit the farm. It's not far from the Millers' house, which would be convenient for church Sundays."

"That's true."

"So why aren't you going to look at the farm?"

She wouldn't give up until he was honest with her. Completely honest.

"A farmer should have a wife and family to help him."

Abby put the skillet into the sink. With soap suds

clinging to her fingers, she faced him and said, "So I guess that means you're looking for a wife. I could say it's about time. You're thirty-five, and most men have been married for years by the time they're your age."

"I haven't found the woman I want to spend the rest of my life with."

"You haven't found the *perfect* woman, you mean." She laughed as she turned back to the sink. "I know you, big brother. You want everything perfect."

"Why shouldn't I?"

"What about falling in love? I haven't heard you say a word about that."

"Love isn't all it's touted to be." What was the use of love when it had driven his *daed* to drinking and almost torn apart their family? "Let me find what I'm looking for, Abby, without your help. I didn't get involved when you found the perfect man for yourself."

"Really?" She arched her eyebrows.

"Okay, I didn't get involved as much as I wanted to."

"That's likely true." She smiled. "I didn't find the perfect man. I've found the right man, and I know we'll be happy when we marry after he's baptized. Right and perfect aren't the same thing."

"They are for me."

"Isaac, you know as well as I do there's only one perfect being—God. How can you expect a mortal woman to achieve a state of perfection?"

"You're arguing over a single word. When I say perfect, I mean perfect for me. Why shouldn't I want that?"

Instead of the pert, teasing answer he'd thought she'd give him, his sister became serious as she looked over her shoulder. "Because you may miss the right woman for you while waiting for the perfect one to come along. I hope you don't make that mistake, Isaac."

He hoped so, too.

Chapter Three

The day-care center, Rachel knew, had been at the community center for almost five months after the flood. Once Reverend Rhee, the retired minister, had moved out of the church basement and into the new house Amish Helping Hands had built for her, the day-care center had returned to its original location at the Evergreen Corners Community Church. While it had moved back almost six months ago, Rachel smiled as she thought of how excited everyone involved had been to have the day-care center once more in the basement of the small white church. It had been seen as another step toward returning the village to what it had been before the storm. The *kinder* had been delighted to go to their familiar classrooms along with their toys and teachers.

Voices reached them as she went with her daughters down the uncarpeted stairs to the cellar, glad to be out of the rain. The bright colors of the classrooms seemed more garish after the dull gray of the early morning.

"Look who's back!" called Gwen O'Malley, the head

teacher, as she smiled at the girls, who gripped Rachel's hands. She was a slender woman with a moon-shaped face. A curly red cloud topped her head, and was always flopping about like the stuffed arms and legs of Eva's bear. She adored *kinder*, and they returned her affection. Both girls flung their short arms around her and began chattering.

"How are you feeling, Loribeth? Eva?" the woman they called "Miss Gwen" asked. "Are your tummies happy?"

Loribeth rubbed her stomach. "It ouched." She'd switched to English easily.

"Ouched," Eva said, echoing her older sister.

"I know." Gwen squatted in front of them. "Your tummies don't ouch now, do they?"

Both girls shook their heads so seriously Rachel had to struggle not to grin. Gwen's lips twitched, too.

"I threw up on I-zak's boots," Loribeth said, telling the story with the drama of a telenovela actress. "He got me out of the tub, but Mommy put me to bed." She couldn't hide her delight that she'd messed up Isaac's boots.

Later, Rachel would have to remind Loribeth that being nice to others, even people her daughter disliked, was important. As she listened to her girls, she wondered why she'd worried. They'd been in Evergreen Corners since the spring, so it would have been bizarre if the girls weren't speaking English while among the town's residents.

Fretting wasn't like her. She'd learned in the Army to have a clear vision of her goals, but her brain hadn't contained many intelligible thoughts since Travis's death. On the day when a knock on her door had signaled the arrival of the local post chaplain, logic had deserted her.

How could there be any logic in a world where her husband and the *daed* of her *kinder* had been killed in the final week of his deployment?

Sorrow flooded her, threatening to drown her in the memories of the *gut* times and plans for the future that would never come to pass. She silenced the thoughts, refusing to let them escape from where she'd locked them away in her heart. She wished she could have buried them along with her husband, as rifles had fired a salute and she'd accepted the folded American flag along with the gratitude of the American people. Knowing the Army was the most important thing in Travis's life had offered her some comfort because he'd died doing what he loved. Yet, she wished he could see how much the girls had grown. He'd missed Loribeth's first words and every milestone Eva had made.

"Right, Mommy?"

At Eva's voice, she escaped the quicksand of her memories. She found a smile and pasted it in place as she stroked her daughter's hair. Not wanting to admit she hadn't heard anything her girls or Gwen had said, she smiled. "I need to get to work, *lieblings*. Be *gut* for Miss Gwen."

She gave them each a kiss and watched as they loped over to where other *kinder* had gathered to listen to a story. There were fewer than half of the normal number of *kinder* in the room.

As if Rachel had spoken aloud, Gwen said, "We've

got a bunch of kids out with the stomach bug. It's going through the staff, too."

"Do you need me to help today?"

Gwen smiled. "Thanks, Rachel, but we're okay at the moment, and I know today is your day to work in the kitchen. Go ahead. We'll be fine."

"If you need me, call the community center and I'll come right over."

"I appreciate that, but I hope I won't have to chase you down."

"Me, either." With a wave, Rachel climbed the stairs and went out the door into the soggy September morning.

She bent her head into the rain, drawing her black cloak over her bonnet, though it was too warm for the heavy garment. When bringing her girls to day care, it was easier to drape a cloak over them rather than try to squeeze beneath an umbrella.

Hearing shouts from the other side of the village green, she watched as a group of men strode north toward the latest building sites. She could pick out Isaac easily. He walked with a steady pace, his head high. The small matter of rain didn't keep Isaac Kauffman from moving forward with his day.

It shouldn't hold her back, either. Bowing her head into the wind, she scurried toward the community center set next to the Mennonite chapel. Water splashed out of puddles and dropped off trees. Her sneakers and black stockings were soaked by the time she threw open the door and rushed inside.

The main room of the community center was filled

with tables and assorted chairs that had been donated eleven months ago, after the flood. Other than the volunteers, only a handful of local villagers continued to take their meals at the community center. Those people would be able to make meals in their own kitchens once the last three houses under construction were finished. In the months since the flood, twelve houses had been built, after the debris left by the high water had been trucked away.

Breakfast had been under way for at least an hour, but fresh food awaited any stragglers at the pass-through window between the main room and the kitchen. After she'd taken off her cloak and black bonnet and hung them near the door, Rachel ignored the stack of cranberry muffins and hurried into the kitchen.

It was warm and smelled of bacon and eggs from breakfast. Two women were cutting freshly baked bread in preparation for making lunch sandwiches. Two others were loading the dishwasher while another cleaned pans in the sink. Abby was taking meats, lettuce and tomatoes from the refrigerator, and carrying them to a counter.

Rachel took a steadying breath. The kitchen was more crowded than usual. She saw two new workers. The one cutting bread was a tall blonde who wore a heart-shaped *kapp* above a lovely face. The other was an *Englischer* whose light brown hair was cut into a bob. She was a couple of inches taller than Rachel, and she moved around the kitchen in a flurry of energy as she stacked dirty dishes in the dishwasher.

Calling a greeting, Abby set the food on the counter

and came over to introduce Rachel to the newcomers. The tall blonde was Nina Streit from eastern Lancaster County. Her voice complemented her beauty. Her curves couldn't be hidden by the simple dress she wore beneath a black apron.

"So glad you've joined us," Rachel said.

The tall woman bowed her head, then went back to work.

Abby turned toward the shorter woman. "Rachel, I don't think you've met Hailee Lennox. Hailee, this is Rachel Yoder."

"So glad you've joined us, too." Rachel steeled herself for another cool reaction.

Instead, Hailee said, "Me, too! The folks here are nice. I'm glad I finally got a chance to come and join in." She grinned. "I can come a couple of days a week and on the weekends when I'm not training with my National Guard unit."

Rachel looked away, hoping her face didn't display her shock at meeting another female soldier. Her eyes were caught by Nina's. The tall woman regarded her with a curious expression and a half smile, as if she'd guessed Rachel's secret.

Don't be silly. Her secret was safe.

Moving her gaze to Abby, she asked, "What do you need me to do this morning?"

"Cupcakes."

"Sounds like fun."

"Why don't you have Hailee help you? You can teach her how we do things here."

Glad that Abby had asked her to help Hailee instead

of icy Nina, Rachel was soon busy showing Hailee where to find the ingredients for the cupcakes they'd serve with lunch. On such a stormy day, warm dessert would be welcomed by the volunteers. They were stirring batter when Nina moved to join them.

"How long have you been here, Rachel?" she asked as she began greasing and flouring the cupcake pans.

"Since spring."

"So long?"

"*Ja.* I'll be staying as long as I'm needed here."

Nina's eyebrows rose. "My family expects me home by the end of October. I have two sisters and a brother getting married, so they want the whole family there. How about yours?"

Abby paused on the other side of the prep table, and Rachel was grateful when her friend asked, "Have you seen the insulated container for *kaffi*?"

"I have." Glad she didn't have to answer Nina's question, Rachel went to the pantry across from the stoves. She'd met people like Nina before—people who had to establish a pecking order with themselves at the top. The best way to deal with them, she'd learned, was to avoid any competition with them.

Opening the door to the walk-in pantry, she stood on tiptoe to reach the blue-and-white plastic jug they used to send hot or cold drinks to the volunteers on the work sites. Her fingertips touched it, but she couldn't get her hands around it. Not wanting to bother getting a chair to stand on, she jumped and tapped one side of the container. She smiled when the jug moved an inch closer. It was enough for her to be able to pull it off the shelf.

A sharp crash sounded behind her. She gripped the insulated jug to her chest and whirled. A scream burst from her throat before she could halt it. Had that been gunfire? A bomb going off? The unforgettable odors of sweat and blood and heat surged over her, and she pressed against the pantry wall.

The pantry!

She was in Evergreen Corners, Vermont. She was—

Her eyes widened when she saw everyone in the kitchen had halted. The women stared at her in dismay. No wonder. She must look like a *dummkopf* cowering in the pantry. If they had any idea of the images rushing through her mind…

They must never know. She had to keep the truth to herself.

Horror rushed through her, wiping away every other thought, when a motion on the other side of the pass-through window caught her eye. Isaac stood there. His face was rigid. Somehow she had to make sure any suspicions he might have were quickly allayed.

Isaac scanned the tableau in front of him. Beside him, Vernon Umble, his cousin, stared through his thick glasses that were, as always, perched on the tip of his nose. The volunteers in the kitchen were as still as statues. They were all looking at where Rachel stood in the door to the pantry. Her face was empty of color, and though she was struggling to smile, he couldn't miss the remnants of fear in her eyes. He wouldn't insult her by assuming she'd been startled by a mouse. She was made of much sterner stuff.

So what had made her scream as if she was afraid for her life?

Rachel straightened and smiled, but he guessed it was forced. "Sorry! I was startled by the crash."

"I dropped a cookie sheet," said Abby.

"The noise echoed through the pantry, and it sounded like a…" She faltered. With an unsteady laugh, she added, "I don't know what it sounded like other than loud!"

As the volunteers returned to work, they continued to aim uneasy glances in Rachel's direction. As Isaac crossed the kitchen, Abby caught his eye. He guessed she was trying to pass some silent message to him, but he had no idea what it might be. If she was trying to urge him to be gentle with her friend, she didn't need to worry. He only wanted to make sure Rachel was okay.

"I'm fine," Rachel said before he could ask. "Please don't say anything. I'm embarrassed enough already."

Embarrassment wasn't the emotion glowing in her eyes, but he wasn't going to argue with her when so many ears were turned toward them.

"The girls must be much better," he said, though he wanted her to be honest with him about what had frightened her. "You wouldn't be here otherwise."

"They're fine and at day care."

"Waiting for choco puddin'?"

Her lustrous eyes grew wide. "Oh, *danki*, Isaac! In the flurry to get us out the door this morning, I forgot to buy cocoa so I can make pudding tonight." Her smile became genuine. "The girls would have been heartbroken if I'd forgotten."

She was babbling. To divert him from asking the questions she wanted to avoid? Every instinct warned him something was amiss, but that he shouldn't push the issue. She had the right to keep her thoughts to herself.

Slipping past him, she carried the jug to where *kaffi* waited in a pot. She poured it in and closed the top.

"Gute mariye," murmured a silky voice from his other side.

Isaac turned and was surprised how he had to raise his eyes almost to a level gaze as he looked at a pretty blonde who stood right beside him. Her eyes were brown, and her lips were full and as red as fresh strawberries. He returned her greeting and introduced himself.

"Oh, you're Abby's big brother," said the blonde after telling him her name was Nina. "I've heard many *wunderbaar* things about you, Isaac." Her voice caressed his name. "I'm glad we've met at last."

"Me, too," he said, but his gaze cut toward where Rachel was packing cookies and muffins left over from breakfast into a plastic box.

"I'm sure we'll become *gut* friends." Nina's pleasant voice made him look at her. "Wouldn't you like that?"

He gave her a quick smile. "Excuse me. We need to get to work."

"See you later. Maybe we can get better acquainted during supper."

He went to where Rachel and another woman had finished packing the box with snacks for his team. The *Englisch* woman stepped aside so he could heft the well-filled box. His cousin Vernon came forward to get the jug holding the *kaffi*. They thanked the women for preparing the food for their midmorning break.

As he left with his cousin, Isaac turned to look over his shoulder. His gaze snagged on Rachel's and caught. Disquiet dimmed her eyes. He couldn't keep from wondering what had caused her to scream.

Isaac stepped outside. The rain had slowed to a drizzle, but the wind had picked up, so drops sliced into his face. He and Vernon walked with care on the slippery sidewalk.

When they reached the street running parallel to the brook, the few people they passed were aiming nervous glances at the water. He wanted to reassure them a rainy day wasn't going to recreate the disaster they'd suffered last autumn.

Isaac handed off the box to someone as he went into the house where the workers had begun hanging drywall. Soon the *kaffi* and the food were gone. The hard work made everyone hungry. After finishing his *kaffi*, he tossed the cup into a trash bag, then went to check the work in the larger bedroom. His team was skilled, but mistakes happened. Finding them before little errors became big problems was part of his job. He was pleased to see everything had been done right.

"She's pretty, isn't she?" asked Vernon as Isaac came back into the main room.

His cousin set a box of flooring on top of the others already stacked there. The boards would need a few days of sitting in the house and becoming accustomed to the humidity before they could be put into place.

Otherwise, the boards would swell or shrink too much and leave gaps in the flooring.

"How many more boxes do we need to bring in?" he asked, ignoring the question.

"About a half dozen." Vernon leaned one hand against the low wall dividing the living room from the kitchen. "I answered your question, so why don't you answer mine?"

"You said someone was pretty. I didn't see a need to answer when I didn't know who you were talking about."

Vernon laughed. "You mean the pretty blonde or the pretty brunette? Some men would be grinning like a *dummkopf* to have two such lookers paying them attention."

"Nina was nice enough to introduce herself."

"Rachel was watching you every second of your conversation." He chuckled. "Except when you glanced in her direction. Guess she didn't want you to know she was keeping a close eye on you."

"You're being preposterous. Rachel was busy packing food for us."

"Me? Preposterous? What do you call yourself? I saw how you were looking at her. Not at the blonde, but at Rachel. Could it be, after all this time, you've found the woman for you?"

"All this time? You're older than I am, and you're still a bachelor."

"Maybe not much longer."

"Really?" He couldn't hide his surprise.

Vernon laughed. "*Ja*. There's this nice widow who's

been helping with the painting over at the library, and she's a *gut* cook. Makes the best mincemeat pie I've ever had. A widow is used to having a man around, so I figure I won't have to change to meet her expectations."

"My step-*mamm* said something similar when she married *Daed*."

"Their marriage is what's made me think about the wisdom of courting a widow. Maybe you should think about it, too, cousin. Rachel Yoder is a widow with two little ones. I'm sure she'd be glad for a steady man in her life." He winked. "Besides, you know she's *gut* having *bopplin*. Her two are close in age, and you know how women are. As soon as one's out of diapers, they're pining for a new *boppli*."

Isaac wondered why his bachelor cousin considered himself an expert on women and *kinder*. On the other hand, there might be something to what Vernon said, but Isaac had learned long ago to make up his mind with facts he gathered himself.

The facts were simple. Rachel was a *gut mamm*, and she was an excellent cook and housekeeper. She wasn't bold with her speech or demeanor, and she never missed a church Sunday. She also kept her little girls entertained during the long service, a sure sign they'd been attending church since they were born. A hard worker, a *wunderbaar mamm*, devoted to God. Everything that would make her the perfect wife he'd been seeking.

Was God giving him a chance to see the perfect wife for him was here in Evergreen Corners?

Maybe, but he couldn't stop thinking of her extraordinary reaction to the commonplace sound of a cookie sheet striking the floor. Was there something she wasn't telling anyone?

He needed to find out.

Chapter Four

❧

"I need someone to come with me," Abby called the next afternoon from the back door of the kitchen. "Anyone free?"

Several voices replied with an enthusiastic affirmative, including Rachel's. Getting out of the kitchen for a short time sounded like a *wunderbaar* idea. Nina had spent the day testing her patience and everyone else's, pushing the volunteers to their limits.

Rachel had never met another plain woman like Nina. She bragged like a sergeant Rachel had known whose platoon always won any challenge on the orienteering course. She'd grown accustomed to such bluster from him, because sergeants liked to rub others' noses in their victories. It was a way, she knew, to build camaraderie within a platoon, which was something invaluable when those men and women faced a real enemy. Even when the stories resembled superhero movies, it was part of the team-building spirit.

That wasn't the Amish way. Nobody boasted about

their accomplishments or their family connections. Compliments were supposed to be met with a subdued reaction.

However, Nina hadn't been taught that. From the time she arrived in the kitchen—at the exact time to take a place front and center to serve breakfast after the rest of the volunteers had spent hours preparing the food—she'd listed the reasons why her family, her district and her community were the best.

Hailee and the other *Englischers* avoided Nina, because the blonde didn't seem to have any interest in impressing them. Her whole focus was on outshining the other plain women.

Rachel guessed it was because Nina was determined to find herself a husband in Evergreen Corners. Though she was surprised none of the men in Nina's home district had offered her marriage, she wondered if the blonde wanted to surpass her sisters, who were getting married.

Or maybe she was as unhappy at home as you were. The thought sent shame through Rachel. She shouldn't judge others when her own life and choices wouldn't have stood scrutiny.

However, her empathy for Nina didn't keep her from adding her voice to the others offering to help Abby with whatever she needed.

When Abby asked her to come grocery shopping, Rachel saw a few women looking relieved they hadn't been chosen. She understood. Wandering along the few aisles at Spezio's, the local supermarket, was often an exercise in frustration. The store wasn't set up to provide for a community kitchen, though the manager was eager to work with the relief groups.

They took the bus to the grocery store on the outskirts of the village. Right after the flood, the residents hadn't been able to get to the store without driving more than an hour each way.

Local people had become accustomed to plain folks in their midst, so nobody paid attention as Abby and Rachel walked into the store. They each got a cart, and Abby pulled out two copies of her shopping list. Handing one to Rachel, she led the way toward the left side, where the fruit and vegetables were stacked in pleasing arrays.

"You find the things on the right half of the page, and I'll do the other side," Abby said.

Nodding, Rachel went first to the onions. She needed to get forty pounds, along with an equal amount of potatoes. Putting the bags in the cart, she had to smile. The bags weighed far less than either Loribeth or Eva, whom she hefted every day. Who'd have guessed toting around her *kinder* would provide a better workout than the two-mile runs she'd done daily in the Army?

"What's funny?" asked Abby as she set an armful of zucchini and squash in her cart. "You're grinning like a cat with a bowl of cream."

Rachel related her thoughts, leaving out the part about her military life. It was getting easier to navigate her way between the two worlds, but she mustn't get complacent. Doing that could ruin not only her hopes for the future, but also her girls'.

"I wonder if someone's written a self-help book on

exercising with toddlers," she added as they reached the end of the aisle.

"It'd be a bestseller." Abby reached for a bottle of chili powder. "I appreciate your help today. My list was too long for me to bring the groceries home by myself."

"I appreciate helping."

Abby giggled. "I saw the look Nina aimed at you earlier."

"At me?"

"You know she doesn't like you, I assume."

It was Rachel's turn to laugh. "I think everyone knows Nina doesn't like me."

"Or anyone else."

"That's sad."

Abby's eyebrows rose. "I didn't expect you to say that."

"We've had a great time working in the kitchen. It's hard work, and it was *hot* work during the summer, but it's been fun." She took another container of baking powder off the shelf. "I learned a long time ago it's better to get along with people than be standoffish."

"Or proud."

"*Hochmut* should never be part of a plain life."

"That sounds like something someone said to you often."

Putting bottles of cinnamon and cumin into the shopping cart, she was glad to avoid her friend's gaze as she said, "Often enough."

She didn't want to think of her *daed* and how he'd snarled those words at her as he'd accused her of the sin of *hochmut* when she tried to explain she was innocent of whatever misdeed he'd believed she'd committed. He'd been furious she didn't dissolve into tears when he towered over her, threatening to hurt her more.

Defiance bubbled in her at the memories. She'd withstood what he'd handed out with his hand and his belt for as long as she'd been able.

Could he have been right? Was she proud she'd survived his abuse? She was, but that had to be different from the pride the ministers preached against. She'd survived by escaping, following the path God must have laid out for her, because she'd had no idea where she was going.

Abby pushed her cart forward a few feet, then stopped. "I forgot garlic cloves, too. It's strange to get them from a store instead of the root cellar."

In spite of herself, Rachel flinched. The root cellar had been *Daed*'s favorite place to imprison her and her younger siblings. Years later, she had begun to wonder if he didn't want anyone to see the welts and bruises he'd caused. At the time, while locked in the dark, she could think of nothing but her pain and her fear, and her wish someone would let her out. Usually one of her siblings did after *Daed* had gone to bed, but once she'd been in the root cellar, forgotten, until *Mamm* came to get some vegetables for the next night's supper.

Mamm hadn't said a word, and Rachel guessed her *mamm* was terrified of *Daed* and embarrassed by how he treated their *kinder* and her inability to stop it.

"I wish Nina would be nicer to everyone," Abby said. "We've had such camaraderie in the kitchen. If you want my opinion, she's hiding some sort of hurt."

"I agree." She was relieved to speak of anything other than her past. "She makes such an effort to show she's superior to the rest of us, but I've found people who act that way often are the opposite. Or they think they are, so they do everything in their power to hide it instead of giving over their insecurities to God."

Abby moved the cart along the aisle to the next item on her list. "You sound as if you've encountered other folks like that."

"Enough to learn what's on the outside may not be the same as what's on the inside."

Rachel busied herself getting a dozen boxes of the pasta that was on sale, so she had an excuse not to say more. If she did, she might say too much. How sweet it'd be to tell Abby the truth!

By the time they reached the cash registers, their carts were stacked so high Rachel kept a cautionary arm by hers. She guided it into the narrow space between two of the three checkout stands.

"It was much easier," Abby said as she began to put groceries on the conveyor to the register, "when Glen ordered the food and supplies we needed."

"Why did he stop?" Rachel asked as she put items threatening to topple from her cart on the belt, too.

"He's trying to bring the project to a close around Christmas. He's been spreading his duties among the rest of us. He handed off obtaining food to me." She pushed her empty cart forward so the young girl at the end of the checkout stand could put filled bags into it.

Rachel was relieved when, after paying, Abby had the store manager arrange for the heaviest groceries to be delivered by van to the community center. However, there were eight bags of perishable food to take with them.

The handles were cutting into Rachel's palms by the time they reached the bus stop. She was grateful when the bus rolled to a stop less than a minute after they arrived. When the doors swung open, the bus driver asked if they needed help, but before he could get up, two men offered assistance. Rachel handed over three of the bags and climbed onto the bus.

"*Danki*—thank you," Rachel said as she slid into the seat next to Abby and the men put the bags on the floor beside them. "You've been a *wunderbaar* blessing today."

The larger man blushed, and both men nodded before hurrying to take their seats as the bus moved onto the road.

Rachel leaned back. "Well, there's one big job done. Except for putting the groceries away. However, many hands should mean light work. Isn't that how the saying goes?"

"Sometimes you sound like Isaac."

"I'll take that as a compliment. Or is it? You complain sometimes he's too exacting in his comments."

"Isaac is exact with every aspect of his life, and I don't think you're any different. You like to have a plan for everything and a way to make the plan happen."

"If I give that appearance, I can assure you it's pretense. Most of the time since I've arrived in Evergreen Corners, I've been following orders. Do you think Isaac is like that, too?"

"My brother knows what he's doing."

"I didn't mean to suggest he didn't."

Abby grinned. "I know you didn't, but he's particular about being questioned about how he does things. I thought you should know."

"I'll keep that in mind, but I don't know if Loribeth will. She seems a little too pleased she threw up on his boots."

"He handled that better than I would have expected, but he needs to loosen up a little if he ever finds the perfect wife he's looking for and has *kinder* of his own."

An odd twist tightened Rachel's stomach, shocking her. Of course, Isaac would be searching for a perfect wife. He liked everything in his life to be in perfect order. That wife wouldn't be her…for more reasons than she could list. The most important was a former military officer was about as far from an ideal Amish wife as possible.

She managed to keep her voice light when she replied, "I should have guessed he'd be looking for a wife with you getting married. He won't have you to cook and keep his house."

"Does everyone in Vermont know I'm getting married?" She wagged a finger at Rachel. "We shouldn't be speaking of that until the announcement is published during a Sunday service."

"Maybe not everyone in Vermont, but anyone who sees you and David together can tell you're in love. Besides, friends always know these things, and I hope you count me as a friend."

"I do!"

Rachel laughed. "Don't you want to save those words for the wedding ceremony?"

Rolling her eyes, Abby chuckled. "Don't make me watch every word I say. I'll go crazy!"

"I would never do that." She'd spoken with too much fervor because her friend gave her a curious look. She wished she could explain she knew too well how it was to have to guard each word, but she silenced the thought. "So are you going to help your brother find a wife?"

"Me?" Her eyes widened with emoted horror. "Not me! Where would I find my brother the perfect wife he's looking for?"

"Is he serious? How could such a creature exist?"

"I asked him the same thing, but he seems to believe it's possible to find himself the perfect Amish wife."

Rachel laughed along with her friend, but she suspected Abby would jump in to assist her brother if she found a woman she thought would be a *gut* match for him. As much as Abby loved her brother, she would find matchmaking irresistible if she encountered a possible wife for him.

As long as Abby didn't consider Rachel a possible candidate. Trying to make such a match would prove to be a recipe for perfection all right. A recipe for the perfect disaster.

The bus came to a stop with the hiss of air brakes. Isaac paused on the sidewalk along with his future brother-in-law, David Riehl. They'd been checking the furnace being put into the last house the volunteers would be able to finish before winter. The ground began to freeze in late October, and they couldn't put in foundations after that.

Isaac appreciated David's skills with electricity and small motors. David had spotted a misplaced wire in the new furnace. It could be corrected before the unit was turned on.

When he saw Abby and Rachel stepping off the bus with bags of groceries, he called, "Could you use some help?"

His sister turned with a warm smile. When Rachel did the same, he was amazed to feel his heart give a peculiar beat he'd never experienced before. There was something about her expressions, open and honest, that made him want to find excuses to make her smile.

"We'd love some help." Abby held out her bags to David, who took more than half of what she held.

"Rachel?" Isaac asked.

"Danki." As always, she didn't say any more than necessary. Her smile had vanished, and she seemed fascinated with something on the sidewalk in front of her toes.

He lifted the bags out of her hands. He was surprised how heavy they were. Had she taken the weightiest ones for herself? He should have expected that, because she seemed to assume any task without complaint.

A hard-working woman is one of your criteria for a wife, said the small voice heard only in his head.

When the others began to walk toward the community center, Isaac followed. David continued to grin as Abby led their little parade. Isaac had come to see the man was, without question, the perfect match for his sister. They couldn't exchange vows until David completed his baptism classes and was more proficient in *Deitsch*. Plans were being made for the establishment of an Amish community in Evergreen Corners. Once that happened, church leaders had to be chosen. Any married man could become a part of the lot when ministers and a deacon were ordained. Isaac was certain his sister's future husband would be included among the possibilities once they were wed.

Rachel walked alone behind them, and Isaac increased the length of his strides to catch up with her.

"How are the girls feeling?" he asked.

"They're fine."

He'd hoped she would give him something other than the same clipped answers.

"I assume Abby's having the rest of the groceries delivered," he said.

"Ja."

His fingers tightened on the bags' handles. "Have I done something to offend you?"

"Offend me?" She stared at him with candid astonishment. "Of course not! Why would you think that?"

"Whenever I talk to you, you don't say anything more than you have to. I know you aren't curt with Abby, because she's told me things you've said that she's found insightful or amusing. So I'm wondering why it'd be easier for me to pull teeth from an angry bull than to pull words from you."

A flush climbed her cheeks, and he couldn't help but wonder if he'd made her more uncomfortable with him. "The truth is you intimidate me."

"I do?" It was his turn to be shocked. "I don't in-tend to."

"You don't need to apologize. It's just…" She paused and took a deep breath, then released it in a slow sigh. "I don't know what it is, but part is you're so impor-tant to the recovery effort, and I feel like I'm wasting your time."

"Nobody is any more important to our work here." The wrong tack, he realized when she edged away on the sidewalk. "Look, Rachel. Let's agree talking to each other without worrying about every word would be a *gut* thing. You and Abby are friends, and I can't think of any reason why we can't be, too. Can you?"

"No." When he thought she wouldn't say more, she added, "No, I can't think of any reason why we can't be friends, Isaac. It'd be easier for Abby if we were *friends*."

Had she put a slight emphasis on the last word, or was it only in his mind? He would have to change *her* mind that they could share more than friendship…if she continued to show how she could be the perfect wife for him.

Chapter Five

Lining up with the men to enter the community center, where they would worship together, Isaac glanced at where the women were doing the same. Rachel stood near the front of the line, one of the oldest of the volunteers, and he was the second eldest among the men. Only his cousin Vernon was older than he was.

The white-haired woman who was holding Loribeth's hand was Minerva Swartzentruber, the widow his cousin was walking out with. It was odd using such a youthful term to describe his cousin courting a woman who must be nearly sixty years old.

Wasn't he thinking of doing the same? Walking out with a woman who'd caught his eye? A woman who wasn't in her twenties any longer, either. He wasn't the same person he'd been when he was eighteen or nineteen and first considering it was time to look for a wife. Then, the idea of having another person to provide for had sent panic rising through him. He'd made their old farm in Lancaster County sustainable, but he'd spent

every minute of every day working to keep people from
knowing the truth about his *daed*'s craving for alcohol.
Too many nights he'd wished he could have slept instead of tossing and turning with worry.

His life was his own. At last.

During the service while he sang, prayed and listened to the sermons from a pair of visiting ministers, Isaac prayed God would show him the best way
to determine if Rachel was the woman he should ask
to be his wife. His thoughts were interrupted when Eva
crossed between the benches where the men sat facing
the women. She climbed beside him and leaned her
head against his arm.

She's fine, he mouthed when Rachel looked at him.

She gave him a grateful smile before bending her
head to hush her older daughter, who was fidgeting beside her. Recalling how difficult it'd been for him when
he was the little girls' ages to sit for the three hours of
a Sunday service, he was glad to keep one of them distracted so Rachel could concentrate on the other.

He didn't have to do much distracting because two
minutes later, Eva fell asleep. Soft breaths moved her
tiny chest against the arm he curved around her to make
sure she didn't fall. When they rose for a hymn, he
shifted her off his legs. She murmured something but
didn't wake until the service came to an end.

With a cheeky grin, Eva ran to her *mamm*. Isaac
didn't follow, because Rachel would be joining the other
women in serving the communal meal. Though they
usually ate together every day, there was something
special about the Sabbath luncheon, when the men gath-

ered and spoke of the past week's work and the tasks awaiting them in the week to come.

Isaac wanted to linger, but went outdoors with the other men while the women and *kinder* ate. He waited for Rachel and her daughters to come outside, but he was called away by the mayor, who began by apologizing for intruding on his Sunday before she pelted him with questions about the current house projects. He was able to answer most of them, but had to call to other volunteers to provide information, taking them away from a game of cornhole, which was safer and easier to play on the village green than horseshoes.

During the conversation, Isaac kept glancing at the community center. Yet he missed seeing Rachel and her girls emerge, because by the time the mayor was reassured everything was going as scheduled, they'd already left. The men tossing the small containers filled with corn hadn't noticed where they'd gone. He asked everyone along the sidewalk, but they'd been too busy with their conversations to pay attention to anything else.

He'd have to go inside the community center. His feet balked. If he went in there and began asking questions about Rachel, he might as well wear a sign around his neck that he was interested in walking out with her.

As he stood, lost in the uncertainty of what he should do—a most peculiar sensation he couldn't recall feeling before—his sister emerged from the community center. A smile warmed her face when she saw him.

Without a greeting, she said, "Rachel is taking her little ones to look at the brook." Her eyes twinkled at him. "I thought you'd want to know."

"Did you?" he asked, not ready to admit he'd wanted to know. He'd wanted to know very much.

"*Ja.* You're looking for a wife, and as a *gut* sister, it's my job to point out when one is available for you to talk to her without a crowd around." She glanced past him. "Or you could wait until Nina Streit devises a reason to come over here."

He gave a cautious look in the same direction. The pretty, tall blonde he'd seen in the kitchen at the community center was surrounded by several lads too young for her. They were vying for her attention, and she was doling out smiles as if each one was the greatest reward on earth.

"I don't know much about her," Isaac said. "I suppose I should go and introduce myself to her."

"You've already been introduced to her. At the community center earlier in the week. Don't you remember?"

"Oh, *ja*," he said, though he didn't. If he did, he'd also have to admit that whenever Rachel was nearby, he found it difficult to notice any other woman.

"So what are you waiting for? Like I said, Rachel is heading to the brook." She gave him a gentle push. "She won't stay there forever."

Isaac settled his hat on his head as he took a meandering path toward the brook. It was a short walk there, and he heard the girls before he saw them among the few trees that had survived the flood.

Rachel had found a bank where the ground slanted gently toward the water. The closest houses were hidden by a thick row of tall, old-growth trees along the bank. Bugs chirped in the high grass, and more whirred in the air.

The little girls squatted until the front of their *schlupp schotzlis*, the white pinafores they wore over their best dresses, touched the clear bubbles caught between the stones. They were slapping the water with small sticks. When they were splattered, they giggled, their voices as sweet and high-pitched as the birds singing overhead. They all looked back as they heard the sound of his footsteps.

"Isaac!" Rachel exclaimed as he neared.

He understood the questions she hadn't asked but had been inferred in her surprised tone as she spoke his name. What was he doing there? Why had he followed them to the brook?

Making sure his smile didn't waver, he said, "I'm sorry if I startled you."

"You did. I—"

Eva ran over to him. Holding up her branch, she said, "See, I-zak!"

"That's pretty," he said, not sure what she was trying to convey to him.

With a frown, she stamped her tiny foot. "Not pretty. Splash!"

"That's what I meant," he answered quickly. "It must make a pretty big splash."

Her smile returned, as if it'd never vanished. "Big splash!" She hopped to the edge of the brook.

As she teetered, he reached out to catch her. He wasn't quick enough because Rachel grabbed her first. He was left with his arms outstretched, facing Loribeth, who regarded him as if he was some disgusting thing she'd stepped into. The *kind* folded her arms over her chest and turned around. She couldn't have made her feelings about him any clearer if she'd shouted.

"Can we go?" asked Loribeth.

"Take off your shoes and socks," Rachel answered, "and give them to me." She picked up a crocheted bag he hadn't noticed on the ground. When the little girls obeyed and ran around barefoot, with Loribeth keeping a wide swath of ground between her and him, Rachel put the discarded clothing in the bag.

"Where are you going?" he asked.

"I saw some late blackberries across the brook, and we're going to pick some." She gave him a tentative smile as she pulled a small basin from the bag. "I hope the girls are still as enthusiastic about picking the berries after they get jabbed by a thorn."

"I never was happy to get stuck by a thorn when I was a kid! I don't think that will ever change."

"Me, either, but the berries are so sweet it's worth it." Her smile became warmer. "You're welcome to join us if you'd like."

"*Danki*. That sounds like fun, and I'm sure you can make something delicious with any berries we pick."

"You're welcome to take what you pick home."

"How?" He stuck his hands into the pockets of his church trousers. "Abby wouldn't be happy to find berry juice in my best pants."

She didn't laugh with him because Loribeth had jumped to a rock protruding from the water. The little girl teetered, then caught her balance.

"Wait for us," Rachel said.

Her older daughter began to pout, but giggled when foam from the water washed over her bare toes before she moved forward another stone.

Taking Eva by the hand, Rachel went to the shore to follow.

"Don't you want to take off your shoes and socks, too?" Isaac asked. "You're going to get them soaked."

Color washed from her face, and he wondered if she thought he was being too forward. He wouldn't have hesitated to say the same thing to one of his male friends, or to his sister, but everything he said or did around Rachel seemed to have shades of gray he hadn't considered.

"The water is low. I don't think I need to worry." She half turned. "Will you help Eva? I need to keep my brave Loribeth from tumbling into the water."

Had she noticed her older daughter's antipathy toward him? How could she not? Loribeth made no secret of it.

Holding out his hand to the littler girl, he asked, "Ready?"

She nodded, her eyes big with anticipation.

He said, "Let's go," then motioned for her to step onto the first flat stone.

The distance was too much for her short legs, so he grasped her other hand and swung her forward. She chuckled when her toes touched a stone.

Though he kept his eyes on Eva, he couldn't be unaware of Rachel a short distance in front of him. She'd convinced Loribeth to hold her hand, and they were skipping from stone to stone as if they were the same age. He paused, watching. He'd never seen Rachel so carefree before, and he had to wonder if this was how she'd been when her husband was alive.

It was odd how she seldom mentioned him. Was she as reticent with her girls? He tried to recall if he'd ever heard them speak of their *daed*. He thought of how Eva had rested her head against him during the church service, and a surge of sympathy filled him for Rachel's husband, who'd never had a chance to experience such a simple gesture.

As he swung Eva onto the opposite bank, she tugged her fingers out of his the moment her feet touched the grass, then ran after her sister.

Isaac stepped beside Rachel, who was watching them run, their arms outstretched as if about to take flight.

"Looks like you didn't get your feet wet."

"I did." She shook one foot, and water trickled out of her sneaker. "It was either my foot or Loribeth in the brook. It's so hard to believe that sleepy brook did so much damage."

"I know, but look around and see the scars that haven't healed yet."

"Will Amish Helping Hands be able to get everything done by Christmas?"

He shrugged. "Guess we'll have to have everything buttoned-up by then. Not that we'll cut any corners. These people have suffered enough. They don't want a house falling down around their ears."

When Eva tumbled, a strident cry cut through the afternoon. Isaac rushed over and picked up the little girl, brushed dirt off her and reassured her she was okay. A moment later, she was chasing Loribeth.

He saw astonishment in Rachel's eyes. He realized his intrusion might not have been welcome.

"Sorry," he murmured. "I guess I spent so much time as a kid making sure Abby didn't get hurt, old habits kicked in."

"That's okay." She seemed as if she was about to add something more to him, then raised her voice and called, "Don't go so far!" She smiled as the girls paused, then kneeled to look at something close to the ground. "Loribeth would scurry to the ends of the earth if I took my eyes off her."

"And Eva would follow."

"Ja."

"Let me give them a reason to stay closer." He bent and pulled out a wide strip of grass. Holding it to his mouth, he blew hard.

A sharp whistle rang through the air, and the girls' heads popped up. They ran to him.

"I-zak!" Eva exclaimed with a wide grin. "Again!"

"What did you do?" her older sister asked.

He opened his hand and showed them the blade of grass on his palm. "It's a grass whistle."

"Me, too!" Eva hopped around in her excitement.

He aimed a wink at Rachel. "You girls need to find a blade of grass that's long and wide." He pulled on another long piece, loosening the sleek, green portion of new growth. "Like this."

Helping them find the proper-size blades, he saw their hands were filthy. Rachel wouldn't want them putting those dirty fingers to their mouths, so he led them to a spot where the bank was flat.

Rachel urged the girls to be careful as they splattered water in every direction. "You only need to rinse the grass, not agitate the water as if it's a washing machine."

"Shake it to get the water off it," he said and was rewarded with drops spraying over him as the girls swung the pieces over their heads. He raised his hand when Rachel was about to scold them. "I asked for it. I need to be careful what I say."

"They take everyone at their word. Their exact word."

"I get that." Motioning for the girls to come closer, he positioned his piece of grass with his thumbs on either side of it. "You need to hold it like this."

He waited until Rachel had helped the girls. Eva's thumb kept slipping until her *mamm* put her hands over her daughter's, keeping them in place.

Curiosity swept him. How would it feel to have Rachel's fingers against his work-hardened ones? Hers showed signs of years of working as well, but they weren't scarred and coarse like his. Hers cupped Eva's fingers as if they were as fragile and perfect as a soap bubble.

Isaac pushed the thought out of his head. Letting himself get caught in his imagination would be foolish. He couldn't become like his *daed* and lose himself in unreality.

"Hold the grass to your mouth and blow." He demonstrated, and another shrill whistle emerged.

The girls tried but couldn't make any sound other than their lips buzzing against their thumbs.

"It's a trick!" Loribeth scowled.

"Be nice," Rachel said. "It is a trick, but a *gut* one. It's one you can learn if you're patient, ain't so, Isaac?"

"*Ja*. Imagine there's a hole to one side of the piece of grass, and try to blow through it."

Eva looked from his hands to hers. Puffing out her already round cheeks, she blew hard. A faint sound emerged.

"Me did it!" Eva twirled in her excitement. "*Mamm*, me did it!"

"You did." She gave her daughter a quick squeeze.

Loribeth pouted. "Not me. I can't make it whistle. Stupid grass." She started to throw it aside, but Rachel halted her with a frown. "It won't work, *Mamm*. There must be something wrong with it."

"*Komm* here," Isaac said to the little girl. "Let me help you."

For a long moment, he thought Loribeth would refuse. Her determination to do everything her younger sister could do must have been stronger than her dislike for him because she edged closer. Not too close, he noted, and with enough space for her to make a quick getaway if he proved to be untrustworthy.

He shaped her hands around the blade. "Try it."

She did, but no sound came out.

"Blow hard," he urged. "Sometimes the grass needs to know who's the boss."

She drew in a deep breath that made her cheeks look like a chipmunk's, filled with acorns. Her face reddened as she blew. He heard a squeak before she whirled away from him and flung her arms around her *mamm*.

He watched while Rachel congratulated her daughter, giving her a gentle hug. She clapped her hands in appreciation as the girls made silly sounds. She was a *wunderbaar mamm*. There was no doubt about how well she met the standards for his future wife.

Rachel was amazed how the afternoon had turned out. In her most absurd fantasies, she couldn't have envisioned Isaac playing with her girls and helping them pick berries. She tried to imagine their *daed* spending time with them, adjusting their hands so they could make a blade of grass whistle. She couldn't.

She wasn't being fair. Loribeth had been a *boppli* when Travis left for his last deployment, and Eva hadn't been born. Travis had been so excited both times she discovered she was pregnant. Though she knew he'd hoped for a son, he'd been thrilled with Loribeth. He would have been as happy, she had to believe, when Eva was born.

As she sat with her back against a tree, she wasn't surprised when Isaac dropped beside her. The girls could wear her out, and she was accustomed to their endless games.

"I'm not as young as I used to be," he said with a sigh. "Maybe I should have been like Eva and taken a nap during the sermon."

"I hope she wasn't a problem for you. She slipped away when I was trying to keep Loribeth quiet."

"She wasn't a problem. She was out like a light within seconds."

"She didn't sleep well last night."

"You'd never guess that to see her."

"Her nap gave her a second wind, it seems." Rachel smiled as she watched her daughters chasing each other through the grass. They paused to examine a leaf that intrigued them, then tossed it in the brook.

"Are your shoes dry?"

"Almost."

"I don't know how you can stand having your wet toes squishing around in your socks."

"It's no big deal. I get my feet wet almost every time I mop a floor." She forced a smile. "I've been called an enthusiastic mopper."

"You're the first person I've ever met who gets excited about cleaning a floor."

The conversation had taken an absurd turn, but she preferred that to explaining the true reason why she hadn't removed her socks. On her left calf, only inches below her knee, was a scattered pattern of scars. The medics had gotten her to the hospital after the improvised explosive device exploded. Nothing vital had been permanently injured, though they'd had to remove a few chips of bones along with the shrapnel. She'd been back to work within days, but the scars remained. Once healed, she'd forgotten about them until a neighbor in her new community asked about what had happened to her. She'd given some half answer about an accident while traveling, not mentioning she'd been in Afghanistan at the time.

Relieved when the *kinder* ran to join them, Rachel welcomed hugs from her girls. She tried to sort out what they were saying while they talked at the same time about the fun they'd been having.

"Me 'un-gy," Eva announced.

"Hungry," Rachel said when she saw Isaac's confusion.

"You 'un-gy, I-zak?" her daughter asked.

"Always," he answered with an easy grin.

Eva turned to her. "I-zak 'un-gy, too, *Mamm. Komm* eat? P'ease?"

Translating Eva's toddler words to mean she wanted Isaac to join them for supper, Rachel wondered if he'd understood that, too. When she gave him a sideways glance, he was smiling at her daughter. Telling him she didn't have enough to share—which would be false—was something she couldn't do.

She hoped her voice didn't sound like fake merriment. "We've got macaroni salad and some cold leftover ham for supper. Would you like to join us?"

"Oh, *komm, komm*, I-zak," cried Eva, dancing about as if she stood on an anthill. "P'etty p'ease."

"How could I turn down an invitation like that?" he asked with a wink.

"Easy. Say 'no *danki*,'" muttered her older daughter.

"Loribeth!" Rachel chided. "What have Miss Gwen and I told you about being polite to others?"

"It's important." Her daughter's stance made it clear she didn't agree. "But Miss Gwen said—"

"There are no *buts*. I'm sure that's what Miss Gwen said."

"But, *Mamm*—"

"No *buts*." Gentling her voice, she said, "Go and get

your shoes and socks, please. Help Eva if she can't get her shoes on."

Loribeth stomped to where her shoes and socks had been left. Anger radiated from her.

"Are you sure it's okay for me to join you?" Isaac asked, his smile gone as his gaze followed her daughters.

"I wouldn't have asked if I didn't think it was okay."

"You may think it's okay, but I don't know if your older one shares your opinion."

"True, but she needs to learn to be nice to everyone."

"Not just people she likes?"

"That isn't what I meant." The familiar swath of heat that surrounded her whenever she said the wrong thing around Isaac—which she seemed to do with horrifying frequency—climbed up her face. "She got along fine with you when you were teaching them to whistle with grass."

"It was more of a truce than the beginning of a friendship."

"For Loribeth, that's a big deal." She sighed. "She wasn't happy when I first brought them here. Eva trusts everyone, but Loribeth's trust has to be earned."

"She dislikes change?"

"I'm not sure if it's that, though she's had plenty of changes in her short life. It may be the way she is."

"Like her *mamm*?"

Rachel's eyes widened, and she couldn't keep from staring at him. Was she as distrustful as Loribeth? She hadn't thought so, but it might appear that way to someone who didn't know how many secrets she was keeping.

"More like her *daed*, I'd say," she replied, knowing she must sound as if she didn't have any reason not to discuss this. "I see him in her."

"What about Eva?" Not giving her a chance to answer, he chuckled. "I'd say she's pretty much a miniature of you. She's warmhearted, and she isn't afraid of doing what she thinks is right."

"Oh, don't let her fool you. She can be more stubborn than her sister."

"Again like you, if I don't miss my guess."

"Well," she said, "we all have our faults, ain't so?"

She held her breath, hoping her words would be a reminder she wasn't the ideal wife Abby had told her he was seeking. If the circumstances had been different, she would have enjoyed spending more time with Isaac—with and without the *kinder*. But he was looking for a wife, and she wasn't ready to think about marriage, not until she was sure her girls would be happy with the choice she made.

"I don't see," Isaac said, "being stubborn as a fault. It means you're focused and persistent and know what you want out of life."

If only that could be true…

"Maybe I'll tell Miss Gwen that," she said, "the next time she says one of my girls is being as stubborn as an old mule."

"Who's Miss Gwen? You mentioned her before."

"She's the head teacher at the day care where the girls go while I'm helping in the kitchen."

"You must have made sacrifices to come to Evergreen Corners."

She wondered if he was curious how she could afford to be there. Few widows would have been able to leave their homes and volunteer their time, as she was doing. He had no idea she received a monthly military pension. She didn't use it for day-to-day expenses, but instead lived on the savings she'd accrued and on Travis's insurance. Her pension went to a bank account, waiting for the time when her daughters married.

"I've been glad to help," she said, "and it's been a *wunderbaar* experience for the girls to meet new friends."

"And you, too?"

She shouldn't look at him, but she did, and her gaze was captured by his dark brown eyes. Her answer to the question was important to him. Oh, how she wished she could come out and say he shouldn't consider her for a wife!

The perfect Amish wife, she corrected herself.

Somehow she needed to find a way to let him know she'd never be a perfect wife, most especially not a perfect Amish wife.

Chapter Six

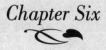

The kitchen drain continued its steady *drip-drip-drip*. Rachel's attempts to tighten it by hand hadn't stopped the leak. She needed a wrench to put a halt to the puddles under the sink.

She pawed through the small toolbox that had been stored in the closet in her bedroom. Who kept a toolbox without an adjustable crescent wrench?

Sitting on her heels, she grimaced. So many times she'd reminded the men and women working in her transportation company to check their tools *before* they needed them. She could imagine the laughter if those soldiers ever discovered their company commander hadn't followed her own orders. She'd been foolish to assume her landlord had provided a complete set of basic tools.

Rachel set herself on her feet. One thing hadn't changed from her life in the Army. If she lacked something necessary to complete a job, she needed to find a way to get her hands on that tool.

She glanced at the clock on the stove. She was already late getting the girls from day care. She'd have to go to the store before she took them home. Glad she'd planned on leftovers for supper, she grabbed her bonnet and tied it under her chin as she hurried out into the warm afternoon.

Grateful that, for once, the girls didn't beg to linger a few extra minutes to play with their friends, Rachel walked with them to the store that wasn't far from the library.

It was tiny compared to the big-box stores on the edge of town, and she hoped somewhere in the muddle of merchandise there would be an adjustable wrench. She went to where tools were stacked in no particular order on the wall opposite the small post-office window. When she found what she was looking for, she tested the adjustments on the wrench. It should be perfect.

She was starting to show the girls what she was buying when Isaac came into the store. He noticed her, too, and he smiled as he walked toward them, as he had three days ago, when he'd joined her and the girls for a Sunday walk through the meadow on the far side of the brook. And just as it had that day, her heart began to dance within her.

Isaac grinned and replied to Eva's enthusiastic greeting. He glanced in Loribeth's direction, but didn't try to engage her in conversation. Though she had no idea why her older daughter had taken a dislike to Isaac, Rachel was relieved they seemed to have called a truce. At least for today.

Finally he looked at her, and her knees wobbled. She straightened them, determined to keep her heart from ruling her head, as had happened when she'd fallen for a man whose first love had always been his military career.

"Trouble?" Isaac asked in lieu of a hello.

She followed his gaze to the wrench she held. "We've got a drain that's leaking. I thought—"

"I'll check it if you'd like."

She halted herself from saying she was capable of doing the repairs herself. Saying that could create questions. An Amish woman would depend on the men in her family to handle household repairs.

"Ja!" Eva shouted before Rachel could answer. "Make it stop, I-zak! P'ease, p'ease!" She began her impression of a dripping sink as she spun around him.

"I guess we'd appreciate your help," Rachel said as Isaac took the little girl by the hand. "Let me pay for this."

"I've got wrenches in my toolbox," he replied.

"I should have one at home. Just in case."

"Ja, you should, and I'll show you how to use it the right way." He smiled. "You're wise to be prepared for emergencies, Rachel."

"I don't know if a dripping sink is an emergency. It's just annoying."

"It's *gut* to be prepared for annoyances, too."

Rachel paid for the wrench with Loribeth close to her side. She noticed for the first time how her older daughter positioned herself to stand between Rachel and Isaac. Had Rachel betrayed her uneasiness about Isaac's interest in some way? She needed to ask Loribeth, but it would have to wait until after the sink was repaired.

Eva kept up a steady babble to Isaac as they climbed

the sloping street toward the trailer. She talked about day care and her toys. Unsure how much Isaac understood, Rachel interjected an explanation here and there, where she could. Sometimes, *she* didn't comprehend what her younger daughter said.

As they passed the mailbox by the road, Isaac said, "Looks as if you've got mail."

She opened the half-ajar mailbox door. Pulling out flyers from local businesses, she saw an official-looking envelope. Her stomach dropped toward her toes. Even after she saw it was junk mail made to look important, her heart continued to thud against her ribs.

Travis's family had seen her decision to return to her Amish roots as an attempt to keep them from spending time with Loribeth and Eva. She'd assured them that she would bring the girls to visit as often as she could. In fact, while she'd lived in Maine, she'd sent letters offering to come to their home in Rhode Island. When she decided to go to Evergreen Corners to assist with the rebuilding and give herself a chance to recreate her life, she'd contacted them. That time their answer had been that, until she set aside her idea of becoming Amish, they wanted nothing to do with her. There had been a veiled suggestion her in-laws intended to consult with an attorney about getting the girls so they could raise them "as their father would have wanted," but nothing had come of it.

Not so far.

They hadn't responded to her subsequent letters. When she'd sent pictures of the girls as *bopplin*—pictures taken before she returned to the Amish—she hadn't received a reply. The situation broke her heart. The *kinder* had lost their *daed*, and she hadn't expected they'd lose their grandparents, too. They'd only known Travis's parents because she hadn't dared to try to sneak them to visit her *mamm*. The chance of encountering *Daed* was too great, and she didn't want him to ruin their lives as he'd attempted to ruin hers and her brother's and sister's.

In the kitchen, Isaac gave each of the girls a task to do so they could feel as if they were helping. Eva was sent to get old towels from the bathroom, and Loribeth was asked to hold a flashlight so it shone under the sink. Rachel was impressed anew about how well Isaac handled the *kinder*, even though it had been quite a while since he'd done the same with his brothers and sister.

He talked through every step he took to repair the drain. At his urging, Rachel leaned in as if she was hearing something new. Her daughters laughed when he explained how to know in which direction to turn the wrench. Rachel had to grab the flashlight from Loribeth as the two girls giggled and danced around the kitchen as they called out, "Righty tighty, lefty loosey."

"Want to try using the wrench, Rachel?" Isaac asked as he pushed himself out from under the sink.

"Sure." She squatted and held out her hand.

He placed it on her palm and explained how she should hold it to get the best torque. When she moved to reach under the sink, he put his hand on her elbow to steady it.

His touch had the opposite effect. Her usual firm grip on a tool wavered as her hand shook from the sensation of his work-roughened skin touching her.

"It's heavy," he said, his words brushing the fine

hairs beneath her *kapp* at her nape. "Use two hands if you need to."

"No, I want to use it the right way. Learning the wrong way won't get anyone anywhere."

She heard his smile in his voice as he said, "True."

Giving the wrench a firm twist, she smiled, too, as the water oozing around the pipe stopped. "I think that's it."

He motioned her aside and checked the pipe. He set the wrench on the floor, then wiped moisture from the drain line. When no more drips appeared, he nodded. "Looks *gut*." Standing, he dried his hands on a towel. "It shouldn't *drip-drip-drip* now, girls." He bent to pick up the wrench.

Loribeth grabbed it. "Want to use the wrench."

"Me, too," Eva said, never wanting to be left out. Her lower lip protruded in a pout to match her sister's. "Use wench."

Trying not to laugh because releasing one emotion might undam the rest of them, and she needed to keep tight control while she stood close to Isaac, Rachel tapped her younger daughter's lower lip with her fingertip. "Leave this stuck out like this, and someone will put a teacup on it."

"No teacup!" asserted the little girl. "Want to use the wench."

"Wrench," Rachel said before she couldn't hold back her laughter any longer. "Wr-r-r-rench."

"That's what me said." Eva regarded her as if wondering whether her *mamm* had lost her mind. "Me want to use the wench."

"I think it's a lost battle," Isaac said with a chuckle. Leaning toward Eva, he asked, "Does your *mamm* have a toolbox?"

"*Ja.*"

"Do you know where it is?"

Eva pointed to a spot in front of the stove. "Right there!"

"Can you two girls put this wrench into the box so your *mamm* can find it the next time she needs it?" He regarded them with a stern expression. "First, you need to get some cloths and make sure it's dry. Rusty tools don't help anyone. Do you think you can do that?"

Eva gave him an excited *ja*, and soon the two little girls were sitting on the floor with the wrench balanced between them as they dried every inch of it.

"*Danki,*" Rachel said as she closed the door of the sink cabinet.

"That should keep them entertained for a while."

"*Ja*, but my *danki* was for your help in fixing the leak."

"I think your final twist did the trick." He gathered the damp towels. "You catch on quickly."

She kept her eyes lowered. Would they give away the truth she kept hidden? "I've got a *gut* teacher."

He beamed as she took the towels and carried them to the hamper in the bathroom.

Relieved he hadn't guessed he'd been teaching someone who was familiar with wrenches, she came into the kitchen to discover Eva had invited him to join them for supper. She hushed Isaac's protests that she didn't need to provide him with a meal, because tonight's supper might go a long way toward proving to him she'd never be viewed as the perfect Amish wife.

Isaac put away the toolbox and returned to the kitchen. He tried to find out if Rachel was okay with him staying for supper, but she brushed aside his words as she bustled around the small kitchen.

"Girls, get your cups and bring them to the table." She smiled over their heads as she added, "They're already learning to help."

"Training up a *kind* is important."

"It's easy when they want to assist me." She motioned for him to leave the kitchen. "And you can assist me by sitting and keeping the girls out from underfoot while I make our supper."

"You heard your *mamm*, girls. We're banished from the kitchen."

When Rachel suggested they color, her daughters collected books and crayons from a small box in the living room. They sprawled on their stomachs, and he had to take care making sure he didn't step on small toes or fingers as he edged out of the kitchen.

He bumped a rocker. Reaching out to slow its rocking, he ran his fingers along the simple carving on the thick wood. He wasn't a finish carpenter, but he could appreciate the artistry of an excellent woodworker.

"This is a well-made rocker," he said. "Where was it made?"

"Germany."

"Really?"

"*Ja.*" She bent to stir the bowl of macaroni salad

she'd pulled out of the refrigerator. She must be making sure the dressing reached the bottom of the dish. "I saw it in a catalog, and I realized how nice it'd be for rocking *bopplin* to sleep."

"So you had it brought from Germany?"

"Ja."

Was she extravagant with everything she set her heart upon?

"My husband," she went on, "saw how much I loved it and insisted we get it before Loribeth was born." A faint smile tipped her lips. "He said it was the least he could do when I was giving him a son to follow in his footsteps." Her smile broadened. "By the time Loribeth was born, the chair had been delivered, and we were happy to have a healthy daughter."

More questions pelted his mind, but Eva jumped to her feet and brought her coloring book for him to admire. She'd colored cows blue and the sky orange, and there was more color outside the lines than inside. She'd also added a few blobs of yellow that she informed him were the people looking at the cow: Eva, Loribeth, Rachel…and him. That he was included sent an unexpected warmth through him.

It stayed with him during the meal of ham, salad and potato chips. The girls had been delighted when he asked for chocolate milk, too. Loribeth thawed enough to tell him about how they'd found the chocolate milk at the store despite it being moved to a different location since their last visit.

When Rachel offered *kaffi* along with dessert, he accepted. The girls ate their apple pie and returned to their coloring on the floor before Rachel had a chance to set a cup and plate in front of him. He picked up his fork, eager to try the pie, which smelled so *wunderbaar*.

He cut through the crust and put a bite in his mouth. The spices exploded, thrilling his senses as he chewed. And chewed. And chewed. Even so, he had to swallow hard. He grabbed his cup and washed down the remainder with *kaffi*. He almost gagged because he'd forgotten to put sugar and milk into his cup.

"Are you okay?" she asked, and he realized she hadn't brought a piece of pie for herself.

"Of course. The pie is delicious. I don't know what special spices you put in it, but they're fabulous."

"You're being too generous." She poked at one of the crumbs on Eva's plate. "My husband used to say he liked my pie crust because it was resilient, like me. I know I'm not a *wunderbaar* pie-maker."

"Apple is my favorite pie, so I'm not fussy about anything but the filling."

"Is that a nice way of saying the crust is chewy?"

He searched for an answer that wouldn't insult her or her pie. "I'd say it's unique."

"*Danki* for your honesty. I'll never be the baker your sister is. Abby's crusts are so light she has to put filling in to keep them from floating away. I appreciate you being honest, as my husband was."

"Were you married for a long time?" he asked before he could halt himself.

"Six years almost to the day from when we said our vows to when he died after we found out Eva was on her way." She sighed. "I'm beginning to remember the *gut* anniversary more than the sad one."

"I'm glad. It's got to be better for the girls."

"I'm not sure it makes any difference to them. Loribeth may remember him, but I think it's more because of what I've told her rather than from her own memories. Eva never had a chance to know him."

"I didn't realize that."

"I try to talk about him to the girls, but sometimes it feels as if the time I had with him is melting away, inch by inch."

"Hasn't his family helped you keep his memory alive?"

"I don't hear from them often." She stood. "Would you like more *kaffi*?"

"If you don't mind." He would rather find out why her late husband's family seemed to have cut off her and the girls, but he recognized the resolve in her voice as she'd changed the subject.

The *kaffi*, once he added cream and sugar, was the best Isaac had had in a long time. Maybe his sister's pie crust was a bit more flaky—or a lot more flaky—but Rachel brewed a *wunderbaar* cup of *kaffi*.

Taking another appreciative sip, he gazed across the table and smiled at her. He was curious about her past, but her averted eyes had made it clear she didn't want to talk about it. He could respect that. Though they'd spent some time together during the past couple of weeks, they remained strangers.

He wished he knew a quick way to break through the barriers she kept in place. Grief must unfold in its own way. He'd learned that by observing his *daed*.

He continued to enjoy his *kaffi* as she put the girls to bed. When she returned, they spoke of the projects he was working on and the chances the work could be finished before year's end. He asked what her plans were when the aid agencies closed their doors in Evergreen Corners, and he wasn't surprised when she said she might remain in the small village. He could understand the appeal, because though he'd traveled often to his family's farm in northern Vermont, something had always drawn him back. Not only the work he could do, but also a community that connected plain folks and *Englischers*.

"I should get going," he said, noticing it was almost ten o'clock. In spite of his words, he didn't move. "*Danki* for the pie and the company."

"*Danki* for the lesson in how to use a wrench."

"Don't you mean 'wench'?" he asked as he stood.

When she rolled her eyes and shook her head, he laughed.

He was glad she was enjoying their conversation as much as he was. He hadn't wanted to leave while she was distressed.

Maybe it'd be better if they kept their conversations on the present, he decided as he bid her *gut nacht*. That would allow him to lead the subject to the future, specifically if they could have a future together.

Chapter Seven

In the clear warm light of morning, as Rachel worked in the community center's kitchen along with the other volunteers, it seemed as if the conversation she'd had with Isaac last night had been part of a dream. She tried to equate the laid-back man who'd faced her across her dining-room table with the person who always seemed focused on the next problem as he was dealing with the present one. She'd never expected the stern man who was obsessed with timetables sitting and enjoying cups of *kaffi* along with her pie.

She was grateful and disappointed he hadn't joined the volunteers at breakfast. Though she wasn't sure what she would have said to him, she would have liked to discover if last evening felt like a moment out of time for him, too.

Shaking her head, she tried to rid it of the cobweb of thoughts she shouldn't have been having. That everything seemed dreamlike could be explained by the gray morning and the downpour that had caught her unprepared after she'd dropped off Loribeth and Eva at day care. She'd been soaked before she could get back inside. With every step, her toes seemed awash in water inside her sneakers.

I don't know how you can stand having your wet toes squishing around in your socks.

She was shocked. The voice inside her head belonged to Isaac. It must have been because she was thinking about their conversation last night.

She was getting too involved with a man who was looking for something she wasn't. Getting comfortable with him could lead to her blurting out the truth. Hadn't she learned that last night, when she'd mentioned the rocking chair had been made in Germany? She'd stopped before telling him it'd been purchased while she was recovering in Germany after being wounded. At the time, Travis had seen it as a peace offering because he'd been insisting she resign her commission to be with their daughter. She'd asked him to become a civilian, too, but he'd resisted until his unit was deployed for what would be his final mission.

"Hey, Rachel! Are you awake over there?"

At Hailee's impatient voice, she wondered how long the young woman had been calling to her. She looked at the cleaning rag that had dripped on the table. How long had she been standing and thinking about things that couldn't and shouldn't be changed?

"Not quite," she called. "Need me for something?"

"Have you seen the big box we use for the midmorning coffee break? Abby can't find it."

"It's in the pantry. I'll get it."

"Thanks!" Whirling to do another chore, Hailee hummed a Clint Black song Rachel recalled from before she'd turned off the radio for the final time.

She went into the pantry and took down the large insulated bag, then carried it to where Abby had gathered food left from breakfast. "Here you go."

"*Danki*, Rachel," Isaac's sister said with a grateful smile. Fatigue had left charcoal shadows beneath her eyes, and Rachel recalled that the youth group Abby oversaw with her fiancé was busy planning a hike before snow closed the mountain trails. "Can you pack muffins along with those chocolate-chip cookies?"

"Let me help," Hailee said.

They filled a box with treats. Rachel got some butter from the fridge and added a few plastic knives to the box. Zipping the top closed, she saw Abby stop on the other side of the table.

"You know how much I hate to ask this," Abby began with a wry smile.

"I know. It's my turn to take the midmorning snacks to the workers. Besides, I'm already wet." She wiggled her toes in her sneakers. "I make strange sounds when I walk."

Abby smiled. "At least take my umbrella."

"I'll be fine." She had no idea how she'd manage the box and the big container of fresh *kaffi* along with an umbrella. "Someone else can take the food for the afternoon break."

"Sounds like a plan." Abby patted her arm. "We appreciate your volunteering, especially today."

"*Ja*," interjected Nina as she paused by the table. "It

wouldn't be right for one of us who's interested in finding a husband to be seen looking like…"

"A drowned rat?" Rachel asked as she hefted the box.

"Men like to believe a woman is always lovely, no
matter the situation, and we shouldn't do anything to
make them think otherwise." She looked at Rachel and
sighed. "I guess you don't remember how it is for us
younger women."

Instead of firing a sharp answer, as she suspected
Nina wanted, Rachel put her hand against her lower
back and leaned forward as if gripping a cane. "You're
right. We old folks don't understand you young whip-
persnappers."

Laughter came from around the kitchen, and Nina's
eyes narrowed with unspoken anger. She flounced away
as Rachel straightened.

"Be careful," Hailee warned. "She could be a dangerous enemy."

"Only if we want the same thing, which we don't."
She felt a prickle of guilt, but she couldn't consider a
future with Isaac when he wanted a perfect wife. Not
that Nina would be a perfect Amish wife, either, but at
least she didn't have a past as a military officer and she
could give him the family Rachel could not.

Abby handed her the thermos. "She thinks her smiles
will reduce men to blithering idiots eager to do her bid-
ding."

"From what I've seen, she may be right." Rachel
shifted the two containers so she wouldn't drop either.

"A blithering idiot isn't what I was looking for in a
husband."

"Maybe Nina is."

"Do you think it would cause too much of a scandal if I told her to go home?" A wistful note filled Abby's voice.

"You're assuming if you asked she'd listen to your request."

"True." Abby smiled. "*Danki*, Rachel. You always put everything in the proper perspective. I'm sorry it's your turn to go to the building site today."

She started to shrug, then thought better of it as the insulated box shifted. She carried the food out to the main room, then put it down long enough to pull on her wet coat and soaked bonnet. She picked up the boxes and thanked Hailee, who helped by tossing Rachel's cloak over her and what she carried.

Rachel went out into the storm. She was certain it'd be easier to walk with the bulky containers than with her daughters, who were always tempted to run and look at something that intrigued them, no matter what the weather.

The village appeared deserted except for a few people who'd gathered on the bridge over the brook. They looked upriver toward the ruined covered bridge and then downstream. She'd seen a handful of residents go onto the main bridge with every storm. A bank of dark clouds above the mountains to the west drew more people to the bridge. She nodded as she walked past them, but didn't stop to ask what they thought they might be able to do if the brook rose to a dangerous level, as it had last fall. They wouldn't be able to stop the wild waters, but she guessed they didn't want to be taken by surprise again.

The buildings were being repaired and the roads repaved. Bridges had been reconstructed, and trees had been replanted. However, it'd be far longer before anyone who'd lived through the flood would have peace of mind.

The building sites weren't far from the covered bridge. One set of wooden arches had been stripped of everything but a few deck boards. Atop the other set, the bridge seemed to tilt more with each passing day. Would it collapse into the brook before it could be repaired? She knew the mayor was fighting red tape to get funds, but so far the state hadn't considered the bridge a priority, because there were alternate ways to get to the homes on either side of the brook.

If her transportation unit had been there, they could have put down a roadbed and erected a temporary structure to protect the antique timbers in no time.

Rachel might as well wish the flood had never happened. She hurried through the strengthening wind to where three partially built houses were set side by side overlooking the brook. The road separated the house sites from the brook. In the hurricane, water had swept the original houses off their foundations. From what she'd heard, furniture from only one of the houses had ever been found, and that had been downstream near a lake. Everything from the other two houses had vanished.

The ground around the building sites had been trampled bare. Grass and weeds tangled beyond the areas where the volunteers worked. Nobody was outside on the rainy day. The two houses without roofs stood deserted, so she guessed everyone was inside the one that offered some shelter.

Going inside, she heard several workers call, "Shut the door!"

She smiled as she shook rain off her bonnet. The warning sounded as if it'd been said enough times to become singsong. With the house weatherproofed, the volunteers were determined to avoid the elements they'd worked in during the past months.

She couldn't blame them. She was grateful every day for the cooler weather, so it was possible to catch one's breath in the community center's kitchen.

"Coffee's here!" shouted a woman dressed in bib overalls and a bright red shirt. She was, if Rachel recalled correctly, a teacher at the elementary school.

Every head turned, and Rachel's eyes were caught by Isaac's. He stood on a board straddling two sawhorses while he worked near the ceiling. She was astonished to see he was wiring a ceiling fan in place, but knew she shouldn't be. Though Amish didn't have electricity in their homes, they did in their barns and businesses.

He jumped down, then took the *kaffi* container and set it on the board where he'd been standing. She put the box of muffins and cookies next to it. She grabbed the box when it wobbled.

"It's okay," he said, chuckling as he handed her a towel to wipe her soaked hands and face. "The sawhorses aren't the same height."

"Are you sure it's not an uneven floor?" she asked,

surprised to hear herself teasing him within earshot of the other volunteers.

A tall plain man she knew was named Michael Miller rolled his eyes like an irritated teenager. "You wouldn't joke about such things if you had any idea how many measurements Isaac insisted we take before we set the first joist."

"And for the second and third," added another man from the other side of the room.

More grumbles laced with laughter came from every direction around her.

"See what you've started by questioning the quality of our work?" asked Isaac.

Rachel joined in with the laughter, and the bad taste left by Nina's snide comments vanished. "I'll know better from now on."

"Do you want to see what we've done?"

"*Ja*, once I pour the *kaffi*."

He motioned to one of the men. "Jose will be glad to do that so he makes sure he gets a full cup today."

The man who wore a cheerful grin said, "I didn't complain much about having only a half cup yesterday."

When several of the volunteers snorted their disagreements, everyone chuckled.

Isaac took the cup held out to him and snagged a pair of cookies before motioning for her to follow him. After taking off her shawl, coat and bonnet so she didn't track water through the new house, she peeked through doorways into rooms set off by two-by-fours. Wiring ran between the studs. Hand tools were placed close to the walls, but she had to slalom around the larger equipment.

"It's beginning to look like a real house," she said as he finished the second cookie. "How much longer do you think it'll take?"

"About four to six weeks. Once the drywall is up, we'll put on joint compound. That needs to dry before we can begin painting. We'll install the cabinets and fixtures. Floors go in after that. At the same time, the exterior will be painted. That will finish the project, and we'll move on to our next-to-the-last house." He gave her a wry smile. "You can see why I'm concerned about finishing by year's end. I think we'll have to divide the team to get both houses done on time."

"I'm sure you'll figure it out."

"Without cutting corners."

"You're going to have to cut some corners off boards."

His mouth quirked. "You know what I meant."

"I did, but it's fun to pull your leg. The girls don't get my sometimes absurd sense of humor."

"Or they're wise enough to ignore your words." Not giving her a chance to retort, he asked, "How are the girls doing?"

His simple question opened the door to the memories of last evening, and she found herself tongue-tied, as she'd been the day he'd helped her take the *kinder* to the *doktor*'s office. "Okay."

"Not making their regular mischief?" He looked at his work boots. "If one shines more than the other, it's because it got a *gut* cleaning after Loribeth threw up on it."

She despised the heat rising along her face. "I should have said this before. *Danki*, Isaac, for being a big help since the day the girls got sick. I should have—"

He halted her by putting his finger against her lips. Shocked by the spark that raced from his skin to hers, she could only stare at him.

Swallowing hard, he drew back his hand. "You've thanked me too much already, Rachel."

He grinned, but the easy expression didn't reach his hooded eyes. What was he trying to hide? That he'd felt something unexpected when he touched her, or he'd noticed her reaction and realized he'd made a mistake?

She wondered how two siblings could be so different. Abby couldn't hide a single thing she felt because it was displayed on her face. Isaac was the definition of a closed book, concealing what he thought behind correct words. Wasn't she doing the same? Last night in the trailer, she'd veiled her thoughts behind an offer of a cup of *kaffi* and a taut smile.

She must respect his secrets if she didn't want him to probe into hers. She must make sure he never suspected she was anything other than the widow he saw in front of his eyes.

Isaac drove a nail into a board, swinging the hammer with the power of his frustration. What a *dummkopf* he was! What had he been thinking? He shouldn't have given in to his yearning to discover if Rachel's lips were as soft as they looked. Not when they were in a house filled with other volunteers. If they'd been seen...

He grabbed another nail and banged the hammer on it, grazing his thumb. Startled, he stared at the reddened digit. He hadn't hit himself with a hammer since he'd been a boy. That had been his first lesson. Keep his eye—and mind—on what he was doing while using tools.

He'd been thinking about Rachel and how her bright blue eyes had widened when his fingertip touched her mouth. She looked away, but not quickly enough because he'd seen more than shock in her gaze. He'd seen a softening there, an invitation he wasn't sure she intended to offer him.

"Having trouble keeping your mind on your work?" asked his cousin Vernon as he brought an assembled light to go onto the fan Isaac had been hanging when Rachel arrived.

"Trying to figure out how we're going to get everything done in time," he said.

"In the house or with something else?" Vernon laughed, then added in a near whisper so nobody else could hear, "So I see you've decided to court a widow, too. Or were my eyes—and everyone else's—deceiving us?"

"I'm not going to dignify that stupid question with an answer." Isaac pulled a tape measure from his belt. "We need to get to work."

His cousin continued to chuckle as he went on to his next task. The older man wore a knowing grin every time Isaac spoke with him that morning. The rest of the crew was more circumspect, but Isaac couldn't help overhearing whispers when he walked past.

When it was time to stop for the day, he was relieved. Today, it'd seemed everyone was more interested in gossiping than working. Why couldn't others mind their own business? The question had plagued him while he tried to keep the neighbors from learning about his *daed*'s alcoholism. He didn't want to deal with it again.

Isaac was fighting a headache by the time he dragged his grim mood up the steps to the garage apartment. He was tired of the sideways glances, tired of whispered speculation, tired of the rain and tired of worrying about the schedule that seemed impossible to meet.

He was met by the aroma of beef stew as he entered the apartment. His sister had changed her work schedule so she cooked meals at home two nights a week, but she often left something on the stove for him and went to David's house to eat with him and his daughter.

Abby came out of the kitchen, wiping her hands on her apron. She smiled. "Did you have a *gut* day, Isaac? Rachel said you're making great progress on the house. She enjoyed the tour you gave her."

"Not you, too, Abby," he grumbled as he placed his hat on the peg by the door with more fervor than necessary. It careened off, and he had to retrieve it and slip it on the peg.

"Not me, too? What are you talking about?"

"Vernon has been bugging me since Rachel brought food for our break this morning. Maybe you should send someone else with the *kaffi*."

She folded her arms in front of her. "I could send

Nina or Hailee, I suppose, but I'd have to explain to Rachel you don't want her there."

"No, that won't work."

"The first part or the second?"

He rubbed his brow. His headache was strengthening and threatened to crack open his skull. "Can't we talk about something else? Let's eat." He took a single step toward the kitchen and gasped when his knees buckled beneath him.

Abby leaped forward and caught him, steering him toward the sofa in one smooth motion. When he collapsed on it, she placed a hand against his forehead.

"You've got a fever, Isaac. I think you've caught the bug that's going around."

"Don't be silly! I've got too much work to be sick."

"As if germs ever check our schedules."

He groaned, unsure if the sound was from the abrupt pain in his gut, or the thought of how many on his team could sicken if he'd passed the bug on to them. They already were cutting it close in their race to finish the houses before the aid agencies shut.

Then he'd have to go home to the family's farm up north. Could he return to the life he'd left behind, a life of secrets and half truths? Could he leave without letting Rachel know he believed she'd be the perfect wife for him?

Chapter Eight

"Look who's back among the living!" someone shouted from the community center's main room.

Laughter reverberated into the kitchen.

Rachel hurried to the pass-through window and was pleased to see Isaac, though gray under his eyes, looked otherwise fine. When she'd learned he was sick, she'd wanted to help, but Abby, while grateful, had been determined to keep Rachel and her daughters from being exposed to Isaac's germs.

She watched as his crew welcomed him as if he'd been gone for two years instead of two days. He grinned at their teasing, but his gaze swept the room. When it struck hers, she gripped the edge of the pass-through and didn't look away. He'd become so much a part of her life during the past couple of weeks that it'd seemed as if a strange void had been opened when he didn't stop by to play with Eva and try—yet again—to persuade Loribeth they could be friends, too.

She missed him.

Plain and simple. Missed him as she hadn't missed anyone since Travis went away on his final deployment.

Would it be as painful when Isaac left Evergreen Corners at year's end? She tried to tell herself his going would be for the best.

But as their gazes connected and locked, she wondered how much longer she could pretend she'd be satisfied with being his friend and nothing more.

Isaac crossed the room toward her, and she stepped out of the kitchen. The other voices in the room became muffled as she said, *"Gute mariye."*

"Gute mariye."

"How are you feeling?"

"As someone said, I'm among the living," he said with a smile that made her fight to catch her breath. "It wasn't the same bug the *kinder* had, though it had similar symptoms. So you don't have to feel guilty that I caught it from your girls."

"I wasn't. They were sick too long ago."

"So why are you on edge?"

She didn't want to tell him how worried she'd been—how worried she *was* about him leaving Evergreen Corners in a few months—but she also refused to lie. "No more than you are, Isaac Kauffman, when I'm sure you spent your recovery time worrying that even a single sick day will keep you from finishing those last three houses before the end of the year."

"Abby shouldn't have said—"

"Abby didn't say anything. I know you and how you've been fretting about the projects."

He squared his shoulders. "A man doesn't fret, Rachel."

"What would you call being concerned about every detail of every project, how it'll be done and when, how much it'll cost and what will happen if everything isn't finished to your standards by the end of the year?"

"Dedication."

She laughed, glad he felt well enough to jest. "Call it whatever you want. It's fretting."

"She's right," Abby said as she joined them. Giving her brother a quick hug, she grinned. "You were worse than ever when you weren't feeling *gut*."

Looking from his sister to her, Isaac said, "I hope she didn't tell you I threw up on her shoes."

Rachel's eyes widened. "You did? How awful for…" She wasn't sure if she should feel sorrier for Isaac or Abby.

"He's joking, Rachel," Abby said as she wagged a warning finger at her brother, who burst into laughter. "He kept everything down fine."

Firing a frown in his direction, Rachel said, "It's not like you to tell a lie, Isaac Kauffman."

"I didn't tell a lie." He struggled to speak past his guffaws. "I said I hoped Abby didn't tell you I threw up on her shoes. Guess I didn't add I hoped she hadn't because it wasn't true."

"See what I have to endure?" his sister asked with a martyr's sigh. "Nobody realizes how he pokes fun at people he's close to."

As brother and sister continued to debate in *gut* humor, Rachel wished she could hold Abby's words inside her heart. Isaac teased people he was close to? That must mean he was feeling close to her. She allowed herself to savor the idea a moment before pushing it aside. Isaac wasn't looking for a friend, she reminded herself. He was looking for a perfect Amish wife to give him a perfect Amish family and a perfect Amish home.

Abby was called away with a question, and Rachel started to follow. She paused when Isaac spoke her name.

"Rachel, I need to ask you a favor." He reminded her of Loribeth when she was unsure if she could get away with something naughty.

Naughty? Isaac? The two words didn't go together. Though she'd discovered other sides to him than the strict martinet she first had believed he was, he walked a very straight path.

"What can I do to help?" she asked.

"I've got an appointment in half an hour to look at a farm that's for sale at the edge of the village."

"You're thinking of buying a farm here?"

"Just looking. I'd appreciate it if you'd give me your opinion."

"Of a farm? I've never run a farm."

"You've lived on one. More important, you've lived and worked in a farmhouse, and I'd like your insight into the house. Is it something that would work for me?"

She translated his question to mean he wondered if the house would become a *gut* home for him and his wife and family. "I'll be glad to look at the house for you. It's the least I can do after all you've done for us."

His eyebrows lowered. "I don't want you to feel

you've got to say *ja*. You aren't beholden to me for anything."

"You've helped—"

"You've helped, too. Keeping score isn't what we're supposed to do. God expects us to offer our hands and our talents to others without obligation."

She lowered her eyes from his frown. "*Es dutt mir leed*, Isaac."

"You don't have anything to be sorry for, so don't apologize. I thought we were friends, and friends do things for each other without keeping track." He paused, then raised his chin and asked, "Rachel Yoder, without either of us fulfilling or creating an obligation of any kind, would you visit the house this morning and give me your honest opinion?"

At the humor in his voice, she looked at him. Even a week ago, she wouldn't have believed anyone who told her Isaac's eyes could twinkle that brightly.

"Ja." She intended to add more, but halted when Nina pushed between her and Isaac.

The taller woman didn't glance in her direction. "Isaac, how lovely to see you!" She wore one of her scintillating smiles as she put a bold hand on his arm. "Did I hear you say you're looking for opinions about a house you want to buy?"

For a moment, Rachel was envious of how comfortable the blonde acted around men. She pushed aside that thought as soon as it formed.

From the kitchen doorway, Abby mouthed *I'm sorry*, but Rachel wasn't sure if the words were for her or Isaac. Nina was already talking as if she was going to make a home on the farm with Isaac. Nina batted her eyelashes at Isaac as she linked her arm through his and steered him toward the door. For a moment, Rachel hesitated. Maybe she should take this as God's way of reminding her she shouldn't stand in the way of what Isaac was seeking.

Then he turned and shot a desperate glance in her direction. Rachel didn't need Abby's murmured urging to follow the two out of the community center and into the cool, crisp morning. As she tied her bonnet under her chin, she caught up with them along the sloping sidewalk. She ignored the pointed scowl Nina aimed in her direction and fell into step with them. Isaac glanced at her and winked, his expression growing serious when he turned to Nina.

Rachel knew he was glad she'd come along, and she was glad, too.

When the real-estate agent, a pleasant middle-aged lady, dropped them off on the dirt road that curled along a hillside above the brook, Rachel wasn't surprised. Ahead of them was supposed to be the farm lane. It had become a field of brambles like the briars enveloping Sleeping Beauty's castle. As long as a fiery dragon didn't hide in their depths… A plain woman shouldn't be thinking about dragons in briar patches or the firepower needed to root out the creature.

Beside her, Nina sniffed with disgust. "Someone needs to cut the brush around here. How do they expect anyone to see the house when it's surrounded by a jungle?"

"The previous owner died," Isaac said as he led the way into the bushes, hacking them with a large knife the real-estate agent had given him before she returned to her car. When he looked at the house, which was half-hidden by trees, he sighed. "His heirs are elderly, too, and that's why they're selling the place."

"It's sad," Rachel interjected into the strained silence left by Isaac's words, "when a farm can't be kept in a family that's been the one to husband the land for so many years."

"It is." He glanced over his shoulder as he added, "Be careful your clothes don't get snagged on the thorns."

Nina made a despairing sound, and Rachel was surprised when the younger woman continued to follow them instead of turning back to the road. In spite of her efforts, Rachel had to unhook her apron twice from prickles, and the second time jabbed her finger. She stuck it in her mouth for a moment as if she was no older than Eva, then continued to push her way through the snarled greenery.

She gave a sigh of relief that echoed Isaac's as she emerged from the briar patch. Waiting for Nina to escape the tangle, she noticed leaves stuck to his suspenders and scratches on his arms.

"I didn't realize," he said in an apologetic tone as the blonde emerged, "how we'd have to hack our way in. If I had, I would have cleared a path before I invited anyone else here. I'll make sure the path is wider before we leave."

"That's so kind of you, Isaac." Nina brushed leaf debris off her light blue dress and regarded him with wide eyes. "You're always thoughtful of others."

"What do you think of the place?" he asked, looking at Rachel.

She appraised the scene before them. Rusty red and muted gold mums needed to be trimmed near the porch. A beautiful sugar maple was a mixture of orange and green, as the leaves began to don their autumn colors. Lilac bushes had grown too close to the house and concealed windows. A section of gutter along the roof was sprouting tiny trees where seeds had taken root in the debris that had collected and rotted there. The small leaves offered the only color because weather had stripped off any paint. Gray clapboards were beginning to curl at the edges.

"I think," she said, "there's potential here. It must have been beautiful once. With the underbrush cut and flowers blooming throughout the summer, it'll look *wunderbaar.*"

"I'm glad you can see that." He smiled, but turned as Nina pointed out the tilting weathervane on the main barn.

Following them toward the house, Rachel was glad the porch steps were intact. Nodding when Isaac handed her a key and suggested she and Nina go inside while he went into the cellar to check the furnace and foundation, Rachel hurried across the porch's creaking boards.

The front-door lock was reluctant to move, but she leaned her shoulder into it as she twisted the key and turned the knob. The door opened with a squeak that grated on her ears.

She walked into the kitchen with Nina on her heels. The house smelled of mildew and neglect. Dust clung to every surface, including cobwebs woven into the corners of the windows. Dead bugs were strewn across any flat surface, and the walls were dim with grime.

However, the kitchen cabinets were maple and not sagging. The large woodstove was from an earlier era, but when she opened one of the doors, she was pleased to see there was no rust inside. Elbow grease and cleanser would have it shining in no time. She couldn't say the same for the nearby range. It was so filthy she couldn't be sure what its original color had been.

A table in the center of the floor had seating for eight. Several more chairs were arranged along the walls wherever there was enough space. She could envision a large family eating at the table, along with the hired men who would have helped in the fields and with the milking a few generations ago.

"It stinks in here," Nina began, then paused as the door opened and Isaac walked in. "However, any *gut* Amish woman could have this cleaned in no time."

Rachel thought Nina was being overoptimistic. Hours and hours of work would be required to get the house into livable shape. Spiderwebs were weighted with dust, and her feet stuck to the floor with every step. She imagined getting a power washer to take the top layers of grease and burned-on food off the stove. She didn't want to think what that oven must look like, and she intended to avoid opening the refrigerator door. She guessed it was filled with mold and other things she didn't want to come face-to-face with.

Isaac gave the kitchen a cursory glance, then walked into the living room beyond it. She explored the first floor with him and Nina, who was struggling to maintain her sunny attitude.

When Isaac wanted to check out the barns, Rachel returned to the kitchen. She opened a door that led to what had been a laundry space. The washer rusting in silence was older than she was by several decades.

Nina waited in the middle of the kitchen, her arms clasped in front of her.

"I can't imagine anyone living in this disaster."

Closing the laundry-room door, Rachel motioned toward the table. "It was a family home at one time."

"Whoever did the cooking for that many people must have spent her whole life in the kitchen."

"Let's hope some chairs belonged to daughters who helped put three meals on that table every day."

"Until they found someone to marry." Turning toward Rachel, she mused, "Speaking of marriage, can I give you a word of advice?"

"If you feel you need to."

Nina didn't take the hint in Rachel's cool answer. "If you think being sentimental is the way to that man's heart, you're wrong."

"Really?"

"*Ja.* Anyone should be able to see Isaac Kauffman is a practical man. Men like him don't like mushy comments about flowers." She gave Rachel a satisfied look from beneath her lowered lashes. "I'm surprised you don't know that. You've been married."

"My husband used to bring me flowers." She didn't

add that the bouquet was almost always an attempt at an apology after he'd been delayed and come home late from hanging out with his men after practice maneuvers.

Nina waved away her words. "What worked with him won't work with Isaac, so if you think you can persuade him to walk out with you, you—"

"I don't have any plans to marry Isaac."

"No? I heard you talking about husbands."

"What? When?"

"When we were stuck in those briars."

Rachel searched her memory, then laughed. It was the wrong reaction, she realized, when Nina's expression became stormy. For a moment, she considered letting the young woman stew in her misunderstanding, but that wouldn't be what God would expect of her. She needed to be honest.

"I was talking about husband," Rachel said, "in the way that a family husbands a piece of land, bringing forth its bounty."

"I knew that," Nina said in a superior tone, though her eyes suggested the opposite, "but I wanted *you* to be prepared if Isaac misunderstood you."

"*Danki* for pointing that out."

"My pleasure."

Rachel saw no reason to continue the conversation, so she headed for the stairs to the second floor. The blonde didn't follow.

After peeking into four filthy bedrooms and a disgusting bathroom, Rachel opened another door. Stairs led up to the attic. They were dotted with half-chewed acorns and dead bugs, but she climbed, her curiosity stronger than her distaste. She peered over the top of the stairs. Boxes and chests were pushed up to one side, and the floor was covered with more than an inch of dust. She started to step onto it, but paused when she heard her name called.

Looking down, she saw Isaac with Nina close beside him. Would he be upset that she was exploring what could become his home? If so, she saw no clue of it on his face as she returned to the second floor.

"Anything up there?" he asked.

"Some stuff in storage." She wiped the hem of her skirt. "And lots of dust. How were the barns?"

"Like the house, they need work. I've seen enough for this visit. Have you seen enough of the house?"

"Enough to know it needs a *gut* work frolic." As they walked down to the living room, Rachel ran her hand along the banister that had been smoothed by many fingers before hers. "It'd be great fun to discover what's stored in the closets and in the chests under the eaves."

Nina wrinkled her nose, but Rachel wasn't sure if it was in disagreement, or she'd caught another of the odors that didn't seem to bother the blonde as much when Isaac was in the house.

"I'm sure it's nothing but junk," Nina stated. "As far as *practical* matters go, the living room is a fair size, but you'll have to take a wall down if you plan to hold church Sunday services here."

"We're few in number."

"The community will grow. At least, I know you're hoping it will." Her eyelashes fluttered.

Rachel pretended to cough so she could hide her annoyance with Nina's blatant flirting. Isaac turned to her with exaggerated concern, and she saw he was having a tough time concealing his amusement at Nina's attempts to beguile him.

When Isaac suggested they take a more roundabout route to the road, Rachel nodded along with Nina. They walked out into a field that, unlike the briar patch around the farm lane, had been cut earlier in the summer. Rachel watched where she stepped because it became obvious a herd of cows had been there not too long ago. She realized she should have mentioned that fact when Nina gave a sudden screech and waved her foot in the air. Her face was so distorted with disgust and outrage, Rachel couldn't hold back a laugh.

"It isn't funny!" Nina cried. "I stepped in cow manure."

"Wipe your shoe on clean grass and be grateful you weren't barefoot," Rachel said.

"It wasn't cow manure," Isaac added. "You stepped in a mud puddle, Nina. Rachel's right. Just wipe your shoe on the grass."

Annoyed, the blonde stamped away in the direction of the road.

Rachel put her hands over her mouth, but couldn't silence her laughter. Nina had looked like Loribeth when her nose was out of joint. It wasn't kind of Rachel to react that way, and she'd have to apologize to Nina later.

She looked at Isaac as a rumbling laugh burst from him. It was *wunderbaar* to share a joke with him, more *wunderbaar* than it should have been. She'd worry later about their relationship, which was becoming too complicated. For now, she gave in to laughter.

Rachel's laugh, Isaac decided, was perfect. Filled with music and glee and honesty. Once she released it, he doubted it could ever be recaptured because it wafted like a robin's song on gentle breeze.

It was a sound he was sure he'd never grow tired of.

"Oh," she murmured, "that wasn't nice of me."

"Of us," he amended with a grin.

"You wouldn't have laughed if I hadn't." She rolled her eyes as she added, "Nina won't make it easy for me to say I'm sorry."

"She will if you assure her that you won't ever tell anyone that she thought some wet mud was cow manure. No Amish woman on the husband hunt would want her potential mate to discover she knows nothing about cows."

"Are you always so deviously clever, Isaac?"

"If I said you inspire me, would that be an acceptable answer?"

When she began to walk in the direction of the road, he matched her steps. She smiled as she said, "That would make me the devious one then, ain't so?"

"Would it?" He chuckled, amazed how easy it was to be himself around Rachel. She didn't expect him to take the lead every time, and when she asked a question, he knew she wouldn't take his answer as the final word. She had a quick and practical mind that he found intriguing.

"I don't know." She glanced at the buildings behind them. "What will you do next?"

"Run some numbers for repair costs. There's no milk tank, so everything will have to be kept in pails until I can get a tank put in."

"Is there electricity for the tank?"

"*Ja*, but I'd want to upgrade it. If I do decide to buy this farm, I'll want to put in a refrigerated tank so I can sell my milk as Grade A."

"There are a lot of cheesemakers in Vermont, and they're fine with Grade B milk. You might want to do other improvements first. You can move to Grade A milk after you've gotten in your first harvest and you're familiar with your herd and what they're capable of producing."

He looked at her with astonishment as they left the field and crossed through the narrow strip of trees toward the road. She had a rare gift for getting to the crux of a problem and presenting a solution he might have overlooked. If she'd been born a man, he guessed she would have been running a successful business.

As they stepped onto the narrow, twisting road, he said, "That's a *gut* point, Rachel, though I'd have to haul around milk pails. I've got lots to consider. Most important, my family lives hours north of here."

"Abby plans to stay in Evergreen Corners after she gets married."

"True." He couldn't add how he continued to worry that his *daed* would lapse into his dependence on liquor if Herman couldn't make a success of the farm in the Northeast Kingdom. "First, I'm going to have to run the numbers to see if it's feasible."

"And pray for God's guidance."

"That goes without saying." But he was glad she'd said that. It showed her faith was strong and as much a part of her as breathing.

Had a potent faith been one of the criteria for the woman he hoped to marry? It must have been.

While he was weighing the pros and cons of purchasing the farm, he needed to do something else, too— figure out how to persuade Rachel that she'd be the perfect wife for him.

Chapter Nine

Isaac sat in the community center the following week and listened to the rain pouring from the eaves. The volunteers had finished their meals, and only Abby and a few other women remained. They were cleaning up from supper and making preparations for tomorrow's breakfast.

So he waited for his sister, who'd forgotten to bring an umbrella with her. He'd offered to go to their garage apartment and retrieve it, but she'd said they wouldn't be much longer and asked him to wait.

That had been over an hour ago.

He looked at the page in front of him. Columns of numbers had been crossed out or erased. He was trying to calculate the cost of getting the old farm into *gut* enough shape that he could make some money to reinvest in it.

The list of what needed to be done was longer than he'd guessed when he paid his first visit to the farm. A second trip with the real-estate agent three days later had shown him even more work that had been delayed almost too long. The roof on the main barn rested on rafters that were beginning to bow. The door to the hay-loft hung by a single hinge. The concrete in the milk-ing area had begun to crack and chip, a danger to any cows that didn't watch where they were going. Or for a man hefting heavy milk cans and carrying them into the storage area.

That was just the main barn. The equipment shed needed its right wall shored up, and what he guessed had been a chicken coop wasn't salvageable. Its future would be as kindling for the stove.

He rubbed his forehead and sighed. The house needed as much attention as the outbuildings. Was he insane? He'd become accustomed to having a crew of skilled carpenters when he worked on the new houses. At the farm, he'd have to work alone until he earned enough money to hire help.

Maybe Rachel was right about selling Grade B milk to begin with, that small voice in his mind counseled.

Rachel…

He was no closer to introducing the idea of marriage into their conversations. Each time he'd seen her since their first trip to the farm, she'd been with her daugh-ters. Talking about the future while she had toddlers in tow seemed ridiculous. He recalled how Abby had talked a couple of days ago about David taking her out for *kaffi* and pie at the village diner again. They'd gone there when they first started working with the teen group, and she said it was a *gut* place to talk.

A smile unfurled on his lips. Was Abby matchmaking again? His sister hadn't mentioned anything about him walking out with her friend, but maybe she'd decided to resort to more subtle methods.

"Oh, Isaac, I hoped that was you!"

At Nina's voice, he folded the pages and shoved them into his pocket. She'd already asked too many questions about when he was going to move onto the farm, and he didn't want to be rude and tell her he was trying to decide *if* he wanted to purchase the property.

"Do you need something, Nina?" he asked.

"Abby mentioned you had an umbrella."

"*Ja.*"

"I don't have one here." She gave a faint shudder as she glanced at the front door. "It's raining hard, ain't so?"

"*Ja*. Would you like to borrow my umbrella?"

"Then you and Abby would be left without one." She widened her eyes. "Would it be too much trouble for you to walk me home?"

"Of course not." He stood, expecting her to back up a few steps. She didn't, and he found his face uncomfortably close to hers. Edging away from her burgeoning smile, he said, "Go and get your things while I tell Abby I'll be right back."

Something flickered in her eyes, and her smile wavered. He didn't wait to hear what she had to say. Instead, he strode into the kitchen. It seemed deserted other than his sister, who was mixing dough for the muffins the women would bake in the morning.

After he'd told her his plans, Abby dropped her spoon into the bowl with a clank that sounded extra loud in the quiet space. She regarded him with an unusual frown that straightened her lips. Her voice wasn't more than a whisper. He guessed she didn't want it to carry past his ears. "I don't know why you let her rope you into taking her home."

"She doesn't want to get soaked."

"Is that what she told you?"

Isaac scowled at his sister, wondering why she was making such a big deal out of doing a fellow volunteer a favor. "Why are you asking silly questions?"

"I asked one question, and it wasn't silly. I know you're interested in finding yourself the perfect wife, but you can't be thinking Nina is the one you're looking for."

He was astonished his sister would speak of matters normally shrouded in secrecy. Even siblings were sometimes surprised when plans to marry were published by a couple they hadn't realized were walking out together. She might drop hints he should walk out with Rachel, but she'd never asked him if he was.

She must have taken his silence as a reprimand because she squared her shoulders and looked him straight in the eye. "Well, don't say that I didn't warn you." She strode away, vexation coming off her like a wave of heat.

He sighed. Nobody would ever describe his sister as tight-lipped or accuse her of hiding her opinions. Everyone knew what Abby Kauffman was feeling and thinking.

Years ago, he'd been the same, but that had changed when the family responsibilities fell on him. He hadn't wanted the community's disapproval to focus on his *daed*, who hid his alcoholism well most days with Isaac's help. If the deacon or the bishop had learned of the problem, they would have come to confront his *daed*. The eyes of the *Leit* would have been upon the whole family, and Isaac hadn't wanted his siblings to bear the humiliation of the truth being shared throughout the district.

After walking out of the kitchen, he put on his hat, found his umbrella and opened it and the door. Nina slipped her hand onto his arm and pressed up against him as they went out into the rainy evening. Too close for his comfort, but he didn't say anything as they crossed the wet grass of the village green. She pointed out the house where she was staying. It had a broad porch, which allowed them to get out of the rain.

"Danki," she murmured as he lowered the umbrella and gave it a gentle shake. "Would you like to come in, Isaac?"

"I need to take Abby home."

She smiled at him. "You could do that and come back. I made some cookies we can share. They're delicious."

"Danki, but I'll say *gut nacht."*

Her eyes snapped with abrupt anger, and he half expected her to stamp her foot as Loribeth might have. At the thought of the *kind*, Rachel's pretty face filled his mind as his sister's words rang through his head.

Abby was right. Nina Streit wasn't the woman who could make him the perfect wife. Rachel was, and he needed to find out if she would be willing to marry him. He'd put it off for too long while he fiddled around with calculations on the funds needed to close on the farm and make it productive. The numbers on the farm were clear-cut, and so was his decision about Rachel.

That was why after leaving Nina on the porch and returning to the community center, he hurried his sister home so quickly she struggled to keep up with his longer strides. He threw open the door at the top of the stairs and motioned for her to go inside. When she did, he remained on the landing.

"Are you going somewhere?" Abby asked in a tone that suggested she already knew the answer.

"For a walk."

"In the rain?"

"I've got some things to think about, and walking always helps me think."

As she began to close the door, she looked around the edge and grinned. "Say hi to Rachel for me!" Her laughter remained after she'd shut the door.

Isaac gave in to a wry grin. He should have known he couldn't fool his sister. Abby had been hinting—and more than hinting—that he didn't have much time to waste in thinking about asking Rachel to walk out with him. He was aware of how little time they had remaining. It was nearly October, and the work in Evergreen Corners was scheduled to be done around Christmas.

He and Rachel weren't youngsters any longer. There weren't singings and other youth-group events for them to ride home from together. She had *kinder* to consider. If it'd been summer, he might have arranged for a van to take them to Canobie Lake Park in New Hampshire. He'd enjoyed trips to Hersheypark amusement park as a youth and had heard fun stories about Canobie. It was too late in the year for that.

By the time he'd walked to Rachel's home, he'd talked himself in and out of a half-dozen ideas. He'd still made no firm decision when he knocked on the door.

It opened, and the *kinder* stood there. Loribeth regarded him with open distrust, but Eva grinned at him. He couldn't keep from smiling back. Rachel's daughters were adorable…like their *mamm*.

A screech came from beyond the girls. Both whirled and squealed with excitement.

"Kitty!" called Eva and raced away.

When Loribeth followed, for once trailing behind her little sister, he stood on the front step, unsure if he should go in or not.

"Shut the door!" Rachel shouted.

He lowered the umbrella, stepped inside and closed the door in a single swift motion. The *kinder* spun about and ran toward him, chasing something small. It ran into his boots, caromed away and stared with unblinking eyes.

A tiny kitten.

It sped around him. The girls gave chase. Backed into a corner by the kitchen cupboards, it turned, arched its back and hissed.

Rachel came into the room, her hair loosening from beneath her *kapp*. There was something endearing about her dishevelment, and she resembled her daughters more than ever. "Isaac! I didn't realize—" She jumped aside as the kitten and *kinder* raced toward her.

"Where did you get a wild cat?" he asked, trying not to laugh. "And why?"

* * *

Instead of answering, Rachel rushed after the kitten. She'd almost captured the little beast twice before. Each time, the kitten had eluded her, skittering away as she reached for the tiny ball of fur. Cornering the tiny cat, she edged closer, then jerked back her hands before they could be scratched—again!—or bitten—again! She watched the four-ounce, long-haired calico fiend race past her and into the girls' room. Her daughters followed, giggling with delight.

"That is Sweetie Pie," she said as she looked at her hands, which were striped with bloody scratches. "Most cats have five claws on each foot. That misnamed creature has seven toes on each of her front ones, and I'm going to have the scars to prove it."

"I didn't know you were planning to get a cat." Isaac set his umbrella against the wall and put his hat on the peg beside her bonnet.

"Neither did I. The girls think she's cute and sweet, which is why they've named her Sweetie Pie. I think she's planning to murder us in our sleep tonight."

When he took her by the arm and led her to the sink, he turned on the faucet and cleaned her scratches.

"Ouch!" she said as the water hit a deep one.

"Sorry." Sympathy filled his eyes, which were far more expressive than Rachel would have guessed they ever could have been when she'd first met him.

"It's okay," she said, though it wasn't. The incisions left by the kitten's claws burned as if she was holding a match to them. "You wouldn't want a maniacal kitten by any chance, would you?"

"Not likely." He glanced at the *kinder*, who were using a string to tempt the cat to bat at it. "I think you'd have a mutiny on your hands if you get rid of their latest pet project."

She groaned, not from pain but from his silly pun. "I know, but a kitten is the last thing I needed."

"So why did you get one?"

"A parent came to the day care today with a box of kittens." She opened a tube of antibacterial ointment. "I was able to talk the girls out of bringing home two, but they refused to leave without one they can share."

"Diabolical of those parents."

"Without question." She dabbed more ointment on the bleeding scratches. Wincing, she said, "I thought they'd enjoy having something to take care of and love. However, as the saying goes, no *gut* deed—"

"Goes unpunished." He gave her a crooked smile. "What are you going to do with the kitten when you have to be at the community center?"

"She's litter-box trained, or so I've been assured. I plan to put her in the bathroom with her box and some food and water until she becomes tame enough not to rip the whole house apart." She smiled and shook her head. "After that, the cat and the house are in God's hands. I hope He leaves both intact."

"I'll add my prayers." He stepped aside as Eva ran into the kitchen after the cat. "You're going to need them."

Rachel watched in amazement when Isaac bent as the kitten and *kind* raced past him. He seized the kitten by the scruff. Her odd paws wiggled as if she was trying to run through the air, then she calmed as he continued to hold her suspended as her *mamm* would have. Waiting while her breathing slowed, he began to pet her. He spoke nonsense words to her as she grew calmer, her eyes blinking as she struggled not to give in to sleep.

"That's incredible," she breathed as Eva stared wide-eyed at the kitten that was still for the first time since they'd brought her home.

Loribeth paused at the far end of the kitchen, her gaze focused on Isaac, but she didn't move any closer.

"It comes from years of chasing kittens in the barn. You learn when to grab them and how," he said. "Do you have a bed for her?"

"Ja," Eva said. "She no like."

"Really?" he asked, squatting in front of the little girl.

Eva reached out a tentative finger and ran it along the kitten. The faint buzz of a purr startled the little girl.

"That means she likes you," Rachel assured her.

"By growling?" asked Loribeth as she inched closer.

"It's not growling. It's a sound kitties make when they're happy."

With a wide grin, Eva said, "She like Eva."

"She does."

"I wasn't sure she could purr at such a young age," Rachel said.

"I read somewhere," he replied, "that young bobcats purr."

"That makes sense, because she's as wild as a bobcat."

Isaac looked at Eva. "Where does Sweetie Pie sleep?"

"With me?" Eva asked, her eyes wide with hope.

"Not tonight. Tonight she's going to sleep in the bathroom." Rachel motioned for them to follow her.

As she passed her older daughter, she caught Loribeth's hand and smiled. Her daughter remained somber, and Rachel gave a silent sigh. She wished she had some idea why Loribeth disliked Isaac. Her attempts to find out had caused her daughter to end the conversation by picking an argument with her sister.

When Loribeth tugged away, Rachel asked, "Don't you want to tuck Sweetie Pie into bed?"

Her daughter looked from the kitten to Isaac, torn.

He must have seen her reaction, because he said, "Let me put Sweetie Pie in her bed, and I'll get out of the way while you say '*gut nacht*' to her."

Rachel put her hand on his arm in a silent *danki* as he slid past her in the narrow hallway. He glanced at her, and the powerful emotions in his eyes nearly staggered her. For the briefest second, before he turned away, she'd seen the truth. He continued to consider her a possibility for his wife.

As her heart reeled with delight, she wanted to shout he was about to make a huge mistake. He didn't even know her real married name, a name she'd never used in the Army, so it'd been easy to set it aside when she decided to return to her Amish roots.

You don't know the real me, she wanted to shout after him. *If you did, you'd walk out the door and never return.*

She shuddered at the thought of Isaac shutting her out of his life, but went with her girls into the bathroom as soon as he'd retreated toward the kitchen. Her daughters sat on either side of the box they'd lined with several towels to make a nest for the kitten.

While Rachel whispered to the girls, the kitten gave a soft hiss, but her heart wasn't in it as she surrendered to sleep. Loribeth put a doll's blanket on the kitten. Instead of growling at her and striking out, the kitten nestled into the towels, curled into a ball with her tail pointed at her nose.

Her daughters were reluctant to go to bed, but did when she reminded them Sweetie Pie would be up early in the morning. After chasing the kitten and her littermates throughout the day, Loribeth and Eva were asleep, too, almost before Rachel turned on their nightlights and closed their bedroom door.

She leaned against it for a moment, trying to steady her breath as she thought of going into the living room, where Isaac was waiting for her. He'd come over in the rain. Why? He wasn't there to ask her to marry him tonight, was he?

Rachel squared her shoulders and walked away from the door. All she could do was pray their friendship could be salvaged. She had to believe that was possible, or she would do something foolish.

Like agree to be his wife when she was the wrong woman for him…

Chapter Ten

Raking leaves was backbreaking work, and Rachel's muscles were threatening to explode from a dull ache into searing pain at any minute. She wasn't accustomed to such physical work, and she hadn't guessed what a chore it'd be to get leaves off the grass. There were only two trees in the front yard, but every tree along the street, and most in the woods behind the trailer, had donated to the collection on her lawn. She suspected she could have called her landlord, and he would have sent someone over to get rid of the leaves. She couldn't, not when he was letting her and the girls stay there while she served with Amish Helping Hands. She must not repay his kindness with demands for a job she could do herself.

The trash-removal company was coming soon to take away any leaves raked to the street, and she wanted as many gone as possible. She hated doing lawn work. It was, she knew, another remnant of her childhood, when mowing the grass and raking the leaves and shoveling the snow had been her tasks. While other young girls had gathered for frolics and had the chance to spend time with young men from nearby districts, she'd had to stay at home and do her chores.

With a laugh, she said aloud, "You know there's a story about that, Cinderella."

"Cinderella?" asked Eva, her ears attuned to anything any adult said, as always. "What Cinderella?"

"Not a what, but a who. Cinderella is a girl who needs to do her chores to help her family, and she never complains." She smiled. Sometimes it was difficult to recall how she hadn't known much about fairy tales when she was a *kind*. Most she'd discovered after she'd jumped the fence and had to read them in order to understand references made in her new *Englisch* life.

Doubt crept into her mind. Were her in-laws right? Was she denying Loribeth and Eva a part of their heritage? As they grew, she planned to share more about Travis and the *Englisch* life they'd lived before his death. It was impossible to live in two such different worlds, and trying to do so would confuse her daughters. They were at an age when they were willing to accept what she offered them. Would they always be that way? She couldn't keep from wondering if, when they were older, they'd decide to jump the fence, as she had. Would they come to resent her, and tell her that she'd deprived them of the life they would have had if Travis hadn't been killed? Or would they come to treasure a plain life, as she did?

Shaking aside the uneasy thoughts, she paused and watched the girls chasing Sweetie Pie around the yard.

There were years ahead of them before Loribeth and Eva had to make the decision of how to spend the rest of their lives. What mattered was that they knew she loved them, no matter what they chose.

She smiled when Eva slid on a small patch of leaves and tumbled to the ground, then jumped to her feet to run after her older sister and Sweetie Pie. Though the kitten had snarled and swiped her paws at Rachel for the first two days she lived with them, the connection between the tiny creature and her daughters had been instantaneous.

When Sweetie Pie rushed to where Rachel stood, the kitten leaned against her leg for a short second before scurrying away. Her smile broadened. That was unexpected. For some reason she couldn't fathom, the kitten had had a change of heart this morning and didn't hiss and scratch each time Rachel got near. Maybe Sweetie Pie had decided if she wanted to be with the *kinder* who doted on her, she had to be nice to their *mamm*.

Or maybe the kitten had figured out which member of the family kept her food bowl full.

"Look at you!" called Abby as she crossed the leaf-speckled lawn, carrying two grocery bags. "Out enjoying a beautiful fall day."

"*Enjoying* may not be the right word." Rachel gave her back a rub. "No, it's not the right word."

"I know Isaac would be glad to help."

Not being honest with her friend about Isaac's visit a couple of nights ago was troublesome, though there really wasn't anything to tell Abby. As soon as she'd gotten the girls settled for the night, the kitten had begun to mew loudly, protesting being left alone. That had upset her daughters, and she'd been glad for Isaac's help in calming the kitten while she convinced the *kinder* to go back to bed. He'd left soon after that, as if he'd been concerned that she'd blame him for the kitten's noise. She'd been sorry he'd headed out so quickly, but she had been relieved at the same time.

She almost told Abby that, but didn't. She couldn't explain her fear that Isaac might propose and that she might listen to her heart.

Her silly heart, which seemed to believe there was a way for her to give it to him and find happiness together despite her past.

Her misguided heart that had already persuaded her to marry Travis when she'd known his career was more important to him than any wife and family could ever have been.

She would be a *dummkopf* to listen to it again.

She couldn't say that. Instead, she shook her head. "Isaac has enough to do already. He wants to have those new houses…" She paused. "What's the word he used?"

"Buttoned-up." Abby set her bags on the trailer's front steps. "Don't let his worrying get to you. He laments every evening how much work needs doing before the houses are weatherproof. He must say 'buttoned-up' at least a dozen times every evening. Do you have another rake around here?"

"No, you're not going to help, either. You've been working every day for the past two weeks at the community center, as well as making supper for your brother and for David and Mikayla."

Abby's smile softened, as it did when anyone mentioned the man she planned to marry and his daughter. "It's an excuse to see more of them."

Rachel leaned her rake against a tree and came to sit beside her friend on the steps. She opened the container next to them, then filled four glasses with bright red juice. She gave two to her daughters and then offered the third to Abby.

"Don't ask what flavor it is or how much real juice is in it," she said. "The girls love it, so I know it's got lots of sugar in it."

"No kidding," Abby replied after taking a sip. "It might be all sugar."

"But it's wet, and that's what I need." She tilted her cup and drained it. "If you drink it fast, you don't have to taste it as much."

They laughed together, but neither reached to refill their cups.

"The girls are having fun with their new kitten," Abby said. "They're going to exhaust the poor little thing."

"Or she's going to exhaust them." She smiled. "Either way, they should sleep well tonight. It's *gut* for them to have something to take care of."

"You sound like Isaac. He's always saying we need to be responsible for ourselves and those around us." Her friend's easy expression fell away. "I shouldn't joke about it. If it hadn't been for Isaac, I don't know what would have happened to our family after *Mamm* died. My *daed* had...a problem." She glanced at Rachel. "He had a problem with alcohol. He never was fall-down drunk, but when he drank, he drank to excess."

"I'm sorry." She was, because she knew how difficult it was to live with a parent who was a disappointment.

"It's better now since *Daed* remarried, but Isaac carried the weight of the farm and raising us during the years when he should have been a carefree teen whose only thoughts were of getting a courting buggy so he could convince some cute girl to let him take her home."

"I had no idea."

"Of course you didn't. He never talks about things from the past." Her eyes narrowed. "Like you don't. You've both buried your pasts and don't let anyone help you."

She didn't have a quick answer for that, because it was the truth, so she shouted to her girls to come closer to the house. "If that kitten goes in the street, I'm afraid they'll follow."

Abby hesitated, and Rachel guessed her friend wanted to return to what they'd been discussing. However, when Abby spoke, it was about the coming week at the community center and the next worship service in the morning.

As her friend turned to go, Rachel reached for her rake. Her back warned that she shouldn't plan on working much longer, but she ignored it. She could hear the rumble of the trash truck a couple of streets away, and getting as many leaves to the street should be her mission.

Mission. She hadn't used that word for a long time. How long would it take before she could feel completely

Amish? There must be a way to smother her past at the same time she built her future.

Then you could be the perfect Amish wife Isaac is looking for, she thought before she could halt it.

The urge to laugh battled with the tears filling her eyes. He considered her a *gut* candidate for his perfect wife, and she had to find a way to persuade him she wasn't. It'd be simple if she didn't want to protect their friendship. She could have told him that he was *ab in kopp* to think he could find that paragon. It'd be easy to say only a crazy man would believe such a person existed.

She didn't want to dash his hopes as her own had been when she'd discovered Travis's first love was his military career. How she'd admired that when they first met, and she'd fallen for the dedicated soldier! She couldn't fault him. He'd never pretended to be something he wasn't.

As she was.

No! She was a plain *mamm* with two sweet daughters who wanted to help in the recovery of the flood-torn village. What she'd been in the past was in the past. What she was now was what she wanted to be in the future, but she was struggling to find her way each day.

Which made her the worst choice for Isaac to marry.

She sighed. Having her thoughts go around and around wasn't leading her to a solution of the problem of how to keep Isaac from broaching the subject of marriage.

As if thinking his name caused him to appear, Isaac strode along the street. He carried his toolbox in one hand and had a step stool balanced over his opposite shoulder.

"Some of you look as if you're having fun," he called as he set the box and the stool not far from where she'd raked the leaves onto the street.

She paused and leaned on her rake. Aware of how her hair was poking out in every direction from beneath the black kerchief she wore on her head, she resisted pushing it in place. That could make him think that she cared about what he thought of how she looked.

"Some of us are having more fun than others," she replied.

"I can see that." He lifted the girls out of the leaves Rachel had gathered near the sidewalk. Leaves were scattered around what had been a neat pile.

Her daughters protested but Isaac murmured something to them, and they nodded before they ran across the yard. Their steps jolted the kitten awake, and the three began chasing each other in a merry game.

After Isaac had carried his tools to a clear spot on the lawn, Rachel asked, "What did you say to them? I can't get them to quiet that quickly."

"I told them if they helped instead of sending the leaves in every direction, I'd take them for ice cream." Smiling, he added, "I may have suggested as well that the sooner the task here was done, the sooner we could have ice cream."

"Bribery!"

"It's a time-honored parenting skill that I learned while dealing with my younger brothers and Abby."

She wanted to ask him why his voice always had

that undercurrent of regret and sorrow when he spoke of his youth. It couldn't have been because he believed he'd done something wrong in helping his widowed *daed*. Was Isaac ashamed his *daed* had a weakness for alcohol?

He wants a perfect wife. Maybe he wanted a perfect daed, *too.* The thought struck her like a blow from her *daed*'s hand. So often she'd heard others state—teasing, but with the assurance of honesty—how Isaac wanted each step of the building process to be perfect before going on to the next.

Maybe she was, she realized for the first time, dodging a bullet not to meet the qualifications he was seeking in a wife.

No! she thought as she had before. Isaac wasn't unbending. He smiled and made a few jokes at his own expense. He was kindhearted and treated her girls, even Loribeth, who avoided him as much as possible, with a gentle humor that impressed her. Abby, who was an amazing woman, had said more than once how much she'd learned from Isaac.

She was right back where she'd started, trying to figure out a way to keep him from asking her to be his wife, so they could remain friends. If she only knew how...

"Hey!" he shouted as he sped toward the road where her daughters had chased the kitten.

An explosion cut through the air. A roar reverberated through her body. She was thrown into a moment she'd tried never to recall. A moment of useless destruction. Of grief. Of death.

She screamed.

* * *

Isaac froze and so did the two little girls as they skidded to a stop next to the piles of leaves at the edge of the yard. Stunned by the shriek that must have been torn from Rachel's throat, he looked from her shocked *kinder* to where she crouched with her arms flung over her head.

"Mamm!" cried Loribeth, racing past him.

He grabbed Eva and ran. He passed Loribeth in a few steps, but slowed as he reached Rachel, who was making sounds that he wasn't sure were words or groans. He couldn't understand anything she said.

"Watch your sister," he ordered as he set Eva on her feet.

Loribeth opened her mouth to protest, but he gave her a swift look that silenced her. She took Eva by the hand and leaned her cheek on her *mamm*'s shoulder.

Rachel flinched away.

The little girl's eyes filled with tears, and Eva began to cry.

Though he wanted to comfort them, he needed to see to Rachel first. He kneeled beside her, ignoring the rumble of the trash truck as it stopped at the edge of the yard.

Not touching her, he whispered, "Rachel."

She didn't react.

He spoke her name again and again, and on the fourth try, she raised her head. Her face was colorless. She blinked as if waking from a long and horrible nightmare.

"Isaac?" Her voice cracked on his name. "What are you doing here? You shouldn't be…" She looked around, her eyes widening as she took in the autumnal scene and the trash truck moving along the street to the next yard. "Oh."

She didn't add anything more as he put his hands under her elbows and brought her to her feet. The girls were silent when he gestured for them to lead the way toward their front door.

Seating her on the steps, he poured out a cup of some juice from the jug Eva tried to heft. He gave the girls each a paper cup, too, but neither of them took a sip as they stared at their *mamm.* Did they have any idea of what was going on? He guessed the answer was no.

So what *had* happened to make Rachel cry out like she had? Not just today, but that day a few weeks ago in the community center, when she'd cowered in the pantry.

"Danki," Rachel whispered as she took the cup he handed her. She sipped, then put it beside her. "That's disgusting." A faint smile warmed her too-gray skin.

"Mamm?" asked Loribeth.

"Ja?"

The little girl hesitated, but her younger sister didn't. "Okay, *Mamm*?"

Rachel curved her hands around each of her daughters' faces. "I will be. Don't worry."

Not soothed by her *mamm*'s words, Loribeth asked the question Isaac wanted to ask. "What happened?"

"I saw— That is, I thought I saw something scary." Her warm smile must have cost her dearly because it wavered as she said, "I was wrong. I'm sorry I frightened you. Go and get Sweetie Pie. It's going to be time to start supper soon."

He wasn't sure if the girls would obey, but after a moment, they scurried away. As soon as they reached the kitten, they began to giggle, their fears forgotten.

It wouldn't be that easy for either Rachel or him.

He held the door open as she went inside. He didn't wait for an invitation to follow once the girls returned, Loribeth carrying the kitten. When he suggested they take Sweetie Pie to their room to play, they glanced at Rachel. Not for permission, he was certain, but to make sure their *mamm* wasn't going to collapse again in front of their eyes.

Rachel sat in the rocker while he went outside. He collected her rake and his tools. After putting them by the front steps, he brought the jug of juice inside with him. He glanced at where she was rocking. When she didn't speak, he went into the kitchen and put the tea-kettle on without saying anything, either.

As sounds of childish glee came from the girls' bed-room, he sat on the sofa. He turned his gaze to Rachel, who was staring straight ahead. "You're acting like a friend of mine."

"How?" Her voice was cautious, as if she'd weighed the simplest word before she let it leave her lips.

"Any loud sound terrified him." When she glanced at him, he held her gaze. "He was in a buggy that was hit by a train when he was a *kind*. His parents were killed, and he never could endure any loud sound. His *doktor* called it post-traumatic something or other."

"Post-traumatic stress disorder," she whispered.

"*Ja*, that's it." His eyebrows lowered. "I'm surprised you know about it."

"I've read about it in the newspapers."

"I have, too. Soldiers coming home from wars and being unable to forget what they've seen and heard." He shook his head. "It made me realize we must continue to pray for them when the wars aren't in the newspapers every day."

"*Ja*."

He waited for her to add more, but she didn't. Instead, she stood and went to remove the teakettle when it began to whistle. She poured hot water into two cups and then dropped a tea bag in each one. After handing him one, she sat in the rocker.

When he held the cup close to his nose, he smelled the distinct sharpness of mint. That was unexpected, but after taking a sip, he realized she'd picked the perfect flavor. It was warming and cooling at the same time. He sipped and waited. He'd said all he could.

"I saw a *gut* friend killed," she said, "and though I don't think about it every minute of every day any longer, the memory lurks. Any loud noise, especially any unexpected noise, resurrects that moment and how powerless I was to save his life."

"I'm sorry, Rachel."

She reached across the small space between them and touched his arm so fleetingly he almost believed he'd imagined her light caress. "*Danki*, but I've learned it's futile to try to change the past. I'm sure you understand that."

"I do indeed," he replied, though he doubted she could guess how sincerely he meant those words.

The two little girls burst into the room, wearing eager expressions. Eva rushed to him and tugged on his sleeve.

"Ice keem!" Eva exclaimed. "'Member? Ice keem?"

"*Ja*, I do 'member," he said, relieved for the chance to put aside the awful topic and smile at the *kind* whose greatest concern was whether he'd do as he promised and treat her and her sister to ice cream. "Shall we go to the diner and see what flavors they've got tonight?"

Rachel began, "If you three want to—"

"They serve ice cream to quartets," he said. Setting his cup on the counter, he offered her his hand. "*Komm mol*, Rachel. You can't prefer mint tea to chocolate ice cream."

"Choco." Eva spoke the word as if it was the sweetest one in the world.

Rachel looked from him to her daughters. Though Loribeth had been silent, anticipation glistened in her eyes.

Letting him bring her to her feet, she smiled at her girls. "Maybe they have mint chocolate chip, ain't so?"

"Who knows?" He took her cup and set it next to his.

She sent her daughters to get their coats and bonnets, then faced him. *"Danki."*

"It does get better. That's what my friend told me."

"I keep reminding myself of that. Days and weeks go by, and everything is fine until…"

"Don't think about it any more today."

"You're right. Let's enjoy our 'ice keem.'"

As she herded the girls ahead of her, he noticed her trembling hands. No other sign of her despair was visible in how she chatted with the girls about which flavor they would order.

He shivered as he stepped outside, though the afternoon remained warm. He thought of how vulnerable she'd looked while huddled on the ground, her hands over her head. Whatever had happened to her must have been horrific.

If there's a way to ease her path away from that appalling memory, Lord, guide me to it.

She was a strong woman. That was one of the criteria on his list for his perfect wife. Would he ever meet anyone—man or woman—stronger than Rachel? So when was he going to match her courage and ask her to be his wife? As he watched her holding the girls' hands and swinging them as they walked along, he knew it had to be soon.

Chapter Eleven

Rachel opened her wallet and put two dimes on the counter at the rear of the general store. That paid for the penny candy she'd let her girls pick out after more than five minutes of discussion.

"Thank you for your patience, Mrs. Weiskopf," Rachel said to the elderly woman behind the counter.

"I know how important such a choice is when you're their age," the white-haired woman said with a smile. "Every child wants to sample as many different items as they can. That's why we've kept the penny candy counter open, though there's no profit in it. Sometimes, it's not about money. Sometimes, it's about memories."

"You're right," she replied, though she would have been as happy to forget most of what had happened while she was a *kind*. "Got your bags, girls?"

Loribeth held up her small white bag, but Eva was too busy looking into hers to pay attention.

Thanking Mrs. Weiskopf, Rachel took her daughters by the hands and led them toward the door.

The breeze had a wintry chill in it when they stepped out onto the porch. She felt her daughters shiver and squatted to button their coats. The sun had been shining when they went inside, but storm clouds roiled over the mountains. Glancing toward the bridge, she saw several silhouettes moving in its direction. She wondered how long it would take before the hint of rain sent chills, icier than the autumnal wind, through the residents of the small town.

Movement on the sidewalk caught her eye. She looked away, then back so swiftly her bonnet bounced. Every inch of her tensed with a fear greater and older than what she'd endured when the sound of the trash truck hitting a pothole had resurrected the memory of death and destruction in the desert.

A pair of men were walking toward the store. They hadn't reached the steps that had been replaced after the flood and were raw lumber. Both wore black coats and broadfall trousers. Only one had a beard, and it fell to his chest, but it couldn't hide the deep chasm of a scar on his left cheek. He was gesticulating as he said something to the man striding alongside him.

She looked away, telling herself she had to be mistaken. There must be hundreds of plain men who wore long, pewter-gray beards and gestured vehemently with their hands. And the scar from the corner of his eye to his lips? There had to be other men with similar gouges in their faces.

That couldn't be her *daed*!

Not in Evergreen Corners, a place where she was sure she'd be safe from his unstable temper.

When Loribeth started to ask a question, she silenced her girls by urging them to select one piece of candy each from their bags. That kept them occupied while the two men walked by, not glancing in her direction. But she saw enough of the older man's face to know the truth.

It was her *daed*! What was Manassas Yoder doing here?

Grateful her bonnet concealed so much of her face, she waited for the men to turn onto the street that led across the bridge. She steered her daughters up the hill. Panic gripped her, making it hard to breathe. Where should she go? If *Daed* had seen her, he could follow her home. She didn't want to be alone with the man who had punished her and her siblings for the slightest infraction. What would her military friends think of her if they saw her fleeing like a frightened rabbit from a bent old man?

What would her friends in Evergreen Corners think of her avoiding her *daed*?

What would Isaac think?

Somehow, while trying not to consider the answers to those questions, Rachel got through the rest of the afternoon until she could concentrate on making supper for her small family. She pushed the close encounter from her head and began to hope that her *daed* hadn't seen her. Evergreen Corners was at a crossroads of two major routes in Vermont. Maybe it was only by chance her *daed* had walked by the store.

She couldn't believe that. Her family lived in Ohio, and she couldn't imagine a single reason her *daed* would be in town other than she was there. She'd been foolish to believe Evergreen Corners could become a haven while she regained the equilibrium to go on with her life. She was no closer to returning to the woman she used to be before tragedy tore apart her life. She'd seen that when she'd overreacted last week to the sound of a backfiring trash truck.

Dear God, show me Your mercy and help me protect my daughters.

She stirred spaghetti sauce on the stove, then wiped her hands on her apron. Stepping around Sweetie Pie, she took out a box of spaghetti. She gave a single piece to each girl and urged them to use them to play with the kitten in the living room. Soon the *kinder* were squealing with delight as Sweetie Pie tried to capture the tip of the spaghetti. They were kept busy until she'd finished preparing their supper. After they shared a silent prayer, the girls ate while Rachel pushed her food around her plate, unable to swallow a single bite.

At a knock at the door, everything stopped for Rachel. She had no thoughts. She couldn't move. She felt nothing but fear.

Loribeth jumped to her feet and raced to the door.

She wanted to halt her daughter, but couldn't make a sound. She watched, helpless as a newborn *boppli*, as the little girl swung open the door, then slammed it shut.

"It's *him*." The disgust in Loribeth's voice broke through Rachel's paralysis. Her daughter used that tone only when speaking of Isaac.

Relief and happiness flooded Rachel. Her *daed* wasn't on her front steps. Standing, she drew in a slow, steadying breath and managed to make her feet work enough to carry her to the door.

When she reopened the door, she looked into Isaac's warm smile and knew that while her relief was because Manassas Yoder wasn't there, her happiness was because Isaac *was*. Before she spoke a single word, she knew Isaac would offer her well-thought-out advice if she told him about her *daed*.

Thoughts of Manassas Yoder fled from her mind as she savored the sight of Isaac on her doorstep. His brown eyes were twinkling with *gut* humor. He wore a white shirt beneath the black suspenders that emphasized the breadth of his shoulders.

Her eyes widened when she realized he held some gold-and-orange mums. When he handed the bouquet to her, she smiled.

"Does this mean what I think it means?" she asked.

"What do you think it means?"

"You've put an offer on the farm. You wouldn't have picked the mums by the house's porch otherwise, ain't so?"

His smile wobbled for a moment, then strengthened. "I can never surprise you, can I, Rachel? You see right through me."

"Oh, how *wunderbaar*!"

"That I'm that obvious?"

"No." She let him into the house. "That you've put in an offer on the farm. Abby must be thrilled, too."

"I'm sure she'll be, assuming the deal goes through."

Asking him questions about what would happen next with his offer, she listened to his answers as she led the way into the kitchen. She filled a glass and carried it into the dining room. She put the flowers in it, smiling as her daughters grinned at the bright blossoms. Her fingers trembled so much that water spilled on the table. She rushed to get a cloth.

"What's wrong?" Isaac asked as he followed her into the kitchen, and she knew his keen eyes hadn't missed how her hands shook.

She didn't dissemble because she knew the answer to one of her questions. She wanted to tell Isaac what had happened and get his insight into her quandary. "I think I saw my *daed* today in Evergreen Corners."

"You think? You didn't go and speak with him?"

She shook her head. "No. After I first ran away years ago, he told me that if I ever defied him and left again, he never wanted anything to do with me."

"Words said in anger aren't always what someone feels."

"I know, but in this case, he meant every syllable." She sighed as she looked toward the living room. "I didn't want the girls to be present if he got angry, as he did so often when I was young."

"You can't avoid him forever, Rachel. He's your *daed*, and you must be the reason he's come to Evergreen Corners."

"I don't know why he's here. I left home over twenty years ago. He never came looking for me."

"He never *found* you, you mean. You don't know how long he's been looking for you. It might have been from the day you left."

Rachel shook her head. She didn't want to listen to

Isaac's usual *gut* sense. To allow herself to imagine *Daed* had been searching for her since she left home would suggest he cared about her other than as an extra pair of hands to help around the farm. If he had, why hadn't he shown that to her at least once during the seventeen years she'd lived at home?

As if in answer to her unspoken question, an assertive knock sounded on the front door. Her defenses rose, as she prepared to use the skills that had kept her alive while deployed. She calculated what would be the best and safest course of action. First, she called out to her girls to stay where they were.

Standing on tiptoe, she peeked out the window over the sink. She could barely see the front steps, but in the last of the twilight, she discovered not one, but two silhouettes there.

Isaac matched her motion. "Is one of them your *daed*?"

"I think so."

"You should talk with him, Rachel. You need to find out why he's come to Evergreen Corners."

"I don't know if—"

Another knock sounded.

"Do you want me to answer it?" he asked.

With all my heart, she longed to say, but she shook her head. If her *daed* was out there, she couldn't use Isaac as a human shield against him.

Telling the girls again to stay where they were, she rushed to the door. She had to unfold her fingers, which were closed in fists, before she could open it. Seeking out to God in silent prayer to be with her, she threw open the door.

She stared. The man next to her *daed* was as familiar to her as her reflection in a mirror. He was taller than she remembered him, but the bright blue eyes in his rugged face identified him as her younger brother, Robert. She could recall the days he and their sister, Arlene, had been born. Like her, as they grew up, they were made to feel worthless.

"Do you recognize me, Rachel?" he asked, his voice far deeper than the one in her memory.

"Ja." She wanted to throw her arms wide and welcome her brother into her life, but she couldn't be unaware of the man standing beside him. "How are you, Robbie?"

"I'm *gut*. How are you, Rachel?"

She started to reply *gut*, but paused, not wanting to ply her brother with a lie. "Surprised. I'm surprised to see you here, Robbie."

"Robert," he corrected. "I go by Robert now. *Daed* says a grown man shouldn't have a *kind*'s name."

"How did you find me?"

"One of the scribes for *The Budget* mentioned the volunteers working here. Your name was included. When someone showed it to *Daed*, he insisted we come here."

Why hadn't she considered the possibility that someone among the plain community would have written regular letters about the flood-recovery efforts to *The Budget*, the newspaper that connected plain people around the world? She'd become too complacent, hadn't been looking over her shoulder every minute as she had when she first moved into the *Englisch* world.

Her brother cleared his throat, then asked, "May we come in? Both of us?"

The words that he was welcome to enter her home, but *Daed* was not, burned on her tongue. She almost spoke them. She halted herself when she felt small hands on her skirt as Eva tried to peer past her, curious to see who was at the door.

"I don't know," she said.

"He's changed, Rachel."

"Are you sure?" She wanted to bite back the words bursting from her foolish heart. She wanted to believe it was possible to have the *daed* she'd always wanted. How many times had she listened to her heart and returned home? Too many, and each time it had betrayed her.

"Since *Mamm* died, he's been nicer to us."

"*Mamm* died?" Tears welled in her eyes, startling her. She'd wished her *mamm* had been strong enough to step between her husband and their *kinder* when he lost his temper and struck out at them. Even so, she'd loved her *mamm* deeply.

"About two years ago. She died in her sleep." Robert gave her a sad smile. "Peacefully." *Unlike how she'd lived.* Her brother didn't say the words, but she heard them in her heart. "Can we come in?"

Like before, she knew she must not make a scene in front of her daughters. It would be better, as Isaac had suggested, to talk with her *daed* and listen to what he'd come to say. After that, she could decide what to do about speaking with him in the future.

"Of course," she said. "*Komm* in."

She stepped aside to let the men in, then edged away another involuntary pace when her *daed* entered her home. Suddenly she felt as young and weak as the *kind* who'd endured his temper.

A hand at the center of her back kept her from continuing to distance herself from the man who'd made her childhood a nightmare. At the touch, her heart skittered within her. Isaac! She wasn't facing her *daed* alone. Her panic ebbed for the first time since she'd first seen her *daed* that afternoon. One of the first lessons she'd learned in the Army was the strength there was in having someone at your side you could depend on. And she could depend on Isaac.

Daed looked older than the image she'd been carrying in her head. With a start of amazement, she realized she was approaching the age he'd been when she'd left home for the final time. He must be in his late sixties now, and his strong nose and narrowed eyes were flanked by thick valleys of wrinkles.

He rolled the brim of his black church hat in his hands as he paused in the middle of her living room. His bushy gray eyebrows lowered when he noted the two little girls standing beside her and Isaac behind her.

"Your family?" her *daed* asked in a creaking voice.

"The girls are my daughters. Isaac is another of the volunteers in Evergreen Corners." She wished she could steal a glance at Isaac to discover what he was thinking about her *daed*.

"You found someone to marry you?"

"Ja." She fought not to bristle at the question that

suggested whoever had been willing to wed her must have been a *dummkopf* of the first order. "We were married for almost six years."

"Where is your husband?"

"He died."

Her *daed*'s eyebrows arched, but for once he didn't make the snide comment she'd expected. When he mumbled something that might have been "I'm sorry," she was startled. Could Robbie—Robert—have been right? Had their *daed* changed?

"As I said, these are my daughters." She put a hand on each girl's shoulder as she said their names and ages.

"They favor you."

"I see their *daed* in them, as well." To her daughters, she added, "This is your *grossdawdi*." When the girls gave her puzzled looks, she bent to whisper in each one's ear. "Your grandpa." A quick glance toward the men showed that none of them had heard her speak the *Englisch* word so the girls would understand the stranger in front of them was her *daed*. "This is Robert." She smiled, though the expression felt alien on her lips when she stood in the same room as Manassas Yoder. "He's my little brother."

Eva tilted her head to gaze at Robert. "You no little. Me little."

"I used to be little but I grew."

"Me, too?" Eva spun to face Rachel. "Me grow, too? No little no more?"

"Ja," she said, stroking her *kind*'s cheek, "but promise you won't grow up too fast."

"It's not our way," *Daed* interrupted, "to make promises. That's something you should be teaching your *kinder*, Rachel." Glancing around the trailer, he wrinkled his nose. "It's not right, raising them among these *Englischers*."

Isaac cleared his throat, then said, "We have a growing plain community here in Evergreen Corners. There are more than thirty plain people here."

"All Amish?"

"Some are Mennonite, but our numbers fluctuate as people come and go. Most have homes they must keep an eye on as well as volunteering here."

"They should be with their real family. They have an *aenti* and *onkels* as well as several cousins."

"What?" asked Loribeth. "We've got what?"

Sorrow erupted through Rachel as *Daed* went on to list the names of Arlene's eight *kinder*. The girls spoke *Deitsch* with ease, but they didn't know the words for their relatives other than *mamm* and *daed*, because she'd never used them with Loribeth and Eva.

To cover her daughter's furtive whisper, Rachel said more loudly, "Girls, you should say hello to your *grossdawdi*."

"Hello," the girls said.

"*Komm* here." *Daed* sat on the sofa and patted his knee.

Both girls wrapped their arms around Rachel and clung to her.

He scowled, and his eyes slitted as he looked at Rachel. His expression told her that he—again—found her lacking.

"They're shy," Isaac said in the quiet tone that warned

he wouldn't be budged by argument from anyone. "Perhaps it'd be better if you talked to them from where you are on this first meeting."

"They're my *kins-kinder*!" he retorted.

"True, but you're a stranger to them. You need to give them time to get to know you."

"You're right, Isaac," her *daed* said, shocking her. She couldn't remember him backing down when someone suggested he was wrong.

Had he really changed? After all, she was different from the young girl who'd jumped the fence, believing everything she wanted and needed was in the *Englisch* world.

"Give the girls some time," Isaac urged. "It's taken them a while to get used to us in Evergreen Corners, but they've come around."

"We can stay for only a few days," Robert said, speaking to Rachel for the first time since they'd come inside.

Rachel made a decision. "*Komm* to supper tomorrow night." By then, she might be prepared to deal with a *daed* who'd found ways to control his temper. She couldn't let her heart betray her into foolishness.

Her gaze slipped toward Isaac. No, she must not let her heart and her longing to belong to a family delude her again.

Isaac tried to ignore his relief when Rachel's *daed* and brother left. Though she'd warned him about how uneasy she was about speaking with Manassas, he'd been shocked that she tiptoed around the man. She'd tried to hide how she flinched whenever he raised his voice, but he'd seen it. Had her *daed*?

Her brother seemed to be a decent man, but was almost as tentative around Manassas as Rachel was. The reactions told Isaac there was more to the story than an Amish patriarch being furious when one of his *kinder* decided not to be baptized and ran away to live among *Englischers*.

Guilt clawed at him when he realized he was grateful that their arrival tonight must have dimmed Rachel's memory of him bringing her flowers. He'd never guessed her first thoughts would be of him and his dream. He'd hoped the flowers would open the door to a conversation about her becoming his wife, but that hadn't happened.

He wasn't being fair, he reminded himself as he stood in the doorway to the girls' bedroom. Rachel had been unnerved by seeing her *daed*. Tonight hadn't been the right night to initiate a discussion. He had to have faith a better opportunity was waiting.

"He's really and truly your *daed*?" asked Loribeth as Rachel bent to tuck her into bed.

"*Ja*, he is, and he's your *grossdawdi*."

The little girl wore a puzzled frown. "He went away, and he came back. Will my *daed* come back, too?"

When Rachel blinked hard, he guessed she was trying not to cry. She sat on the side of Loribeth's bed. He looked at where Eva was listening from the other bed and knew Rachel had to choose her words with care. As if for the first time, he realized what a hard task she had of raising two little girls alone.

He admired her strength as she forced a smile that looked genuine enough to comfort the *kinder*. Knowing how much each motion was costing her, he watched as she bent to kiss Loribeth's forehead.

"No, your *daed* won't be coming back." Her voice softened to a tender whisper. "Remember? Your *daed* is with God, and he's waiting for us when it's our turn to—"

"To meet God," Isaac quickly interjected when her voice faded into uncertain silence. She was, he knew, struggling not to cause the youngsters more pain.

She never spoke of how her husband had died. Isaac had no idea if the man had been ill or if there had been a terrible accident.

"That's right," Rachel said, drawing his attention to her. "You must wait until God calls you home."

"Until then," Isaac said, "it's important you treat others with kindness and be *gut* girls who listen to your *mamm*."

"Even Alyssa?" asked Loribeth, shocking him because she'd avoided speaking to him. The girls were as distressed as their *mamm* over the unexpected guests this evening.

Though he had no idea who Alyssa was, Isaac said, "*Ja*, you must treat Alyssa with kindness."

"She broke my blue crayon and told Miss Gwen I did it."

"That wasn't nice, ain't so?" he asked.

The girls shook their heads.

"Some people aren't as nice as they should be, but

that means we need to be nice ourselves, so they can see how they're supposed to behave."

"Oh," Loribeth said, her eyes widening. "Like being a roller mob-el?"

"Ja." He glanced at Rachel, who was fighting a smile, though her eyes glistened with unshed tears. "At least I think so."

Standing, Rachel smoothed the covers. *"Ja,* you need to be a role model like Miss Gwen says."

"Okay," the little girl said, but didn't appear persuaded.

"'Kay," her sister said, then added, "And forgive, ain't so, I-zak?"

"Ja." He wondered if Eva had any idea what it meant to forgive…or if he did.

He ignored thoughts of his own *daed* while Rachel said a prayer with the girls and gave them each another kiss before turning on their night-lights. She closed their door after checking the kitten was napping on the kitchen floor, one paw pinning down a piece of uncooked spaghetti.

"Kaffi?" she asked as they went into the kitchen.

"Not for me. Get some for yourself if you want."

"I don't think I need caffeine tonight."

He translated that to mean she was already too on edge to sleep. Or maybe she wanted to be alone to sort out what had happened that day. Her life had been upended, and she must need time in prayer to seek guidance for how to handle tomorrow night's conversation with her brother and *daed.*

"I should be going," he said, though he wanted to remain and offer what help he could.

"You're welcome to join us tomorrow for supper." She took a breath and let it go. "I'd like you to come tomorrow night, Isaac, but I'll understand if you don't want to."

"I'll be there."

Her shoulders sagged with relief. "*Danki*, Isaac."

"I enjoy coming to your table."

"My thanks isn't for that," she said as he reached for the doorknob. "Loribeth's question threw me for a loop."

"Having your *daed* here tonight has rattled you." Before he could halt himself, he brushed a strand of her ebony hair toward her *kapp*, curling it behind her ear. His fingers lingered for a moment, then he drew them away.

How he longed to touch her soft cheek and tilt her mouth toward his! He couldn't guess anything else that would have been more foolish. He wished her pleasant dreams and let himself out before he gave in to his yearning to kiss her.

Something had gone wrong with his plan for finding the perfect wife. He was falling in love with Rachel Yoder, and that could make him as witless as his *daed* had been after *Mamm*'s death.

As he hurried across the deserted village green, he knew Rachel wouldn't be the only one reaching out to God tonight. He needed help himself before he lost his head and, for the first time in longer than he could recall, listened first to his heart.

Chapter Twelve

Pausing by the table that was set for six, Rachel hoped *Daed* would appreciate how much work her daughters had done to make it special for him. They'd made cards from folded sheets of construction paper and pictures they'd cut out of magazines at the day-care center. Loribeth had been able to sign her name, but Eva drew a pair of stick figures that were supposed to be her and her *grossdawdi*. A sun shone in the sky above their heads, a sign that Eva believed made it a happy scene.

Rachel wanted to believe it'd be a joyous reunion to-night. She longed to believe her *daed* had changed as much as she had during the past two decades. When she'd left home, she couldn't have imagined she'd find a career in the Army, marry and have *kinder* and find her way back to a plain life. If someone had told her what path her life would take, she would have laughed, saying it was impossible.

But it had happened, and she was in Evergreen Corners, Vermont, ready to offer her *daed* a home-cooked meal.

Her uncertainty must have infected her daughters because the girls were subdued while she helped them dress for the meal, which was cooking in the oven. They hadn't pleaded to sample the cake she'd baked earlier, and she wasn't sure if she'd heard them speak much above a whisper all day. Sweetie Pie had been ignored except when Loribeth had fallen asleep after day care on the couch with the kitten curled into the curve of her body.

"You look *wunderbaar*," she said as she smiled at her daughters.

"Cute as a button," Loribeth replied. "That's what Miss Gwen says. Why are buttons cute, *Mamm*?"

"I don't know. Plain women don't use them, ain't so?"

"Cute as a pin?" asked Eva, looking at the ones holding Rachel's apron in place.

Hugging her daughters, Rachel sent up a prayer of gratitude for these two precious gifts God had given her. She would have done anything for them, and hosting her *daed* tonight was proof of that.

She left the girls to their coloring books while she oversaw supper. She was making scalloped potatoes and pork chops. The casserole was in the oven, and she had green beans waiting to be cooked on top. Chow-chow and applesauce were already on the table. She would put the rolls in to warm while she served the rest of the food, and planned to bring them and butter and apple butter to the table once the water for the beans was set to boil.

It was a meal *Mamm* had made for special occasions. The thought of her *mamm* having died without

Rachel being able to say goodbye staggered her, especially when she realized her death and Travis's must have been within months of each other. If God had been making sure the news was postponed so she had no more pain than she could handle as her life was turned inside out, she was grateful to Him. She'd felt so alone in the wake of Travis's death, having a young *kind* and pregnant with another.

You don't have to be alone. The words whispered in her head. If only she could be the wife Isaac wanted, the wife he deserved...

Rachel focused on supper preparations to halt her thoughts. She poured sweet cider that one of the volunteers had brought from his orchard to share. Arranging the glasses on the counter, she checked she had milk for Eva, who didn't like cider. When a knock sounded on the door, she was taking the lid off the casserole so the pork chops would brown during the last fifteen minutes of cooking. She set it on the stove and went to answer the door. She shot her daughters a smile when they began collecting their crayons and books and putting them in the toy cubby by the sofa.

Opening the door, she smiled at Robert and their *daed*. They were dressed in their Sunday best, and she was glad that she also had chosen the light blue dress she wore to worship services.

"*Komm* in," she urged. "It's getting chillier with every passing evening."

Her daughters scurried to her side, their eyes wide as they stared at the men. Robert bent to greet them, but *Daed* strode past everyone and looked into the dining room.

Facing her, he asked, "Why is the table set for six?"

"Isaac is joining us, too."

"Are you walking out with him?"

She hesitated, unsure why she'd heard what sounded like venom in her *daed*'s voice. Why would he speak so of Isaac? They'd met briefly. Had *Daed* taken offense when Isaac's comment made him admit he was mistaken?

Glancing at her brother, she saw he was as bothered by their *daed*'s tone as she was. That made her more ill at ease.

"No, we aren't walking out together," she replied, as if there hadn't been a break in the conversation. "Isaac is, as I said, another volunteer in the recovery efforts. He's been kind to us as have the rest of the plain folks— as well as the *Englischers*—in town."

He gave her a quelling scowl, but she didn't cower as she had in the past. She'd had too many other frowns aimed in her direction when she'd given orders to her transportation company that weren't popular. Looks couldn't kill, though there had been plenty of other ways for the people under her command to die.

She squelched the shiver racing along her spine. She needed to keep her mind from the past. She couldn't change it.

"*Daed*, would you like some cider?" she asked in a tone she hoped sounded cheerful.

Before he could answer, a knock at the door announced Isaac had arrived. She thrust one of the glasses of cider into her *daed*'s hand, urged him and her brother to sit in the living room, and turned to get the door.

Her smile widened at the sight of Isaac on the steps. He, too, was dressed in his *mutze* coat and dark pants, and she wondered if he'd ever looked more handsome than he did when he whispered, "Am I on time?"

"You're here at the perfect time." She realized what she'd said and wanted to take back the words in case Isaac thought she was making fun of him and his quest for a perfect wife.

"Gut."

Leaving him to talk to Robert, *Daed* and the girls, she rushed into the kitchen to finish preparing the food. Her fingers were clumsy as she worked and listened to the stilted conversation from the other room. She didn't shoo away her daughters when they came in to be with her.

In spite of having to walk around them each time she moved, she got supper on the table. She swung Eva onto the bench, where she'd sit, too, and moved Loribeth's chair to her other side. Calling to the men to join them, she motioned for each of them to take a seat.

Robert chose the chair across from her when *Daed* pulled out the one at the head of the table, next to where Loribeth sat. That left the one next to Eva for Isaac, who asked her *daed* to lead them in silent prayer.

She took her daughters' hands and bowed her head. She raised it when her *daed* bumped his knee against the table leg, the sign he'd always used to announce he was done. Serving the little girls and cutting their food into bite-size pieces, she was kept busy while the men spooned out the fragrant casserole and passed around vegetables and rolls.

Isaac turned the conversation to the work the volunteers had been doing for almost a year in Evergreen Corners. Her brother had a lot of questions, and the two men soon were talking as if they'd been friends for years. *Daed* didn't speak often unless he was asking for more food to be passed to him. Keeping her girls quiet and eating occupied Rachel.

Conversation halted as if a switch had been flipped when her *daed* held out his hand to her older daughter. "*Komm* here, girl."

Loribeth shrank away from her *grossdawdi*'s outstretched hand and giggled nervously.

"They're bashful," Robert said in a consoling tone. "Remember? Isaac mentioned that last night."

Daed glared at Rachel, who was trying to divert Loribeth into eating the rest of her roll spread with apple butter. "I suppose you've been telling them more of your made-up stories about your pitiful childhood, so they hate me."

"I've never said a word about it to them," Rachel said quietly.

"I'm sure you've told him." *Daed* flung a hand in Isaac's direction and made a baleful sound deep in his throat. "You never could keep your mouth closed about private family business."

"I haven't said anything to anyone," she said as Loribeth put her hand over her mouth, but began to laugh when Eva did. Rachel was sure the girls didn't find anything funny about the situation, but they didn't know how else to react to their *grossdawdi* growling like a rabid dog.

"Why should I believe that when my *kins-kinder* avoid me? You've lied all your life, daughter."

She hadn't. She'd always been honest with him, and during her childhood, that had enraged him more. She sought an answer that wouldn't set him off, but she delayed too long.

Daed surged to his feet, and she was again the frightened little girl she'd been. She was facing a tyrannical parent and fearing she'd suffer the back of his hand or the lash of his belt. She cowered, unable to halt herself, when he reached toward her.

Then she realized he wasn't interested in her. He glowered at Loribeth as he said, "Stop that infernal giggling, girl!"

"Her name is Loribeth," Rachel said, trying to batten down her instinctive fear. She wasn't that helpless *kind* any longer. She was a woman who'd been taught, through the tough lessons of boot camp and deployments, to remain calm when facing her enemies.

Was that how she thought of her *daed*? As the enemy? She shouldn't—

That thought was interrupted when he snarled, "She needs to do as she's told. Every *kind* needs to learn to obey its elders." He grabbed Loribeth's arm and jerked her out of her chair.

The little girl screeched more in surprise than in pain, but Rachel knew how it would go. First horrible words spewing from her *daed*'s mouth, words aimed at tearing her apart, and then would come the blows.

Every ounce of her rebelled against him inflicting his idea of parenting on her *kinder*. Every moment of training she'd had in the military came to the forefront.

Standing so fast that the bench skidded backward across the floor, she stepped between Loribeth and her *daed*. She didn't raise her hand, simply bent her elbow, putting her forearm across her body. In her mind, she heard her self-defense instructor explaining the bones in her lower arm were among the strongest in her body. Her arm would help ward off a blow from any direction.

"Don't touch my *kinder*," she warned softly as she put her left hand against Loribeth's narrow chest so she could push her daughter away if necessary.

Beside her, like a miniature warrior, Sweetie Pie arched and hissed. Her fur fluffed out until she looked almost twice her tiny size.

"Step aside," *Daed* ordered. "It's clear you shouldn't be responsible for these *kinder* when you can't carry on a respectful discussion."

A gentle hand cupped her other elbow. As warmth seeped up her arm, she was grateful she wasn't alone in facing the man who'd abused her and her siblings. Isaac stood behind her, ready to get her girls to safety. That he hadn't spoken told her more than any words could. He might not approve of her taking such a defensive stance, but he wouldn't gainsay her because he was coming to understand why she'd been so upset at *Daed* returning to her life.

Robert began, *"Daed—"*

"That's right," their *daed* said. "Listen to your brother.

I'm your *daed*, Rachel. You'll do as I say. Honor your *daed*."

"I have tried to, but I'm also my *kinder*'s *mamm*, and I'll do what I must to keep them safe." She didn't let him force her into shifting her gaze away as she said, "As their *mamm*, I'm saying you must not ever lift your hand to either of my girls. Violence isn't our way. If you lay a hand on them, I'll call the police."

"We don't bring *Englischers* into our business."

"I will when someone threatens my girls. I don't think you realize…" She swallowed hard, holding back the words she once would have spoken if someone tried to browbeat her or one of the people in her command. Those sharp retorts belonged to another life. Just as Manassas Yoder did.

Could he have any idea how much she was aching inside? She'd dared to believe her brother was right when he said that their *daed* had changed. She'd trusted the hope in her brother's eyes when he spoke of *Daed* being in control of his temper at last. She'd imagined he could be the *daed* she'd longed for when she'd been cold and scared and in pain when he banished her to the root cellar after a beating.

Rachel drew her daughters closer and put her hands on their shoulders. "You need to leave."

"So you're throwing out your *daed*?"

"Please leave," she said in the same calm voice. It took every bit of her willpower to keep it serene, but she refused to let him see how he'd crushed her hopes that he had set aside his cruelty.

He stared at her, and when she didn't shift her gaze

away, he lowered his eyes. Pushing past her, he grabbed his hat. "Let's go, Robert!" He stormed out, slamming the door in his wake.

Rachel exchanged horrified glances with Isaac and Robert. Isaac's face was grim, but Robert's was filled with shame.

"I'm sorry, Rachel," her brother said as he came around the table. "I thought… That is, I never would have…" He hung his head.

Giving him a swift hug, she said, "I wanted to believe him, too, so don't blame yourself."

"If he'd hurt your girls…" He hugged her again, then he was gone, too.

Eva flung her arms around Rachel's legs and pressed her face to them. She began to cry.

Bending, Rachel picked up her younger daughter. She hoped her trembling hands wouldn't make her drop Eva. As she snuggled the *kind* close, she looked at her other daughter. Loribeth had no more color in her face than she did the day she'd thrown up on Isaac's shoes.

"Mamm…" she began, then started to sob.

Squatting in front of Loribeth, Rachel balanced Eva on her legs while she put an arm around her older daughter. Loribeth pressed against her, almost knocking her backward. Only Isaac's hand on her shoulders kept her from tipping over onto the floor.

"It's okay," Rachel murmured to her daughters as she raised her gaze toward Isaac's face.

The cold severity remained, but as she watched, it eased into a gentler expression. For the first time in her life, after a confrontation with her *daed*, she didn't feel alone. She hadn't ever believed someone beyond her equally helpless brother and sister could be on her side, and she treasured the moment in the most secret place of her heart, where she'd been trying to hide her growing love for Isaac from herself.

Isaac watched Rachel and her *kinder*, and another wave of anger surged over him. He had fought to keep from lashing out at Manassas Yoder. Though the man had left, rage still bristled along Isaac's skin like an itch he mustn't scratch.

He said little while Rachel served slices of chocolate cake with scoops of ice cream. He barely tasted the few bites he managed to swallow.

When she gave the girls a bath and put them to bed, he was surprised Loribeth didn't shy away from him. She must have been more frightened by her *gross-dawdi* than he'd guessed. Another rumble of ire resonated through him, but he silenced it, not wanting to upset the girls more.

He offered to help Rachel clear the table once the girls were in bed, but she waved aside his offer and walked into the living room. When he joined her there, she faced him. "I'm sorry, Isaac. I know I shouldn't have confronted him as I did."

"Turning the other cheek isn't easy, especially when doing so leaves your *kinder* in danger." He cupped her chin and tilted her face toward him. "Rachel, you didn't strike your *daed* or raise your voice to him. I can't say I could have spoken with such serenity if I'd been in your place."

"When I get angry, I get quiet." She gave him a smile filled with regret. "That's something everyone who's ever known me has had to learn."

"I'll keep that in mind." His fingers played along her cheek, savoring the texture of her silky skin.

Her eyes grew big with wonder, and he knew that she must be savoring the same luscious sensations that were trickling up his fingers. She breathed his name. Was this the right time to pull her into his arms and kiss her? To ask her to be his wife because he believed she was the perfect one for him?

No, argued his common sense. *She tossed her* daed *out of her home an hour ago. She isn't thinking straight right now. Neither are you.*

When he sat on the couch, he was surprised when she sat beside him. It was the first time he'd seen her choose any spot in the living room other than her beloved rocking chair.

"You should talk to Cora Miller," he said.

He saw that she recognized the name of a fellow volunteer, who'd been one of the first in Evergreen Corners to receive a new home after the flood. "Why?"

"Cora has experience with *daeds* who are bad to their *kinder*. She came here to protect her nephew and niece from theirs." He held her gaze. "You need to forgive Manassas, Rachel. Not for him, but for yourself. Carrying around anger eats at you. Besides, as we're taught, we can only hope for forgiveness if we offer it."

"Could you forgive a man like that?"

He hated the sound of bitterness in her voice, a sound

he'd heard in his own too often. "I already have. My *daed* wasn't the best, either."

"Abby mentioned that he drank too much and too often."

He was startled. "Abby knew?"

"Do you think you could pull the wool over *Abby's* eyes? She doesn't miss much."

"No, she doesn't." He wondered why he'd never considered how readily Abby saw behind the facades people built to protect themselves and others. "I should thank her for keeping me in the dark, so I didn't have to worry more about her."

"I don't think you could worry more about her. Or her about you. That's what love does."

"My sister doesn't know the whole truth." He sighed and pushed himself to his feet. "Our *daed* drank every day. Sometimes he could function. Other times he couldn't, and I had to take over when he was unable to do chores. I didn't want the younger *kinder* knowing because I kept praying one day God would open *Daed's* eyes to what he was doing to himself and us. Though it took more time than I'd ever imagined, God did reach out to *Daed*. He opened not only *Daed's* eyes, but his heart, so the grief left by *Mamm's* death could be replaced by love for the woman who became his wife."

"God is *gut*."

"True, but I can't help wishing He'd acted sooner. It was more than twenty years from *Mamm's* funeral to *Daed's* second wedding. Those years were challenging. I know there are those who say that God doesn't give us more than we can handle with His assistance, but there were times when I wanted to throw in the towel and walk away."

She folded her hands as if in prayer and murmured, "I know how difficult overdrinking can be for a family."

"Your *daed*—"

"I'm not talking about him. I'm talking about my husband." She swallowed hard, and her gaze turned inward.

He recognized the pose. He'd experienced it himself far too many times when he had to acknowledge that, no matter what he tried, he couldn't succeed in changing his *daed*.

"Will you tell me about him, Rachel?"

She continued to stare into her memories, and he wondered if his heartfelt words had reached her. When she spoke, he didn't know if it was in response to what he'd said, or if she was giving voice to the past's pain.

"He liked to drink beer with his friends. Sometimes too often and too much. I tried once to talk to him about it, but he told me I didn't know what I was talking about. When he was in an accident after he'd been drinking and almost died, I thought the truth might come out, but he somehow kept it hidden. I know he didn't want his boss to know because that might have caused trouble at work."

"So he wasn't a farmer?"

She shook her head. "No, but his job was everything to him."

"Not everything when he had you and your daughters."

She wore a sad smile. "Travis loved his job first and foremost."

"Travis? That was your husband's name?"

For a moment, as she stood, he thought she'd change the subject as she had so many times when he asked questions about her past. Instead she filled two cups with *kaffi*.

"Isn't that an unusual name for a plain man?" he asked.

She paused in the middle of the room as if she didn't know which way to go. "His parents must have liked it if they gave it to him." A spasm of something he couldn't define seemed to make her face tighten as tears glittered in her eyes. "They seem comfortable making their own rules." She hiccuped a sob. "Just as my *daed* did. I hoped, Isaac… I really hoped he'd changed. That he'd want to change, but he hasn't."

"I'm sorry." He stood and put his arms around her.

She pressed her face to his chest and began to weep, as deeply and as openly as her young daughters had earlier. He guided her to the sofa. Sitting beside her, he held her as she cried for the dreams that had died in the crucible of her *daed*'s uncontrolled rage tonight.

Chapter Thirteen

It wasn't easy to be cheerful for her daughters the next morning, but Rachel did everything she could to wash away the caustic memory of last night's debacle at supper. She let Abby know she needed the day to spend with Loribeth and Eva. She stopped at the day-care center and told Gwen that the girls wouldn't be attending.

She took them to the Saturday farmers market in a parking lot of a bank across from the high school. It was the final week for the market, and she wanted to get more of the delicious apples she'd bought there. Though the day was unseasonably warm, not many people had come to the market. She was able to let the girls skip around without worrying they'd trip someone or fall over a bag of vegetables in front of a table.

Wherever she stopped, everyone was talking about the odd weather and reports of a strengthening tropical storm churning the seas to the south. Reports said the storm would remain at sea and bypass New England. That didn't halt the speculation. Vermonters always loved to talk—and complain—about the weather, but she heard the faint edge of worry in their voices. After Hurricane Kevin's devastation last year, the residents of Evergreen Corners were more anxious than usual.

No matter how many conversations she was part of, she couldn't stop thinking of how she'd sobbed in Isaac's arms last night. He hadn't implored her to stop or soothed her with platitudes about everything being okay. He'd held her until she finished mourning what she'd never had with her *daed*. When she regained some control, he'd handed her a handkerchief and let her wipe her eyes and blow her nose. He'd squeezed her hand and, before he'd left, urged her to go to bed and leave the dishes for the next day.

She hadn't, and a few more tears had fallen into the soapy water before she'd gone into her small bedroom and her bed that seemed too large and too empty. She'd found a few minutes of sleep as the sun was about to rise, then woke the girls and began a new day.

She had to let go of old dreams and look for new ones. She didn't need to look far, because she had her beloved *kinder*. She might never be able to kiss Isaac, as she'd longed to last night before he left, but she could dream. She could…

Rachel stopped in midstep when a too-familiar form stepped in front of her. Ignoring her first instinct to run away as fast as she could, she waited for her *daed* to speak. She noticed Robert standing behind him. Her daughters were checking out some wooden toys, oblivious to what was happening, but the space was filled with merchants. Her *daed* wouldn't be *dumm* enough to try to hurt them in public.

She hoped.

When he opened his mouth, she tried to prepare herself for whatever vitriol he would fire at her. "I want to say goodbye, daughter."

She nodded, not sure what she could or should say in response. He'd used her words against her throughout her childhood.

"And to apologize."

Shocked, she whispered, "*You* want to apologize?"

"I didn't mean to scare your daughter. My temper gets the better of me sometimes." He sighed. "I told myself I wouldn't lose it when I was with you and your *kinder*, and I did keep it for a long time."

"*Danki* for trying." What else could she say? It wouldn't get her anywhere to argue that an hour in her company wasn't a long time to hold on to his temper.

"I know you never understood that what I did was in your best interests."

"You're right. I'll never understand that."

He shuffled his feet as if unsure what to say next. Did he expect her to forgive him? She had tried for years, but she'd come to realize he wouldn't be anything more than he was. She couldn't forget the horrors she and her siblings had survived.

"Before I go," he said, "I've got one question— Where have you been?"

"As far away as I could be." She wasn't going to reveal the truth to him, because she didn't trust him. Not as she wanted to trust Isaac.

He nodded, then turned and began to walk away. She was appalled when a wisp of sympathy seeped into her heart. He'd lost almost everything by not being able to keep his temper. That was so sad.

You need to forgive Manassas, Rachel. Not for him, but for yourself. Carrying around anger eats at you. Besides, as we're taught, we can only hope for forgiveness if we offer it.

Isaac had spoken the words with the clarity of his faith. She wished she could be as sure he was right. Not about forgiveness. She understood that to be forgiven, she must learn to forgive. Was offering forgiveness to a man who had beaten her and driven her from home even possible?

It had to be. She knew that as she knew she needed air to live.

"I forgive you," she said to his back.

He faltered but didn't look at her as he continued in the opposite direction.

She closed her eyes as God's grace suffused through her. All the times she'd cried out for Him to come and rescue her, she hadn't realized that she only needed to open herself to forgiveness. She had to forgive *Daed* and to forgive herself as well, for believing on some level that she'd deserved every beating she'd received. She hadn't. She was born of God's love and worthy of being loved.

"Rachel?"

She looked at her brother, who'd come to stand in front of her. "Robert, are you leaving, too?"

"*Ja*. I must warn Arlene to keep a close eye on her

kinder, though I think she already knows." He sighed. "I so wanted to believe *Daed* had changed that I stopped noticing how she sends them off to play with friends or do chores when *Daed* visits. She and her husband have been talking about moving to Indiana, and that may be why. How could I have been so blind?"

"Don't blame yourself for this. I was taken in, too, because I wanted to believe we could have the family we always wanted." She gripped his arm. "Robert, move far away from him and find yourself someone *wunderbaar* to love."

"As you plan to do with Isaac?"

She wouldn't be false with her brother. "Isaac wants a wife who's something I'm not, Robert."

"Are you so sure of that? I've seen how he looks at you." He gave her a sad grin. "He didn't hesitate to leap to the defense of you and your daughters. Even *Daed* couldn't be oblivious to that." His smile warmed. "I know *hochmut* is a sin, Rachel, but I don't think I've ever been prouder of someone than I was of you when you defended Loribeth." He glanced at the man striding away toward the green. "Would it be okay if I came to visit sometime?"

"Anytime."

"I'm intrigued by the work everyone is doing here, and I'd like to lend a hand." He gave her a small smile. "As a *danki* for what this village has done for my sister and my nieces."

"The projects here are planned to be finished by year's end."

"They plan to get that covered bridge fixed by then?"

"Apparently the original funds for the bridge were sidetracked to a different project. Are there more? I don't know. I don't know what's going to happen after Christmas." She put her hand on his forearm again. "Please come and visit us, Robert. I've missed you and Arlene. Tell her that."

"I will, and maybe sometime you'll come to Ohio to visit us."

"Maybe." Her gaze slid past him. "Not in the near future."

Looking over his shoulder at their *daed*, he nodded. "I understand. Let me get him home and settled, and I'll write to you about coming for a longer visit."

She embraced him. "I can't wait."

"Me, either." He gave her another hug, then turned to follow their *daed* toward the bridge at the center of the village.

Eva slipped her hand into Rachel's. "*Grossdawdi* angry. God says be happy. I-zak says so."

"Isaac is right," she replied as she wiped her hand against the sweat on her forehead. It was far too hot for an autumn morning. "Let's finish our shopping."

She held out her hands to her girls. Eva grabbed hold, but Loribeth didn't.

"Your *daed* came to see you," her older daughter said as thick tears fell over her lashes. "Why won't mine come to see me?"

Rachel squatted in front of Loribeth, wondering how she could have failed to notice that her daughter missed her *daed* so deeply. "He would if he could."

"He hasn't come to see me." Her small voice broke. "It's because of *him*, ain't so?"

"What him?"

"I-zak! *Daed* doesn't want him here, pretending to be our *daed*."

"Isaac isn't trying to pretend to be your *daed*. He knows he and your *daed* are two different people." She doubted her daughter could conceive how dissimilar the two men truly were.

Maybe Loribeth couldn't, but she'd sensed the ways Isaac and Travis were alike. Both were dedicated to any job they took on, and worked hard until it was completed to their satisfaction. They assumed leadership roles with ease and had earned the respect of those around them. Most important, they cared about her small family.

"I miss my *daed*."

She drew her daughter to her and held Loribeth's cheek against her heart. "I miss him, too."

"You do?"

"With every breath I take, but I'm grateful God gave you to us because you're so much like your *daed*. Not only do you look like him, but you're strong and smart like him."

"So he can't come back?"

Looking over Loribeth's head, she motioned for Eva to come closer. Eva was on the edge of tears, too, though Rachel doubted the little girl understood what they were talking about. Eva knew only that her sister and *mamm* were upset.

Rachel put her arms around her daughters. Meeting

their watery gazes, she said, "Your *daed* is with God, and both he and God are watching over you every day and every night. Your *daed* loved you. Don't forget that. Not ever."

The girls nodded gravely.

"Here in Evergreen Corners, Isaac is a part of our life." *At least for now.* Taking a steadying breath, she added, "Nobody will ever take *Daed*'s place in your heart."

"Or yours?" asked Loribeth, uncertain.

"Ja." She smiled as she tapped the middle of her daughter's narrow chest. "Did you know that hearts are balloons? Hearts get bigger the more love you put into them like balloons get bigger when you put more air into them. However, while balloons can only get so big before they burst, your heart can keep getting bigger and bigger to hold every bit of the love you want to put into it."

"Really?"

"Think about it, Loribeth. When we first came to Evergreen Corners, you had love in your heart for me and Eva and *Daed*, ain't so?"

"Ja."

"Then you found room in your heart for Miss Gwen and Abby and Pastor Hershey and your new friends."

"Me, too?" asked Eva.

"You, too." She put her fingers over the little girl's heart. "I can tell you've got lots of room in your hearts for love."

The *kinder* considered her words in silence, and Rachel knew she'd implanted a new idea in her daughters' heads.

Standing, she smiled. "While we're here, let's get some fresh eggs so we can bake an applesauce cake tomorrow."

As she'd hoped, the mention of their favorite cake distracted her daughters. They debated the merits of white eggs over brown eggs, though Rachel and the lady selling the eggs assured them the only difference was the color of the shells. Loribeth wanted the biggest eggs while Eva declared that the smaller ones would make a cuter cake. Selecting a mixture of brown and white eggs in a variety of sizes, Rachel paid the woman and turned her daughters toward home.

Eva ran to a nearby table and pointed at a box of tiny birthday candles. "Pretty."

"Aren't they?" Rachel smiled. "Shall we get them?"

"My birthday, *Mamm*?" asked Loribeth.

"No, your birthday is in March, and Eva's is in April. That's not until spring."

"*Mamm*'s birthday?"

"Mine was a couple of months ago. Remember? We had carrot cake."

"No birthday," Eva said, her lips trembling and great tears filling her eyes.

Loribeth looked ready to cry, too.

"I know someone who's having a birthday soon. Isaac." Rachel wasn't sure when his birthday was, but the girls wouldn't care. They wanted a birthday cake and a celebration.

"I-zak?" asked Eva and looked at her sister.

A message Rachel couldn't decipher passed between her daughters before they grinned. As she imagined an impromptu birthday party tomorrow, she hoped that Isaac would play along to keep the little girls smiling.

And her, too.

Isaac set his toolbox on the floor of the closet beneath the stairs to the apartment over the mayor's garage. It was a compromise that he and Abby had worked out. She'd wanted him to leave his tools at the building site, and he'd wanted to bring them into the house. They'd settled on the secured storage area. He'd trusted the other volunteers, as well as most of the people of Evergreen Corners, until several thefts had occurred during the building of the previous house. He—and most volunteers—toted their tools back and forth to the work sites.

When he opened the door, Abby came to greet him, as she did often. Tonight, however, she said nothing as she held out an envelope to him.

"What's this?" he asked.

"A message from Rachel. She stopped by earlier and asked me to give it to you."

He took the envelope, surprised. Why would Rachel send him a note instead of speaking to him herself?

"Is everything all right between you two?" Abby asked.

"I thought so." Had he been mistaken about what had happened at supper last night? Or after? Maybe she'd wanted him to kiss her and had been annoyed when he hadn't. He was vexed that he'd let the moment pass without sampling her lips, but he hadn't wanted to take advantage of her despair.

"She didn't come to work at the kitchen today."

"I'm not surprised."

"Why?"

He related what he'd witnessed last night.

His gentle-hearted sister's eyes were awash with tears. "Poor Rachel. But I still don't understand why she sent you a note in a sealed envelope."

"Let's find out." He opened it and drew out a single sheet of paper. His worry vanished when he saw the colored figures at the top and bottom of the page. While Loribeth's drawing resembled trees and a shining sun, Eva's scribbling was indecipherable. It might have been a dog or a car or a pumpkin. It had wheels and legs and was orange. Beyond that he couldn't guess.

He looked at the center of the page and began to smile. Rachel had sent him an invitation from her and the girls to join them for the supper tomorrow. The words *Eva wants me to be sure to tell you that there will be cake* were under the time and date.

"They're inviting me for supper tomorrow," he said. Because it wasn't a church Sunday, the few plain folks in Evergreen Corners would spend the day at the community center enjoying quiet conversation and discussing the progress they'd made on the last three houses during the previous week. Some, however, took the time to visit one another.

"So I can see." She tapped the paper.

He turned it over and read the words: *Please come. We want to thank you for your many kindnesses.* He guessed Rachel had added the words before sealing the envelope. Grinning, he folded the page and put it in the envelope for safekeeping. Tomorrow, he decided. Tomorrow, he'd ask the perfect Amish woman to marry him and become his perfect Amish wife.

Chapter Fourteen

What a difference between today and the night her *daed* had sat at the table! Rachel looked out from the kitchen and smiled. Loribeth was shy with Isaac, but she wasn't spitting at him like Sweetie Pie did when provoked. However, Eva was leaning against him, chattering about a secret she couldn't tell him.

"Big one!" the little girl said.

"Eva, don't say anything else," scolded her sister.

Eva paid her no attention as she gazed at Isaac with adoration. "I-zak, big surprise. You see. Soon."

"Gut," he said. "A surprise isn't a surprise if someone talks about it." He moved his fingers in front of his lips as if he was turning a key in a lock.

Eva copied his motion, then asked, "Know what, I-zak? Big surprise!"

Knowing that the little girl was about to spill everything including her glass of milk, which was close to her arm, Rachel shook out a handful of candles and stuck them in the cinnamon cream-cheese frosting covering the applesauce cake. She struck a match and lit them before carrying the cake into the living room.

"Birthday cake?" asked Isaac.

"Surprise!" Eva exclaimed.

"Happy birthday, Isaac!" Rachel said, trying to catch his eyes.

"It's not my—" He halted himself when he glanced toward Loribeth. Her bright smile wavered. Before her *grossdawdi* had shouted at her, she never would have given Isaac any expression but a scowl. She was warming to him. "Wait a minute! My birthday is right around the corner."

Eva ran to look into the living room. "Where?"

Rachel laughed as she put the cake in front of Isaac. "It's a saying, Eva. It means something is coming soon."

Sending the girls to get paper plates and the pint of ice cream she'd left on the counter, she said, "*Danki* for playing along. The girls saw the candles at the farmers market, and they wanted to have a birthday cake. So I hope you don't mind we're celebrating your birthday early or late or whatever." She smiled uneasily. "You know them well enough to know they don't like to wait for something like your actual birthday."

"My birthday is actually the first of November. We're just celebrating it early." He chuckled as she caught the ice-cream container as it began to slip from Loribeth's hands. When he winked at her daughters, he said, "This is a *wunderbaar* surprise. To be honest, I'd forgotten my birthday was coming up."

"You forgot? How could you forget your birthday?" scoffed Loribeth.

"Grown-ups do that sometimes when they're busy with other things," Rachel quickly replied. "Isaac has been busy getting roofs on the houses before the first snow."

"*Ja.* I've had a lot on my mind."

The twinkle in his eyes told her he wasn't talking about the houses. She looked away before her thoughts could wander in the wrong direction, such as imagining *she* was what had distracted him.

"Aren't you going to blow out the candles?" Loribeth pointed to the cake. "*Mamm* said this was the right amount."

"Are you sure?"

She counted as seriously as a judge announcing a felon's sentence, "One, two, three, seven, six, nine, one-teen, two-teen, three-teen, ten. There are ten candles."

"Ten," added Eva, not willing to be left out as she climbed up and kneeled on her chair. She folded her arms on the table.

"That's old, ain't so?" asked Loribeth.

"Old enough," said Rachel, "to know that if someone doesn't blow the candles out soon, we'll have wax in the frosting, and that won't taste *gut.*"

Two small faces turned to him, eager to sample the cake. He blew out the candles. The girls cheered and Rachel clapped her hands, then held out a knife.

"Do you want to serve, Isaac, or do you want me to?"

"You. I'm accustomed to cutting drywall, not cake."

That made Eva giggle again.

After plucking out the candles and putting them on

the plate beside the cake, Rachel cut four pieces. She made sure that each girl got the same amount of frosting.

She sat as Loribeth said, "*Mamm* had a birthday."

"Did she?" His tone was as serious but his eyes glittered with amusement. "Did she have a cake with candles, too?"

"*Ja,*" her daughter said. "Four candles because it was her big oh-oh-four."

Rachel stopped with her fork halfway to her mouth when Isaac turned his gaze on her. Seeing the surprise on his face, she asked, "Too young or too old?"

"I'd say forty is the perfect age for you right now."

She concentrated on her cake. His easy grin and his use of the word *perfect* should have been a flashing yellow light for her. She needed to be cautious and not give him the opportunity to speak about his search for a wife.

The *kinder* began to sing "Happy Birthday to You" in two different keys, but their enthusiasm was obvious, and she laughed along with Isaac. Making the girls a part of the conversation was the best course. She'd keep everything light and frothy through the rest of the evening while she avoided any chance that he might propose.

Because she feared she might say *ja* and ruin their lives.

Isaac knew when he was being given the run-around. His *daed* had taught him early how simple it was for someone to avoid a topic they didn't want to talk about, or to use someone else as a way to steer the conversation in a specific direction. *Daed* had been able to discuss everything he'd been doing without mentioning how he'd finished off a bottle of vodka and somehow made it sound as if he was relating every detail of his day.

Rachel was doing the same. Each time he tried to engage her in conversation, she found a way to switch the topic to the birthday cake and how excited the girls had been to bake it for him. The one slip she made was when she mentioned saying goodbye to her *daed* and brother at the farmers market. He listened as she explained how she'd offered Manassas Yoder forgiveness. When he told her that he'd welcome Robert on his team if her brother returned before the aid associations left, gratitude gleamed in her smile.

Yet, she'd resisted his offer to help her with the dishes, telling him the birthday boy should never have to do chores. He couldn't insist, so he sat in the living room and listened to the dishes clatter in the sink, and wondered how long she would take to finish the task.

Eva paddled into the room on bare feet. She carried something that glittered in the light from the lamp hanging from the ceiling. He smiled. There were electric lights in the apartment where he lived with his sister, too. He couldn't wait to return to a plain house, where propane lamps offered a softer light along with the gentle hiss that had been a part of his life until he came to Evergreen Corners.

"What do you have there?" he asked.

"My *daed*."

His eyebrows lowered, then he raised them, not wanting to frighten the little girl. He could see she was carrying a picture frame. Was it a drawing she'd made of Rachel's late husband?

"See?" She thrust the picture frame toward him. "My *daed* is a so-der. Look."

Isaac took the frame, turned it over and stared at the picture of a man standing next to a woman who was unquestionably Rachel, though she wore *Englisch* clothing. She held a newborn in her arms, and she was smiling, her pretty face alight with joy.

His eyes focused on the man beside her. The man wore a military uniform. It was printed with some sort of camouflage. His trousers were tucked into combat boots. Isaac couldn't read the name embroidered on his chest, but he could tell it wasn't Yoder because there were too many letters.

Who was this soldier with his arm around Rachel?

As if he'd asked the question aloud, Eva tapped the picture. "My *daed*. Cutie pie, ain't so?"

"Are you sure this is your *daed*?" He wanted to be certain he hadn't misunderstood the *kind*.

"*Daed. Mamm.* Loribeth." She touched each face as she spoke the names. "No Eva there." She frowned for a moment, then brightened. "Not yet. *Mamm* says, 'Not yet.'" She looked at him with wide eyes. "What 'not yet' mean?"

He struggled to find words to answer her as his gaze remained riveted on the picture of the *Englisch* soldier with his arm around Rachel's shoulders. After telling Eva they'd talk more later, he went toward the kitchen because he wanted Rachel to explain why her daughter believed the soldier in the photo was her *daed*. He needed her to be honest with him.

Right now.

Rachel looked over her shoulder and smiled when he walked into the kitchen with Eva in tow. Her eyes widened when he raised the picture frame.

"Why did you keep this a secret?" he asked.

"I want my daughters to be accepted among the Amish, and my past can't keep that from happening."

"Your husband was a soldier."

"An Army major." She wiped her hands. "Let me put the girls to bed, and then you can ask me your questions."

"You'll give me answers?"

"Ja." She met his gaze. "I've never lied to you, Isaac."

"Just hedged on the truth."

"More that I didn't offer any information unless someone asked." She looked at the *kind* by his side. "Is it time for a story, Eva?"

The little girl clapped her hands eagerly and ran to her bedroom, where her sister was playing with the kitten.

For once, Isaac didn't join Rachel in getting the *kinder* ready for bed. He heard their hushed voices and the occasional laugh from where he sat on the sofa. He tried not to look at the photo he'd put on the table by the rocking chair, but his gaze kept returning to the happy family, which had been torn apart when her husband died.

He gasped under his breath. *How* had her husband died? He remembered her talking about an accident.

Had that been her husband or someone else? He found himself questioning everything she'd ever said, weighing it for the truth.

When Rachel came into the living room, she went to the table and placed the photo facedown. He guessed she didn't want to chance anyone else seeing it.

She sat in the rocking chair and clasped her fingers. "Go ahead. Ask your questions."

"That's your husband?"

"*Ja*. He was Travis Gauthier, and he was a career soldier."

He hadn't questioned that her married name was the same as her maiden name. That happened fairly often among the Amish because there were so few surnames. Clearly, he shouldn't have assumed he knew the truth. It was time to get the facts out on the table.

"How did you meet?" he asked.

"We met after I ran away from home that last time, and I fell in love with him. He died while deployed."

"I'm sorry."

A faint smile tilted her lips. "*Danki*, Isaac. I appreciate that."

So many questions hammered at his lips, but he asked the first he'd thought of when she confirmed the woman in the photo was her. "Were you shunned after you married him?"

She shook her head. "No, I left before I was baptized. By the time I met my husband, I'd been living as an *Englischer* for almost a dozen years. Travis—my husband—was a career soldier. The Army was his first love."

"After you, you mean."

"No, the Army came first, and I knew that when I married him. He loved me, and he adored Loribeth. He would have adored Eva, too, if he'd ever had the chance to meet her. However, I knew when he was offered another deployment, he'd take it. When I developed complications before Eva was born, Travis refused to leave his men and come home." Clasping her hands together as if in prayer, she bent her head as she murmured, "He was proven to be right because he died ensuring they survived an ambush."

Her face was colorless as she raised her eyes to meet his. He wondered what she saw reflected in them. Shock? Dismay? Sorrow? He felt those things and many more he couldn't name.

A single emotion burned in her eyes. Anger. He understood why when she spoke.

"The Army sent a chaplain to the house to express the government's gratitude and sympathy at the loss of my husband. They said he died doing what he loved and serving the country he loved, as if that should wipe out any traces of our loss. They called him a hero, as if hearing that word should make everything okay. Don't you think Loribeth and Eva would trade having a *daed* who's a hero for a *daed* who tucks them in each night?"

"Eva speaks well of her *daed*."

"She's only repeating what I've told her, because she's never known him. Travis was a *wunderbaar daed* when he was home. He spoiled Loribeth and showed her off as his 'little recruit' to the soldiers in his command." She put her face in her hands. "Loribeth hardly remembers him. She used to talk about him, but now she doesn't."

"Maybe because you don't talk about him."

"I do. All the time, but only with my girls. If I were to speak about him with other folks, there would be questions. Not just from the plain people. *Englischers* would remark about how proud they should be that their *daed* died fighting for our country. I don't want his death to become more important to them than his life."

As she looked at the floor, silence oozed into the room, blanketing everything and sucking the air out of the space. It was as if a million miles separated them, though he could have reached out and touched her.

The *gut* Lord knew how much he longed to touch her, to draw her into his arms and hold her so close they could savor the melody of their hearts beating in harmony. His fingers had brushed her cheek lightly, and they longed to uncurl around her nape as he tilted her mouth beneath his.

He was on his feet and walking toward her before he was aware he'd moved. When she continued to stare at the floor, he whispered, "Rachel?"

She raised her head to meet his eyes. In her eyes were shadows left by the experiences of losing her husband, as well as the past days when her *daed* had burst back into her life and threatened to tear it apart.

"I'll understand if you want to leave," she said softly. "Please don't spread the truth. Not for my sake, but for my daughters'. They don't deserve to be punished for what their parents did."

Did she think he'd run around the village green shouting out the story like a town crier?

She stood and put her arms around him, leaning into him, as one slender hand on his neck steered his mouth toward hers. Amazed by the sensation, which was as powerful and fiery as lightning at the moment their lips touched, he didn't move for the length of a single heartbeat. Then his arms enfolded her as he explored her lips. They were as sweet as he'd dared to imagine. The soft warmth of her in his arms made his senses reel.

His breath was uneven when he raised his head to gaze into her pretty face. He'd be happy to do the same every day for the rest of his life. Because…

Because I love her, he thought to himself, though he'd tried to halt it.

He stepped back from her, shutting off his thoughts. Love had never been part of his plan for finding the perfect Amish wife. He didn't want to fall victim to love and become its *dummkopf*, as his *daed* had. But he didn't want to lose her, either.

"Rachel, I have something to ask you." He put his hands on her shoulders and gazed into her eyes. "I've been wanting to for days, and it seems now is the best time."

Ice filled Rachel's veins.

Run!

The warning burst through her head, startling her. She wasn't a coward, one to race away from challenges. She'd stood her ground while in the Army and had kept bullies from pushing her aside as an ineffectual female.

She'd halted the eager hands of men who believed that, in spite of so many years of proof otherwise, women joined the military because they were desperate for a man's touch. She'd served with courage and dedication. She'd held the hand of a man while he took his last breath.

"It's late. Can't this wait for another time?" She hated clichés, but didn't want to hurt his feelings.

"I don't think so. I know this isn't the right time to do this. It's the wrong way, but we aren't *kinder* any longer, and we don't live in a normal plain community. I can't go to the deacon and have him approach your *daed* before I speak with you of a future together."

No! He couldn't be about to ask her to marry him.

He kept going while words refused to form on her lips. "You're a *wunderbaar mamm*, not only to your *kinder*, but to that kitten. You're a great cook. I've seen how hard you work, and I admire your strong faith. Everything a man could want in a wife."

What about love? her heart demanded while her mind was shouting, *No, no, no!* He shouldn't be asking her to marry him. He had no idea who she was. If she'd told him weeks ago, they could have avoided this. He was seeking the perfect Amish wife, and she was anything but.

"Rachel, would you do me the honor of becoming my wife?" Hope warmed his smile.

Oh, God, why didn't You help me find the right words to halt him from asking that question?

She couldn't say *ja* when she hadn't been honest with him. If she spoke the truth, he'd walk out of her life and never return. Her heart shattered in her chest at that thought. She'd fallen in love with him in spite of her efforts not to. Her heart was breaking, and she must wound his. Too late, she realized by trying to protect her and Isaac's hearts, she'd made the whole situation worse.

Far worse.

Chapter Fifteen

Holding his breath, Isaac waited for the answer Rachel had given him so many times in his dreams. He'd imagined her throwing her arms around his neck with wild abandon and kissing him after saying *"Ja."* Or would she flush with pleasure and whisper the word that would change their futures forever before he put his fingertips beneath her chin and lifted her face so his mouth could meet hers? He'd pondered how she'd grasp his hands and her daughters' while they danced around in a merry circle.

That last one always made him laugh as he pictured Abby's shock at her staid oldest brother capering about like a *kind*.

Rachel did none of those things.

Instead, she backed away from him, shaking her head.

Was she saying no?

How could that be? Didn't she realize, as he did, that she would make him the perfect wife? Didn't she know that he didn't care that once she'd been married to an *Englisch* soldier? Isaac had been shocked by the revelation, but he'd set aside those feelings and asked her to be his wife.

"Rachel," he said when she remained silent, "you've got to see that we could build a *wunderbaar* life together. Your daughters are as precious to me as they are to you. I'll be the best possible *daed* I can be to them and to any *kinder* God brings into our lives. We've had *daeds* who failed us, so we know how a *gut* parent should treat his or her *kinder*."

"I know, but I can't marry you, Isaac." She edged toward the dining room as she added, "I'm sorry."

Then she was gone, her soft footsteps fading as she went to the far end of the trailer, leaving him standing in the middle of her living room. His arms, which had been filled with warmth when she kissed him, grew cold. He was overwhelmed by something he hated.

Indecision.

Should he go after her and plead with her to listen to *gut* sense? Should he wait and see if she returned? Why had she kissed him if she had no intention of marrying him?

He stood in silence for two minutes—what seemed like a lifetime—as thoughts raced through his mind, before he went to the front door. He switched off the lights as he left.

Rachel would have preferred to remain at home the next morning, but she was scheduled to work at the community center. She'd ruined one relationship in Evergreen

Corners. She didn't want to risk doing the same with others, though she wouldn't have been surprised if Abby told her to leave and never return. That her friend greeted her with her customary smile suggested Isaac hadn't said anything to his sister about what had happened last night.

Why would he have spoken of it? Though Isaac fought his *hochmut*, he was a proud man. She couldn't understand how his quest for perfection had led him to her, the least perfect woman in their community.

The rumble of voices vanished, and Rachel saw Mayor Gladys Whittaker walk in. Gladys's face was lined with strain and her lips were set in a firm line.

Without a preamble, the mayor called out, "I assume none of you have seen or heard the latest weather forecast."

Isaac spoke, as he often did, for everyone gathered there. "No, but we've heard other people talking about a storm that's going out to sea."

"It isn't."

The mayor's words hung in the abrupt quiet like the last notes of "Taps" in the silence hovering over a casket. Only instead of fading, they seemed to grow larger and more malevolent.

Rachel wrapped one arm around herself and the other around Hailee's shoulders as the mayor went on, "The hurricane, which they've named Hurricane Gail, has begun following an identical path to the one Hurricane Kevin did last year." Her gaze swept the room as her voice grew dark with despair. "It's headed toward Evergreen Corners."

No one moved.

No one spoke.

Then everyone seemed to speak at the same time.

Gladys tried to call for order.

Nobody paid her any mind.

Anxious to hear what the mayor had to say, Rachel moved to the kitchen doorway. She put two fingers in her mouth and whistled as loudly as she could. The sharp sound shocked everyone into silence.

Gladys nodded her thanks to Rachel, then said, "I know you've got lots of questions. Let me tell you what I know. The governor has been in touch with the National Weather Service and the National Hurricane Center, as well as the mayors and town managers in this watershed. We're forewarned this year. Whether the storm remains a hurricane or is downgraded to a tropical storm, we won't let our guard down. Speaking of that, the governor asked if we could use a unit from the Vermont National Guard, and I said yes. They've got heavy equipment to keep the channel clear under the bridges, which will halt the water from being dammed and rising as high as it did last year."

"We've got some equipment here, too," someone called from the rear of the room. "Not all of the heavy pieces have left."

"Aren't you in the Vermont National Guard?" Rachel asked Hailee. The combination of the experienced workers in Evergreen Corners and the unit from the National Guard might prevent last year's disaster from happening again.

"I am, and I got an alert to be ready to be activated yesterday." She pulled out a cell phone from her apron pocket and ran her fingers along the screen. Her eyebrows rose. "Great news! The unit coming here is mine." She looked at the worried faces around her. "They're good people, well-trained. If there's a way to prevent another flood, they'll do it."

"Another flood?" asked Nina from behind them. "I'm not *dumm* enough to sit here and wait for it." She pulled off her apron and threw it on a counter, not caring that one end fell into a bowl of pancake batter.

The blonde strode out into the main room and repeated her caustic words before heading for the door. If she'd hoped to turn everyone's attention to her, she failed. Instead, the gathering began to pepper the mayor with questions about timing and the amount of wind and rain the storm forecast. It had decimated areas of Florida's east coast and was hovering over the Carolinas, dropping stupendous amounts of rain that threatened to cause historic flooding.

Rachel clapped her hands, startling the women in the kitchen out of their despair. "Let's go! We've got a ton of work ahead of us." As she turned to listen to instructions from Abby, her gaze was caught by Isaac's.

His eyes were narrowed with a determination that matched hers, but she saw the flickers of pain in those dark depths before he looked away. Somehow, she was going to have to find a way to apologize to him. Not now, though, when they had to work to try to save Evergreen Corners from being washed away.

The National Guard vehicles rolled over the bridge and parked along the village green later that afternoon.

The dull-colored vehicles looked out of place beneath the bright leaves on the trees and the pumpkins sitting on the steps of many of the neighboring houses.

When the volunteers surged out to mingle with the villagers watching the guardsmen unpack their gear, Rachel didn't join them. She remained in the kitchen, making sure the *kaffi* pots were full and fresh. Later, she'd ask Hailee how it'd gone. The younger woman had left hours ago to collect her equipment so she'd be ready when orders were given.

"Rachel Gauthier, is that you?"

At the surname she hadn't heard for nearly three years, Rachel spun to see a tall, black-haired woman dressed in camouflage peering through the pass-through window. Sergeant Lorea Zabala had been under Rachel's command several times during her military career, but Rachel had never expected to see her friend in Evergreen Corners.

Fright rushed through her, but she suppressed it. Lorea was her friend. She wouldn't expose Rachel's past. At least, not intentionally.

"What are you doing here?" Rachel asked as she drew her friend into the kitchen so they could speak unobserved. An ironic laugh burst from her throat. "That was a stupid question."

"I could ask you the same, and it wouldn't be stupid."

"I live in Evergreen Corners. We moved here after Travis was killed."

Her friend's face lengthened. "I heard about that. I wanted to let you know how sorry I am, but I didn't know how to get in touch with you, and nobody seemed to know where you were."

"Being Amish and a veteran don't go hand-in-hand."

"I can imagine." Her eyes brightened. "Where's that cutie you named after me?"

Rachel smiled as she recalled the day she'd told her sergeant that her *boppli* would be named Loribeth in her honor. "At day care with her little sister."

"You've got two girls?"

"I found out I was pregnant after Travis deployed. He never met Eva." She glanced toward the door. She guessed everyone was gathered around the National Guard transports. "Lorea, I need to ask a big favor."

"Anything. You know that."

"I don't want anyone here to know I was in the Army."

Lorea's eyebrows arched in astonishment, then she frowned. "Am I hearing you right? Weren't you the one who always insisted being honest was not just the best policy, but the only one? You want me to lie to these people?"

"No, but don't mention I'm a vet." She raised her eyebrows. "I could make that an order, Sergeant."

"Try it, and see how well I'll listen to a civilian." Lorea's stern frown changed into a grin. "I'm sure you've got good reasons for your request."

"I do." She plucked at her skirt. "As you can see, I've returned to living plain, and my past and my present don't fit together."

"So who is he?"

"What do you mean?" she asked, though she knew.

"The man who's not supposed to know about your

amazing career in the Army because you want him to be part of your life."

"It's not just one person. Everyone in town believes I've been Amish my whole life." She was hedging, and she could tell her friend sensed that. "I'll explain further when the storm is past. We'll make time to catch up."

Lorea looked past Rachel. "Does she know the truth?"

Turning, Rachel saw Hailee coming into the community center. "No. Like I said, nobody knows." She raised her voice, making sure it sounded nonchalant. "I assume you know Hailee."

"We've worked together before. How do you know—?" She held out her hand to the younger woman, who skidded to a stop beside them.

"I was sent to find out what was delaying the coffee." She looked at Rachel. "Is it ready? Do you want me to get the big containers?"

"You know each other?" asked Lorea.

Rachel let the younger woman answer. "We've been working together here to make meals for the volunteers who've been rebuilding the town."

"*You're* working in the kitchen? I didn't know you knew which end of a potato peeler to use."

Hailee chuckled. "You know I've done my fair share of KP, Sarge."

"Get the coffee, and then join the others to unload our supplies. We need locations to store them where they'll be safe from flooding or wind damage."

Rachel bit her lower lip as she listened. She couldn't keep from flinching when Hailee mentioned which buildings were the most vulnerable. Only when her new hometown could be left in ruins once more did Rachel realize how precious Evergreen Corners and its residents had become. If debris clogged under the bridges as it had last time, the volunteers' hard work could be destroyed.

A possible solution flashed in her head. It'd worked when she was in charge of an Army reserve company repairing levees along the Mississippi, and it might work here.

"Excuse me," she said, edging past her friends.

She heard one of them ask a question, but she didn't pause to answer. Grabbing her bonnet, she rushed outside. Wind tugged at her skirt and apron, and the air was too warm and too humid, signaling the storm was getting closer. She scanned the green. Near the gazebo that bore signs of damage from last year's flood, Gladys was talking to Isaac.

She faltered, then knew she couldn't let personal issues stand in the way. Hoping that they'd be willing to listen to her when she couldn't tell them about her past experience, she crossed the green. She waited until the mayor greeted her. Isaac's eyes narrowed, but he didn't speak.

"Rachel, I'm quite busy," Gladys said. "If what you've got can wait—"

"It can't. I've got a way to save Evergreen Corners." She tried to ignore their expressions of disbelief and launched into her idea. Keeping her eyes on the mayor's face, she watched as Gladys's skepticism became excitement.

"Wait here," the mayor said before Rachel was done. "I want to get Captain McBride and his sergeant over here, so they can hear this, too." She held up a single finger. "Don't go anywhere."

As the mayor rushed to find the company commander and Lorea, Rachel felt Isaac's steady gaze on her.

"I hope you know what you're doing," he said.

"I hope so, too." She prayed he would somehow understand she was talking about last night, as well as the hurricane. Was there any chance they could remain friends?

As he walked away when someone called his name, she knew with a sinking heart the answer was the same one she'd given him when he'd proposed last night.

No.

Chapter Sixteen

Less than a half hour later, Isaac stood in the mayor's office with Rachel and Glen Landis, the project director for the aid agencies. They were waiting for the mayor and the National Guard commander.

A television in one corner of the room kept up the unrelenting weather coverage. He glanced at the screen and saw the storm had moved farther north than he'd guessed. He couldn't keep from feeling as if they were being stalked by a great monster crawling along the coastline.

Watch over everyone in the storm's path, he prayed as he'd been doing since Gladys had first announced the oncoming hurricane.

As Rachel and Glen spoke in hushed tones, Isaac went out into the hallway. He needed something to wet his dry throat. He almost laughed at his thought. When had he started lying to himself? He was thirsty, but what he really needed most was to get out of the cramped room while Rachel was there. Every word she spoke and every movement she made reminded him of his humiliation when she'd turned down his offer of marriage. She was trying to treat him as if the conversation had never happened, but he couldn't match her poise.

He stopped by a water fountain and bent to take a drink. From his right, he heard two people talking. Their words became clear as they came closer.

"You remember the unit that saved that town in Missouri during the big floods about eight years ago?" a woman asked.

A man replied, "Of course. Their plan's part of the manual that's become required reading for flood-preparedness work." Surprise heightened his deep voice. "Are you saying an *Amish* woman has had exactly the same idea?"

"Yes, sir."

"Strange, huh?"

"Not so strange when…" The woman stopped talking as the two came around the corner and stared at Isaac.

He appraised the duo in their military uniforms. The man was Captain McBride, and the woman's name tag listed her as Zabala. She looked away, but not before he noticed a flush on her well-tanned cheeks. Though he wanted to ask why it wasn't strange Rachel's idea was the same as the one in some textbook, he didn't have a chance.

The mayor rushed toward them, talking into her phone. She waved for them to come into her office.

"There's no time to waste," Gladys said as they gathered in the small space. "Not when the new houses and the whole village are at risk. Tell everyone about your idea, Rachel."

Isaac followed when Rachel pointed out the window at the meadow where he'd joined her and her daughters after services on a sunny Sunday—a Sunday that felt like part of someone else's life. When she glanced at him, then away, he guessed her thoughts were similar.

"Who owns that field?" she asked.

"The town." Gladys's voice caught. "We'd planned to put baseball fields out there, but that got put on a back burner when our resources had to be committed to flood recovery."

"The banks on this side are higher than on the other side. Last year, debris clogged beneath the bridge until the water pressure became so strong it popped like a cork, sending a wall of water and boulders and everything else along the brook's bed."

"What do you propose we do to change that?" Glen asked.

Isaac wasn't the only one who flinched at the word *propose*, but Rachel launched into her plan. As he listened, he had to admit it was simple but could be effective if they had the time to do the work.

She suggested they dig a trench from north of the bridge. It would go past the village and into the meadow. Diverting the water would ease the power of the flow and keep debris from piling so high.

"Can your people do this, Captain McBride?" she asked.

"We'll do our best." Turning to the mayor, he asked, "Do you have a topographical map of the village?"

Gladys rushed to a file cabinet and yanked out a drawer. She pulled out a rolled page and spread it across the desk. Isaac joined the others as they crowded in to look at it, but said little as Rachel outlined her plan. He listened in astonishment as she used terms he'd never heard. Confusion was displayed on the mayor's face and Glen's as well, but the captain nodded, showing he understood every word she spoke.

"You don't have to dig too deep," Rachel finished. "Just enough so the brook will overflow its banks on the lower side. The water will pool in the field like it's a retention pond." She looked at him. "I suggest you work with Isaac. Every new foundation in Evergreen Corners was put in with his supervision."

"So," the captain said, facing Isaac, "you're familiar with construction?"

"You'll find many of the volunteers are," he replied.

"Will you help Sergeant Zabala find those with the most construction experience, Mr. Kauffman?"

"Isaac," he corrected. "Plain folks don't use titles."

"I'll try to remember that. Zabala, go with Isaac and get this going. It's a long shot, but it's all we've got."

"Sir?" asked the sergeant. She gestured toward the door.

Isaac complied, hearing the intense conversation resume in their wake. As he walked through the hall to the stairs, he glanced at the sergeant and found her regarding him with open curiosity.

"Sorry," she said, realizing he'd caught her staring. "I haven't met many Amish people before."

"That's okay. I haven't met many military people."

She laughed, then began asking him insightful questions about which of the volunteers had the most experience with earth-moving equipment. Within an hour, volunteers who knew how to run the heavy excavation machinery and soldiers were working side by side as they dug a trench into the field across the brook.

The wind began to come in uneven gusts, and rain misted around Isaac as if the air had become too humid to contain the moisture. Through the afternoon, word was passed that the storm had slowed. There might be enough time to dig the rudimentary channel to divert the water cascading through the narrow brook's bed. He often saw Rachel from a distance, always conferring with Captain McBride or one of the soldiers. He kept asking himself why she seemed to fit in with them as well as she did with the plain community.

By the time the faint rays of the sun were swallowed by the roiling clouds amid grim reports of the oncoming storm, he'd assisted in evacuating more than a dozen families from low-lying areas into the high-school gym. He'd helped board up their homes. Each time he emerged from a building, he'd eyed the increasing slice into the middle of the meadow. It led to the brook above the bridge in the center of the village. Would the ruined covered bridge survive another onslaught? They had no time to try to protect it, too.

He saw someone walking toward him and realized it was Rachel. She paused in front of him.

"We need to talk," she said without preamble.

"About your trench? It looks as if it'll work."

"No, about the questions I've seen in your eyes all day. I can see it bothers you how much time I'm spending with the soldiers."

"We're plain people who have refused to fight, but you speak their language of abbreviations and half words." He swallowed hard. "Tell me the truth, Rachel."

"I will. I've never lied to you. I understand Army lingo because four years ago, I was in Afghanistan and in charge of a transportation company."

He stared at her. Rachel Yoder, the woman he'd asked to marry him, had been a soldier?

"But before you came here, you lived in a plain community in Maine," he insisted, then wondered with whom he was arguing. Himself? "Were you honest with them?"

"No, but I didn't lie to them, either."

"How was living there possible if you didn't tell them about your past?"

"I waited for someone to ask, but they assumed I was what I appeared to be. A widow with two *kinder* who wanted to live a plain life."

"As I did. How could I have guessed you were a... soldier?" He was having a tough time even saying the words. Probably because as he looked at Rachel standing in front of him, dressed in a simple dark green dress beneath her black apron, and with her pleated *kapp* on her head, he couldn't envision her wearing the uniforms of the soldiers swarming around the village green.

"You couldn't," she said. "That's why I wanted to tell you the truth before the storm arrives. You deserve to know why I could never marry you when you're looking for the perfect Amish wife. That's not me."

He started to reply, but she'd already turned on her heel and was walking away. He took a single step to follow, then halted himself. She was right. She wasn't what he'd been searching for in a wife. He could tell his mind that, but his heart rebelled. He gritted his teeth. He'd be foolish to heed his heart, so why was every cell in his body urging him to run after her?

Isaac had no idea how much time had passed when he stood in front of the final piece of plywood from the pile outside the community center and waited for the whir of the battery-operated screwdriver he held to stop. During the night, they'd screwed wood over window after window, a task he hadn't been sure they'd be able to finish before the hurricane's strongest winds arrived. The storm couldn't be worse than the tempest playing havoc with his gut as his memory replayed the images of Rachel's face when she told him about her past.

He had to acknowledge the courage it'd taken her to be honest with him. As well, he had to admit she'd never lied to him. She'd let him keep his assumptions.

Not wanting to think of that, he ran through the list of tasks he'd been keeping in his head, checking off each one as done. Many of the residents who'd helped in the wake of last year's flood were stepping up again.

They'd helped elderly residents near the brook move to higher ground.

They'd secured the equipment and supplies. Glen had popped into the community center less than a half hour before to announce that everything had been moved away from the building sites and onto the farm Isaac was buying. After a quick call to get permission from the real-estate agent handling the purchase, Isaac had told the construction volunteers to store everything in and around the barns.

They'd gotten the town's records out of the way. Gladys Whittaker and her staff had carried those records from the town hall to the high school. The day-care center had been relocated out of the church cellar. Sandbags encircled the library and homes. They wouldn't offer much protection against a raging flood, but if Rachel's ditch worked as everyone hoped, a wall of water wouldn't come through the center of Evergreen Corners again.

His jaw worked as he tried once more to push Rachel out of his mind.

"Isaac?"

His future brother-in-law, David, was regarding him with puzzlement. How long had Isaac been standing there, lost in thought, with his screwdriver lifted like the Statue of Liberty's torch?

"Ja?" he replied.

"We're done here," David called over the rising wind. "Abby's got drinks inside for anyone who wants them before going home."

Most of the men thanked him, but hurried in the direction of their houses. They intended to be with their families when the damaging winds and rain swept up the valley and into the village.

Isaac went inside the community center, too aware his only family in Evergreen Corners was inside. He could have… No, he wasn't going to lose himself in visions of what might have been with Rachel and her *kinder.*

The building seemed oddly quiet. He realized he'd become accustomed to the screaming of the wind outside. With the door dampening the noise, his ears rang in the silence.

He was surprised when David followed him inside until he saw David's daughter working with Abby and other women in the kitchen. Collecting two cups of *kaffi*, Isaac brought them to a nearby table.

The building quaked as a powerful gust struck it. The sound of rain against the roof and the plywood over the windows would have been loud if it hadn't been drowned by the howling of the wind.

Abby rushed to his side. "I'm glad you're inside."

"Me, too." He grimaced as the gale grew stronger. The storm must have accelerated north again. "If Rachel's idea works, we may have saved the village. If it doesn't…" He took a sip of the *kaffi*, but the strong caffeine couldn't ease his exhaustion.

"It's a *gut* idea."

His eyebrows lowered. "Nobody said it wasn't."

"Everyone else is excited about the idea. If you want to know the truth, Isaac Kauffman, I think you're afraid."

"Of another flood?"

She grimaced. "No! You're afraid of Rachel."

"What?" Maybe he was too tired to follow the conversation, because it wasn't making any sense to him.

"Okay, maybe you're not afraid of her, but you're afraid of giving your heart as *Daed* did and falling apart as he did when *Mamm* died. You've always thought you were the stronger man because you picked up the pieces and kept us together. That was easy."

"It wasn't."

She raised one eyebrow. "It was a whole lot easier to watch *Daed* fall apart than to suffer that sorrow yourself. You care about us, but not as you care about Rachel and her girls. All you had to lose when you stepped in to take over the family and the farm was having us separated among our relatives. Oh, and your *hochmut* that you'd been there to save the day." She wagged a finger at him. "Don't tell me you weren't proud of what you'd accomplished."

"I was, but I didn't brag to anyone."

"In part because you didn't want everyone to know how far *Daed* had sunk. That was a battle you were ready to wage, but it's a whole other thing when you think of losing Rachel."

He hung his head in his hands as he leaned his elbows on the table. "I get it."

"Do you?"

"Ja."

"So are you going to throw in the towel because you're afraid of a future that might never happen?"

"I asked her to marry me, and she said no."

Abby's mouth became round with surprise. "You did?"

"Ja, and she turned me down."

"That doesn't make sense."

He wasn't going to reveal the secret of Rachel's military experience, not even to his sister. "I know it didn't, but she said no."

"When you proposed, did you think to mention that you love her?"

He flinched at the question. Had he? He was too tired to remember.

"There's no use talking about it, Abby. She said no. She doesn't want to be my wife. Me thinking otherwise was all a big mistake."

"We make mistakes, but God doesn't. Did you ever consider that He sent Rachel to you because He wanted you to see that perfect isn't all you believe it is? Only God is perfection, Isaac. He knew that when He sent His son to die for our sins and teach us the importance of forgiveness. Perfect people don't need forgiveness, ain't so?"

Before he could respond while struggling not to surrender to the world's biggest yawn, the weather radio on the counter screamed an alarm. What worse tidings could it bring them?

"Turn it up!" someone shouted.

David leaned forward to adjust the volume, and a voice echoed through the community center.

"Tornado warning for the following locations until 5:00 p.m., Eastern Daylight Time." The man listed off several nearby towns, then said, "Evergreen Corners."

"A tornado? In a hurricane?" someone asked. "Is that possible?"

Nobody replied as the room exploded into action. Abby sent her volunteers into the kitchen to make sure the stoves were off. The door to the cellar was thrown open, and David's daughter, Mikayla, began herding the *kinder* to the lower level.

Isaac's eyes widened, his fatigue forgotten. Where were Rachel and her girls?

He spun and raced toward the door. From behind him, Abby shouted, "Have you lost your mind, Isaac? There could be a tornado coming!"

"Rachel's not here. I've got to make sure she's okay."

"She's a smart woman. She'll find a safe place."

"In a trailer?"

Abby blanched. "I forgot that."

He kissed the top of her head. "Get in the cellar with the others."

"Be careful. Please." She grasped his hand. "Isaac, you falling in love with her wasn't a mistake. It's the best thing that's ever happened to you."

"I know."

"Don't be afraid to let love into your life."

"I won't!" He gave her a not-so-gentle shove. "Go! Now!"

"I'll pray for you and Rachel and her *kinder*."

"Pray for everybody in the path of the storm."

"I have been." She gave him a quick hug, then ran to where David was standing beside the cellar door, waiting for her.

Isaac stepped out of the community center, fighting to close the door after him. His hat flew off his head. It danced in a crazy spiral. He left it. A hat could be replaced. Lives couldn't.

He raced across the deserted green. He kept flicking his gaze skyward, where the clouds contorted in agony, curling in on themselves. The wind rose, then dropped before gusting so hard it nearly knocked him off his feet. Rain drilled into his face. Leaves plastered his left side as they were stripped from trees and sent rocketing across the grass.

He reached the trailer and groaned. Only a few of its windows had been covered with boards. Through the rest, lights blared into the day that was growing as dark as night. He jumped onto the steps and reached to knock. The shrill creak of a breaking tree beyond the school changed his mind.

Grasping the door, he yanked it open. He held on to it before the wind could send it crashing against the railing.

"I-zak!" cried Loribeth as she ran toward him. She gave a frightened cry when the trailer shook with the concussion of the falling tree.

Or maybe more than one being uprooted. He couldn't tell any longer because the noise inside the trailer was almost as loud as outside. Wind and rain clattered on its metal walls, shaking it like a dog with a toy. A window in the living room had been shattered, shards on the floor and wind invading the small space.

"Where's your *mamm*?" Isaac shouted over the roar.

"Something's wrong with *Mamm*!" she cried, flinging herself against him. "In the bathroom."

Horror erupted in his mind. Had she been hurt? He scooped up the little girl and ran.

By the tub, Eva held on to her kitten, her toy bear and her *mamm*, who was sitting on the floor, her legs drawn up and her face hidden on her knees. A low, keening sound came from Rachel.

He pushed past Loribeth, then edged aside Eva and

the kitten. The *kind* started to protest but he didn't listen as he kneeled beside Rachel. She appeared as terrified and cut off from reality as she had the afternoon she'd been raking leaves. Had the storm triggered what she'd called post-traumatic stress disorder?

He put a single finger under her chin and raised her face. Shining trails of tears scarred her cheeks, and she stared at him as if she'd never seen him before.

"You've got to get out of here," he said.

She shook her head and pressed her face against her knees.

"You can't stay here. The girls can't stay here. This place isn't safe."

She grasped his sleeve. Putting her face close to his, she said in a desperate whisper, "We can't go outside. Can't you hear the explosions? We'll be killed."

"You'll be killed if you stay here."

"No, it's safe here. Inside. Where there aren't any bombs."

"Bombs? You're not in Afghanistan. You're here with your *kinder*. Rachel Yoder, come back to us."

It was her name that tore Rachel out of the prison of panic created by her mind. It was her name from a time before there had been any improvised explosive devices or bombs dropping out of the sky.

Rachel raised her head and opened her eyes. She stared at Isaac, who looked as if he'd walked through a wind tunnel. The noise continued outside, but it was, she realized, the roar of the wind. Not fighter jets plowing a path for ground forces toward the enemy. A sharp sound struck the window.

Hail. Not gunfire.

He was right. She wasn't in Afghanistan. She was in Vermont. The trailer rocked, and she gasped.

The hurricane!

As if she'd said the words aloud, Isaac shouted, "There's a tornado warning. You've got to get out of this trailer."

Jumping to her feet, she wobbled a moment, but it was a moment in the now, not in the horrors of the past. She forced her mind to work.

"Blankets," she ordered.

"I'll get them." He ran toward the girls' room.

Rachel stuffed the kitten into a cloth bag. The little creature screeched its outrage as Isaac returned with the blankets from her daughters' beds.

"Where can we go?" she asked as she draped one blanket over Eva's head.

"The high school. We evacuated other families there."

He swathed Loribeth in another blanket, lifted her into his arms and took the bag with the kitten from her. As he rushed through the narrow hallway, Rachel followed. She cringed at what sounded like continuous explosions.

Thunder, she realized while she stared at the broken window in the living room. Thunder and wind. Not bombs. She must not let her memories suck her into the past. If she did, her *kinder* could die.

She fought to stay on her feet as she stepped outside.

Eva was crying. Rachel could feel it, but her daughter's sobs vanished in the cacophony around them.

Isaac raced toward the school. Rachel tried to keep up, holding Eva's head close to her shoulder. The wind pushed her backward, but she didn't stop running and praying. If the doors were locked, they might not have time to reach another haven.

The wind died slightly, and she realized they'd reached the high school, which was blocking it. Isaac yanked open the door and shouted something to her. She didn't understand his words, but his intent was clear.

She stepped forward, then was shoved back again by the wind. As he set Loribeth inside, he stretched an arm out to Rachel. She gripped it. The wind pushed her away. His hand tightened on her arm, and she knew he'd never let her go.

That gave her the strength to plant her feet and drive herself toward him. She ducked as something whirred over her head. She stared at a large tornado poised along the ridge above town. Awe mixed with terror as she watched it slice through the forest, tearing trees and electric poles from the ground like a *kind* plucking toothpicks out of pieces of cheese.

She ran into the school gym. Bending, she put down Eva. She leaned her hands on her legs as she struggled to catch her breath, but somehow croaked out, "It's coming! A tornado!"

People fled the wide-open space to a pair of doors at the far end of the gym. She grabbed her daughters' hands and followed. They ran into a locker room, then into an equipment room at the far end. Balls caromed across the floor as others sought sanctuary among the racks that held equipment and towels.

Rachel dropped to her knees and arched her body over her daughters as the walls came alive, moving in and out as if a great beast hovered on the other side. There was, for the storm was a monster ready to destroy everything in its path. When arms went around her, she drew Isaac's head into her shoulder, splaying her fingers over his skull. It was the only protection she could offer.

"Protect us, Lord," murmured Isaac against her ear. "You're our haven in the storm. We ask You to calm the winds as Your son did while sailing upon the sea. Be with Your *kinder* and hold back the storm."

She opened her mouth to add to his prayer, but the lights overhead blinked once, then went out, leaving them in a darkness so deep it looked the same with her eyes closed or open. The floor shivered beneath her, and she heard a strange rattling sound.

The roof! The wind was trying to tear the roof right off the school.

Her ears popped, and the wind's scream rose in pitch while creating a rumble she felt in her bones. Something struck her shoulder, and she struggled to breathe as the very air was sucked out of her.

Then silence.

Only for a second before the hurricane's howl returned. It was almost welcome in the wake of the tornado.

She raised her head and groaned as the motion shifted her shoulder. It wasn't broken because she could move her fingers, but breathing added to her pain. Knowing she should be grateful she could draw in a breath, she looked at Isaac. In shock, she realized she could see him. The roof over their heads had vanished. Rain struck them and washed through the blood that ran from his forehead along his face. Wind rose to another shriek, and stacks of towels rose like a flock of albino birds. He reached out to touch her cheek before they checked the *kinder* and the furious kitten. None of them was hurt.

Around them, other people were looking around. Some were hurt, but none of the injuries seemed to be life-threatening. As one, everyone scrambled to their feet to find a better place to ride out the storm.

Rachel grabbed a towel that hadn't flown away and handed it to Isaac. He wiped away some of the blood, then tossed aside the towel before they found shelter in one of the nearby restrooms. Overhead, the wind tried to batter its way into the school, but it couldn't.

When Isaac drew her head to his shoulder, she cuddled into him. Her daughters curled up beside them, Loribeth holding on to Sweetie Pie, who seemed content to stay right where she was. Someone had raided the nurse's office, and Isaac now had a bandage across his forehead with gauze wrapped around his wet hair.

"*Danki* for coming to our rescue, Isaac," Rachel whispered.

"*Danki* to the *gut* Lord for letting me get to you in time and letting us find a haven in the qym's equipment room." He grinned. "'Haven in the equipment room'? Words I never thought I'd ever say." He grew serious again. "I'm so grateful. If something had happened to you or the girls…"

"Because of you and God's grace, nothing did. I didn't expect my PTSD to erupt in the midst of a storm."

"It's caused by something more than an accident, ain't so?" His words resonated beneath her cheek.

"*Ja.* My nightmares started the night after a roadside bomb detonated right outside the vehicle where I was riding. One of my team died instantly. Another got to the field hospital, but lost both legs and an arm." She drew up her skirt enough to reveal the scars on her calf. "There was concern if the surgeons could save my leg, but they did. However, I never returned to duty because the nightmares began invading my days, too." She looked at him. "As you witnessed."

"You shouldn't have kept this to yourself. If you'd talked to others—to me!—you might have healed."

"Maybe, but the therapists I've had said it may be with me for the rest of my life."

"If that's God's will, then it'll be so, but you need to ask the greatest *Doktor* to grant you His healing." He shifted and cupped her chin. "Do that by opening your heart to Him fully."

"I've been trying." She paused as the building shook with the power of the storm. "The episodes don't happen as often. I'm getting better, but it's slow."

"Let me help."

"You have. More than you can guess."

"So why did you turn down my proposal?"

"Because of my past."

"What if I said I don't care about your past? Would you marry me then?"

"No," she whispered.

He moved to face her. "Is it because you don't love me?"

She curved her hand along his cheek. "Of course I love you. I've tried not to, but my heart won't listen. What I was—"

"Isn't what you are now. We can go together to the bishop and have him listen to your story. He will help you reach the point where you can be baptized. Then you can bury your past."

"Not all of it. Not the *gut* parts."

"God had His reasons for giving you the path you've walked. With prayer, you can learn how to keep the memories that give you joy and release all that has hurt you."

"Is it possible?"

"Everything is possible when we give our lives and our hearts over to God." He gave her a quick smile. "Of course, as I'm saying that, I realize I want to give my heart to you. Marry me, Rachel."

She shook her head. "I can't. I know you want *kinder*, and I can't give them to you. I told you that there were complications with Eva. The *doktors* were worried I would die if I became pregnant again. I had surgery to make sure I wouldn't."

Knowing her face was aflame, she looked away. She didn't want to see his expression as she'd admitted another way she was far from the perfect wife he was seeking.

His fingers steered her gaze to his. "Do you think that matters to me?"

"You've talked about having *kinder* of your own. The perfect wife would be able to give you many."

"I'm not looking for a perfect wife."

"Abby said—"

"I'm not looking for a perfect wife because I've found one. You. What other Amish woman knows how to save a whole village by diverting floodwaters? And has two impish daughters, including one who's not afraid to throw up on my boots? And makes a unique piecrust?" His voice softened into a whisper. "Do you know where I might find someone like that who loves me?"

"I might." Joy danced through her as she realized Loribeth and Eva were listening. "However, my girls have a few qualifications for the perfect Amish *daed*."

"Do they?"

Loribeth sat. "My *mamm* needs a handsome man."

"Will I do?" he asked.

Instead of answering right away, she conferred in whispers with her sister.

Eva smiled and gave him a thumbs-up.

"What else?" He tried not to smile.

"*Mamm* needs someone to kill spiders," Loribeth announced.

"*Ja*, no spiders." Eva shivered.

"I think your *mamm* knows how to kill spiders," he said. "Anything else?"

"Ice keem!" Eva interjected.

As she laughed along with Isaac, Rachel wondered

if she'd ever comprehended the true breadth of happiness until this moment.

"So it seems that I met the girls' qualifications, and you meet mine. Do I meet yours?"

"Ja."

As his lips found hers, his arms encircled her, holding her close as if he never wanted to let her go. She didn't want him to.

Epilogue

The farm's dirt road, with its potholes, announced the arrival of every vehicle as soon as it turned onto it. Each type of vehicle created a different sound. The tires on the milk truck spewed rocks out to strike others along the shoulder. If one of the half-dozen buggies now in Evergreen Corners came toward the house, metal wheels rolled over the loose stones and fought to emerge from the soft dirt.

Rachel came out to stand on the front porch as a car rumbled toward her home. She and the girls had moved into the tumbledown house in the wake of the hurricane. The damage to the trailer had left it less livable than the old farmhouse. Isaac would join them after their wedding.

The week after the National Guard left Evergreen Corners, Rachel shared the truth of her past with the Amish community in the village, accepted their offer of forgiveness and began working with the local bishop so she could be baptized in the spring. Once that happened, she and Isaac could exchange their vows and truly become a family.

In the meantime, they'd been kept busy working in Evergreen Corners and on the old farmhouse. Though the excavated trench had prevented most of the flooding, the damage from the hurricane's wind and the tornado's fury had left its marks on the small town.

The houses built during the past year stood, though one had lost shingles when a nearby tree brushed its eaves as it'd toppled. The main bridge hadn't had to be closed, though one of its railings collapsed into the brook. The old covered bridge had lost more boards, and there was to be discussion about whether it should be torn down or repaired by the aid agencies, which planned to extend their stays into the New Year. They'd expanded their work to nearby villages that hadn't fared as well.

None of that was on Rachel's mind as she watched the car with Rhode Island plates stopping by the snowbanks in front of the house. Isaac put his hand on her arm before she went to greet the people emerging from the car.

The white-haired woman wore a navy blue coat over khaki trousers. The man, who'd been driving, was almost as tall as Isaac. He had hints of gray in his hair that was the same dark red as Eva's.

"I'm glad you're here," Rachel said simply.

The couple exchanged a glance, uneasiness on their faces. They looked past her.

"I'm Isaac Kauffman," said her future husband when

he came to stand beside her. "Welcome to Evergreen Corners."

Rachel bit her lip as Travis's parents seemed to be choosing between replying and fleeing. She'd been amazed when Bianca and Gordon Gauthier had accepted her most recent invitation to come to visit.

"The girls are eager to see you," she said and motioned toward the front door.

Her daughters emerged onto the porch. Loribeth took her little sister by the hand as they walked toward the grandparents they didn't remember ever meeting.

"Are you my *grossmammi* and *grossdawdi*?" asked Loribeth.

"In English," Rachel said. "Remember?"

"It's all right," Bianca replied as she bent toward the girls. "I understood enough. Yes, I'm Grandma Gauthier. You must be Loribeth. You're the spitting image of Travis." Bianca wiped away a tear. "You must be Eva because you've got the Gauthier hair."

"That's me!" She put her hands on her head. "My hair. Nobody else's!"

Eva's retort broke the tension in the yard. This time, when Isaac urged her in-laws to *komm* into the house, they did, chatting with the girls as if they wanted to make up for the years of separation.

In the kitchen, their grandparents gave each girl a brightly wrapped box. Rachel watched the *kinder's* excitement. Each girl pulled out a faceless doll dressed in plain clothing. As the girls hugged their new toys and thanked their grandparents, Rachel blinked away tears. No words had been spoken, but the gifts showed, more than any long explanations or apologies could have, that Travis's parents were okay with their granddaughters being raised Amish.

Isaac touched her fingers, confirming the connection that would last until their final breaths. He smiled, as pleased as she was that another connection—one she feared would be lost forever—was strong again. One more would be reforged when his *daed* and stepmother came for Abby's wedding next month.

"You know," she whispered as the girls introduced Travis's parents to Sweetie Pie and the latest addition to their house, a puppy named Floppsy because of his big ears, "we both may have been wrong."

"About what?"

"About perfection." She smiled at him. "Because being here with you and them today is as close to perfection as I can imagine."

Squeezing his hand, though she longed to taste his lips, she went to where Eva was trying to get the puppy to do a trick for her grandparents. She couldn't wait for his kisses, the perfect gift for a lifetime of love.

* * * * *

HER AMISH SUITOR'S SECRET

Carrie Lighte

For my nieces—my youngest readers—
and in loving memory of my great-aunt Marce.

Lay not up for yourselves treasures upon earth,
where moth and rust doth corrupt,
and where thieves break through and steal:

But lay up for yourselves treasures in heaven,
where neither moth nor rust doth corrupt, and
where thieves do not break through nor steal:

For where your treasure is,
there will your heart be also.
—*Matthew* 6:19–21

Chapter One

"**Y**ou want me to pretend I'm Amish?" Caleb Miller repeated in a hushed whisper. He'd come from Madison, Wisconsin, to the Chicago suburbs to visit his brother, Ryan, and six-year-old nephew, Liam, who was asleep in the next room. "I can't do that."

"Why not? You loved living on that Amish farm when you were in college," his brother reminded him.

Caleb recalled the experience fondly. As a college student, he was a German language major with a minor in anthropology. His professor had strong ties to the Amish community, and for three summers in a row, Caleb had lived with an Amish family on a soybean farm in Pennsylvania, not far from where he went to school. "That was ten years ago. I've probably forgotten almost all of the *Deitsch* I learned," he protested.

"C'mon, you're a German language professor! You'll pick it up again in no time," Ryan countered. "You'll blend right in."

"I'm an *adjunct* faculty member. And I'm not concerned about blending in. I'm concerned about being deceptive. What you're suggesting is unethical. It wouldn't be fair to the Amish community. Posing as someone I'm not is… It's fraud. I could lose my job!"

"Tell me about it," Ryan muttered, closing his eyes and pressing his fingertips to his temples. In mid-May Caleb's brother had been suspended from his position as an archivist at the city museum after an inventory audit revealed nearly a million dollars of rare coins was missing. Two other employees had access to the collection, but the card reader indicated only Ryan had opened the storage area since the previous audit. That was almost a month ago and Ryan was losing hope of ever being reinstated. His eyes watered as he dropped his hands and looked squarely at Caleb. "I appreciate there's a risk— a very small risk—that if you do this and the university finds out, you could lose your job. But if I go to prison, there's a very high probability I'll lose my *son*."

Caleb winced at the thought. After a lengthy separation, Ryan's wife, Sheryl, had recently filed for divorce. She often held the threat of petitioning for sole custody of Liam over Ryan's head. Ryan was an excellent father, so there had been virtually no chance of the court agreeing to the request. But once the FBI investigated him and his standing at work was jeopardized, Ryan began to worry his parental rights were on shaky ground, too. He told Caleb his fear of being incarcerated was secondary compared to his fear of losing Liam. The possibility was agonizing Caleb, too, since he was crazy about his nephew, who was probably the closest Caleb would ever come to having a child of his own.

His resolve wavering, he argued feebly, "The FBI said they found no evidence of the coins at the cabins. No evidence anyone connected to the crime had been there, either."

The first week in June, Ryan received in the mail a flyer from a small Amish lakeside camp in Serenity Ridge, Maine. The sender had circled a line of text reading: "If you can't find what you're looking for within walking or canoeing distance of your cabin, it isn't worth finding."

At first Ryan thought the anonymous message was nothing more than a marketing campaign or a hint from a colleague that he needed to take a vacation. But on the other side of the flyer someone had scrawled "Matthew 6:19–21." Ryan was familiar with the Bible verse reference, which said, "Lay not up for yourselves treasures upon earth, where moth and rust doth corrupt, and where thieves break through and steal: But lay up for yourselves treasures in heaven, where neither moth nor rust doth corrupt, and where thieves do not break through nor steal: For where your treasure is, there will your heart be also."

Ryan deduced the message was related to the stolen artifacts and he turned the note over to the FBI, who thoroughly searched the cabins and the property. Agents also interviewed the camp's owners, who were reluctant to get involved, not solely because they were Amish but also because the law enforcement's presence on-site was disruptive to their business. The FBI was equally frustrated with their record-keeping process, which amounted to little more than taking reservations by cell phone and writing the customers' last names and dates in a notebook. Furthermore, because they were Amish, the owners only accepted cash, check or money orders from their guests, which meant several of their customers were practically untraceable.

In the end, the FBI found no credible evidence to suggest the coin theft from the museum was linked to the Amish camp or its guests. The agents proposed someone with a grudge against Ryan or someone who wanted to send the FBI on a wild-goose chase had deliberately provided the false tip. They also questioned whether Ryan had convinced someone to forge the note and mail it from Maine. The suggestion was outrageous—it meant Ryan still wasn't above suspicion and left him feeling depressed.

"Just because they didn't find any evidence doesn't mean it's not there," Ryan insisted. "The detective I hired said it was possible the thief changed his mind. Maybe he heard about the FBI's investigation and figured selling the coins would be too risky."

"If that was true, wouldn't he have simply abandoned them? Why send a note hinting they're hidden near the camp in Maine?"

"The Bible verse makes me think he had a guilty conscience. The Amish don't typically evangelize, but you've said the way they put their faith into practice can be inspiring. Perhaps something the camp owners said or did made him decide he couldn't keep stolen property."

"Then why wouldn't he tell you exactly where the coins were hidden? Why just give you a vague clue?"

"I don't know. Maybe he was buying time so he could get to Canada first. Maybe another note is coming—"

Caleb interjected, "You sound a little crazy right now, Ryan."

"I *am* a little crazy right now. I can't think. I can't sleep or eat. I'd go to Maine myself if I wasn't prohibited from leaving the area while the investigation is ongoing. And I can't afford the detective I hired any longer—I'm supporting two households as it is. If I end up being arrested, I'll need every penny I have for a decent lawyer." Ryan's pallid face contorted into a grimace. "Please, Caleb. I need your help."

"Couldn't I just stay at the cabins as a guest?"

"I already called and they said they're booked for the season. That's how I found out they need a handyman—the lady made a joke about hoping I was calling about the advertisement in *The Budget* for a resident groundskeeper. Don't you see? The timing is providential. It *has* to be."

Caleb grunted. He wasn't so sure about that. Although he'd been a Christian since he was a young boy, lately his relationship with God amounted to little more than attending church on Sunday and saying grace before a meal, if he remembered. But whether it was God's will for him to go to Maine or not, one thing Caleb did know for certain: his brother needed him. His *nephew* needed him. They were the only family he had and he couldn't let them down. "I might as well go. It's not like I'm doing anything else this summer," he said wryly.

At thirty-one, Caleb had already declared himself

a confirmed bachelor. When the academic year ended each spring, he spent more time cultivating his vegetable garden than he spent cultivating personal relationships, especially with women. Having grown up in a home where his parents bickered from sunrise to sunset—eventually divorcing when Caleb was in his senior year of college—he had no desire to marry. Sure, he'd had several short-term relationships over the years, but the minute a conflict arose, Caleb broke up with the woman. He'd rather be lonely than wind up as miserable as his parents had been. Or as his brother was now.

"Are you being serious?" Ryan asked.

"Yeah, I'll go."

"Woo-hoo!" Ryan yelped, and practically crushed Caleb's shoulders in a bear hug until Liam padded into the room.

"What's wrong, Daddy?" he asked, bleary-eyed.

"Nothing, son. I was shouting because Uncle Caleb told me good news. He's going away this summer. On a nice long vacation."

"You are? But you just got here." Liam looked as if he was about to cry. He'd become very clingy since Ryan moved into an apartment and saw him only on the weekends. "Can we come, too?"

Caleb winced at his plea. "It's not going to be a real vacation, Liam. I'll be working. I'll tell you what—next time I come back, you and I can go camping together. How's that?"

Liam nodded slowly. "Okay. But when will you get back?"

"Soon," Caleb promised. "Just as soon as I can."

* * *

"I hope everything goes smoothly for you and the girls while we're away," Rose Allgyer's aunt Nancy said at the end of Rose's second week helping run Serenity Lake Cabins.

"I've owned and managed a restaurant in one of the busiest tourist areas in Lancaster County, so don't worry about us," Rose said. "You've got enough on your mind." Rose's aunt and uncle were traveling from Maine to Ohio to participate in an eight-to ten-week clinical trial for patients with renal cell cancer and wouldn't return home until the last week in August.

"*Gott* willing, this treatment will be exactly what Sol needs." Nancy angled her face toward the lake. It was the third week in June and the temperatures were already in the mideighties, but a cool breeze stirred the water and drifted up the hill to where they were relaxing on the porch. "It will be so *gut* to see my *schweschder* and her *familye* in Ohio again. It's been almost ten years since we moved away. I love it here, but I do miss everybody back home."

A couple of years after relocating from Ohio to a new Amish settlement in Serenity Ridge, Maine, Nancy and Sol had purchased the Maine camp. They earned their living by selling produce and renting the cabins to fishermen, young families, older couples and artists and writers who enjoyed solitude and simplicity. *And* good cooking—Nancy and her sixteen-year-old twin daughters, Charity and Hope, along with one other staff member, served a full breakfast and supper and a light lunch in the main dining hall every day except Sunday.

As Rose had discovered during the past two weeks, harvesting produce and cooking for that many people, as well as cleaning the cabins and washing linens on Saturdays, was hard work. But, as she told her aunt, the guests here were generally less demanding than the *Englischers* she encountered at the restaurant in Pennsylvania.

"*Jah*, our guests are very respectful of the property and each other's privacy. Many of them have been coming here every year since we opened. That's why I regretted the tumult I told you about with the FBI at the start of the season. It was so disruptive to all of us. You can't imagine how intrusive some of the agents' questions were. And they went through our record keeping with a fine-tooth comb."

If only I'd gone through my *business records with a fine-tooth comb, perhaps I wouldn't be broke right now,* Rose thought bitterly. Earlier that spring she'd discovered her fiancé, Baker Zook, had been taking money from the restaurant she owned. The small eatery originally belonged to Baker's mother, but when she passed away two years ago, Rose became the new proprietor. Baker, a horse trainer by trade, had been handling the accounting successfully until that time, and Rose saw no reason to hire anyone else once she took over the business. During the course of the following year, her professional relationship with Baker developed into a romantic courtship and the pair had planned to get married in the upcoming autumn wedding season.

That was before she learned Baker had been skimming money from the restaurant's account to buy and resell racehorses. He admitted his wrongdoing only when one of the most expensive horses he'd invested in strained its suspensory ligament, rendering it incapable of competing. Unable to hide the financial loss, Baker confessed to the church leaders and apologized to Rose. The deacons had helped him devise a bimonthly repayment schedule, but it would be another two years before Rose would be fully recompensed. Meanwhile, she had defaulted on a business loan and had to forfeit the lease on her restaurant.

The irony is that I was drawn to Baker because, unlike any suitor I ever had, he seemed to respect that I was an independent business owner. In retrospect Rose realized Baker probably only valued her professional success because it funded his equine wheeling and dealing. She felt utterly humiliated she'd been bamboozled, and her embarrassment was compounded by her family, who hadn't wanted her to buy the restaurant in the first place.

"If you had gotten married when you were young like your sisters did, you wouldn't be in this predicament now," her mother had lectured. "You're twenty-nine, and you have no husband and no income. Who is going to provide for you once *Daed* and I are gone?"

Trying to convince her family she'd been better off without a man in her life and that she could take care of herself was futile, so she decided she'd have to *show* them instead. Rose set her sights on leasing a small café when she returned to Pennsylvania at the end of the summer. However, even though the salary her aunt and uncle were paying her was generous, it still wasn't enough for her to be able to afford the initial rent and deposit for the new location.

"Would you and *Onkel* Sol mind if I come up with a way to bring in extra income on my own time while

I'm here?" she asked Nancy. As a business owner herself, Rose's aunt had been one of the few people who had supported Rose's endeavors with the restaurant.

"Of course not, as long as it doesn't hinder your service to our guests or disrupt their privacy. And don't wear yourself too thin. Charity and Hope are *gut* workers, but as you've probably noticed, Eleanor sometimes talks quicker than she works," Nancy warned.

Rose chuckled. She *had* noticed that Eleanor Sutter, the twenty-one-year-old woman who came in the late afternoon to help prepare and serve supper, was a real chatterbox.

"Once Caleb Miller arrives, he'll take over the upkeep of the fields and the two of you can work together on harvesting the produce. Sol usually manages the finances, but I'd rather not assign that to Caleb, since we don't know much about him, except he said he's a distant *gschwischderkind* of the Miller *familye* in Blue Hill, Ohio, where I grew up. And any relative of theirs is a friend of mine. Do you feel confident handling the accounting?"

"Absolutely!" Rose declared. *There's no way I'm going to make the mistake of delegating that responsibility to someone else again.* As it was, after Rose learned the camp's usual caretaker had broken his leg, she had tried to convince Nancy and Sol it wasn't necessary for them to hire a resident replacement. Rose suggested they could save money by employing an hourly worker to make any urgent repairs the cabins needed, and she insisted she and the twins could manage the gardens on their own. But her aunt was resolute, claiming so much had been left undone because of Sol's illness she didn't want the camp's condition to deteriorate further. Also, Hope and Charity both served as nannies for local Amish mothers from after breakfast until almost supper on weekdays, which meant they wouldn't be available to pitch in during the day.

Rose sipped her lemonade and then asked, "When is Caleb arriving anyway?"

"Tomorrow afternoon around four o'clock."

Rose frowned. "It's odd that he'd travel on the *Sabbat*, don't you think?"

"*Neh*, not especially. We travel when we visit our friends after church on *Suundaag*."

"*Jah*, but you don't pay someone to transport you— you take your own buggy. Isn't hiring an *Englisch* driver or taking the train kind of like conducting business or going shopping?"

"The bishop allows it, so…" Nancy said with a shrug. Then she gently added, "I know Baker broke your heart, Rose—"

"He didn't break my heart. He broke my trust," Rose cut in. She would *not* give Baker credit for breaking her heart, even if that was exactly what he'd done.

"*Jah*, he definitely broke your trust," Nancy acknowledged. "But not every young man you meet is going to be as unscrupulous as he was. I hope you'll give Caleb a chance to demonstrate what kind of person he is before you come to any conclusions about his character."

"Of course, I will," Rose assured her aunt. *Although, I can't imagine spending much time getting to know him.*

"*Gut*. Working together will be a lot easier if you

do. And maybe the two of you will wind up becoming friends," Nancy suggested.

I need to make money, not friends, Rose thought, biting her lip. But when she noticed her aunt scrutinizing her, she smiled and said, "Who knows, maybe we will."

After the van driver dropped him off at the end of the long dirt driveway—which appeared more like a road—leading to the lakeside cabins, Caleb inhaled the piney scent, trying to calm his nerves. He'd spent nearly every moment since he called Nancy the weekend before preparing for his arrival here. He'd ordered an Amish hat and clothing and listened to as many recordings of people speaking *Deitsch* as he could find online. He'd even considered traveling the hour and a half from Madison to Green Lake County to hang out at the Amish market and practice the language, but he didn't want to do anything to draw attention to himself.

He surveyed the fields as he ambled past them. Nancy had told him most of the acreage was used for berries and potatoes, but they also grew a variety of fruits and vegetables, from asparagus to watermelons and everything in between. From what Caleb could discern, their crops were flourishing. He'd developed an interest in horticulture as a teenager, when being alone outdoors provided him with an escape from his parents' quarrels, and Caleb anticipated managing the gardens would be the most pleasant part of his role here, too.

The open fields gave way to a little forest of pine trees and once he'd trekked another quarter of a mile, Caleb spied what appeared to be the main house, as well as the roofs and back walls of several small cabins. He dallied a moment in the shade, his heart thumping in his ears. He felt as nervous as if he were waiting offstage, about to perform in a play—and in a way, he was.

"Wilkom," a trim middle-aged woman called from the porch of the main house as Caleb approached. She pushed herself up from the wooden glider and waved to him.

"Guder nammidaag," he replied, his voice cracking dryly.

"I'm Nancy Petersheim," she said when he climbed the steps. "You must be Caleb Miller."

"I am, *jah*," he answered awkwardly, and set down his suitcase. Some Amish shook hands and others didn't, so he waited for Nancy to take the lead.

"You walked in from the road? You must be parched. I'll bring you a cool drink and a slice of Rose's *aebeer babrag boi*. Take a seat."

Caleb knew *aebeer* meant *strawberry* and *boi* meant *pie*, but his mind went blank on the word *babrag*. He sat in a glider and scanned the grounds. The property in front of the main house sloped down toward the lake. From where he was situated on the porch, Caleb's view of the water was partially obscured by trees, but he could see enough of the lake to understand why it was referred to as *pristine* on the flyer his brother had received. He counted nine small cabins tucked beneath the pines, each one angled toward the water. To his delight, he noticed the ground was covered in needles. *No grass means no mowing.* His least favorite part of yard work.

He turned toward the door as Nancy emerged with a tray of goodies. *That's right.* Babrag *means* rhubarb.

Caleb hadn't realized how hungry he was until he took a bite of strawberry-rhubarb pie, the perfect marriage of tart and sweet. He briefly closed his eyes as he savored the flavor, amazed he'd forgotten how scrumptious Amish food could be.

"*Appenditlich*, isn't it?" Nancy beamed. "My niece, Rose, makes the best *boi* I've ever tasted. She's the one who will be doing most of the cooking while we're away."

"*Jah, appenditlich,*" he agreed, shoveling a large forkful into his mouth. Caleb figured by keeping his mouth full he could avoid answering questions until his nerves steadied. Fortunately, as he was finishing the dessert, Nancy cocked an ear toward the screen door.

"I hear my husband, Sol, stirring. When he first gets up from a nap, he's a little woozy. You'll get to meet him at supper. For now, why don't you familiarize yourself with the grounds and make yourself at home in your cabin?" She pointed toward a tiny structure on the water's edge. "You'll be staying in that one, cabin number nine. Actually, we sometimes call it cabin eight and a half because it's so small, but it has the best location."

Caleb meandered happily down the path, relieved his initial interaction with Nancy had gone off without a hitch. *Maybe this won't be as difficult as I imagined,* he hoped. Of course, convincing his employer he was Amish was a minor accomplishment compared to finding the evidence his brother needed him to find. But at least he'd made it over the first hurdle.

The humidity caused the cabin door to stick in its frame, and Caleb had to nudge it open with his shoulder. Once inside, he found the one-room structure contained a single bed, an armchair, a desk-and-chair set, a bureau and a gas lamp. There was a separate stall with a toilet, sink and shower. *I guess this is what the flyer meant by simply furnished,* he thought. But the view through the picture window more than made up for the scarcity of furnishings: not ten yards away Serenity Lake sparkled with sunlight, and in the distance, hills abundant with verdant trees encircled the shoreline.

After a little experimenting Caleb figured out the picture window opened perpendicularly instead of horizontally. He swung it toward himself on its hinge and then fastened the bottom sill with hooks to the beams overhead. Within seconds a soft breeze wafted across his face and he closed his eyes to relish the sensation. *I'd better keep moving or I'm likely to doze off and miss supper,* he thought, so he began unpacking his suitcase.

It didn't take long. Aside from a couple changes of clothes and toiletries, all Caleb had brought with him was his cell phone and a solar-powered charger. He and Ryan had agreed that for the duration of his stay Caleb would call his brother only on Saturdays. Caleb would have to keep the phone muted, although they'd text or leave messages with each other about any urgent developments. Caleb stashed the phone in the middle drawer before removing his final possession from the side pocket of the suitcase: a photo of Liam, grinning broadly to show he'd lost a front tooth. On the back of the photo he'd written "I love you!" Caleb smiled before sliding the picture into a Bible he'd found in the top drawer of the bureau.

Stepping outside, he noticed the camp was unusually quiet, not a guest in sight. Maybe they were out fishing? As he walked toward the narrow stretch of sand in front of the dock, he noticed a sign that read No Swimming or Sunbathing. Doubtless, the Amish owners found *Englisch* swimwear too immodest to allow guests to wear it while on their property. However, according to the flyer the camp did provide two canoes and two rowboats for their guests' use, as well as a shed full of fishing gear they could borrow. *I wouldn't mind vacationing at a place like this myself,* Caleb thought. *Too bad Liam couldn't come here with me.*

He'd been so nervous anticipating his meeting with Nancy and Sol, he hadn't noticed until just then how much his feet ached. He hadn't gotten a chance to break in the new work boots he'd bought before he left Wisconsin, and he was sure he had blisters on his heels. As he bent to unlace the boots so he could dip his feet in the water, he spotted a flash of color from the corner of his eye. A woman wearing a cobalt blue dress was paddling a canoe around a large rock that jutted into the water some two hundred yards down the shoreline.

That must be Rose, he thought as she drew closer. She looked too mature to be one of the sixteen-year-old daughters Nancy had told him about on the phone. The woman's strokes were smooth and sure, and in no time she'd bypassed the dock, apparently preferring to disembark on the shore. Deeply tanned, she had a kerchief instead of a prayer *kapp* fastened over her dark hair, and her forehead glistened with perspiration. Her face was all broad planes and sharp angles and if Caleb didn't know she was Amish, he would have claimed for certain she was wearing rose-red lipstick—was that how she'd gotten her name?

"Don't just stand there—move!" she hollered as she propelled the fore end of the canoe onto the shore, nearly bowling into him. He jumped back just in time.

No, Caleb decided. *Her parents probably named her Rose because they knew how prickly she'd be.*

As Rose got out of the canoe, the man greeted her. "*Guder nammidaag.* I'm Caleb. Caleb Miller. You must be Rose."

"*Jah*," she answered tersely, pulling the canoe farther onto shore. *We haven't even started working together and he's already getting in my way.* She knew she should welcome him or say she was glad he'd arrived, but she didn't appreciate the way he'd been gawking at her. The most she could ask by way of hospitality was, "How was your trip?"

"*Gut, denki*," he answered as he helped her flip the canoe over in the sand. His dark curly hair poked out from beneath his hat, and when he looked at her she noticed he had the longest eyelashes she'd ever seen on a man; they made his blue eyes appear all the more luminous. Or was that a trick of the light off the lake? "How was yours?"

"My what?" Rose was annoyed at herself for being flustered by him. Gut-*looking doesn't mean* gut *acting*, she thought, remembering her sisters frequently commenting about how handsome Baker was.

"Your canoeing trip." He pointed toward the water.

"Oh, it was fine." It hadn't been fine. It was hot and buggy, and the only reason she'd stayed out all afternoon was because she didn't want to be at the house while Eleanor's twenty-four-year-old brother, Henry, tried to flirt with her under the guise of visiting Nancy and Sol. Rose unfastened her life vest and hung it in the shed nearby.

When she emerged, Caleb handed her her sneakers and grinned. Wisconsin must have something special in their water, she thought—his teeth were as white as the *Englisch* celebrities on the covers of magazines at the superstore. The clanking of a bell interrupted Rose's thoughts. "That's *Ant* Nancy's signal supper is ready."

Although she was still barefoot, Rose trod easily on the path up the hill, with Caleb lagging behind. *I hope he doesn't* always *move as slowly as what I've seen so far.* There was a bin of water and a towel outside the door on the porch. Rose dunked one foot into the bin and then the other, rinsing them free of pine needles and then drying them before going inside with Caleb.

"Ah, I see you two have met, Caleb and Rose," Nancy said. She introduced her husband to Caleb and explained Hope and Charity had gone to a singing that evening and wouldn't be joining them for supper. Then everyone took a seat at the kitchen table.

"I'll say grace," Sol announced, giving Caleb a moment to remove his hat.

Don't they have any manners in Wisconsin? Rose wondered when Caleb didn't take the hint.

"There's a hook near the door for your *hut* or you can hang it on your chair, Caleb," Nancy kindly suggested.

"My apologies," Caleb replied, sweeping his hat off his head and balancing it on the back of his chair. Rose noticed his face was still aflame after Sol finished praying and everyone lifted their heads again.

"What is your occupation in Wisconsin that allows you to come all the way to Maine at this time of year?" she asked.

"I'm a teacher."

Rose cocked her head, intrigued. "I've heard some settlements are so small they have male teachers instead of female teachers, but I've never spoken to one. What's your favorite part of working with *scholars*?"

"I, uh, enjoy teaching *Deutsche*," Caleb said, taking an enormous bite of his ham-and-cheese sandwich. When he finished chewing he addressed Sol. "Your wife told me on the phone I'd be taking care of the *gaerde* and *baamgaarde* as well as maintaining the grounds and cabins. What kind of repair projects have you been working on?"

"There will be time enough for discussing work when the *Sabbat* is over," Nancy said, and again Caleb's cheeks went red.

Like Rose, her uncle must have noticed Caleb's embarrassment, because Sol waved his hand and commented, "Nancy's just worried if you find out how much work there is to do, you'll turn around and go back to Wisconsin in the middle of the night."

That wouldn't be the worst thing in the world, Rose thought facetiously.

"I'll take you around tomorrow morning and show you everything," Sol continued. "I've made a few to-do lists, but most of your responsibilities will be typical gardening and maintenance projects. Making sure everything is functional and tidy for our guests. And keeping shifty-looking types from prowling around the property."

"Shifty-looking types?" Caleb coughed, wide-eyed. "Have you had a problem with unwelcome people on the property?"

"Perhaps not unwelcome, but uninvited, *jah*." Sol winked at his wife before explaining to Caleb, "Our Rose hasn't even been here a month and we've already had more bachelors visiting us the past couple *Suundaage* than we've had all spring. I get the feeling once Nancy and I leave they're going to find excuses to *kumme* by during the week, too. So if you notice any young men hanging around or acting strange, feel free to tell them to scram—"

"Onkel!" Rose was sure her face was even redder than Caleb's had been. She didn't need the likes of a slow-moving, ill-mannered man like Caleb looking out for her. She didn't need *any* man looking out for her, for that matter.

"Something tells me Rose would chase away any unsavory characters long before I got to them," Caleb remarked, and she didn't know whether it was a compliment or a criticism. Either way, she didn't care.

"You've got that right. The only fishy behavior I'll put up with is from the bass and trout in Serenity Lake," she declared. Everyone cracked up, and Rose laughed along with them even though she couldn't have been more serious.

Chapter Two

Caleb woke shortly after first light. The battery-operated clock on the desk said it was only a little past four; the sun wasn't even up yet. But since he'd turned in early the night before and he'd had such a refreshing sleep, he got up and dressed anyway. Now what? He wished he'd brought something to read; the Bible was the only book in the cabin. He leafed through it until he got to the sixth chapter of Matthew so he could review verses 19–21. By now he had them practically memorized, but he still wasn't convinced they had anything to do with the stolen coins from the museum. As he flipped the page back and skimmed the chapter from the beginning, the words of the Lord's Prayer caught his eye and it occurred to him he should pray.

It had been so long since he'd spent any time in prayer he felt sheepish talking to the Lord now, but Caleb bowed his head and mumbled, "God, I know I haven't been very faithful lately, but Ryan is desperate, so if there is something here at the cabins that will help prove my brother's

innocence, will You please show it to me?" Caleb medi-
tated silently for several minutes, listening to the rhyth-
mic slapping of water against the shore before opening
his eyes and rising.

Sol had said to meet him on the porch at six o'clock,
which was also when Rose or one of Sol's daughters collected eggs and milked the cow. Caleb kind of wished that
would be his responsibility. He'd enjoyed milking when he
lived on the Amish farm, but he was out of practice. Surely
the *meed* would appreciate it if he did it for them, he thought
as he headed toward the barn on the other side of the main
house and then went inside. Even with the door open it took
a moment for his eyes to adjust to the lack of light.

Scanning the organized interior, he glimpsed the family's milk cow and horse. The buggy and harness were also
housed in the barn, as well as hay, feed and sundry farming tools and supplies. Caleb briefly considered whether
the coins could have been stashed among them, but on first
look he saw nothing resembling the carrying case or small
safe Ryan said the thief would have been likely to use to
transport the valuables. Besides, the barn was a highly
trafficked area. *If I were concealing stolen goods, I'd hide
them someplace that was off the beaten path. Like in the
woods.* Taking a fresh pail from the hook and removing
the stainless steel lid, Caleb set about milking the cow
and he was surprised by how quickly the process came
back to him. "Good girl," he said, patting the gentle animal when he was finished, grateful she'd been so passive.

The sun was up and the sky bright when he walked
outside. Still, he doubted it was six o'clock yet and he
figured he might as well gather the eggs, too. Maybe by

doing a few extra chores he'd get on Rose's good side. Although he would usually avoid a young woman altogether if she seemed peevish toward him, Caleb couldn't afford to alienate anyone at the camp. Besides, he surmised maybe he shouldn't take Rose's snippy attitude personally. During supper he learned she'd been in Maine for only a couple of weeks herself; maybe when she saw him onshore she mistook him for another uninvited caller. Sol indicated she had several men vying for her affections, which must be irritating since she clearly wasn't interested in being courted.

Caleb set down the milk pail, entered the coop and unlatched the door to the henhouse. The chickens were less cooperative than the cow had been and he incurred a few pecks on his wrist and hand as he wrested a couple of broody birds from the nesting box. After successfully retrieving his first egg, he realized he didn't have a basket, so he swept his hat off his head and deposited the egg inside it. He'd collected a good dozen when he heard a woman's voice behind him.

"Exactly what do you think you're doing?" It was Rose, and she sounded every bit as thorny this morning as she had yesterday evening by the lake.

"*Guder mariye,*" he replied congenially. "I'm collecting *oier.*"

"That's *my* responsibility. Or Hope and Charity's."

"I don't mind."

"*I* do. I need every one of those to make breakfast for the guests. Your *hut* isn't sturdy enough for you to pile so many on top of each other in it—they'll break."

"Sorry." Caleb carefully supported the bottom of

his hat as he extended it to Rose so she could transfer the eggs into her basket. When she'd taken the last one, he turned on his heel and hightailed it away from her.

He was halfway across the yard when she squawked, "Hey! You didn't shut the door—the *hinkel* are getting out!"

Spinning around, Caleb saw three chickens had escaped the coop and several more were streaming out. He dashed toward them with his arms spread wide to herd them back into the coop, but his feet were still sore from the blisters so he wasn't as nimble as he needed to be. Rose came to his aid and by the time the chickens were inside again and she had secured the door behind her, she was red-faced and scowling. She picked up the egg basket and waited for him to retrieve the milk pail from where he'd left it in the grass earlier.

"Are you sure you're Amish?" she asked as they walked toward the house.

Uh-oh. "Wh-what do you mean?" he stuttered.

"My four-and five-year-old nieces and nephews know better than to leave the coop door open. They also know you should do the milking after collecting the *oier*, so you can bring the *millich* inside right away. We can't drink this now. I'll have to make *sauer millich kuche* instead."

Relieved his *Englisch* identity hadn't been found out, Caleb smiled. "If your *sauer millich kuche* is anything like your *aebeer babrag boi*, then I'm glad I didn't bring the *millich* inside right away."

Rose rolled her eyes—he noticed they were amber, not brown as he'd first thought. "Flattery will get you nowhere," she said, but a tiny smile decorated her lips. "I'm just glad you didn't leave the *corral* door open. The *gaul* is much harder to round up than the *hinkel*."

"Are you speaking from personal experience?"

Caught, she giggled. "*Jah.* I suppose you're not the only one who's careless the first morning after a long day of travel."

Caleb laughed. "Tomorrow I'll do better, I promise." If he lasted that long without blowing his cover.

When they returned to the house, Sol was waiting on the porch to give Caleb a tour of the property and review his to-do list, which included maintaining the grounds, cabins, dock and boats, cultivating the gardens and orchards, caring for the livestock and completing a host of other minor chores, as well. How would he ever keep up with all of this and still have time to look for the coins, Caleb wondered.

When they circled back to the porch, Sol gazed down the hill toward the water. "There's a lot to be done, but be sure to have a little *schpass* while you're here," he advised. There was a catch in his voice as he added, "It's a shame there's not enough time for me to take you out on the lake to show you the best fishing spots…"

Sensing Sol was nervous about his upcoming treatment, Caleb assured him, "You can show me when you return." *If I'm still here.*

"I'll look forward to that," Sol replied, grinning again.

After the last guests departed the dining hall and while Hope and Charity were clearing their dishes, Rose prepared the family's breakfast. Usually, her aunt would have been helping, too, but on Mondays Nancy went to the bank first thing in the morning. Rose didn't mind— she liked being in charge.

Serving guests here seemed easier than at her restaurant in Pennsylvania, probably because at the camp everyone ate together, family-style, at long picnic tables. Instead of ordering individual meals, for breakfast and supper guests were offered two main entrées, homemade bread or buns, various garden fruits and vegetables, and of course, something sweet, such as doughnuts in the morning and desserts in the evening. For the noon meal, guests could make their own lunch or help themselves to the platters of bread, fruit and cheese Nancy or the girls set out for them, buffet-style. If guests had special dietary needs, they were welcome to use the kitchen to prepare their own meals either before or after the regular meal hours, but otherwise, everyone ate as much or as little as they liked from what was offered. Nancy said in the seven years since they opened the cabins to the public, she'd never received a single complaint.

Glancing through the large window-like opening in the wall that separated the kitchen from the dining area, Rose reminded Charity to set an extra place at the table for Caleb.

"*Mamm* said you met him yesterday. What's he like?" Hope asked casually, causing Rose to suppress a smile. Having just turned sixteen, the twins were allowed to court now, and Rose had observed subtle signs of flirting when they interacted with certain boys at church. She remembered being that naive and optimistic about romance. It was *gut* to enjoy it while it lasted.

"He's probably a little older than I am," she said, knowing Caleb's age would dash their hopes of having him as a suitor.

Sure enough, Hope moaned, clearly disappointed. "Aw, that's too bad."

"He's also rather *doppich*." Rose only added that he was clumsy by way of consolation.

"Doppich?" Charity echoed from the dining area. "How so?"

"Well, let's just say he's not very light on his feet. Not very quick, either," Rose replied with a laugh. "I almost ran him over with the canoe yesterday—and he was standing onshore! And this morning he let the *hinkel* out and it took him five minutes to round them up again."

"That's because my new boots are giving me blisters," Caleb clarified.

Uh-oh. When did he kumme *in and how much did he hear?* Rose was mortified she might have been caught talking about Caleb, especially in unflattering terms. "Oh, uh, that's too bad. After breakfast I'll give you a couple adhesive bandages," she offered. She ducked her head and pushed eggs around in a skillet as she listened to him introduce himself to Charity and Hope. A moment later she heard Nancy and Sol enter the dining hall, too.

As they ate, Rose noted she'd have to make more food next time: Caleb had a voracious appetite, and he hardly gave himself time to swallow in between bites of scrapple and eggs. After everyone's plate was empty, Sol reached for his wife's hand and cleared his throat, but it was Nancy who spoke.

"We want you all to know how much it means to us that

we can count on you to keep the camp running smoothly. These next couple of months are going to be challenging and—" Her eyes filled and she stopped speaking.

Rose got up and walked around to the other side of the table. Squeezing in between Sol and Nancy, she gave them each a sideways hug. "It's a privilege to help and we'll be praying faithfully for you." Then she offered to finish cleaning up so Hope and Charity could accompany their parents to the house until the van arrived. Caleb solemnly shook Sol's and Nancy's hands—such a formal gesture, but perhaps that was what the Wisconsin Amish did, Rose thought—and after they left, he gulped down a final swig of coffee and took off for the fields. It wasn't until Rose was bringing the tray of dirty dishes into the kitchen that she remembered he needed an adhesive bandage. *Oh, well, I'll give him one later.*

For now, she was reveling in the solitude. She liked being alone, even if it meant she had to do all the work by herself, because it gave her time to flesh out her plan for earning more money without neglecting her responsibilities at the camp. Since she needed to be available to the guests, she couldn't take another part-time job in town. *Too bad I couldn't open the dining hall to the public*, she thought. But that would definitely ruin the camp's tranquil, isolated atmosphere—a huge no-no in her aunt's book.

The roadside fruit-and-vegetable stand was as close as Nancy and Sol allowed the general public to come to the camp. Typically, the Petersheims sold whatever produce they didn't serve to the guests or use and can for themselves. However, so far this season they seemed to have a bumper crop of almost everything they grew, so

Rose decided she'd put up the extra vegetables and use the fruit to make jam and sell it at the stand. She'd split the proceeds with her aunt and uncle, of course, since it was their harvest. *Englischers* back home were willing to pay a pretty penny for homemade jams and naturally preserved foods, and she imagined the same would be true of the *Englischers* in Maine. The extra income wouldn't be enough to secure the lease for the café, but it would be a start until Rose could devise a more lucrative plan.

In between completing the rest of her chores at the camp, she took a trip into town for jars and other supplies, and then she spent the afternoon strawberry picking so she could make a double batch of jam the following day. She was pleased with her progress but exhausted by the time Eleanor arrived and the twins returned home to help her prepare the guests' dinner.

"What's Caleb Miller like?" Eleanor asked, undoubtedly for the same reason the twins had inquired about him.

This time, Rose answered more carefully. "You'll get to meet him soon yourself."

Blithely Eleanor tugged Rose's sleeve. "Just tell me one little thing about him."

"He's in need of a bandage for a blister on his foot," Rose retorted, her patience wearing thin. "Now, chop that asparagus, please. It's already been washed."

"Is he tall?" Eleanor persisted. At five eleven, she was even taller than Rose.

"That's two things." Rose pointed to the heap of stalks on the cutting board. "The asparagus, please."

"*Jah*, he's tall," Charity told Eleanor. "But he's old."

Eleanor picked up a knife. "How old?"

"At least thirty, maybe older."

"Kind of strange he's not married yet," Hope remarked.

"Thirty's not so old to be single. Not for a man anyway." Eleanor shot Rose an exaggeratedly contrite look.
"Oops, sorry, Rose."

"Don't be," she snapped. "I'm not."

After spending the day repairing the dock, groom-
ing the livestock and cleaning their stalls, fertilizing
the gardens, digging up tubers and harvesting asparagus, as well as pruning the shrubbery around the camp,
Caleb's arm and back muscles were so sore he didn't
give a second thought to the blisters on his feet. While
his work allowed him plenty of opportunities to scope
out the property, he was discouraged to discover how
thick the undergrowth was in the woods on both sides of
the camp. The coins could be anywhere—or nowhere.

He'd stopped moving only long enough to eat lunch
in the dining hall around one thirty. By then, the guests
had helped themselves to the light buffet, and two empty
pie tins were the only evidence that Rose had set out
pies for dessert. Caleb made a mental note to take his
break earlier the following day. He suspected Rose
would have baked more pies by then, as he'd crossed
paths with her in the strawberry patch about a half hour
ago. When he'd asked if she needed help picking berries,
she waved him away. She seemed almost proprietorial
about her duties, and Caleb remembered many Amish
women considered their houses and gardens to be their

domain. Not that Rose was like any other Amish woman he'd met, but still, Caleb figured it would be wise to give her a wide berth. After what he'd overheard her saying about him that morning he didn't want to be considered intrusive, as well as clumsy and slow.

At suppertime he felt slightly out of place as the only man among four women. To make matters more uncomfortable, Eleanor riddled him with questions about his life in Wisconsin. He tried to keep his answers as honest as he could, but his replies sounded evasive to his own ears.

"Wisconsin is so far away. Won't you miss your *familye*?" she asked.

"My *eldre* died years ago, so it's just my *bruder* and me now." Caleb didn't mention his nephew for fear it would lead to questions about Sheryl. He didn't want to slip up and mention the pending divorce, which would be a giveaway since the Amish never divorced.

"What about your friends? Or your girlfriend?"

Caught off guard because most Amish people weren't so candid in inquiring about romantic relationships, Caleb admitted, "I don't have a girlfriend, and I'll be too busy to miss anyone else."

Eleanor fluttered her lashes. "If you need my help with anything, just let me know. I've worked here every summer for the past five years, so I know this camp inside and out. If you'd like I could show you around the lake, too."

That could come in handy in his quest for the coins. "*Denki*. I might take you up on that offer."

"The guests have first dibs on the canoes and rowboats during the week," Rose quickly informed him. "*Suundaag* is the only day we're allowed to use them."

"Why? Don't the guests go fishing or canoeing on *Suundaag*?"

"Sometimes they do, but since we don't serve meals on the *Sabbat*, most of them take the opportunity to go boating on Black Bear Lake, across town. The fishing isn't nearly as *gut* but they can use motorboats there. Or they spend the day hiking or sightseeing, and shopping or dining in the area."

Caleb filed this bit of information away in his mind. Might the crook have taken advantage of the empty camp to hide the coins then? "Have you, uh, ever had any problems with unruly guests?" he ventured.

Rose tipped her head quizzically. "Why do you ask that?"

Fortunately, Eleanor was more forthcoming. "*I* have," she complained. "Hope and Charity, remember that guy who yelled at me a few weeks ago?"

"Because you tipped over his *millich*, right?"

"*Jah*. He was *narrish*. Your *daed* very politely told him that's not how we treat each other at the camp, and he stormed out of the dining hall." Eleanor snickered. "They apparently were so offended they left that night and it was only the third day of their vacation."

Caleb's pulse quickened. "They? Was he here with someone else?" *An accomplice?*

"*Jah*, he was with his wife, I think. Or maybe she was his girlfriend. You know how *Englischers* are. They think nothing of—"

"That's enough, Eleanor," Rose cut in, glancing at her nieces. "We're here to serve our guests and to be an example of *Gott*'s love, not to pry or gossip about their private lives."

Caleb's cheeks burned, but he was grateful for the information Eleanor disclosed. If he could gain access to the reservation book, maybe he could figure out which cabin the couple had stayed in. Not that they were necessarily the thieves, but it was worth noting their behavior seemed out of the ordinary. If he determined which cabin they'd rented, he could turn it inside out once Saturday rolled around.

According to Sol, Saturday was changeover day. The current guests had to depart by ten in the morning, and the new guests weren't allowed to arrive until two o'clock. Meanwhile, the girls cleaned and put fresh linens on the beds, while Caleb was expected to give the cabins a once-over, to be sure everything was in working order.

"I didn't mean to meddle," Caleb said. "I, er, just wanted to know what to expect in case you ever needed me to, uh, step in…"

"That won't be necessary." Rose's tone was as vinegary as Eleanor's was honeyed.

"Speaking of stepping in," the younger woman cooed, "Rose mentioned you needed a bandage for your foot. If you *kumme* up to the *haus* with me, I'll give you one."

"*Neh.* I'll get it," Rose sternly objected. "You stay here and wash the dishes."

Caleb loitered in the dining hall until Rose returned, as it was clear she didn't want him to accompany her, either. Too bad—going with Eleanor might have provided the perfect opportunity to sneak a peek at the reservation book, since she appeared eager to gain his favor.

By Saturday Caleb had settled into his daily routine and he'd made great strides in his use of *Deitsch*, but he was no closer to figuring out where the couple Eleanor mentioned had stayed. He gave the cabins a thorough search, which wasn't difficult since they were so small and uncluttered. Virtually identical to each other, each one consisted of an open living area with a picture window overlooking the lake, and two tiny bedrooms, as well as a compact bathroom. The furniture was exactly like his, except in addition to an armchair every cabin contained a small sofa. Caleb even examined the floors for loose boards and checked the dirt around the buildings' foundations to see if it had been overturned. Nothing unusual jumped out at him. The only stray items he found left behind were a damp towel and a pair of sunglasses.

He regretted having nothing of importance to share with Ryan when he called him on Saturday evening at their agreed-upon time. Caleb lowered the picture window and closed the door so no one would hear him talking.

"How was your first week?" Ryan's question was casual, but his voice was tremulous.

"*Gut*—I mean good. I'm beat, though. I always prided myself on staying in decent shape, but putting in an honest week of physical labor was tougher than I expected. Still, it was worth it. You should taste the produce here. Asparagus, broccoli, potatoes. And strawberries—oh, man, the strawberries!" Caleb rambled. "I can't figure out what makes everything tastier than anything I've ever grown, if it's the soil or fertilizer..."

"You sound more like a farmer than a detective," Ryan replied, cutting to the chase. "Have you turned up anything interesting in regard to the coins?"

Caleb hesitated. "No, but I've eliminated the cabins as potential hiding places, so that's a start. I think if the thief stowed anything on the property, it must be in the woods. Don't worry, I'll keep looking. How's Liam?"

"Great. Today he swam the length of the community pool without stopping," Ryan said. "That's one good thing about my suspension—I get to spend a lot more time with him. Surprisingly, Sheryl has agreed I can have him on Wednesdays, as well as on the weekends."

That was because she got together with her friends for scrapbooking on Wednesdays, Caleb thought, but he didn't say it. Ryan had a tendency to interpret any small concession on Sheryl's part as a signal she wanted to reconcile, and Caleb didn't want to burst his bubble. Ryan needed to stay optimistic. "I wish I could take Liam swimming in Serenity Lake. It's gorg—" Caleb was interrupted by a sharp rapping. "Uh-oh, gotta go," he whispered and slipped the phone under his pillow before opening the door. Rose was standing on the step, holding a stack of linens. Sweat trickled down both sides of Caleb's neck.

"Is everything okay?" she inquired.

Borrowing a line from her, he replied, "*Jah*, why do you ask?"

"It's awfully hot to have your cabin all sealed up. I thought maybe it meant you had the chills."

"*Neh*, I'm fine," he stated without further explanation. "Are those linens for me?"

"*Jah*, I forgot to ask Charity and Hope to remove

your dirty sheets and make up your bed for you today when they changed the guests' bedding. *Muundaag* is laundry day so I can strip the bed for you now if you want—"

"*Neh!* I'll do it myself," Caleb exclaimed, thinking of his cell phone tucked beneath his pillow. "I'd prefer you *meed* not *kumme* inside my cabin."

Rose was taken aback by Caleb's vehement response. Did he think it was inappropriate for her to be alone with him in the cabin? That was why she was going to suggest he could take a walk—but he hadn't let her finish talking. She sure hoped he didn't think she was behaving coquettishly, the way Eleanor had been acting. "Okay, I'll leave these with you and you can bring your dirty linens and clothes to the *haus* by *Muundaag* morning."

"*Denki,*" he said as Rose scurried away.

There had been no mistaking the look of relief on his face when Rose had said she was leaving. She was abashed to remember that, after changing the sheets, she'd planned to invite him to join her on the porch of the main house for tea and dessert. Hope and Charity had gone out bowling, so this was the first real break Rose had taken all week. She was drained, but at least her jam-making efforts were paying off; of the forty-eight jars of jam she'd made that week, she had sold all but seventeen.

A guest had bought a dozen jars to take home to her family and friends as souvenirs of her trip. However, the woman expressed disappointment there wasn't a label on the jar indicating who'd made it. She told Rose,

"I think if people knew the jam was homemade by an Amish woman, they'd realize I was giving them something special. Of course, once they taste it they'll realize how special it is anyway, but, you know…"

Rose did know. The woman was suggesting she could sell even more jam if she changed the packaging. And since increasing her sales was exactly what Rose wanted to do, she spent the rest of the evening sketching a design for the labels. She was so excited about her final logo that by Sunday morning she'd forgotten all about her awkward interaction with Caleb.

She and the twins met him outside the barn, where he'd already hitched the horse and buggy and was standing beside the carriage waiting for them to go to church together. A rivulet of perspiration ran from his temples along his hairline even though the day had dawned cool and dry. He asked if Rose wanted to take the reins.

"Jah," she answered. The girls climbed into the back of the buggy, and she and Caleb sat up front. "Are you sure you're not feverish? You look a little peaked."

"I—I guess I'm a little nervous about attending worship services," he admitted as he donned his hat, which Rose noticed was the same straw hat he'd worn all week. "I'm not sure you'll do things at *kurrich* the same way we do them in Wisconsin and I don't want to offend anyone."

She assured him, "There's only one big difference here in Maine—we meet in a building instead of in each other's homes. But otherwise, I think you'll find *kurrich* here is very similar to Old Order services in Wisconsin. The *leit* are very *freindlich* but you're *wilkom* to sit with us so you won't feel awkward about not knowing anyone yet."

Ordinarily, the twins sat with a group of their female friends, while Nancy, Sol and Rose sat together as a family, but Rose had already privately requested Charity and Hope sit with her and Caleb today. Since she wasn't related to him, she would have felt uncomfortable sitting with him alone, something not even courting couples did. As it turned out, though, the deacon's sermon on God's sovereignty was so thought provoking it wouldn't have mattered where Rose was seated; she was entirely absorbed in what he was saying and she completely lost track of her surroundings.

The worship services were followed by a light lunch during which time the men ate with men and, after serving the men and children, the women ate with women. As she brought a pitcher of water to the men's table, Rose noticed they were including Caleb in their lively conversation and when she caught his eye, he nodded at her as if to confirm she'd been right about how friendly everyone was. Maybe now he'd relax a little, she hoped, realizing she'd be nervous, too, if she went to Wisconsin or someplace where she didn't have any friends or family.

After they'd eaten, Charity and Hope hurried off to spend the afternoon playing volleyball with their friends. Caleb and Rose decided they'd leave, too, and they were heading toward Sol and Nancy's buggy when Eleanor traipsed across the lawn with her brother at her side.

"Caleb! Rose!" she beckoned. After introducing Caleb to Henry, she raved, "Isn't it pleasant out? Not too humid, not too breezy. My *bruder* and I were just saying we think it's a great day to go canoeing."

"Jah," Caleb agreed. "It sure is."

"Terrific!" Eleanor exclaimed. "Henry and I will go home and change, then we'll meet you and Rose down by the dock."

Inwardly Rose groaned. If Eleanor and Caleb wanted to spend time together that was fine with her, but Rose had no intention of being stuck with Henry all afternoon. "I'm kind of tired so I just planned to laze around on the porch and soak in the sunshine. You three will have to navigate the lake without me."

"I'm kind of tired, too," Henry said. "I'll hang out with you instead, Rose."

This situation had just gone from bad to worse and it was all Caleb's fault!

Later, when she was alone with him in the buggy, she accusingly asked why he'd do such a thing.

"Do what?"

"Invite Eleanor and Henry canoeing? If you wanted to go off alone with Eleanor, be my guest, but don't expect me to entertain Henry all afternoon."

"Wait a second! For one thing, I didn't *invite* them canoeing. I only agreed it was a pleasant day. For another thing, I'd like to explore the lake, *jah*, but not because I want to *go off alone* with Eleanor," he said. "And as far as Henry goes, if you don't want him around, why don't you just tell him that outright? You don't seem to have any problem letting me know when you don't want *me* around."

Rose's mouth dropped open. She was aware she'd

had a few uncharitable *thoughts* about Caleb, but had she actually come across as that intolerant of his presence? Ashamed, she admitted, "You're right. It's not your fault they're coming over. Eleanor would have contrived a way to *kumme* even if it was raining cats and dogs. And I haven't meant to make you feel unwelcome. I think I've been so caught up in... Well, it doesn't matter, there's no excuse. I'm very sorry."

Even Caleb's profile was handsome, especially when he smiled. "It's okay. I think I have a solution that will help us both out of this predicament."

"I'm all ears."

"You and I will go together in one canoe and they can go in the other. I'll do all the paddling, so you can sit back and relax."

Rose giggled. She liked the way Caleb thought, but he was underestimating how persistent Eleanor and Henry could be. "Those two will never agree to this."

"They won't have a choice if we get to the lake and claim our canoe first."

Grinning, Rose flicked the horse's reins. "Giddyap," she urged.

Chapter Three

"What are you doing out there, Rose? I thought you were tired!" Eleanor wailed. Rose and Caleb waved to her and Henry from where they were idly rocking in the water, some thirty-five feet from shore.

"Why do you think I'm letting Caleb paddle by himself?" Rose answered back.

Caleb smiled. He got the sense Rose didn't relinquish the oars, the reins, the kitchen or any other kind of control very easily. She must *really* not have wanted to spend time alone with Henry if she was willing to let Caleb take charge.

Henry unlaced his boots swiftly and took off his socks as Eleanor sullenly dragged her feet across the sand, her arms crossed against her chest. When she finally climbed into the bow of the canoe and Henry pushed them off from shore, she scolded, "Careful! You're going to tip us over!"

"Which way first?" Caleb asked as the brother and sister neared him and Rose.

Henry pointed to the right. "We'll work our way around the lake counterclockwise."

As Caleb paddled, Rose explained that her aunt and uncle had bought their camp from a wealthy, eccentric *Englischer* who owned all of the land surrounding the one-hundred-and-fifty-acre lake. Mrs. Hallowell also owned a summer mansion on the opposite side of the water, but in the past, whenever her children and grandchildren had come to visit, they'd preferred to rough it together as a large group at "the camp," which Mrs. Hallowell's parents had built for her and her siblings when they were youngsters. Eventually, the brood stopped vacationing there when her children's offspring began attending college. Although Mrs. Hallowell had received countless offers on the property, she'd refused to sell it because she feared developers would turn the land into one giant parking lot and ruin the "rustic charm" of the little structures by building a resort.

According to Rose, Sol had first met the owner when he'd answered an advertisement looking for a farmer and groundskeeper the final summer Mrs. Hallowell's family got together there. They'd struck up such a good rapport that a year or two later she sold the camp to him and Nancy, knowing the Amish wouldn't even install electricity in the cabins, much less build up the property or allow motorboats on the lake. Granted, Mrs. Hallowell still owned virtually all of the property surrounding the lake, but Nancy and Sol had acquired the camp and the acreage near the main road.

Observing the tall pines and rocky inclines bordering the water, Caleb grew overwhelmed—how would he ever search it all? "Does Mrs. Hallowell allow you and your guests to go ashore on her property?"

"*Jah*, but only in designated areas." Rose explained they were welcome to disembark at either of the lake's two small islands, a clearing near a rock the Amish referred to as Relaxation Rock, and at a smaller area leading to a trail up a ridge called Paradise Point.

"What would happen if someone went ashore where they weren't supposed to?" Caleb asked.

"No one is going to shoot you, if that's what you're worried about," Rose said with a laugh. "But when Mrs. Hallowell comes to stay, she does allow her dogs to roam freely near her home and supposedly they're pretty fierce. Plus, she installed surveillance cameras in the woods and at her mansion. It's a common practice among the *Englisch* here. If owners aren't year-round residents they feel they need to make sure no one is breaking into their homes or vandalizing the area while they're away. Mrs. Hallowell told my *ant* and *onkel* about the cameras because she knows how the Amish feel about photography. But it's not an issue because we don't trespass on her land, and out of respect for our beliefs, she disabled the cameras in the places we're allowed to disembark."

Surveillance cameras? Surely the FBI would have obtained the footage from Mrs. Hallowell, right? Since they hadn't found any evidence, Caleb figured he could likely rule out searching the grounds near her mansion and focus on scoping out the areas where there were no cameras. "But how do your guests know where they're allowed to go and where they aren't?"

"There are no-trespassing signs. And information about where they *can* go is included in the guests' *wilkom* pamphlet."

"*Wilkom* pamphlet?" Caleb repeated. That might provide other helpful information...

"*Jah.* We didn't give you one because you're not a guest, but don't worry. We'll show you where you can go without getting in trouble," Rose teased him over her shoulder.

"There it is, Relaxation Rock," Eleanor announced from behind them. "Let's stop and get out."

Once they pulled their canoes ashore, the foursome went around to the opposite side of the boulder, where its numerous cracks and rounded shape allowed them to scale it easily, even without footwear. The rock had a flat top, which Henry claimed made it an ideal location for picnicking or napping, although more adventurous Amish teenagers—those who could swim—preferred to use the level surface as a platform for plunging into the water ten feet below.

"That path you see over there leads to a dirt road and the dirt road takes you to the main highway," he explained, pointing to an opening through the woods. "Cars are prohibited on the dirt road, but Mrs. Hallowell lets us hitch our buggies at the other end of the path. The district keeps a cart there so the *leit* can wheel in rowboats and canoes when they *kumme* fishing."

Eleanor added, "The last Saturday in August before Labor Day weekend, the camp hosts a fish fry and canoe race for our settlement. Sometimes people *kumme* from Unity, too. Relaxation Rock is where the race begins."

"Sounds like *schpass*. I wonder if I'll be around for it," Caleb commented before he realized what he was saying.

"Why wouldn't you be? Didn't Nancy and Sol tell you the camp is still open then?" Eleanor asked but she didn't wait for an answer. "See, once the guests depart on that Saturday—I think it's August 27 this year—the next guests aren't allowed in until the following Monday so we have the camp completely to ourselves. Everyone has a *wunderbaar* time."

"*Gut*. I'll look forward to it," Caleb said.

Henry smacked an insect against his arm. "The blackflies are eating me alive. Let's go." He scooted to the edge of the rock and slid down the way they'd come up. Eleanor and Caleb followed, and Rose was last. As Henry pushed his canoe into the shallows, Eleanor scampered over to Caleb's canoe and planted herself on the seat in the front.

"C'mon, Caleb," she wheedled sweetly, handing him the paddle. "I want to show you where Kissing Cove is."

Rose had no choice but to join Henry in his canoe. She was glad he didn't paddle as quickly as Caleb because from this distance she couldn't hear Eleanor flirting. For some reason, it really grated on her nerves. Realizing she legitimately *was* a bit weary, Rose exhaled heavily and rode in silence with her eyelids lowered until they arrived at so-called Kissing Cove,

fittingly named by the Amish youth who found the se-
cluded area perfect for a little romantic privacy.

"It's too rocky to paddle any closer to shore," Henry
warned. "How about if we race to Paradise Point?"

Always up for a challenge, Rose taunted, "*Jah*, last
team there is pair of pungent pickerel!"

Henry and Rose hadn't journeyed as far into the cove
as Caleb and Eleanor, and they had a head start on their
way out. Henry must have been saving his strength because suddenly they glided through the water, agile as
a loon. Caleb, however, was even more vigorous, and
within a few minutes he and Eleanor pulled alongside
them. Rose scooped handfuls of water sideways, causing Eleanor to squeal. Caleb used his paddle to splash
back at Rose, and in the process he somehow managed
to knock off his own hat and had to reverse in order to
pluck it from where it floated on the water's surface.

"What took you so long?" Rose jeered impishly when
the couple eventually joined her and Henry onshore
near the trail marker for Paradise Point. "You're all
wet. Did you fall in?"

"*Voll schpass,*" Caleb replied, flashing those shiny
white teeth at her.

She fetched a bag of paper cups and a thermal jug
from his canoe. Rose and Eleanor perched on a fallen
log, and Caleb and Henry leaned against individual
rocks as they drank the sun-brewed mint iced tea Rose
had brought. When they were done, she collected
the used cups to discard at the camp and picked up a
crushed beer can nearby, too.

"One of the guests must have left this, even though

we warn them not to litter," she explained to Caleb. "We don't want our hiking privileges revoked."

"Anyone want to jog up to the Point?" Henry asked, obviously showing off.

His sister objected. "Barefoot? No way. My feet are too tender and Caleb already has blisters. We'll stay here, but you and Rose can go ahead if you'd like to."

"I *wouldn't* like to," Rose said. She was sick of Eleanor trying to fob off her brother so she could be alone with Caleb. "I'm getting *hungerich* and I want to go back to the *haus*. It's our turn to race. You against me, Eleanor."

"No fair," the younger woman whined. "You're a lot more muscular than I am. Look how broad your shoulders are compared to mine!"

Oh, brother. If Eleanor was trying to be insulting, she'd have to try harder than that. Rose liked her athletic build, and she carried herself with confidence. Turning Eleanor's words around, she admitted, "You're right, you probably *are* a lot weaker than I am. I'll just have to race Caleb instead."

Caleb looked amused. "You think you're up for that?"

"I could beat you blindfolded."

"You're on," Caleb agreed. "Eleanor, hand me your kerchief, please."

"Why?"

"Rose thinks she can beat me blindfolded."

"That was a figure of speech," Rose said. "I'm not really going to race you blindfolded."

"Afraid you'll lose?" Caleb's eyes twinkled charmingly, but not irresistibly.

"I'm not *afraid* of anything," Rose declared. "But if one of the canoes capsizes and sinks, I'll have to re-place it."

"C'mon, Rose, this will be *schpass*," Henry spurred her on. "Nothing will happen to the canoes. I'll direct you straight to shore. Trust me."

"Rose doesn't trust *anyone*," Eleanor goaded.

Bristling, Rose responded by taking a seat in the bow of the canoe and placing the paddle across her knees. Then she unpinned her kerchief and folded it into a long rectangle to tie over her eyes. Caleb sat down and began to do the same with Eleanor's head covering.

"No peeking," he warned.

Rose stuck her tongue out at him before she realized he couldn't see her anyway.

"On your mark, get set, go!" Eleanor yelled, and Rose paddled with all her might.

"Go, Rose, go!" Henry yelled. "Right, paddle on your right side! Now left. Left."

Rose followed his instructions but she could barely hear him over Eleanor's screams. "Hurry, Caleb, hurry! You're passing her, you're passing her!"

Fighting the urge to laugh—this really was a crazy thing to be doing, and it was a lot of fun—Rose pulled through the water in deep, hard strokes, her muscles burning until Henry finally announced, "We're almost there. This is the final stretch, Rose! We're winning—"

Not five seconds later, Caleb and Eleanor's canoe knocked into theirs so forcefully Rose felt like her mo-lars were vibrating. She lurched sideways, nearly top-pling into the water. When she peeled the kerchief from her eyes she saw they were headed straight for a rock that peaked just below the water's surface. There was no time to change course and she winced as it scraped against the hull of the canoe, nearly bringing them to a standstill as they passed over it.

Onshore, Eleanor was getting out of the canoe, shouting, "You did it, Caleb! We won!"

Caleb paid her no attention. "Are you okay?" he called to Henry and Rose.

"We're fine, but I'm not so sure about the boat," Henry replied.

Rose propelled them the rest of the way to shore, where Caleb and Henry flipped the canoe to take a look. Sure enough, a gouge marred the hull and a deep scratch ran half the length of the vessel. *And* this *is exactly what happens when you blindly trust someone*, Rose thought. "Great, just what I needed—one more thing to try to rebuild," she uttered in disgust.

Too exasperated to say anything else, she stormed toward the house, but not before Eleanor remarked to Caleb, "Kind of a sore loser, isn't she?"

Caleb pressed his fingertips gently against the dent on the canoe's hull, but it didn't give way—a good sign. It meant the damage was mostly cosmetic and he could easily fix it if he picked up a few supplies. He asked Henry to help him carry the canoe to the barn since he didn't want any of the guests using it until it was repaired.

"I hope Rose doesn't blame me for causing her to run over the rock. It's not my fault we bumped into them," Eleanor insisted as she trailed after the men. "I couldn't see around you, Caleb, so I didn't know we were about to collide."

"If it's anyone's fault, it's mine," Caleb reassured her. "I shouldn't have suggested we race like that in the first place. But, uh, right now Rose seems pretty upset and it's time for me to *millich* the *kuh*, so—"

Henry got the message. "*Jah*, we should leave now. We'll go get our shoes and, uh, can you tell Rose I said *mach's gut*?"

"Sure," Caleb agreed. *If she's still talking to me.*

"See you tomorrow, Caleb," Eleanor said. "I hope Rose doesn't chew you out too bad."

I hope the same thing. When he had finished with the evening milking, Caleb brought the pail to the house, but Rose didn't answer the door. Since he didn't want to spoil more milk by leaving it outside in the heat again, he opened the door and called, "Rose?"

She must have been upstairs or in the bathroom because she didn't answer, so Caleb tentatively scanned the entryway. A few feet farther inside was a narrow desk, and atop of it a notebook labeled Reservations caught his eye. *Aha!* He tiptoed to the desk. With trembling hands, he flipped the book open to scan the entries. He wasn't sure how he would identify the strangely behaved couple's names or cabin number, but he figured any information he could glean would be helpful.

"What are you doing?" Rose demanded, leaning over the banister halfway down the stairs. He slapped the book closed without finding the late-May entries.

"I, uh, brought in the *millich*. You didn't *kumme* to the door when I knocked or called so I let myself in."

"I can see that. But why are you rifling through that paperwork?"

"I wanted… I wanted one of the *wilkom* pamphlets you told me about." It wasn't an outright lie—Caleb *did* want a welcome pamphlet—but this time he somehow felt guiltier for misleading her than when he'd given vague responses to Rose's other questions.

She bustled down the stairs, reached in front of him and pulled a tri-fold sheet of paper from a folder beneath the reservation book. "Here."

"Denki." He exchanged the pail for the paper. "I also wanted to say I'm really sorry about the canoe. I'll pay for the supplies to repair it—which I'll do myself. The damage is minimal. I'll have it shipshape again by midday tomorrow."

She peered at him through narrowed eyes. "I'd appreciate that and so will our guests." She moved toward the door and held it open, obviously dismissing him.

Ordinarily he would have beaten a path back to his cabin, but Caleb felt compelled to get back on better terms with Rose again. "So, uh, does this mean you're not making me any supper?"

Shifting the milk pail to her other hand, she kept the door propped open with her foot. "Seriously?" She arched an eyebrow at him. "You've got some nerve, you know that?"

He shrugged. "What can I say? I'm *hungerich* and your meals are the highlight of my day."

Watching the smile come over Rose's face was like

watching a flower open. "Fine," she conceded. "Since it's the *Sabbat*, we're just having leftovers. You can wait on the porch while I prepare them."

Caleb hummed as he rocked in the glider and reveled in the view of the lake until Rose emerged from the house with a tray. He immediately recognized the dish as being Amish haystack, which was a combination of cooked hamburger and pork mixed with tomato sauce and chopped vegetables—asparagus and broccoli in this case—served on a bed of lettuce and topped with melted cheese. Somehow, no matter what was included in the mishmash of ingredients, a haystack dinner always turned out to be delectable, and Caleb was glad Rose hadn't skimped on their portions. He was even gladder to see the tray also contained two slices of strawberry-rhubarb pie.

"So Hope and Charity still aren't home?" he asked, his mouth half-full.

"*Neh*, not yet. I hope they don't stay out too late. Their *rumspringa* began a couple months ago. They're bright, sensible, Godly *meed*, but they're also a little naive about people's intentions. I don't want them to wind up hurt because someone has taken advantage of them."

Caleb forced himself to stop eating long enough to comment, "I understand your concern. If I had *gschwis-chderkinner* like Charity and Hope, I'd want to shield them from the influence of *Englisch* teenagers, too."

"*Englisch* teenagers? It's not the *Englischers* who worry me—it's their Amish peers. Just because they're Amish doesn't mean their behavior is always honorable, you know." Rose's expression clouded. "And that goes for me, too… I'm sorry I was so short-tempered about the canoe cracking. I know it was an accident."

"*Jah*, but I shouldn't have badgered you into racing blindfolded. You didn't want to."

"Only because if anything goes wrong at the camp, it's ultimately my responsibility to fix it." Rose chewed her bottom lip as she served him a slice of pie. "As a business owner, I haven't always made wise decisions, so I'm trying to change that."

"You own a business?"

"I used to. A restaurant. But, well, I had to give up my lease." She picked a crumb from where it had fallen on her lap, her voice brightening as she added, "I intend to rent a new place in the fall if I can afford it. That's why I've been making so much jam—I'm trying to earn more money on the side to cover what I'll need for a down payment on the café."

Aha. So that explained why Rose sometimes seemed so uptight; she was financially pressured. Caleb felt honored she had confided in him. Smacking his lips, he laid down his fork. "If it's money you need, you really ought to consider selling pies, not jam. People can polish off a pie quicker than they can consume a jar of jam. With dessert this tasty, they'd be coming back for more the next day. You'd make a fortune."

Rose would have been inclined to think Caleb was flattering her again, but he'd devoured his pie with such gusto she believed he genuinely meant what he said. "That's actually not a bad suggestion."

"*Jah*, it sure beats my idea about canoeing blind-folded," he joked, making her giggle. Then his fore-head wrinkled with sincerity as he apologized again, "I really am sorry about that. Like I said, I can fix the damage right away, but that means I'll need to take the buggy into town tomorrow morning."

If Rose was going to make pies, she'd need to buy ingredients and aluminum foil pie plates, and she also had to make a deposit at the bank, so she said she'd like to accompany Caleb. They were working out a mutu-ally agreeable time to go when Charity and Hope came around the side of the house—one of their friends must have dropped them off near the barn—and plodded up the stairs. They looked upset.

Caleb seemed to notice their frowns, too. "Hello, you two," he said. "Is something wrong?"

They exchanged glances before Charity responded. "First of all, we really were playing volleyball at Miriam Lapp's *haus* for most of the afternoon…" she began.

Rose was instantly alarmed. "But?"

"But afterward we went to Black Bear Lake. Mir-iam knows some *Englisch* kids whose *eldre* let them use their speedboats. So we cruised around for a while with them."

Although it gave her the chills to imagine her young cousins tooling around a crowded lake in a speedboat with a teenager at the helm, Rose resisted the urge to express her disapproval. She didn't want to make Char-ity and Hope reluctant to talk openly with her in the future. Besides, the girls were such hard workers, and with their father being so ill for so long, Rose was glad they'd been enjoying a little summer recreation with their friends. "Was someone hurt?" she asked as calmly as she could manage.

"*Neh*, nothing like that happened. We were really careful—we all wore life vests," Hope assured her, fidgeting. "But one of the *Englisch* kids, Oliver Graham, made a point of telling the other *Englischers* we were the ones whose camp was raided by the FBI."

"*Jah*," Charity chimed in. "Oliver said the thieves they were looking for are drug abusers who stayed at our camp and that they're still hanging out in the area. He claimed *Mamm* and *Daed* covered for them because they're afraid of what'll happen to us if they turn them in."

Rose went off on an uncensored tirade. "That's absolute *hogwash*! First of all, your *mamm* and *daed* told the authorities everything they knew. Secondly, nothing ever came of the FBI's search—and if you or anyone else was ever in danger, they definitely would have warned us. Furthermore, didn't you hear what the deacon said in church today about how nothing happens outside of *Gott*'s sovereign will? That *baremlich bu* was just being a pest. I can't understand why he'd want to scare you like that, but what he said is complete rubbish."

"See?" Charity said to Hope. For Rose and Caleb's benefit, she explained, "I told Hope Oliver was being vengeful because when he asked her to go in his speedboat alone with him, she turned him down in front of everyone."

"I wasn't trying to embarrass him. I just didn't want to go," Hope said, twisting her mouth to the side.

"You used sound judgment, and there's no need to justify your refusal to go anywhere with any *bu*." Caleb spoke up before Rose could express what would have amounted to the same sentiment. "What did you say his name is?"

Hope hesitated, glancing at Charity again before answering. "Oliver Graham. His *eldre* own Graham Cabins on Black Bear Lake."

"Did he mention how he heard that the thieves were still hanging out in the area?"

Charity shook her head and Hope shrugged, but Rose got the feeling they knew the answer. What was Caleb planning to do? Tell the *bu*'s *eldre* on him? For the twins' sake, she wanted him to drop the subject.

"Why does it matter?" she questioned. "You know how rumors start, especially among kids. The less attention we give that kind of gossip, the better off we'll be. Hope and Charity, I saved you some *boi*. Let's go inside and I'll get it for you."

She thought she'd made her point, but before she could say good-night and follow the girls through the door, Caleb stopped her. "Uh, can I talk to you privately for a minute, Rose?"

"*Jah*, what is it?" Rose raised an eyebrow at Caleb after the girls were out of earshot. He feared he was about to damage his newly established rapport with her, but his concern was too important to leave unspoken.

"You're probably right. What Oliver told the girls was likely a *lecherich* rumor, but I still think we should be on the lookout for anyone whose behavior seems odd."

Rose's mouth dropped open and her eyebrows jumped up in mock horror. "You mean like…like people canoeing blindfolded on the lake?" she whispered furtively.

Caleb wasn't amused. "*Neh*, I mean like strangers on the property."

"The only people who ever come to the camp are our guests or our friends, so I don't think we have anything to worry about."

"Still, I've noticed you don't lock the door to the *haus*…"

"Of course I don't—I go in and out of it all day."

"Exactly! Anyone could wander in while you're gardening or down at the dining hall."

Rose snapped her fingers as if she suddenly remembered something. "*Jah*, you're right. Just this evening a man drifted into the *haus*. He claimed to be bringing me *millich* and looking for a *wilkom* pamphlet, but he had a funny accent. Clearly he wasn't from around here. Maybe I should call the police?"

Any other time, Caleb would have responded with a wisecrack of his own, but tonight he frowned. "Rose, I'm serious."

Her levity extinguished, Rose huffed. "As I said, my *ant* and *onkel* told the agents and detectives everything they knew, and law enforcement was satisfied there was never any thief staying here. As for someone wandering into the *haus*, the only cash on-site is what we receive from guests when they check in on *Samschdaag*. And I keep that money well hidden until I can deposit it at the bank, usually the following *Muundaag.* I doubt the earnings from our produce stand and my jam would be enough to entice anyone to steal."

"It's not the money I'm concerned about. It's you and the *meed*—"

"Whatever happened to you telling my *onkel* Sol you thought I could chase away any unsavory characters myself?"

"I meant guys from *kurrich,* not potential thieves or drug abusers. You can't be too careful, you know."

"You sound like an *Englischer.* What's next? Is locking our doors being prudent enough or should we install surveillance cameras the way Mrs. Hallowell does?" she gibed. "As I said, we *do* take precautions, but beyond that, we have to believe the Lord will watch over us."

"I *do* believe that. But I also believe the Lord wants us to be *gut* stewards of our resources. To safeguard what He's given us—including our lives."

Rose exhaled loudly. "Listen, I'm not going to lock the door during the day—with everything else I have to do, I can't be bothered to keep track of a key, too. I don't even know if Nancy *has* a key. But I will start locking up at night while we're sleeping, and I'll ask the *meed* to do the same."

They hadn't been locking their house at night while they were inside asleep? Caleb shivered. "*Denki.* That will help put my mind at ease."

But the conversation actually heightened his anxiety. As soon as he got back to his cabin, he closed the windows and door and called Ryan to report what Hope and Charity had told him. "If the thief really is hanging around nearby and he decides to come back here, I'm concerned things could get dangerous."

"I wouldn't give a teenager's gossip much credence. Remember the kinds of stories that used to circulate when we were kids?" Ryan countered. "Think about it—why would the thief send me a note indicating the coins are at the camp if he was going to come back and collect them himself?"

Caleb rubbed the sweat from his forehead and looked at his hand absentmindedly before rubbing it on his trousers. "Maybe it wasn't the thief who wrote the note. It could have been an accomplice who got cold feet or who turned on his partner."

There was a weighted silence before Ryan replied. "I still think it's just gossip, but I wouldn't want to put you in harm's way. If you're uncomfortable, you should leave."

Caleb could hear the heaviness in Ryan's voice; he didn't want to let him down. And now Caleb had another concern to consider: If he left, who would keep an eye out for Rose and the twins? Even if Rose thought they *were* in danger, she probably wouldn't go to the police, so there was no chance she'd go now, when she scoffed at the suggestion she needed to be careful. At least if Caleb stayed here, he could monitor the situation. "I can't leave yet. It's too soon," he told his brother. *And I'm already in too deep.*

Chapter Four

Because Monday was wash day and Rose used her spare time in between making breakfast and lunch to go to town with Caleb, she wasn't able to go berry picking until the afternoon. Kneeling between the long rows of strawberry plants, she had a clear view of the main road, and she was pleased to see how frequently cars either stopped to make purchases or at least slowed down to survey the shelves of fruits and vegetables in the little three-sided shed. It occurred to her that the roadside sign simply said Produce, so she'd need to make another one for drivers to know she was selling pies, as well as fruits and vegetables.

She was thinking about how she wanted the sign to read when someone honked a horn. Glancing up, Rose noticed a tall, slender woman had pulled over by the produce stand. She was leaning into her car's open window and pressing the horn with one hand while waving at Rose with another. When Rose waved back, the woman gestured for her to come to the car. *Ach*. What did she want? The produce stand operated on an honor system, with customers putting their money in the plastic mayonnaise jar used as a till and taking out what was due back to them. Rose hoped the woman wasn't going to ask her to make change for a big bill, because she didn't want to take the time away from picking berries to run back to the house. Rose would rather the woman take the produce now and come back with the money another day.

But the woman apparently wasn't interested in buying anything. "I'm looking for Serenity Lake Cabins," she said. The woman wore bright lipstick and brilliant diamond earrings. Rose never understood the appeal of either; she imagined lipstick felt greasy, like after you'd eaten fried chicken, and that the earrings pinched one's earlobes. Then she caught sight of herself in the woman's dark sunglasses and thought, *I suppose* you *might wonder how* I *can stand to have dirt beneath my fingernails.* She straightened her kerchief.

"The cabins are down there," she said, pointing to the dirt driveway. "I'm managing the camp. What can I do for you?"

The woman grinned; except for a smear of fuchsia across her front tooth, her smile was as white as Caleb's. "I'm Julia, the one who called on Saturday to inquire about a vacancy."

Rose remembered. "Right, but as I told you, we're full for the season."

"I know," the woman replied. "But I hope to stay here next year and I was passing through on my way back to Portland. So I thought I could take a peek at the accommodations."

"I'm sorry, but the cabins are occupied and we can't disturb our guests," Rose said. *Besides, I don't have the time to show you around.*

Julia pouted. "Really? I couldn't find any information about the camp on the internet, and I don't really want to rent sight unseen."

"I understand, but—"

"I won't disturb anyone, I promise. It's just that this is the only time I'll be in the area this summer so I made a point of stopping by. And I'm glad I did because I want to buy some of this amazing-looking produce before I leave…"

Rose understood what Julia was implying: if Rose let her have her way, the woman would make a purchase. "I suppose I could show you around the grounds," she compromised. "I can't let you inside any of the cabins, but I can give you a pamphlet describing them."

"Denki," the woman said, her pronunciation making it sound like *donkey*, and Rose had to suppress a snicker. "Is it close enough to walk or should we go in my car?"

It would have been quicker to get into the woman's car to drive the quarter of a mile to the camp, but as Rose glanced down at her skirt, she realized it was stained with dirt and strawberry juice, and she probably smelled from perspiring in the afternoon sun. Furthermore, while it was permissible for the Amish to accept a ride from *Englischers*, Rose felt self-conscious about riding in the car such a short distance—it seemed lazy. What would the guests think if they saw her?

"It's just down the driveway. We can walk," Rose

said, so the woman grabbed a hat with a big floppy brim from the passenger seat, rolled up the window and pressed her keys to lock the car doors. Unfortunately, Rose noticed too late she was wearing sandals with very high heels and she could take only slow, mincing steps down the uneven dirt lane.

Julia was going to have to purchase a lot of produce to make up for the time Rose was wasting. Immediately, she felt a stitch of remorse at the thought. Her aunt and uncle expected her to be courteous to all guests, and Rose imagined that included future guests, too. She slowed her gait so Julia could keep up.

When they finally made it to the main house, Rose dashed inside and returned with a pamphlet, which she extended to the woman, who had taken a seat in the glider.

"How many cabins are there?" she asked. "I've counted nine."

"Eight—it's all in the pamphlet. We don't rent out that little one. It's the one our groundskeeper stays in." She pointed toward Caleb's cabin.

"Are boats allowed on the lake?"

"We have canoes and rowboats for guests to use, or they can bring their own kayaks. Motorboats are prohibited anywhere on the lake."

"I'd love to see the waterfront," the woman hinted.

Why? You can see the lake as plain as day from here, Rose thought, her patience wearing thin. The "waterfront" was just a little patch of sand. Just then she noticed Caleb rounding the corner and she was suddenly inspired. "I'll ask Caleb to give you a quick tour," she said, waving him over to join them.

* * *

Caleb hopped up the porch steps. "Hello," he said. "*Gut* news," he told Rose. "I fixed the canoe and it's dry enough to put in the water." He expected her to be pleased; instead, she winced.

"Caleb, this is Julia," she said. From the angle he'd approached, he hadn't noticed the woman sitting on the other side of where Rose was standing. "She's considering renting a cabin next year."

Caleb immediately understood why Rose had pulled a face. He shouldn't have mentioned the canoe was damaged in front of a potential customer. With a nod to Julia, he said, "If you do, you'll enjoy your stay. It's very peaceful here. And Rose's cooking is delicious." *Although, I can't imagine someone who dresses like you do would like the "rustic charm" of this place. Doesn't look like you eat much, either.*

"Rose said you'd give me a tour of the waterfront," the woman replied.

Rose interjected apologetically, "I know you're busy, but I left a flat of strawberries unattended in the field. I'm afraid the chipmunks will go after them."

A tour of the waterfront? It was no bigger than a child's sandbox and he had a to-do list a mile long. Still, Caleb was flattered Rose entrusted him with the task. Besides, how could he resist her imploring amber eyes? "Sure," he agreed. "I can show Julia the beach. Not that it's very big, but it does provide an unobstructed view of the lake."

Rose's grateful expression was worth the time it took Caleb to accompany Julia down to the lake. Surveying it, Julia peppered him with questions about the hiking trails in the hills encircling the water, how many houses were built on the lake and whether the public had access to it, too. Although he was relieved he'd learned enough about the area to accurately field her questions, Caleb felt conspicuous when Julia remarked, "If you don't mind me saying so, for an Amish person you actually sound like you have a Midwestern accent, you know that?"

"Is that so?" Caleb pivoted to walk toward the main house so Julia couldn't see his face, which he was sure was glowing with embarrassment.

As she painstakingly made her way up the incline, she asked, "So, how long have you and your wife owned this camp?"

"My wife? You mean Rose?" he questioned. "She's not my wife."

The woman stopped in her tracks. "You *live* with her? I didn't think the Amish allow—"

"They *don't*," he said emphatically before she could complete her thought. Then he realized he should have said "*we* don't," since he was supposed to be one of the Amish. Fortunately, the woman was so chatty she didn't seem to notice his error.

"Oh, sorry. I thought this was a family business, so I assumed she was your wife. Is she your sister?"

Caleb felt conflicted about answering. On one hand, he understood in the *Englisch* world her question wouldn't be considered intrusive. On the other hand, he knew the Amish kept their private lives private— especially from *Englischers*. "No, she's not my sister," he said simply. "I have to get back to work now, so we should keep walking."

"Oh! Of course," the woman agreed gamely and continued up the hill. "You go do whatever it is you need to do. I can find my way back to my car myself."

"I need to speak to Rose, so I'm headed that way, too," Caleb said, and, within minutes, he wished he hadn't. He could have completed three or four tasks on his list in the time it took Julia to practically tiptoe down the dirt road. Her shoes were completely inappropriate for the uneven surface and when she stumbled, Caleb instinctively held out his arm for her to steady herself. She latched on and didn't let go until they arrived at the car.

"Thanks for the tour," she said as she took her hat off and tossed it onto the passenger seat. Flipping her long blond hair over her shoulder, she gave him a once-over and remarked, "I hope I get to see you next summer."

Caleb recognized the sultriness in her tone. He had only been living as an Amish man for a week, and already he was appalled by how brazen the *Englisch* woman seemed to him compared to…to Rose. He eagerly trod across the field to where she was picking strawberries.

"Sorry about mentioning the damaged canoe in front of a potential customer," he said. "But I think she'll end up renting a cabin next year anyway. She seemed to really like it here."

"*Jah*, I noticed. *You* seemed to like her being here, too," Rose retorted without looking up.

Once again, Caleb had thought Rose would be pleased with his efforts, and when she appeared annoyed instead, he began to lose patience. "What, exactly, do you mean by that?"

"I mean you were walking arm in arm with her!" She snapped a rotten strawberry from its stem, briefly inspected it and then chucked it over her shoulder.

She's jealous! The thought gave Caleb a strange twinge of delight.

Then Rose lectured, "I don't know how your district does things in Wisconsin, but here in Serenity Ridge, we don't make a public show of hugging strangers— especially not when they're *Englisch*!"

Caleb's cheeks smarted from the chagrin of realizing how mistaken he'd been to think Rose was jealous. She didn't envy Julia for holding his arm; she was angry at Caleb for acting in a way that was considered to be disgraceful. Although his first impulse was to argue he hadn't done anything inappropriate, Caleb's anthropology background helped him consider the situation from Rose's perspective. After all, he was supposed to be Amish, and no Amish man he'd ever met would have allowed an *Englisch* woman to clasp his arm like that. It was no wonder Rose was disgusted.

"I wasn't embracing her," he said calmly. "She kept stumbling so I gave her my arm for balance. I thought it was the courteous thing to do for a customer."

"We don't need customers *that* badly," she said, shielding her eyes as she squinted up at him. "What would our guests think if they saw the two of you coming up the driveway like that? It would give them the wrong impression."

"You're right," Caleb admitted. "But I was genuinely

afraid she'd twist her ankle or trip and hurt herself. You have no idea how litigious some people can be—"

"Litigious? What does that mean?"

Caleb realized the more he tried to wiggle out of this, the more *Englisch* he seemed. "It refers to someone who likes to bring lawsuits against someone else. I was concerned if she got hurt she might try to sue your *ant* and *onkel*. Try to take away their home and lakeside property. She'd say it was negligence because the road was too bumpy."

"Pah," Rose uttered. She relaxed visibly, sitting back on her heels. "She was the one wearing impractical footwear so she couldn't blame my *ant* and *onkel* for something that wasn't their fault. I doubt anyone would make an unfair accusation like that."

That's because you don't know the Englisch *like I do.* With thoughts of Ryan running through his mind, Caleb replied sorrowfully, "It happens more often than you think."

As Rose looked into Caleb's forlorn eyes in the silence that followed, she regretted having been so angry at him. No, not just angry. When she'd seen him walking with Julia, she felt as if she'd bitten into an unripe strawberry. What was that bitter emotion—jealousy? That was *narrish*. She was not envious of the attention Caleb paid to any woman, especially an *Englischer*. An *Englischer* who, by the way, took up both of their time yet ended up not buying any produce!

While Rose still didn't think it was right of him to allow the woman to wrap her arm through his, she knew she could have brought up the subject in a more tactful way. After all, she appreciated that he had done her a favor by giving Julia the tour, and she told him so. "I shouldn't have asked you to do something that was my responsibility, but I appreciate that you did and you did it so cheerfully. It allowed me to get back to berry picking so I could start on the pies as soon as possible," she said. "The season peaked early this year, and it's just about over now. I need every berry I can get."

"I was *hallich* to help." Caleb crouched down beside her and ran his palms over the tops of the strawberry plants. "Looks like you've almost picked the patch clean."

"Almost, but not quite. I still have to pick all of those rows over there by Wednesday, since it's supposed to rain on Thursday and Friday. The berries always taste washed-out after a hard rain, and if I wait until Saturday they'll be overly ripe," she said.

"I could help you," Caleb offered.

"*Denki*, but it's my endeavor." *And I've learned it's best to manage my business by myself.*

"I don't want any part of the proceeds, if that's what you're worried about."

"That's not it. Still, it wouldn't be fair to accept your help and not share the profit with you. Picking berries for pies I'm going to sell goes above and beyond what's expected of you as an employee."

"What if I just want to help you as a friend?" Caleb plucked a fat berry from its stem, dropped it into the tray and looked back at her. His eyes were *so* blue.

I'm parched, she thought, suddenly woozy. *It must be*

the sun. Rose dipped her chin and reached for a berry. "*Denki*, but—"

"But you'd rather not make as much money as you can?" he ribbed her. "If it makes you feel better, you can owe me a favor in return."

"All right, it's a deal," Rose finally conceded. The truth was that she really could use his help, and she was starting to not mind his company, either.

Caleb wasn't sure why he insisted on helping Rose other than being grateful she wasn't holding a grudge against him for his blunder with Julia. Few women he'd ever been in a relationship with had demonstrated that kind of grace before. Not that he was in a relationship with Rose, but he was glad she didn't dismiss his notion they were friends, as well as coworkers.

He started picking at the beginning of the row next to her, and he worked so fast he quickly caught up to where she was, so that they were kneeling side by side. As they worked, she told him she was going to make a new sign advertising the pies.

"I saw some paint and a stack of plywood in the barn. You could use that," he suggested. "I'll pull it out for you after supper."

"*Denki*," she said, stopping to lift a berry to her mouth. She bit into it and closed her eyes, the juice dripping from her fingers. "Mmm, that's *gut*. I was really thirsty," she said. "Is it this hot in the summer in Wisconsin?"

"*Jah*, it can be roasting there, especially because of the humidity. We get some big thunderstorms, too." Weather was a safe topic; Caleb hoped Rose wouldn't question him more about his family or his teaching. He quickly redirected their conversation. "Have you been hiking in the woods here, by the camp?"

"These woods?" She pointed to the areas bordering both sides of the fields and Caleb nodded. "*Neh.* They're too buggy and there aren't any real paths to follow."

"How about on the islands on the lake?"

"*Neh*, I've just paddled around them. Why?"

"I was wondering if they're worth exploring." *If they'd make good hiding places for stolen property...*

"They're pretty small, but I've heard they provide a nice shady place for a picnic or shelter from the rain if you're out fishing and can't get back to the camp in time. But Paradise Point is my favorite place to get out. It's a steep climb, but the view makes it worth it. It was too bad we weren't wearing shoes on Sunday or we could have gone to the top."

"Maybe next time," Caleb suggested, figuring it would be helpful to his search if he went with someone who was already familiar with the landscape. And better Rose than Eleanor. Or Henry. Or anybody else, for that matter.

"Mmm-hmm," Rose murmured distractedly. It wasn't a commitment, but it was better than a refusal.

Whistling, Caleb continued picking berries so swiftly he soon moved far ahead of Rose in the parallel row, which made further conversation impractical.

"Show-off," she called to him some forty minutes later. "It's almost quitting time. I need to make supper pretty soon."

"You go ahead. I'm fine here alone."

"*Neh,* I can't leave until you do. That wouldn't be right."

"Just five more minutes then. There are lots of ripe ones over here," he bargained.

It must have been fifteen minutes later when he felt a little thump between his shoulder blades. Then another one a few inches lower. "Hey!" he shouted. As he stood and turned toward her, Rose lobbed a rotten strawberry right at his chest. Then at his head. Apparently she had stockpiled the unusable fruit in a fold in her apron and was chucking them at him in rapid fire. His white shirt was already grimy, and now it bloomed with crimson.

He bent to retrieve the berries she'd thrown and tossed them back at her. One caught her right in the forehead and another bounced off her arm. They volleyed fruit back and forth until finally she held her palm up and yelled, *"Absatz!"*

"Then drop what you have in your apron," he demanded.

"You drop what you have in your hand first."

"Why? Don't you trust me?" Although Caleb had been teasing, to his surprise Rose let her apron fall flat. The mushy berries spilled to the ground for the birds to enjoy later.

"I'm beginning to," she said, wiping juice from her forehead with the back of her hand. "Truce?"

Caleb opened his fists, letting the fruit bounce at his feet. "Truce," he said, smiling. Contention between him and a woman had never been such fun.

After Caleb scraped the last bit of cheesy sauce from his plate, Rose stood and prompted the girls. "Let's get these dishes cleared. I've got a big tray of strawberries to wash, hull and quarter." She intended to sell pies only on the day she made them, which meant she'd have to wake by four thirty on Tuesday morning. By preparing all of her ingredients this evening, she'd ensure she had enough time to bake the pies before starting breakfast for the camp guests.

"I took the plywood out of the barn and brought it to the house," Caleb said as he pushed the bench back so he could rise. "I brought up a pint of paint and a brush, too."

"*Ach!* I forgot all about my sign. *Denki* for doing that for me. I'll have to get to it in the morning."

"It won't be dry enough to put out on the roadside if you wait until the morning. I'll do it for you," Caleb offered.

Rose touched her hairline. There was something sticky there even though she'd washed her face after her strawberry fight with Caleb. "You just want me to owe you another favor," she teased.

"*Neh*, there's no payback necessary. Although, if you felt inclined to make a spare pie for the staff to eat, I wouldn't object."

Rose chuckled. "I was going to make one for us anyway."

"*Ach*, then I should have asked for two," Caleb said, snapping his fingers. "What do you want the sign to say? Pies Made by an Amish Rose?"

Even though Rose was her name, there was something about the way Caleb called her *an Amish Rose* that made it difficult for her to meet his eyes. "I guess it should just say Rose's Pies." She added, "*Denki.* I appreciate your help—again."

And she did, at the same time aware she couldn't let it become a habit. It wouldn't be fair to accept Caleb's help without compensating him in some way, especially since she realized he was running off so fast because he had to complete chores their berry picking had prevented him from finishing that afternoon. So, later, when she was measuring the ingredients she'd need for the crusts, she was sure to include enough extra to make a batch of individual-sized pies just for him as a token of appreciation, as well as an extra pie for all the staff to share together.

After she'd prepared the berries and taken the remaining rhubarb she'd frozen out of the freezer, she set out the other ingredients and mixing bowls. She was rummaging through the cupboards in search of extra pie tins when she thought she heard the dining hall screen door creak open. "Hello?" she called, but no one answered. *All that sunshine I got today must be playing tricks with my mind*, she thought and stopped to drink a glass of water.

By the time she left the dining hall, it was almost ten o'clock. All of the guests' cabins were dark, and from the direction of the lake, a loon cried. The sound was so eerily beautiful it made Rose shiver. She was almost to the house when something rustled loudly in the thicket of bushes on the side of the path. "Is someone there?" she asked. A branch snapped and then there was utter silence, which for some reason was even more unsettling. Was something—or someone—watching her? Rose fled up the porch steps, entered the house, slammed the door behind her and quickly turned the bolt.

"What's wrong?" Charity asked as she descended the stairs.

Rose panted. "Nothing. I'm probably being *lappich*. I heard something in the bushes and my imagination ran away with me." It was Caleb's influence—all that talk about criminals lurking nearby.

"It could have been the moose. Miriam's *daed* saw it on *Freidaag* morning." There was at least one young bull moose known to roam Serenity Ridge, but Rose doubted that was what she'd heard.

"*Neh*, it wasn't loud enough to be a moose—and a moose wouldn't have suddenly stopped walking, either. It was probably one of the guests. Or a raccoon." But now she would check to see if the back door was locked, too.

Fortunately, Rose's fatigue overshadowed her trepidation, and she fell asleep quickly and slept soundly until morning. When she headed toward the dining hall at first light, she noted deer tracks on the path and felt foolish about her jitteriness the evening before. As she rolled out the pie dough, she prayed for her aunt and uncle and asked *Gott* to bless her efforts that day, especially with her pie making. She thanked the Lord for Caleb's help, too. Ah, Caleb. *He's not at all like I thought he was the first time I met him*, she thought. *I guess that's what* Ant *Nancy meant by giving him a chance to demonstrate his character instead of judging him.*

Thanks to the large oven, Rose was able to make half a dozen pies before breakfast. After the guests had been

served and she, Caleb and the girls had eaten, Rose retrieved the little wagon from the side of the house to
cart the pies, jarred goods and any produce still fresh
enough to sell to the roadside stand. Caleb walked with
her, carrying her new sign. "The pies will sell out by
noon, you'll see," he said.

Later, as she was restocking the shelves with freshly
picked vegetables, she discovered he was right—all of
the pies were gone and it wasn't even lunchtime yet.
The early success motivated her to pick berries again
that afternoon and she gladly accepted Caleb's help.
Not only did he pick even faster than she did, but talking to him made the work seem less tedious. While she
noticed he asked more questions than he answered, she
figured since his parents had died, talking about family made him lonely, so she didn't push.

On Wednesday the pies sold out by ten thirty—Rose
couldn't keep herself from checking the produce stand
every hour or so—and that afternoon Caleb joined her
in the strawberry patch again, which was a good thing,
since a torrential rain broke out at suppertime. "Looks
like we picked all the *gut* berries in the nick of time,"
she commented, telling Caleb she'd freeze the surplus
strawberries or keep them in the cool of the basement
so she could make strawberry-raspberry pies the following week, when she hoped the raspberries would be
ripe enough to pick.

"I doubt any *boi* could taste as delectable as your *aebeer babrag boi*, but I'm willing to be proved wrong,"
Caleb offered. "Rarely happens, though."

"Nice try," Rose countered, but she'd already decided

she'd make a few individual-sized strawberry-raspberry pies for him to sample.

On Friday morning, as she rolled the wagon to the stand, Rose noticed a car idling near the roadway. A middle-aged woman got out and opened a large green umbrella. "Are you Rose?" she asked.

"I am." Rose didn't mind the rain and she'd covered the wagon with a big piece of cardboard so its contents wouldn't get wet, but the woman extended her umbrella to shield Rose's head, too.

"I'm Helen Berton," she said. "We own the Inn on Black Bear Lake."

Rose squinted at her. "How may I help you?"

"I bought a couple of your delicious pies this week and I wanted to put in an order for more. Yesterday someone bought them all before I could get here. Full disclosure—I do serve them to our guests, but meals are included in the cost of their stay, so it's not as if I'm directly reselling or profiting from your pies."

Rose didn't answer right away. She wasn't sure she could commit to taking orders—her first commitment had to be to the guests at the camp. So far nothing had happened to prevent her from making pies to sell, but if there was an issue with a guest or a cabin she had to attend to, Rose might not have time for extra baking. There were always legitimate excuses for an occasional lapse, but it wouldn't reflect well on the Amish—or on Rose—if she agreed to an arrangement and then didn't honor her word. "I don't really take orders. I have more of a first-come, first-served policy," she said.

"Please? I'll pay double what you're charging per pie. They're well worth it."

Now, *that* was tempting. Maybe if Rose shared her concern about something urgent arising at the camp they could work out an arrangement in advance. Like, Rose could keep a few frozen pies on hand? Frozen pies were good, but freshly made pies were better and when it came to her baked goods, Rose was a perfectionist, so she was conflicted. As much as she needed the money, this wasn't a matter she could decide on the spot. "I—I would have to think about it and get back to you with an answer," she said.

Helen thanked her profusely for her consideration. Then she pointed to the wagon. "You must have pies in there—I can smell them. There's nothing stopping me from buying three or four of them today, is there?"

"*Neh*, of course not," Rose answered, and after the woman paid her, she helped load the pies into the trunk of her SUV. "I can let you know my decision tomorrow morning."

"I understand. You probably need to sleep on it, right?" Helen guessed. "Or is it that you have to talk it over with your husband first?"

Rather than informing the woman she wasn't married, Rose lifted her chin and said, "*Neh*. I don't need my husband's opinion, but I do need to pray about it. I'll be here at nine o'clock and we can talk then."

Because Caleb had spent Monday, Tuesday and Wednesday afternoons helping Rose pick berries, he'd had to complete several of his usual afternoon chores in the evening instead. Not that he regretted helping her, but it meant he hadn't been able to search the woods near the property after supper as he'd intended. On Thursday he'd had some spare time, but it was pouring outside and Caleb couldn't think of a convincing explanation for why he'd be walking around in the woods in that kind of weather, in the event someone saw him. Finally on Friday the rain tapered off and he seized the opportunity to go investigate the area while Rose, the girls and the guests were all in the dining hall serving and eating supper.

But it turned out the fern and undergrowth were so dense he had barely covered a hundred yards before he became discouraged, realizing that if a thief had buried something there in the spring, it would be covered completely with foliage by now. How was he going to tell Ryan about this? After another twenty minutes of plodding through the forest, Caleb gave up and turned around.

Tomorrow was a new day and he'd try again then. For now, his muscles ached and his mind was weary. If he were back in Wisconsin, he'd probably unwind by ordering a pizza and catching a Brewers game on TV, but tonight all Caleb wanted to do was to eat a big meal, take a shower, read the Bible and go to bed. It occurred to him he was becoming a little more like the Amish every day, and he hummed as he headed toward the dining hall for supper and a piece of Rose's pie.

Chapter Five

After praying and giving careful consideration to Helen's request, Rose decided she'd agree to make and set aside four extra pies for her daily, except on Sunday. This was in addition to the pies she'd put out on the stand for the general public. When she told her plan to Caleb and the girls at dinner on Friday night, Caleb sounded bewildered.

"But she's essentially a competitor," he said. "Wouldn't Sol and Nancy object to you helping her business?"

Like so many of Caleb's notions, this one struck Rose as odd. "How is she in competition with us? She runs a luxury *Englisch* inn on a busy lake. It's not as if our customers will suddenly choose to go there instead, simply because she serves my pies. My *ant* and *onkel* would be pleased someone else could benefit from the farm *Gott* blessed them with, and they'd be happy I could earn extra money, too."

Eleanor chimed in, "And if you think about it, she could just show up early at the produce stand every morning and buy the pies before anyone else gets there. At least this way Rose will get double the money."

"*Neh*, I won't," Rose said. "I've decided it wouldn't be right to charge her double."

Caleb seemed as nonplussed by this as Rose had been by his suggestion she shouldn't help Helen's business succeed. "It's not as if you're cheating her—she *offered* you double."

"*Neh*. A pie is a pie. The Lord despises unfair scales," she responded, loosely quoting the Biblical proverb. Rose couldn't fault Caleb and Eleanor's reasoning as she'd wavered about the issue herself, but in the end, she knew charging one customer more than her other customers wouldn't be pleasing to God.

When Rose told Helen on Saturday she'd make the pies but couldn't accept double payment, Helen seemed as puzzled as Caleb had appeared. She tried to persuade Rose to at least agree to what she called a "special order fee," but Rose held firm. She explained the other terms of their arrangement—that Helen or her staff would pick up the pies at the produce stand so as not to disturb the guests by coming to the dining hall. "And I'd appreciate your understanding if unusual circumstances prevent me from baking on rare occasion," Rose said.

"Of course," Helen chirped. When Rose extended her hand to shake on the deal, the way the *Englisch* did, Helen hugged her instead. Rose was surprised and pleased by the warm gesture.

Since it was Saturday, Rose's changeover chores kept her busy until almost four o'clock. She stole a moment to check on the raspberry bushes—it appeared some of them would be ready for harvesting next week—when she walked to the main road to retrieve the mail from its box. There were letters for the girls, as well as two for herself: one from Nancy and one from her mother. She waited until she was seated at the desk in the hall to read them.

The letter from Rose's aunt began with a description of the landscape. *"I love the height of the trees in Maine but I'd forgotten how much I miss the wide-open farmland here in Ohio,"* her aunt wrote. Then she said Sol had completed his first week of treatment with few adverse side effects so far. *"Gott is good and we trust in His Providence."*

Her letter continued, *"As I wrote to Charity and Hope, I forgot to tell you we asked the deacon and his wife to worship with you on off-Sundays, so expect a visit from Abram and Jaala. I imagine you'll have plenty of leftovers to serve for lunch."*

Off-Sundays referred to every other Sabbath, when the Amish worshipped with their families at home instead of together as a congregation. Although Rose would have been perfectly comfortable worshipping with Hope, Charity and Caleb, she welcomed the opportunity to get to know Abram and Jaala better. Also, there was less chance Henry would come over and hang around for hours if the deacon was there.

Nancy ended with a postscript: *"How is Caleb working out? He seemed very nervous. I hope he feels at home and has settled in by now."* Recognizing her aunt's not-so-subtle reminder to be welcoming and patient toward Caleb, Rose chuckled. Nancy would be pleased to know how well they were getting along.

After refolding Nancy's letter and setting it aside to read again later, she slit open the envelope from her mother. She took a deep breath and began to read. *"Dear Rose,"* it said. *"This note probably finds you enjoying cool northern weather, but it is unseasonably hot and humid here. I noticed you didn't take either of your sweaters with you when you left, so if you need me to send them, let me know."*

Admittedly, a breeze off the lake kept the house relatively cool, but it was every bit as muggy in the fields here as it was in Pennsylvania, and Rose guffawed at her mother's offer. She had tried to convince Rose to pack warmer clothing before she'd left, but Rose had argued, "I'm only going to Maine, *Mamm*, not to the North Pole." Apparently, her mother still had her doubts.

Rose read on. *"Your father's gout is acting up again so he hasn't been able to walk, much less put on a boot to go to work. By the time you receive this, he should be better, Lord willing, but please remember him in your prayers."*

Rose felt a pinprick of guilt. She hadn't been praying consistently for her parents lately—her focus had been asking the Lord to heal her uncle and to help her earn the money she needed. She offered a silent prayer for her mother, father, siblings and their families before reading further. Her mother had devoted another paragraph to news about her brothers' carpentry business and her sisters' households.

In closing, she wrote, *"Baker came to visit on Tues-*

day. He told your father and me he felt terrible about what he did and that he's working three jobs in order to repay you sooner than he agreed. He seems truly repentant. If you've really forgiven him, you ought to reconsider him as a suitor, Rose. You wouldn't want to look back someday and regret not reconciling with him."

"Ugh!" Rose didn't think she could possibly be more exasperated until she read her mother's final line: *"I gave him your address as he intends to write to you."*

Rose closed her eyes and shook her head. How could her mother do that to her? Obviously, she'd been taken in by Baker's smooth talking. Just like Rose had been once. She seethed. And what does she mean by "if you've really forgiven him"? Furthermore, how could her mother suggest she reconsider Baker as a suitor? Rose couldn't believe a mother would prefer her daughter to be courted by a man who'd behaved so duplicitously than to have her remain single. She felt sold out.

She slid a sheet of decorative paper from the desk drawer and inscribed, *"Dear Mother, Thank you for offering to send my sweater, but I am so hot here in Maine it's all I can do not to jump in the lake each afternoon!"*

I'm sorry to hear Dad has had gout again. I hope he remembered to use ice on his toe—last time that seemed to help him almost as much as the steroid shot he got from the doctor. I will continue praying for him and for all of you. The picnic you described sounded like fun. I wish I could have helped bake desserts. I also enjoyed hearing

*about Mary's new baby and I hope he continues
to be a good sleeper.*

*I have forgiven Baker but I wish you hadn't
given him my address, as I don't want to enter into
a correspondence—or a courtship—with him.
However, I'm pleased to hear he intends to pay
me back earlier than he agreed. If he does, I'll
be able to repay the bank loan he caused me to
default on sooner than expected, too.*

Rose paused. She'd deliberately included the phrase
"he caused me to default on" to emphasize the conse-
quences of Baker's actions, but her mother might see it
as proof Rose hadn't genuinely forgiven him. She blotted it out and kept writing.

*I've found a way to earn extra money so I'll
be able to lease the café on Maple Street once
it becomes available in the fall. I'm baking pies
and selling jam.*

She wanted to add, *"So you needn't worry about my
future as a single woman; I'll be fine on my own."* Instead, she requested her mother greet everyone for her
and then she signed the letter, *"With love from Rose."*

Since it was past time to start supper for the guests,
Rose put aside the stationery to write to her aunt later
and flew down the path to the dining hall. Eleanor was
already there for once and she'd prepped all the vegetables, so Rose had enough time to bake fresh pies
for the new group of guests to eat for dessert. The pies

were still warm when she served them à la mode, and the ice cream melted atop of the crust.

"Don't tell Nancy this, but that was the best strawberry-rhubarb pie I've ever eaten," one of the guests confided on his way out of the dining hall. According to Hope and Charity, the gruff old fisherman had been coming to the camp for five years, yet he rarely spoke a word to anyone.

"I'm glad you enjoyed it. The Lord *has* blessed us with a *wunderbaar* crop of strawberries this year," Rose answered modestly, although she couldn't have felt more tickled.

The moment was ruined when the fisherman clapped Caleb's shoulder before shuffling out the door and advising him, "You'd be wise to take good care of a wife who cooks and looks like yours does!"

Caleb is not *my husband and I* don't *need to be taken care of!* Fuming, Rose ducked out of the room.

As Rose disappeared into the kitchen, Caleb cringed. He understood the man intended to pay her a compliment, but even by *Englisch* standards, his remark was boorish. It was sexist. And by the way the nape of Rose's neck turned from tan to red, Caleb recognized how rankled she'd been by it. He wished he had spoken up in her defense, but it all happened so fast. Besides, what would he have said? *Rose isn't my wife, but I'm blessed to know her for reasons other than what she looks like or how she bakes?* That only would have embarrassed Rose more. *I'll have to speak to her about it in private*, he thought.

But when Rose returned to the dining hall with a tray of food for him and the others to eat, she was stone-faced, and he thought it better not to acknowledge the man's remark unless she brought it up.

As usual, Eleanor kept the conversation at the table going. "Caleb, you have *got* to see the fireworks on *Muundaag* evening."

"Fireworks?"

"*Jah.* It's the Fourth of July on *Muundaag.* A big group of us goes up to Serenity Ridge for the best view of the display. You'll join us, won't you?"

Caleb had been so involved in his responsibilities at the camp he'd lost track of the date and didn't realize it was almost July Fourth. During his summers with the family in Pennsylvania, Caleb learned the Amish didn't pledge allegiance to the flag because they considered their allegiance to be to God above all, but they were patriotic and enjoyed firework displays.

On one hand, he'd like to get away from the camp for a break, but if everyone else was going, staying behind would give him an opportunity to poke through the woods without being seen, especially if they left before dark. "Are you going, Rose?" he asked. Then he quickly added, "And you, too, Charity and Hope?"

"We're going with Miriam and her *breider, jah,*" Charity said. "They're picking us up."

"*Neh,* I'm not going," Rose answered. "I have pies to bake in the early morning. The fireworks don't start until ten and it takes half an hour to get home from the ridge, so being out until eleven is too late for me."

No sense in me sticking around here, then. "That's

too bad because it sounds like *schpass*," Caleb said. Then he told Eleanor and the twins, "I'll meet everyone there after I finish my evening chores."

"Getting to the ridge can be complicated, especially since the *Englisch* will be on the road, too, and we'll need to take the long way around," Eleanor said. "You're *wilkom* to *kumme* home with me when we're done serving supper. A couple of our friends are meeting Henry and me at our *haus* and then we're all traveling in the same buggy. We can bring you home afterward."

"I, uh, appreciate that, but I'm sure I can find the ridge myself. Rose will draw me a map, won't you, Rose?" One morning when Rose caught Caleb wandering through the woods near the field, he claimed he had no sense of direction, so she teasingly offered to draw him a map that showed how to get from the house to the garden. He made reference to her joke now, hoping to elicit a smile, but her expression and posture remained wooden.

"Jah," she agreed in a faraway voice.

The next morning Rose still seemed distracted as she, Hope and Charity sat with Caleb on the porch, waiting for Jaala and Abram. When they arrived, the six of them went inside and seated themselves in the gathering room. Since it was his first time this far inside the house, Caleb scanned his surroundings. This was the largest room in the house, but it was still small by Amish standards. Hope, Charity and Rose sat on the sofa and Jaala took the armchair, which Caleb noticed was the same type as those in the cabins. He and

Abram sat in the straight-backed wooden chairs across from the women.

"Shall we pray?" Abram asked, and the women murmured their agreement. In the pause that followed, Rose touched her head and Caleb instantly realized she was signaling him to remove his hat. *I'm always forgetting to put it on or forgetting to take it off*, he thought sheepishly. As everyone else bowed their heads, Caleb mouthed *"denki"* to Rose, who nodded, her lips curving slightly before she bowed her head, too. If his embarrassment was the price of returning the smile to her face, Caleb was glad to pay it.

After singing hymns they knew by heart—fortunately, Caleb also remembered them from the Amish hymnal, the *Ausbund*—the deacon chose to read Colossians 3:1–14 from the Scriptures. The second verse especially captured Caleb's attention. It read, "Set your affection on things above, not on things on the earth," and reminded him of the text from the book of Matthew that was quoted in the note sent to Ryan. A chill swept up his spine. *The Bible is full of passages that echo or quote other passages*, he told himself. *It doesn't mean Abram knows anything about the note.*

Yet when the deacon read the first part of verse nine, which said, "Lie not one to another," Caleb would have claimed for certain Abram cleared his throat for emphasis; for condemnation. Or maybe that was Caleb's guilty conscience speaking.

He hadn't outright lied to anyone in Serenity Ridge, but he hadn't exactly been truthful, either. Prior to coming to the camp, Caleb had been concerned about being considered a fraud, being unfair to the Amish and possibly losing his job; now he was more concerned about how the Lord looked at what he was doing. Did the ends justify the means in God's sight? *But if I tell the Amish who I really am, I'll have to leave and my brother might lose his son...*

Hope's voice jarred Caleb from his conflicting thoughts. "The verse about setting our affections on things above, not on things on the earth reminds me of the sermon you gave this spring, Abram," Hope observed.

"*Jah*, me, too," Charity agreed.

The deacon beamed. "I'm glad you were listening so closely!"

He delivered a sermon on those verses earlier this spring? Caleb's pulse hammered his eardrums. *Is it possible the person who wrote the note is Amish?* Then his mind made an even bigger leap. *Could it have been Hope and Charity who wrote it? Or Nancy and Sol? Or...* No, Rose hadn't been at the camp when Ryan received the letter. It couldn't have been her. What if it was Abram himself?

"Caleb?" Obviously the deacon had asked him a question he hadn't heard.

"Excuse me?" Caleb felt the heat rising up his neck.

"I asked if you wanted to comment on any of the verses that struck a chord with you."

While everyone was waiting for him to say something, Caleb drew a blank. Now his ears were burning, as well as his neck and cheeks. He was grateful when Rose broke the silence.

"Verse 13, that part about forbearing and forgiving

one another as Christ has forgiven us…" she began tentatively, her voice soft. "Sometimes I believe I've forgiven someone, but when I really consider my attitude toward them, I wonder if I've forgiven them as fully as *Gott* has forgiven me. Maybe I'm holding on to a little grudge."

"I understand what you mean," Jaala said. "We can pray about that for you—and for each other."

All Caleb could think was, *Who hasn't she forgiven completely? The guest from last night?* If she had difficulty forgiving a stranger for his impropriety, how would Rose ever forgive Caleb for masquerading as an Amish person?

He continued to fret as Abram led them in prayer and then in a few contemporary church songs. By the time they finished worshipping, it was almost noon, but for once, Caleb didn't feel hungry. His insides coiled into a tight lump, but he knew it would be rude not to eat with the others. Afterward he would go out on the lake by himself, he decided. He couldn't keep up this charade. He needed to find the coins and leave as soon as possible.

But while he and Abram were sitting on the porch waiting for the women to prepare lunch, the deacon suggested, "Let's take the canoe out to do a little fishing after we eat. Might not be the best time of day for it, but as long as I'm here…" And Caleb knew he couldn't refuse.

Rose was glad when Sunday was over. The Scripture had left her unsettled about whether she'd truly forgiven

Baker. Forgiving him and accepting him as her suitor again were two different things, weren't they? *But I told* Mamm *I didn't even want to enter into a correspondence with him. If I'm really not harboring any ill will, why do I resent the idea of him writing to me?* Rose's thoughts vacillated so much she couldn't wait to get up and make pies on Monday. Sometimes it was easier to *do* than to think, and Rose's work was particularly rewarding that morning because Helen was delighted she was baking on the holiday.

Since the raspberries weren't quite ready for picking yet, Rose spent the afternoon putting up vegetables and making jam until it was almost suppertime. Most of the camp guests were either eating in restaurants or they were having Independence Day cookouts on Black Bear Lake, so preparing the evening meal for the few still at the camp was a cinch. For the staff's supper, Rose and Eleanor baked the trout Caleb caught the day before when he was fishing with Abram.

"This is *appenditlich*," Charity enthused when they'd finished their meal. "You should catch supper more often, Caleb."

"*Jah*, I wish *Daed* were here to go fishing with you. He loves being on the lake," Hope said wistfully. "Maybe if he's strong enough when he gets home, you two can go then."

"I'm sure he'll be well by summer's end," Caleb replied, nodding, yet somehow his reassurance was less than convincing.

Rose sighed. This wasn't the first comment the twins made that indicated how worried they were about their father's health. Hoping to cheer them, she instructed, "Okay, you'd all better get going. I'll take care of the cleanup tonight. Have *schpass* and be careful."

When she finished washing, drying and putting away the dishes, Rose removed the last of the rhubarb from the freezer to defrost it, and then she washed, hulled and cut strawberries. The process was becoming so familiar she imagined she could do it with her eyes closed; yet, she didn't seem to be getting any faster at it. It was almost nine when she finished and stepped outside into the near dark. The camp was unusually quiet, not a single guest on the property, and as she neared the main house, Rose was startled by a flickering movement ahead of her. *I have to quit this foolishness,* she thought. *I'm fine. Nothing's here.*

But as she set her foot on the bottom stair of the porch, she realized something definitely *was* there: a small and dark animal stood near the front door. A cat. But what was with it? Kittens? Then she recognized the telltale white stripe—it was a mother skunk with a surfeit of kits! There was just enough light for Rose to see the animal lift its tale, so she quietly and rapidly backed away before the creature became more agitated.

Now what was she going to do? she wondered from a safe distance. She had locked the back door and the basement hatchway, on Caleb's advice, and she didn't think she could climb into one of the first-story windows. It seemed her only option was to return to the dining hall and wait for the skunks to leave. After fifteen minutes, she crept toward the house and found they were still there. She left and came back a second time, but they appeared to have taken up permanent residence on the porch, so Rose decided this time she'd wait near the lake.

I would have been better off going to the fireworks display. The thought inspired her; although the hill of trees on the opposite shoreline would obscure the fireworks from view here, if she went to Paradise Point, she'd be able to see into the valley on the other side. *Why not? It's not as if I can go to bed anyway.*

In addition to a life vest, Rose retrieved a flashlight from the nearby storage shed. As she was flipping the canoe right side up, Rose distinctly heard footfalls on the path and she held her breath. It had to be a moose or a deer; no one else was at the camp. Or could it be a bear? Reflexively she picked up the canoe paddle and raised it over her head, hoping it would make her appear bigger, which in turn might frighten an animal away. "Who's there?" she shouted, just as something stepped into the clearing by the water.

"Don't swing!" a man warned. "It's me, Caleb."

"You scared me!" she scolded, lowering the paddle. "What are you doing here?"

"I thought I heard something, so I came to see what it was."

"*Neh*, I meant what are you doing back already? The fireworks haven't even begun yet."

"Well, someone agreed to draw a map for me and she forgot, and I didn't want to disturb her since I figured she was intent on making pies…"

"Oh, *neh*! I'm sorry. You should have asked me again."

"I was kidding. Actually, I got about halfway there and ran into a huge traffic jam, and since I'm pretty bushed anyway, I decided it wasn't worth the effort. What are *you* doing down here at this hour?"

Rose explained the skunk situation and couldn't resist needling him. "I blame you for this, you know. I never would have locked the back door and hatchway if you hadn't made such a *schtinke* about our safety."

"I'd say I'm sorry but I'm not. I still think it's for the best that you lock up."

"Jah, jah," Rose grumbled good-naturedly. "Anyway, I was just about to go up to Paradise Point to watch the fireworks from there."

"Alone? In the dark?"

"I have a flashlight." She shone it in his face, and he swatted at the ray of light as if it was a bug until she turned it off.

"Do you mind if I *kumme* with you?"

"You just said you were tired."

"Jah, but I'd feel personally responsible if anything happened to you," he said. "Or to anyone who crosses your path."

"Voll schpass." She laughed. "Okay, but hurry up—and wear your boots."

As they paddled across the lake, Rose pointed out the fireflies blinking brightly beneath the trees along the shoreline. "Look. Our own private fireworks display."

"And the best thing is they're *silent* fireworks."

"You don't like how noisy fireworks are?"

"Let's just say I've really *kumme* to appreciate the serenity of Serenity Lake."

"Isn't it quiet where you live in Wisconsin?"

"It's not *this* quiet. This peaceful. There's something about being here, where sometimes the loudest sound I hear is water lapping the shore… It makes me feel so calm. I feel like that when I'm working in the fields, too. Probably because when I was young I used to escape to the garden when—"

Rose stopped paddling, eager to hear the rest of his sentence. He hardly ever talked about his youth. "When what?" she pressed, looking over her shoulder to get a glimpse of his face.

Over the past couple of weeks while chatting with Rose, Caleb had occasionally forgotten to guard his *Englisch* identity, but until now, he'd always guarded his emotions, especially those concerning his upbringing. He hadn't meant to disclose his feelings tonight— he hadn't even intended to spend any time alone with Rose. But opening up to her seemed to happen naturally, in spite of yesterday's resolution to put distance between himself and the Amish of Serenity Ridge. So he continued, "My *mamm* and *daed* bickered a lot and it helped to go outdoors to get away from them. When I was gardening, I forgot about their troubles. Tending to *Gott*'s creation made me feel… Well, it made me feel tranquil." *Kind of like how I feel right now.*

Caleb had also stopped paddling and mild waves gently rocked the canoe. In the moonlight, he could see Rose's eyebrows were furrowed and she appeared to be contemplating what he'd just said. After a quiet spell, she questioned, "Does gardening still bring you a sense of tranquility?"

"*Jah*, it does." Caleb's mouth went dry as he anticipated her next question: she was going to ask why he'd become a teacher instead of a farmer, and he couldn't drum up a credible reply.

Instead, she gave him a fetching smile and, before twisting forward in her seat again, she added, "I'm glad. For our sake, as well as for yours."

Caleb let his breath out slowly. He dipped his paddle into the water and Rose did, too. As they journeyed he thought about how amazing it felt to confide in her. Maybe he wasn't being honest about the facts of his life, but tonight he'd been honest about his emotions. And even though Rose's back was to him as she sat in the bow, there was something so…not necessarily *romantic*, but so *personal* about being with her that he'd never felt with his friends or any of the women he'd ever dated. *Rose seems to enjoy spending time with me, too*, Caleb rationalized. *So what's the harm in continuing to develop friendships here as long as no one finds out I'm* Englisch?

When they pulled onto the shore near the trailhead by Paradise Point, Caleb hopped out and dragged the canoe several feet up the embankment so Rose wouldn't get her shoes wet, and then they headed for the forested path. It was much darker beneath the trees than on the open water, so Rose shone the flashlight on the ground in front of her. Caleb initially tried to follow in her footsteps but after tripping twice, he decided to accompany her side by side on the narrow path in order to get the benefit of the light.

"I think we should talk so we don't startle any animals," Rose announced loudly. "Or we should sing."

"My singing *would* frighten the animals," Caleb jested.

"In that case, you should have serenaded the skunks on the porch—maybe they would have left."

"Or they would have sprayed me," Caleb said. "This probably isn't the right time to ask, but are there many other kinds of animals in these woods?"

"Serenity Ridge has a family of moose that sometimes make their presence known. The other night when I was coming back from the dining hall, I thought I heard one in the bushes behind me, but then it went quiet."

Caleb's ears perked up. "What night was that?"

"I think it was last Monday or Tuesday, but don't worry, it turned out to be a deer—I saw its tracks on the path. That's the thing about animals and *buwe*—they always leave tracks. When my *breider* were young, my *mamm* always knew when they'd been exploring down by the swamp instead of doing their chores because of what her kitchen floor looked like. You'd think it would occur to them to take off their shoes before they came inside, but it never did," Rose said, giggling.

For the rest of their hike Caleb asked questions about her siblings and their families, and he told her a couple anecdotes about Ryan, too. Finally the trees thinned out and Rose announced they were nearing the summit. Caleb was about to remark he wished they'd brought refreshments when he heard a noise in the distance, almost a metallic sound, or like something scraping against a rock. He came to a halt and tugged Rose's arm to make her stop, too. With his chin nearly resting on her shoulder, he whispered into her ear, "What was that?"

"I didn't hear anything," she whispered back, and flashed the light into the woods on one side of the path and then the other. Caleb didn't see anything unusual. He didn't hear anything unusual, either, other than the thundering of his pulse, which was probably more from standing so close to Rose than from being alarmed. Half a minute passed and nothing stirred in the woods.

He must have imagined it, Caleb thought, merely two seconds before an earsplitting shot reverberated through the night air.

Chapter Six

Rose giggled when Caleb nearly leaped out of his skin—he was even jumpier than she'd been lately. "Quick, they're starting the fireworks!" she exclaimed as a volley of initial explosions resonated in the valley. She hurried the last few yards up the wooded path into the clearing. From there they'd have to scramble up a gravelly incline in order to gain enough height to see beyond the trees, but they wouldn't have enough time or light to scale the larger rocks comprising the ridge. "It's treacherous up here. Don't trip."

A few more separate booms sounded as Rose led Caleb to a rounded boulder. They hoisted themselves onto it right before the sky erupted into a dazzling kaleidoscopic array of designs and the accompanying cacophony ricocheted off the surrounding ridges and hills. Rose nudged Caleb and pointed to the lake below, which reflected splendorous patterns flaring across the sky.

"It's doubly beautiful," he mumbled—exactly what she'd been thinking.

Rose glanced at his profile, which was illuminated by the prismatic flickering of the exploding fireworks. He'd removed his hat, and his head was tilted slightly upward, damp curls sticking to his forehead and temples. He was slack jawed and motionless except for the occasional lowering and lifting of the long dark fringe of his eyelashes. Rose was nearly as mesmerized by his astonishment as he was by the fireworks, and she had to force her gaze back toward the sky.

"Ooh," she sighed, touching her throat as resplendence shattered the dark.

"Ahh," Caleb exclaimed after a particularly radiant shower of color rained down from above.

When neon green, yellow and purple streaks zigzagged through the night, simultaneously they said, "Wow." Then they looked at each other and burst out laughing. Rose didn't know what was so funny, but she couldn't contain her glee. And when the grand finale rocketed through the atmosphere with chromatic explosions too spectacular for words, they hopped to their feet and applauded while vehicles in the distant valley honked their horns. As it quieted, Rose and Caleb stood shoulder to shoulder, watching the cloud of smoke drift over the far hills.

"That was…" Caleb appeared to be searching for a word.

Rose understood without him saying it. "*Jah*, it was." She pushed the button on her flashlight, which cast a feeble glow. She shook it and smacked it against her palm, but the light remained dim.

"Here, let me try." Caleb unscrewed the top, took

the batteries out and reinserted them; this time the light wouldn't come on. "We'll just have to take it slowly. Let me go first," he said. He made his way down the incline sideways, bracing his forearm at a perpendicular angle so Rose could lean on it for balance. As she did, she thought of Julia. Rose supposed if someone saw her and Caleb just now they might jump to conclusions similar to those she'd been afraid they'd make about Caleb escorting Julia to her car. *I hope we get back to the camp before the* Englischers *do*, she fretted. *I don't want to give anyone the wrong impression.*

When they reached the beginning of the path through the woods, Rose released her grip, but at that second something flapped erratically between the trees. She screamed and grabbed Caleb's arm with one hand, using her other hand to cover her head.

"It was just a bat," he informed her.

"Ick!" Rose crouched lower.

"How can someone who doesn't sleep with her doors locked and who's willing to hike up a mountain in the dark alone be afraid of bats?"

"I'm not *afraid* of them." Rose burrowed her face into her arm. "I just don't like them swooping at my head."

"You know it's a myth that they make nests in women's hair, right?"

"*Jah.* So?"

"And they won't bump into you by accident. They use echolocation and they can catch insects midair, so they have really good aim," he reasoned.

"They also have rabies," she said, peeking over her elbow at him. "Some of them do anyway."

"Well, you've seen what happened to the canoe when you tried traveling blindfolded, so you can't walk down the trail with your eyes covered." Rose understood Caleb was trying to quell her anxiety with humor, but it wasn't working: she really, really loathed bats. "Do you want to wear my *hut*? You can keep the brim lowered so you won't notice them."

"*Them?* There's more than one?" she whimpered.

Caleb pried her fingers from his arm and tugged her hand from her head so he could place his hat on her. Even atop of her prayer *kapp*, the hat wiggled loosely, and as Rose tilted her head to look at him, the brim slipped forward, reducing her vision. "I can hardly see."

"That's the point. You keep looking down at your feet while I lead you forward," he said definitively, clasping her hand in his.

"But it's dark. How will *you* see?"

"I'll manage."

"We're going to go back the same way we came up, right? Because you don't know the way on the other paths and they're difficult to follow even during the day."

"*Jah.* We're going back the same way we came up," he assured her. "Ready?"

Rose took a deep breath. "Ready."

Although she was nervously chatting nonstop, after a few minutes Rose loosened her grip so her fingertips weren't pressing into the back of Caleb's hand. *If only she weren't so anxious...* Then what? She might enjoy walking hand in hand with him? Caleb quickly dismissed the thought, reminding himself that she wasn't holding his hand because she wanted to.

The difficulty of navigating through the dark, combined with Rose's halting pace, made for a slow descent and it probably took them twice as long as usual to get to the end of the trail. "We're almost to the bottom," Caleb told Rose. "Finally."

"Sorry I was so slow. You must really regret not going to Serenity Ridge instead."

"Not at all," he answered honestly as he led her into the clearing. "This has been much more—hey! Where's the canoe?" It wasn't resting where he'd left it on the embankment.

Rose dropped his hand and lifted the hat from her head. "What in the world...? Oh, look, there it is, over there." The boat was floating to the west, some twenty yards from shore.

"How did that happen? Is this a prank?"

"Neh," Rose assured him. "It must have drifted off. We probably didn't pull it out of the water far enough."

Caleb was already taking off his boots. "I made sure it was secure. Those tiny waves couldn't have carried it away—a person had to have moved it." He unlaced his other boot.

"But there weren't any other boats here when we came. And no one can access Paradise Point from the other side—it's private property."

"That doesn't mean it can't be accessed. Besides,

someone might have *kumme* here after we started hiking."

"Maybe," Rose said. "But who would do that?"

Who, indeed? "I'll be right back." Caleb waded into the chilly water until it reached his waist, and then he dived forward and swam to retrieve the canoe, tugging it to shore by its rope.

"*Denki* for doing that," she said. "You must be cold."

"*Neh*," he said. "Just wet."

"At least your hat is dry." Rose pointed to her head.

"My boots are, too." Caleb picked up his footwear and held the canoe steady for Rose to climb in. They both donned their life vests and then he pushed off from shore.

"*Now* are you sorry you didn't go to Serenity Ridge instead?" she asked as they paddled across the lake.

"*Neh*," he answered. "Aside from almost getting clobbered with a paddle and going for a midnight swim in my clothes, this has been the most *schpass* I've had in ages. I didn't even mind your tantrum about the bats."

"I'd splash you for that, but you're already wet so it wouldn't do any *gut*."

"With the way things are going tonight, we'd probably capsize," Caleb said, chuckling. *Yet even if we did, I'd still choose hanging out with you over being anywhere else.*

When they pulled ashore, Rose was relieved to see all the cabins were dark—undoubtedly the guests had already returned and were in bed. Not wishing to wake them or be seen coming home with Caleb, she whispered, "Look, a light is on at the *haus*. That means the *meed* must have gotten home and the skunks are gone."

"*Gut*—otherwise I would have had to pop a screen and boost one of you through a window."

Rose realized she was actually glad he hadn't thought of that earlier, because she would have missed out on an adventurous evening. They flipped the canoe on the sand, and put the paddles and life vests in the shed. Just as they reached the fork in the path veering off to his cabin, a bright light shone in their eyes.

"Rose? Caleb?" Charity questioned loudly. "Are you okay? Where have you been?"

"Shh, you'll wake the guests," Rose scolded. Suddenly Hope stepped forward and threw her arms around Rose, sobbing audibly into her neck. "What's wrong, Hope? *Kumme* to the *haus* and we'll talk about it there."

Rose's heart drummed her ribs as the four of them hurried toward the house. Had the girls received news about Sol? *Please, Lord, show me how to comfort them*, she prayed desperately. Or had something happened that upset them at the fireworks? Maybe Oliver Graham had said something to them again…

Once they were in the gathering room, Hope sank into the couch and covered her eyes with her arm, much like Rose had after seeing the bats. Rose settled beside her and placed a hand on the middle of her shoulders while Charity paced across the rag rug in the center of the room. Caleb, still wet, stood in the doorway.

"What's wrong? Why are you crying?" Rose asked at the same time Charity questioned if Rose and Caleb had capsized on the lake.

"*Neh*, we're fine. You tell us what's wrong, first," Rose insisted.

Charity explained, "Caleb never showed up to the fireworks, and when we got home you weren't here, either, Rose. We didn't know what happened to you. We waited and waited. Hope recalled what Oliver Graham said about the thief, and the longer we waited the more worried we got. I thought Hope was going to hyperventilate. Why didn't you leave a note?"

"Oh, Hope," Rose moaned, patting her back. "I'm so sorry I gave you such a fright—both of you. A skunk and her kits were on the porch so I couldn't get into the *haus* to leave you a note. I thought I'd be home long before you got here."

"I'm sorry, too," Caleb said. "There was a traffic jam so I decided not to go to the ridge after all. Rose wanted to see the fireworks from Paradise Point and I didn't think it was *schmaert* for her to go alone, so I went with her. Somehow our canoe floated off and I had to swim after it. Otherwise, we would have been back before you were."

Rose was grateful he didn't tell the girls her disdain for bats had caused an additional delay. "I really didn't mean to worry you," she repeated, leaning closer to take Hope's hand from her eyes.

"Well, you *did*," Charity said accusingly before slumping into the armchair. She muttered, "*We're* the teenagers. The two of you are supposed to worry about us, not the other way around."

Rose chuckled, glad the tension was dissipating. "We promise not to do anything that will make you worry in the future, okay? But I can see we're all letting our imaginations run away with us. We never worried about criminals harming us before, and we don't need to worry about them now. And I think we ought to leave the back door unlocked during the day like we used to, so this kind of thing doesn't happen again. Especially with the skunks coming up on the porch."

As remorseful as he was the girls had suffered such distress, Caleb didn't agree that they should leave the back door unlocked. "I'll put something out to deter the skunks from coming around, so it's fine to keep the back door locked," he suggested lightly, hoping to change Rose's mind about locking up.

"As long as you use something natural that won't harm our guests or their children, I'd appreciate that," Rose said, but she didn't commit to keeping the back door locked. "Speaking of our guests, we'd better get to bed so we can be up in time to make them breakfast tomorrow."

Caleb bade the women good-night and walked down the path, shaking his clothes so they wouldn't cling to his skin when he moved. Once inside the cabin, he reached to take a dry change of clothes from his dresser and noticed the drawer wasn't closed all the way. *That's odd. I'm usually careful because that's the drawer I keep my cell phone in*, he thought and immediately pulled the drawer open. But no, his cell phone was beneath a stack of socks, right where he had left it. *Maybe Rose is right—maybe I'm being paranoid*, he thought as he rubbed his head dry with a towel.

Stretching out in bed a few minutes later, he reflected on the chaotic evening. Despite the minor calamities, Caleb felt oddly sedate and when sleep carried him away, he dreamed about fireflies and fireworks.

The next morning over breakfast, Charity commented, "Was the view worth the climb up to Paradise Point last night, Caleb and Rose?"

"Absolutely," she replied without hesitation.

At the same time, Caleb answered, "*Jah*, it sure was."

Eleanor glanced at him and then at Rose and then back at him before complaining, "You should have been honest from the start, Caleb. If you didn't want to *kumme* to the ridge, you should have told me and I wouldn't have wasted my time looking out for you."

"I *was* being honest," Caleb protested. "But there must have been an accident because there was a huge traffic jam, so I came back. Rose just happened to—"

"You don't need to explain. I won't tell the deacon." Eleanor stuck her chin in the air.

"Tell the deacon what?"

"That you and Rose are courting."

"We are not!" Rose and Caleb said, again in unison.

Then Rose added, "Even if we were, it wouldn't be anyone else's business and I don't see why the deacon would care."

"Because you hardly know each other. And what would the *Englischers* have thought if they'd seen you sneaking back from Paradise Point in the dark? It's unseemly."

Caleb was indignant. "I'd never do anything to jeopardize Rose's reputation. Or mine."

Rose stood up and declared, "We haven't been *sneaking* anywhere!" She pushed her chair back and went into the kitchen.

"What's she so angry about? I said I *wasn't* going to tell the deacon. I didn't say I *was*," Eleanor grumbled, her cheeks pink.

The twins looked down at their plates and quickly gobbled their food. Caleb no longer felt hungry. "I've got some skunks to track down," he said and strode out the door.

Does anyone else think Rose and I are courting? Or, worse, did anyone think they were "sneaking around," or otherwise acting inappropriately, as Eleanor suggested? Caleb didn't want a rumor like that getting back to Nancy and Sol—they might worry Caleb and Rose weren't setting a good example for the twins. He couldn't let that happen. As much as he resented it, Caleb once again decided it was in everyone's best interest if he spent less time with Rose.

It was probably just as well. Searching for the family of skunks provided him a unique opportunity to look for the coins, too. Skunks frequently nested beneath porches, in hollow logs and even in patches of vegetation in warmer weather. So Caleb had the perfect excuse for poking around the property again and searching the woods without arousing suspicion.

After placing citrus peels around the perimeter of the main house to prevent the skunks from returning to the porch, Caleb set out to scrutinize the forested area on both sides of the camp. But after a week of looking, he hadn't discovered any trace of the smelly little critters or of the artifacts. He'd hardly seen hide nor hair of Rose, either, except at mealtimes. At first he figured her raspberry picking and pie making was keeping her as busy as he was, but after a while he began to wonder if she was more intimidated by Eleanor's comment than she'd let on. Was it possible she was as concerned about her immature coworker spreading rumors as Caleb was? If so, then she probably appreciated him keeping his distance.

However, by Saturday he was so restless and irritable from prohibiting himself from socializing with her, Caleb called Ryan an hour early, even though he had no news to report. No good news anyway. "I've been foraging through the woods all week. Granted, the overgrowth is awfully thick, but I haven't come across anything that looks remotely like something's buried or hidden there."

Ryan sighed so heavily into the phone it sounded like a rush of wind. "Well," he said after a pause, "I appreciate it that you're still trying."

"Don't lose heart. I haven't even begun to search the islands or the places where the Amish are allowed to hike. I'll do that tomorrow after church, since that's when I can use the canoe," he said, trying to encourage his brother. "So, how is Liam doing?"

"Not great. I think he picked up a virus from the pool. And whenever he's sick, he wants Sheryl to take care of him, so I won't get to see him this weekend."

Caleb heard the note of loneliness in his brother's voice, and as he surveyed the glittering lake and felt the soft current blowing through his window he wished he could invite Ryan to Serenity Ridge for a while. The lake would do him good. "That's got to be—"

Rose's sudden appearance at his door caught him off guard; Caleb had completely forgotten to close up the cabin before making his call. He disconnected, but it was too late.

"Who are you talking to?" she asked, peering through the screen.

"I—I—I…" He couldn't think of an answer quickly enough and if he tried to hide his phone, he'd only draw more attention to it. He held it up for her to see and stepped outside. "I called my *bruder*."

"You own a cell phone? I've never heard of an Old Order *Ordnung* that allows the Amish to use cell phones for personal calls," she commented, pinching her brows together. Before he could respond, she added, "But then again, I'd never heard of Old Order Amish men being allowed to wear mustaches until I came to Maine, either."

"*Jah*, the mustaches men wear with their beards here surprised me, too," Caleb agreed. Although he felt guilty for not contradicting the conclusion Rose had made about his cell phone use, he was relieved she didn't quiz him further on it. He added, "I only use this to talk about urgent matters with my *bruder* while I'm away."

"Is there an emergency?" she asked, and the lines of concern etched across her forehead made Caleb wish he'd shut his mouth while he was ahead.

"*Neh*, but his *suh* is ill, so I was, uh, just checking in…" Yes, Liam was ill, but it wasn't his illness that had prompted Caleb's call, and he felt ashamed for implying it was. "He's getting better, though. Anyway, are those for me?"

"Jah." She extended a stack of folded sheets. "Before Hope and Charity went out they mentioned they forgot to drop these off today."

"Denki." The back of Caleb's hand grazed her arm as he took the linens, and her smooth skin made him shiver. "I also came to invite you up to the porch for a piece of *aebeer hembeer boi*. I'm experimenting with the recipe and I need your expert opinion."

"I, uh... *Denki*, but my stomach is a little off, so I'll have to pass," he said, which was true; misleading Rose was making Caleb feel sick.

Rose wished she could fly away like the swallow she spied from the corner of her eye. At least, she *hoped* it was a swallow. She managed to squeak, "Oh, okay. I'll see you tomorrow for *kurrich*." Then she beat a path to the main house. *He's never refused food before, especially pie. I wonder if he's still embarrassed by what Eleanor said about what the* Englischers *might think if they saw us together. Especially since some of them already think we're married...*

Rose had been concerned about that herself, even before Eleanor opened her big mouth, but that was why she'd intended to visit with Caleb on the porch in plain view before the sun set. It was also why she'd allowed nearly a week to pass without so much as crossing his path when she saw him outdoors. She wanted to prove to Eleanor—and to anyone else—there was absolutely nothing going on between them. Besides, raspberry picking kept her occupied and Caleb seemed to be on a perpetual hunt for the skunks, wolfing down his meals and then running off to the woods. However, after five or six days of barely speaking an extra word to each other, Rose had hoped he'd be as eager to catch up with her as she was to chat with him. She was crushed he'd turned down her invitation.

Now what am I going to do tonight? Charity and Hope were helping Miriam bake a cake for her brother's birthday on Sunday, so Rose was stuck home alone with nothing to keep her company except the letter she'd received that afternoon from Baker. *I might as well read it*, she silently conceded.

After serving herself a big slice of pie—*Caleb's loss is my gain*—she carried the dessert and letter to the porch and settled into a glider. She took a bite and allowed it to dissolve on her tongue. Then another. Nope, too sweet. She shouldn't have added that extra tablespoon of sugar. She opened the envelope and removed Baker's letter.

"Dear Rosie," he'd written, using his nickname for her as if they were still courting. She was already annoyed and she hadn't even made it past the salutation! *"Your mother gave me your address so I could send the enclosed money order for twice what I owe you."*

"It's not twice what you owe me," Rose said aloud. "It's a *fraction* of what you owe me. It's just two installments paid at the same time."

Don't worry, I haven't been selling horses again, just training them. I've also taken an eve-

ning and Saturday job at Detweiler's hardware
store. I hope this shows how sincere I am about
earning back your trust so things can go back to
how they were between us.

Rose threw her hand in the air and brought it down
against her thigh with a slap. Baker was mistaking earning money with earning trust. Repaying a debt wasn't
the same thing as reconciling a relationship. It was as
if he thought her trust could be *bought*. As if it were a
simple financial transaction.

> *Do you go canoeing often at Serenity Lake?*
> *Remember when we rowed across the reservoir?*
> *I think of that often.*
> *Yours,*
> *Baker.*

"Ugh!" Rose crumpled the letter into a ball. Yes, she
remembered when they went out on the reservoir in a
rowboat. It was where they first kissed. At the time,
she'd found it very romantic, but it bothered her that
Baker thought about that part of their past. She certainly didn't. And she didn't think about a future with
him, either. She'd told him as much when she broke up
with him. Why wasn't it sinking in? Did he think with
time she'd change her mind?

When she returned to Pennsylvania, Rose was going
to have to disavow him, for once and for all, of the notion
she'd ever accept him back as a suitor. For now, though,

Rose was going to savor her pie and the view. Alone. Without Baker, without Caleb. And that was just fine by her.

Caleb regretted declining Rose's invitation to join him for a slice of pie; not only did his stomach settle down a few minutes after she left, but he missed hanging out with her. More important, he sensed she felt slighted by his rejection of the offer. Hurting Rose's feelings was exactly the opposite of what Caleb intended by turning her down, and he stayed awake most of the night wrestling with his conscience. Shortly before the sun came up, he concluded he'd do more harm than good by continuing to steer clear of her. And as for Eleanor or anyone else gossiping about him and Rose... Well, Caleb would be careful not to do anything to give them that impression. Or at least, he wouldn't go off with Rose after dark again. *But I sure could use her guidance on the side trails at Paradise Point, since she said they were difficult to follow.*

So, the next day after church when the twins left with their friends and Caleb was riding home alone with Rose, he asked if she'd like to go hiking to the Point when they got back.

Rose hesitated before answering. "*Jah*, okay. If you anticipate we'll be gone awhile, I'll pack a light supper, but I'd like to be home before dark."

Either she didn't want to meet up with bats again or else she had the same qualms he had about what Eleanor said. Either way, it didn't matter; they'd be home long before the sun set. Caleb hadn't realized until just then how much he'd missed hanging out with Rose, and he bit his lip to keep from whistling.

"I saw you in the woods a couple times this week," she remarked a little farther down the road. "Was your search successful? Did you find them?"

Caleb's head jerked backward in alarm. *She can't possibly know about the coins!* "Find what?" he stalled.

"The skunks. Or their nest."

His heart resumed beating and Caleb blew air from his cheeks. "*Neh.* I'm going to keep looking, though."

When they arrived at the barn, he stayed behind to unhitch the buggy while Rose dashed off to change her clothes and fill a small cooler with food. They agreed to meet down by the lake, but as Caleb was pulling the life vests from the shed, he glanced toward the main house and noticed a small group of Amish visitors gathered on the porch. One of them—it appeared to be the deacon—waved. Waving back, Caleb groaned. *Not today! It's the first time I've been alone with Rose in a week, and it's the only day I can search the trails.*

Within moments, Abram and two other men traipsed down the hill carrying fishing equipment. Caleb recognized Levi Swarey, who owned a Christmas tree farm, and Abram introduced Caleb to the younger man, a carpenter named Isaiah Gerhart.

"Hello, Caleb," the deacon greeted him. "We figured you could use some male companionship for a change."

Why? Did Eleanor tell Abram I've been spending a lot of time with Rose, or is he saying that because I'm the only Amish man at the camp? Caleb forced a grin and said he was glad they'd come. After he'd distributed life vests and gathered fishing equipment for himself from the shed, Caleb climbed into a canoe with Isaiah. As the foursome paddled onto the lake, Levi commented, "I can still hear the *bobbel* crying from here."

"Levi and his wife, Sadie, have a newborn. A *maedel*," Abram explained. "So he's on high alert."

"Sadie says I worry more about little Susannah than she does," Levi admitted.

Caleb asked Isaiah, "Is the other woman I saw on the porch your wife?"

"*Neh.* That's Irene Larson," he answered curtly. Then Caleb realized of course she wasn't his wife; Isaiah was clean-shaven.

Caleb immediately tried to compensate for his error. "I meant to ask if she's your girlfriend."

This time Isaiah didn't answer at all and the other men acted as if he hadn't spoken, too. *Ach! Now I've come across as being as nosy as Eleanor*, Caleb realized.

Later, when there was more distance between the two canoes, Caleb quietly apologized for being intrusive. "Sorry about asking you about Irene back there. In my, uh… In Wisconsin we're not as discreet about our courtships as people are here. I didn't mean to put you on the spot—especially in front of the deacon."

Isaiah chuckled. "I think Abram was more shocked by your question than I was. You see, Irene's *Englisch.*"

Caleb was floored. "But she was wearing Amish clothing!"

"*Jah.* That's because she's going through the convincement process to become Amish. The *kurrich* recently voted to accept her and she'll be baptized in the fall."

"Aha." Now Caleb understood: the Amish were strictly prohibited from dating *Englischers*, and until Irene was baptized, she was considered to be *Englisch*. So even if Isaiah was interested in Irene romantically, he could never let on. *Kind of like if Rose were interested in me*, Caleb thought before quickly dismissing the unbidden comparison.

"Irene's one of three *Englischers* who will be baptized this fall."

"Three?" Successful *Englisch*-to-Amish conversions were very rare, so three at once seemed like a high number to Caleb.

"Because our community here is small and relatively isolated, our district is more open to *Englischers* joining us than they are, say, in central Pennsylvania."

Why this information should fill Caleb with hope he wasn't sure, because it wasn't as if *he* could permanently join Serenity Ridge's Amish community, not after deceiving them the way he'd been doing. But he felt buoyed by the conversation all the same. In fact, Caleb enjoyed the long afternoon on the lake with the other men far more than he expected to, even though he didn't get to look for the coins or spend time with Rose.

It was close to six o'clock when the four men approached the porch, where Sadie was beckoning her twins, Elizabeth and David, to come inside for supper. Everyone took turns washing their hands in the bathroom. Caleb was the last to enter the kitchen, and as he scanned the table for an empty seat, his eye settled on Rose. Sitting near the far end of the table, she was cooing to baby Susannah as she cradled her in the crook of her arm.

Rose appeared as striking and strong as she had the first day Caleb spotted her paddling on the lake. But instead of scowling at him now as she'd done then, when Rose glanced up she smiled. It was enough to take Caleb's breath away and he was certain the deacon heard him gasp, so he quickly covered his mouth and coughed, as if something had tickled his throat instead of his heart.

Chapter Seven

"I can take the *bobbel* now, Rose," Sadie offered after the deacon said grace.

"That's okay. You probably never get to use both of your hands during your meal." Rose sniffed the dark, wispy hair on the chubby baby's head. "She's so sweet. If she were mine I don't think I'd ever put her down."

"You would if you knew how much her *windel schtinke*," eight-year-old David said, plugging his nose and waving his hand in front of his face.

"Mind your manners, *suh*," Levi reminded the child gently, but everyone else cracked up.

"Talk about *schtinke*, the other night I had a *familye* of skunks on my front porch." Rose delved into the story of how the creatures had blocked her from entering the house. She left out the parts that might be scary, such as why the back door was locked. And the parts that might not reflect well on her and Caleb, merely saying she had to wait a long time until the animals left.

Elizabeth's eyes were big. "Did they ever *kumme* back?"

"*Neh*. Not yet anyway. Caleb put citrus rinds around the *haus*. Skunks don't like the smell of citrus."

"What hypocrites," Irene joked, and everyone laughed again.

And that was how they passed the evening—with laughter, pleasant conversation and good food. They also squeezed in a game of horseshoes between supper and dessert. Rose was on Caleb's team, and although they didn't win, she found she preferred being on his side instead of competing against him, the way she'd done when they'd raced blindfolded.

"You and Caleb ought to pair up for the canoe race in August," Jaala suggested as she helped Rose serve pie afterward. Sadie and Irene quickly echoed the idea.

"*Neh*, absolutely not. It wouldn't be right," Abram interjected, nearly causing Rose to upset the tray of dessert. *Why would he forbid us to pair up?*

His wife asked him the same question. "What's wrong with them being a team?"

"With the lake in their front yard, they have an unfair advantage. They can practice paddling together all the time," he said.

"*Ach!* When do they have time? The work here at the camp keeps them running ragged and on *Suundaag*, the one day when they actually could spend a little leisure time on the lake, you show up to go fishing," Jaala lectured Abram sternly. But Rose noticed a twinkle in his eye; he'd been teasing. She giggled and glanced at

Caleb to see his reaction, but he seemed too preoccupied with his pie to look up.

"I promise I won't *kumme* here to fish next week, so you two can practice paddling to your hearts' content," Abram said with a wink at Rose.

Relieved the deacon didn't appear fazed by the idea of Rose and Caleb canoeing together, Rose said, "That's okay. You're *wilkom* anytime. You *all* are." She meant it, too. The *leit* in Serenity Ridge were so warm she already felt as if they were close friends.

In the week that followed, the first blueberries began to ripen, so Rose made haste to pick as many raspberries as she could before she started harvesting the blueberries, too. Because her aunt and uncle didn't have enough land or the right soil for growing wild, or lowbush, blueberries—the kind Maine was famous for—they grew cultivated, or highbush, blueberries. As with the raspberries, Rose would have to pick the blueberries by hand instead of using a rake.

While she hardly had a free moment, she was glad things had returned to normal between Caleb and her, and she couldn't wait to go hiking with him the following Sunday. But as it turned out, the day dawned with a severe thunderstorm, and a steady rain persisted into the evening hours.

Nearly another week passed in the blink of an eye, and Rose was astounded on Friday morning when Hope reminded her at breakfast the blueberry festival was only eight days away.

Rose was incredulous—and frantic. "I thought the blueberry festival wasn't until the last weekend in July?"

"*Jah*, it's on July 30 and 31 this year. That's next Saturday and Sunday."

"What's the blueberry festival?" Caleb asked. He must have forgotten to put his hat on again because his face was nearly as bronzed as his arms, which in turn made his eyes appear nearly as blue as…as *blueberries*. Rose glanced away.

Charity explained the festival was an *Englisch* celebration to kick off the blueberry season. A lot of Maine communities hosted a blueberry festival later in the summer, but Serenity Ridge held theirs early to avoid the competition. Every year women in the district pitched in to rent a tent on the festival grounds so they could sell their goods to locals and tourists. "It's not just baked goods, either. Some women sell blueberry candles or dishcloths with blueberries embroidered onto them. This year Jaala is selling quilts. As long as they're blue or have berries on them, they're fair game."

"You'll sell pies and jam, won't you, Rose?" Caleb asked.

"*Jah*." Rose explained Jaala and Abram would pick up the items on Saturday morning and sell them for her, since she would be checking guests out and helping the girls prepare the cabins for the next group. "I'll be so busy this week I won't know if I'm coming or going."

"I can help pick berries," Caleb volunteered.

"*Denki*, but I'll manage." Rose hadn't meant to complain; she was only thinking aloud.

"Is there anything I can do to make the week more pleasant for you?"

Warmed by his offer, Rose responded, "*Jah*, you can start it off by canoeing with me on the *Sabbat*."

"That would be a pleasure for me, too," Caleb replied, and Rose thought she heard Eleanor snicker. *Go ahead and tell the deacon you think we're flirting. He won't care!*

But on Sunday, a pair of families who were vacationing together took the canoes and rowboats out on the lake and didn't return until evening. And since Hope and Charity were both feeling under the weather, they came straight home after church. The four of them hung out on the porch, chatting and working on a jigsaw puzzle, which was engaging in its own way, yet not quite the kind of afternoon Rose had hoped to share with Caleb.

The following week Rose spent so much time picking raspberries and blueberries and making jam she gave up trying to remove the little prickles from her wrists or scrub the purple stains from her fingers. One morning she told the twins she'd even had a dream about making jam that was so real she could smell the sweetness in her sleep—only to wake and discover it was her own hands, tucked beneath her cheek, that she'd smelled. But her efforts paid off and by Saturday morning, she had two crates packed with blueberry and mixed-berry jam.

She'd risen at three thirty to make an extra dozen pies for the festival, as well as those for Helen and the produce stand. Jaala and Abram were supposed to arrive at eight, but they still hadn't shown by the time everyone finished breakfast. Checking out guests and cleaning the cabins was always a race against time and

Rose didn't have a moment to spare, so Caleb offered to jog to the phone shanty about half a mile down the road to check for a voice mail message.

Some twenty minutes later he reported, "Abram said unfortunately they're both sick. Jaala sends her apologies, but they won't be able to take the pies and jam to the fair."

"Oh, *neh*!" Rose wailed. "Of all the days for this to happen, it had to be changeover day!"

Caleb offered to deliver the goods to the fair himself, but Rose reminded him there was a picture window that needed patching in cabin five and a problem with the bathroom sink in cabin seven. Besides, she doubted he'd want to stick around the festival—he'd be the only man among the half-dozen Amish women selling their wares. And she didn't feel right imposing on one of them to share their display space. "I'll put the pies out on the stand with the others. At least some of them will sell. And the jam will, too, over time…"

"I'll go," Charity volunteered. "You'll be short one person cleaning the cabins and making supper, so it will be tough, but we've managed it before."

Though Rose was skeptical, Caleb convinced her, saying, "I need to run to the hardware store to get screening for the window anyway. So I'll drop Charity off and I can help her cart everything to the tent, too." Hope agreed it was a good idea.

Eleanor was the only one who voiced an objection. "If Hope and I are going to have to work twice as hard, will we get paid twice as much?" she asked, a sly glint in her eyes.

With an equally impish smirk, Rose retorted, "Considering you usually work *half* as hard as you're expected to, you're already getting paid twice as much as you should."

"Hey! I was only teasing!" To Rose's surprise, tears instantly replaced the glint in Eleanor's eyes.

"I was, too," Rose said quickly, even though that was only half-true. "When you're not chatting, you're a *gut* worker. Otherwise, Nancy wouldn't keep you on here." Eleanor crossed her arms over her chest and looked away without acknowledging Rose had spoken.

Caleb broke the tension by announcing he'd go get a folding table for Charity to use and then hitch the horse. Eleanor skulked off to start cleaning, and Hope and Rose carried pies to the buggy while Charity wheeled the wagon full of jam behind them. As she was handing a crate off to Caleb in the back of the buggy, Charity let go before Caleb had it firmly gripped in his hands, so that his end tipped downward. He managed to right it, but the glass jars clinked hard against each other inside the wooden box.

"Careful!" Rose barked. Maybe she should try to sell these at the stand after all.

Caleb was surprised at how harsh Rose sounded, especially considering he and Charity were doing their best to support her. Her comment to Eleanor hadn't been very kind, either. But he knew how hard she'd labored to make the extra jam and pies this past week and how important earning extra money was to her, so he mumbled an apology before he and Charity took off for the festival.

Within an hour, he was back. As he entered cabin five to patch the screen, he noticed the hinges on the door, as well as on the side window, were rusty. There wasn't enough time to remove and replace them, so he sprayed them with oil and scrubbed them as clean as he could for now. As he worked, the rust brought to mind the verses in Matthew warning against storing treasures where rust or moths could ruin them, and Caleb silently said a prayer for his brother.

Ryan seemed to be growing more despondent the longer the investigation dragged on without resolution and without him being reinstated to his position at the museum. After two weekends of not being able to use the canoe, Caleb was eager to get back on the lake and explore Paradise Point, and he intended to ask Rose to go with him after worship services on Sunday. Although Caleb highly doubted he'd find anything of significance, he at least wanted to be able to tell his brother he was exhausting every last possibility.

It was nearly four o'clock when Caleb finished his other groundskeeper and maintenance duties, including repairing the sink in cabin seven. On his way to the barn he stopped at the dining hall to tell Rose there had been a big crowd at the festival so he was hopeful her pies and jam would sell out. He found her in the kitchen, bent over the sink. She was peeling potatoes so vigorously the skins were flying everywhere. When he entered the room, she turned toward him, glowering. She had a strip of potato in her hair.

"Please don't tell me something went wrong when you took Charity to the festival. I can't take one more bad thing happening today."

"*Neh*, nothing went wrong. The tent is right near the entrance so it was getting a lot of foot traffic, and unloading the jam was a snap," he assured her. "Why, what went wrong here?"

"What didn't?" Rose scooped the peels out of the sink and plopped them in the compost bin. Then she took out the cutting board and a knife and began quartering the potatoes as she recited a litany of mishaps. First, she hadn't realized she'd run out of egg noodles until she began preparing supper. Hope had had to go to town to buy more. Meanwhile, Eleanor claimed to have a stomachache, so Rose didn't want her handling the food and she sent her up to the main house to check in the late arrivals. There were three more *familye* who still weren't there yet, and one of them was lost and kept calling to ask for directions. "I don't know how I'm going to serve supper on time if I keep getting interrupted."

"I'm not familiar enough with Serenity Ridge to give directions, but I can run the phone up to Eleanor," he volunteered. "And when Hope comes, I'll take care of the buggy so she can hurry back here to help you."

"That would be *wunderbaar*." Rose handed him the cell phone. "And if it seems like Eleanor is slacking off, send her back down. She might not be able to serve food, but she can empty the compost and sweep the floors. We're not paying her to sit on the porch."

But Eleanor wasn't on the porch when Caleb got to

the house. He knocked loudly and opened the door just as she teetered down the hall. Her eyes were watery and her skin was pallid.

"Are you okay?" Caleb asked.

She shook her head. "I just, um…got sick in the bathroom." Shaking, she sat down beside the desk.

"You should go home," he told her.

"*Neh.* Rose needs my help checking guests in. She's making supper alone because Hope had to go get noodles."

"*Jah*, she told me. Listen, I'll go hitch your horse for you and then I'll *kumme* back and check the guests in myself."

Eleanor leaned her head back against the wall and closed her eyes. "*Denki*, Caleb," she said feebly.

When Caleb returned, Hope had the reservation book open on the desk and she pointed to the names of the guests who still hadn't shown up and the numbers of the cabins they'd be staying in. "When they *kumme*, you put a single line through their names so we know they've arrived. If they pay by check, write 'CH' next to their names. If they pay by cash, make a dollar sign. Then initial the entry. I'll show you where we store the money once they've paid."

She led Caleb to the bookshelf in the gathering room and showed him where the key was hidden beneath the clock and a lockbox was obscured behind tall volumes of encyclopedias. "There are only two more *familye* arriving, so hopefully they'll *kumme* soon."

After Eleanor departed, Caleb took advantage of the opportunity to peruse the reservation book for informa-

tion about who had stayed at the cabins in mid-to late
May. He instantly understood why the FBI was frustrated with Nancy and Sol's record keeping: all they'd
recorded were dates, family names and cabin numbers—they didn't even list how many people stayed in
each cabin. The most suspicious entry he saw was the
name *Smith*, simply because it was so common it could
have been used as an alias. After so much anticipation,
Caleb was disappointed. *But not nearly as disappointed
as Ryan will be when I call him tonight.*

Fortunately, the two families arrived within minutes of each other, and Hope returned shortly after they
did. Caleb rushed to the barn to tell her not to unhitch
the buggy, since he needed to pick up Charity anyway. He asked Hope to tell Rose that Eleanor needed
to go home, but the last customers had arrived and he'd
checked them in. At least that was one less interruption Rose would have to contend with while she was
preparing supper.

When Caleb got to the tent, Charity exuberantly informed him all of the pies and over half of the jam had
sold. Furthermore, Gloria Eicher was staying until the
festival ended at eight, so she offered to sell the remaining jars. "Rose will be so pleased, won't she?" Charity exclaimed.

I hope so, Caleb thought. *Because I need her to be
in a* gut *mood when I ask if she'll go exploring at Paradise Point tomorrow.*

When Caleb and Charity strolled in as Rose and
Hope were clearing the guests' dessert plates from the

table, Rose was in a snit. What nerve for Eleanor and Caleb to take it upon themselves to decide Eleanor was going to leave and Caleb was going to check in guests!

"Guess what, Rose? All your *boie* sold—and more than half of the jam, too!" Charity said as she burst through the door.

"Only half the jam?" *That means half the money I was counting on bringing in.*

"*Jah*, but we left the rest with Gloria Eicher. I'm sure even more will sell this evening. The place was packed when we left."

"Oh, so that's what kept you," Rose said, thinking aloud. "Traffic must have been bad."

"*Neh*, we're a few minutes late because on the way out I treated Charity to cotton candy, since one *gut* turn deserves another," Caleb said. "I never saw *blohbier* cotton candy before."

"That was nice of you, but, as you know, Eleanor isn't here, and Hope and I have had to serve supper and clean up ourselves. So now I'm running behind putting our meal on the table." Rose saw the three others exchange glances, but what did they expect of her? She could only work so fast.

After supper was over and the dishes were done, the girls took off with their friends and Caleb left, too. Usually Rose was glad to have the kitchen to herself, but tonight she was utterly exhausted. Since she wasn't serving meals or baking pies the following day and she'd likely have jam left over from the festival to sell on Monday, she closed up and returned home.

I hope Eleanor doesn't miss work on Muundaag, *too,*

she thought as she entered the gathering room. *That's the day I go to the bank, which always cuts into my time.*

After taking the key from its hiding place, she pulled the lockbox out to make sure Caleb had secured the rental payments. She counted the cash and added it to the amount of money they'd received by check. She came up short by one week's worth of rent, so she recounted it. Again, she was short. There were three checks, which meant five families should have paid in cash. Yet when she tallied the cash a third time, she was still short one week's worth of rent.

She had checked in five *familye*. Three paid by check, two paid in cash. The three guests Eleanor or Caleb had checked in must also have paid in cash or by check. Rose opened the reservation book and discovered Eleanor's initials and a dollar sign next to the Williams family name, which had a line drawn through it. Neither the Jackman nor the Garcia family names were scratched out or had any marking or initials beside them. Obviously Eleanor or Caleb had forgotten to put the payment for one of the *familye* in the lockbox, just like they'd forgotten to record it in the reservation book. Rose regretted ever sending Eleanor up to the house in the first place.

After securing the money, she tromped down to Caleb's cabin to get to the bottom of the matter. Once again, the door was closed—he must have been talking to his brother again—and it took a moment for him to open it.

"I noticed we're missing one week's worth of rent,"

she told him. "I wondered if you forgot to deposit a payment into the lockbox?"

Caleb wrinkled his forehead. "*Neh.* I checked in two *familye*—the Garcias and the Jackmans. They both paid in cash, and I put their money in the lockbox, just like Eleanor showed me."

"Are you sure? Because the Jackman and Garcia names aren't crossed out and initialed in the reservation book. Didn't she tell you you needed to do that, too?"

Caleb snapped his fingers. "*Ach!* You're right, I completely forgot that part of the process. But I was very careful to put the cash with the rest of the money."

"Are you positive? You were doing a lot of running around today, so maybe you set the money aside before you went to pick up Charity or—"

Caleb squared his shoulders and crossed his arms. "No matter how many times you ask, my answer is going to be the same. I put both payments in the lockbox," he enunciated loudly. "Did you ever consider you or Eleanor forgot to deposit the cash *you* received?"

Rose didn't understand why Caleb was being so defensive—she was only trying to jog his memory. "I'm certain *I* didn't forget. Obviously Eleanor isn't here, so I can't ask her, but since she initialed the one guest she checked in and you didn't initial either of yours, it seemed more likely *you* forgot to lock up the cash, too. Or something."

Caleb didn't appreciate Rose's tone. He felt she was coming dangerously close to accusing him of stealing.

"What do you mean, *or something*? I certainly didn't *take* the money, if that's what you're implying."

"I'm not *implying* anything," Rose echoed scornfully. "I'm trying to figure out why we're one week short of rent."

"Who knows. Maybe someone stole it. Maybe if you had listened to me and locked the doors to your *haus*, we wouldn't be having this conversation."

Rose rolled her eyes. "That's *lecherich*. The *haus* might not have been locked up, but the money was. And even if someone found the key and the lockbox, why would they steal only one week's worth of rent? Why not take *all* the cash that was in there? That doesn't make any sense."

Caleb shrugged. "Then figure it out on your own. All I know is I checked two *familye* in today and I put two weeks' worth of rent in the lockbox. Which, by the way, you never thanked me for doing."

"*Thanked* you?" Rose's voice was shrill. "I never *asked* you to check them in! And *this* kind of mess is exactly why I didn't!"

Caleb's heart felt like a fist of snow. "You're right, you didn't ask. I volunteered. My mistake. It won't happen again." He stepped inside and shoved the door shut with the heel of his boot. His temper flaring, he stood in the middle of the room snorting like a bull before retreating to the bathroom to splash cold water on his face. He'd been about to call Ryan when Rose appeared, but he was too angry to talk right now, so he reopened the front window, as well as the door. Not even the splashing of the water against the shore could calm him.

I've totally wasted my summer, he thought as he peered out over the lake. *I'll spend another week here so I can search the islands and the trails, and then I'm going back to Wisconsin.*

If I don't find that money, I'll have to repay it from my savings. Then how will I ever afford to lease the café? Rose agonized as she lay in bed. Her body desperately craved sleep, but her mind was wide-awake. *And what right did Caleb have to act so indignant?* She hadn't been *accusing* him of taking the rent money. But considering how careless he'd been about recording what he'd received in the reservation book, couldn't he see why she'd wondered if he'd forgotten to lock up the cash, too? If anything, *he* was the one who was judging *her* unfairly by implying she was unappreciative of his help when she'd always tried to express her gratitude...

Eventually, sleep won out and Rose drifted off, but the next morning she felt annoyed all over again, especially when Caleb hardly spoke a word to her or the twins as they waited on the porch for Abram and Jaala to arrive for worship. After nearly half an hour had passed, Charity suggested maybe they were too ill to come, so the four of them read aloud from the book of James and then sang a few hymns, but the atmosphere was so somber it felt more like a funeral than a worship service. Rose was relieved when Hope volunteered to end with a prayer.

No sooner had she said "amen" than someone rapped at the door—Henry stood there with a pink envelope in his hand. After greeting everyone, he handed the note to Rose. "It's from Eleanor. She's sick and wanted you to know she won't be coming to work tomorrow."

Rose thanked him and asked if he'd like to stay for lunch, hoping his presence would lighten the mood, but Henry said his parents were sick, too, so he needed to get home. "My *mamm* wanted me to ask if you have any peppermint tea or ginger root she can have."

"*Jah*, I'll get it," Charity said.

"And I'll box up some mac and cheese, and cut you a piece of *boi*," Hope offered. "If your *mamm* and *schweschder* are both ill, they won't be preparing meals today."

Henry followed the twins into the kitchen, leaving Caleb and Rose alone.

"So, Eleanor is actually sick," Caleb said after an awkward pause. "Imagine that."

"What do you mean?" Rose asked.

"You acted as if she wasn't really ill. I suppose you thought *she* was lying, too."

"I never said anyone was lying!" Rose protested. But deep down, she knew he was right—about Eleanor anyway. Rose *had* suspected she *was* feigning illness, maybe to get back at Rose for her wisecrack. She justified her attitude by telling herself, *Caleb would have thought the same thing if he knew Eleanor like I do.* "I'll go make lunch," she said.

"Count me out. I'm not *hungerich*."

Now who's lying? Not that she cared if he joined them; it had been a long time since she'd eaten alone with her cousins and she was looking forward to it. But after they sent Henry off with a container of remedies and food, Hope and Charity told Rose their friends were picnicking on Black Bear Lake. "We'll stop to see if Jaala and Abram need anything on our way there," Hope said.

So, after changing out of her best dress, Rose made a sandwich and carried it to the porch, where she began writing a letter to Nancy. After inquiring about Sol's health, she wrote, *Because of the blueberry festival, we had a chaotic day yesterday, but Charity and Hope came to the rescue...* Rose set down her pen and reflected on all that the girls—and Caleb—had done to help her sell jam and pies at the festival, and she was overwhelmed with shame. Caleb was right; she'd hardly so much as uttered a word of thanks. Instead, she'd snapped at them and bellyached about all the work *she* had to do.

Bellyache—the word reminded her she hadn't read Eleanor's note yet. She retrieved it from the house and opened it to discover a wad of bills folded inside. *"Dear Rose..."* She read as she stood near the porch railing. The word *dear* made Rose feel even guiltier about her attitude toward the young woman. *"I have a high fever and won't be able to come to work until it's gone. I had to run to the bathroom so quickly yesterday I didn't have time to lock up the rent from the Williams family. I tucked the money into my sleeve and forgot about it until I changed last night. Hope you weren't looking for it!—Eleanor."*

Rose didn't know whether to laugh or cry. But she did know she had to apologize. She locked the money in the box and ran to Caleb's cabin. Halfway there, she spotted him on the beach, donning a life vest.

"Caleb, wait!" she called, but he continued preparing to go out on the water. She dashed toward him. "Eleanor had the money—it was in her note. She'd collected it but, because she was sick, she forgot to put it in the lockbox."

"Is that right?" he said dryly, not looking up as he pushed the canoe across the sand. Rose tugged on the side so he couldn't propel it into the water.

"Caleb, please, *absatz*. This is important." He scowled at her, but at least he made eye contact. "I'm sorry I thought you misplaced the rent."

"You didn't think I misplaced it—you thought I *stole* it."

She gasped. "*Neh*, that's not true. I didn't think you stole it, not for a second. I know you're not a thief. I just thought you were, you know, careless or forgetful or something."

"Am I supposed to be flattered? You don't think I'm a thief, just that I'm incompetent?"

Rose's eyes brimmed. "*Neh*, I don't think you're incompetent. You were doing so much to help me yesterday I figured your head was spinning as much as mine was, that's all." She let go of the canoe and straightened her posture to wipe away the tears that were now streaming down her cheeks. "But I was wrong to think you'd been careless. And wrong to think Eleanor was faking being sick. As you said, I was terribly unappreciative yesterday. My behavior didn't reflect how highly I think of you and how grateful I am for your support. I'm sorry from the bottom of my heart. What can I do to make it up to you?"

* * *

Caleb was moved by Rose's words and pained by her tears. How was it possible he could be so angry with her one day and want to take her in his arms the next? He'd never experienced anything like this in a relationship before. Oh, he'd experienced his share of arguments, but he'd never received an apology like Rose's, perhaps because he'd always run away instead of reconciling. He'd intended to run this time, too, but Rose's contrition changed everything. "You can help me paddle to the islands. I want to go exploring."

"Th-then you'll forgive me?" She sniffed and blotted her eyes with her apron.

"*Neh*, I already forgive you," he said, and it was true. The bitterness he'd felt was gone, just like that. "*Kumme*, before someone from *kurrich* shows up and wants to go fishing with me."

But Rose said she needed to leave a note for Hope and Charity, and she dashed off to the house. She returned a couple minutes later carrying a cooler and a jug. They paddled to the smallest island first, which was exactly as Rose had described it: a lump of land with a few rocks and trees poking out of it. Caleb doubted anyone would hide anything there. It looked as if a good rain could raise the water high enough to submerge it. The second island was only slightly larger, so after a quick stop there, he suggested they take a detour to Relaxation Rock before heading to Paradise Point.

They were almost to shore when the white sky spit a few hot, fat raindrops at them and thunder rolled in the distance. Fortunately, they made it to land before the clouds really let loose. This time, they took extra care to pull the canoe completely out of the water.

"Follow me," Rose called over her shoulder. She led him down a trail to a wooden birding pavilion, which contained a bench barely big enough for two people. Rose set the jug between them and Caleb placed the cooler at his feet. After pouring them each a cup of lemonade, she shifted sideways to face him. Her eyes were clouded and he hoped she wouldn't cry again. "It's really important you know I never thought you'd stolen the rent, Caleb."

"I do know," he acknowledged. Her expression was so concerned Caleb found himself admitting, "I probably overreacted to what you said because, well, because my *bruder* was once wrongly accused of being a thief and it's nearly destroying—it nearly *destroyed* his entire life. His job, his *familye*, his well-being..."

Rose inhaled sharply. "That's *baremlich*!"

"Jah." Caleb realized he'd better stop talking; Rose was so sympathetic and easy to talk to he might just break down and tell her everything.

"No wonder you were upset when I questioned you about the money," she acknowledged. "But I never, ever thought you'd stolen it—"

"Rose, you don't have to keep apol—"

"Shh, please let me explain," she said, putting a finger to her lips. Oh, her rosy lips. "I think I've told you about my former fiancé, Baker... Well, the fact is he stole money from my business account. He confessed to it and everything, so it wasn't as if he was wrongly accused. My point in telling you this is to say I know

you're absolutely nothing like Baker. I know you're a man of integrity."

Caleb's mind was spinning like a tornado. He was simultaneously delighted and devastated to hear Rose's words. *Would she still think that if she knew I'm Eng-lisch? Would the reason I've been pretending to be Amish make a difference?*

"Caleb?" she said, touching his arm lightly. It set his skin afire.

"*Denki.* I appreciate you sharing that with me," he responded.

"Then why are you looking at me like that?"

Because I can't look away from you. A teeny spider dotted the white kerchief Rose was wearing as a head covering. He reached toward her. "There's a little insect by your ear, here," he said. She lowered her eyelids as he wiped it away with his thumb. His fingers were so close to her chin he wanted to cup it in his hand. To draw her near and kiss her. Neither of them moved. The air felt charged, the way it does right before a lightning strike.

But no, he couldn't. It was one thing to pose as an Amish man: that was a necessary deception. But he couldn't cause Rose to break the rules of the *Ordnung* by unwittingly kissing an *Englischer.* Reluctantly, he withdrew his hand and cleared his throat.

"Looks like the rain has let up. How about if we go for a walk?" he said.

Chapter Eight

"Kiss and make up." The expression occurred to Rose several times during the week following her conversation with Caleb at Relaxation Rock. She was so sure he'd been about to kiss her as they sat together in the pavilion, and she was equally sure she'd wanted him to. For a fleeting second anyway. But the more days that went by without any additional signs Caleb was romantically interested in her, the more preposterous the possibility seemed in hindsight. Yes, Rose valued his friendship as much as he seemed to value hers, but they weren't courting, so a kiss wouldn't have been appropriate. Besides, in less than a month, they'd go their separate ways. *I have too much to do to be distracted by a passing moment of attraction. I'm glad Gott brought Caleb and me here at the same time, but a suitor doesn't fit into my long-term plans.*

Since Rose projected she was still several hundred dollars short of securing the lease on the café, she intended to double up on her baking and jam-making efforts. But Eleanor's absence meant Rose had to leave the fields earlier than usual to prepare supper, and cleanup took her and the twins longer, too. When Eleanor returned, Rose needed to let her know how much she'd missed her help. Unfortunately, her young coworker's illness lasted through the week and by Friday, Rose was so drained she forgot all about collecting the money jar and unsold produce from the roadside stand until after supper.

As she approached the little building, she spied a pair of crows pecking at the ground in front of it. At first Rose guessed a customer must have spilled a pint of berries, but then she saw it was piecrust the birds were eating. *Ach! I wonder if the customer paid for that pie before dropping it.* But when Rose got closer, she noticed a thick purple splat across the "Rose's Pies" sign and she realized someone had smashed the pie against it on purpose. She couldn't imagine anyone in their district wasting food like that.

It was probably an Englischer, she grumbled to herself. It must have been one of the tourists she'd seen slowing their cars to photograph her in the fields lately—the local *Englischers* were too respectful to snap pictures or destroy property like this. Rose sighed. Sometimes it felt like for each step she took forward, she took two steps backward and three steps sideways, getting further and further from her goal, and it made her wonder if *Gott* really wanted her to have a business of her own after all.

She loaded the wagon with unsold items and carefully balanced the sign atop them. Back at the barn she scrubbed and scrubbed until the stubborn blueberry stain faded, and then she trekked to the road again to put the sign back in its place. There was still a faint blotch of blue clouding Rose's name and she hoped Caleb wouldn't notice it. Knowing what he was like, if she told him about the vandalism—which was actually more like graffiti, really—he'd probably suggest they needed to bolt their windows now, in addition to their doors.

When she got back to the house, Rose tallied the amount of produce and jam that hadn't been sold, and then counted the money deposited in the mayonnaise jar. She was heartened to find she had a dollar more than she would have expected, which meant someone had actually paid for the smashed pie. It was a trifling amount, but Rose received the additional profit almost as if it were the Lord encouraging her to keep going. She returned to the dining hall and prepared the ingredients for Saturday's pies with a smile on her face and a song of thanks on her lips.

She was even more joyful on Saturday morning when Eleanor showed up in the dining hall. "I'm *hallich* you're back," Rose said as she embraced her tall, thin coworker. "I really struggled without you here."

Eleanor pulled away to meet Rose's eyes. "*Jah*, but it was probably a lot quieter without me around, wasn't it?"

Rose bit her lip, but then Eleanor giggled and Rose knew she didn't have to answer; everything was all right between them again. "Since you're here, I'm going to run to the produce stand, okay? Helen needs to pick up her pies early today."

With her hair sticking out and a coffee stain on the front of her shirt, Helen looked as frazzled as Rose had felt all week. "I had a rowdy group at the inn last night," she explained. "Looks like you might have had trouble here, too. What happened to your sign?"

When Rose told her, Helen responded much the same as Caleb would have reacted—by suggesting Rose call the police. Rose shook her head. "It was probably just a group of bored kids playing a prank. And they paid for the pie—there wasn't any money missing from the jar."

"I wouldn't care whether they paid for the pie or not. It wasn't right of them to ruin your sign!" Helen exclaimed. "You're a lot more forgiving than I am."

Helen's comment returned to Rose later that afternoon when she saw Baker's penmanship on an envelope she pulled from the mailbox. She was racked with guilt. *I'm so unforgiving I don't even want to read anything he has to say*, she thought, and tossed the letter on the hall table.

It wasn't until she was headed upstairs for bed that she resigned herself to reading it. *"Dear Rose,"* it began, and Rose was grateful he hadn't taken the liberty of using his nickname for her again.

> *Your mother told me you've been busy baking pies to sell—she said that's probably why I haven't heard back from you myself. I hope it's not because you're still angry at me. I know what I did was wrong, but I really* have *changed, Rose.*

I've been learning a lot from working at the hardware store. It's got me thinking about opening a harness shop since I have so many connections with horse and stable owners. Maybe you and I could even co-lease that little building on Fourth and Main—you know, where the bookstore used to be. They sold food there, too, so there's got to be an oven for you to use, and I could set up shop in the rest of the space. What do you think?

Won't be long until you're back home. Meanwhile, I wanted you to know how much I've missed you.
Yours,
Baker.

Rose closed her eyes and shook her head. If it wasn't that Caleb would come running to see what was wrong, she might have screamed her lungs out. Instead, she smacked her mattress with her fist. *He just doesn't get it! I don't want to be his business partner and I don't want to partner with him in a courtship, either! Why won't he leave me alone? Our courtship is over! It's in the past.*

And that's when it really sank in: she *had* forgiven Baker for stealing from her; she was no longer angry about that. She'd released him. But *he* hadn't released *her*—and *that* was what was angering her now. For her own sake, as well as for his, she couldn't put it off any longer; she was going to have to set him straight.

Rose dropped to her knees. *Oh, Lord*, she prayed. *Please give me the words to express what I need to say, and please give Baker the ears to really hear me. I don't want to hurt him,* Gott...

After meditating a long time, Rose stood and pulled a sheet of paper from the drawer. *"Dear Baker,"* she began. *"Thank you for your letters and for the payments. I do believe you are changing and growing. So am I, by God's grace. While I honestly don't hold any ill will toward you, neither do I have any interest in a courtship or a professional relationship with you in the future. But you will always be my brother in Christ, and because of that I'll pray for God's best for you. (For me, too!) Take care, Rose."*

After folding the letter and sliding it into an envelope, Rose changed into her nightgown and then stretched out on her bed. She expected she'd feel at peace now that she'd finally written to Baker. Instead, she felt agitated by her own words. Was staying single and owning a restaurant really *Gott*'s best for her? And if it was, why couldn't she stop imagining what it would be like to have Caleb as her suitor?

Caleb had been calling his brother all evening, but Ryan wasn't answering. It was eleven thirty in Maine, which meant it was ten thirty in Chicago. *Why isn't he picking up? He never misses our weekly calls.* It was too hot to keep the windows and doors closed the way he usually did when he called Ryan, so Caleb reopened them. A rush of cool air lifted Caleb's hair from his forehead. That was better, he thought as he sank into the armchair.

His thoughts turned to Rose, as they tended to do

lately. Ever since she had apologized to him and he'd confided in her about his brother, Caleb had been tormented by his feelings for Rose. He'd never been in a relationship with a woman that involved the kind of emotional vulnerability he'd shared with her, and because of this closeness, a part of him regretted not kissing her when he'd had the chance.

But not kissing her had been the honorable thing to do. To *not* do. A hundred times a day Caleb reminded himself that no matter how drawn he was to Rose, he couldn't deceive her by acting the way a boyfriend would act. Reminded himself that even if she were drawn to him, a courtship with her would be impossible. He might be able to hide it awhile longer, but eventually she'd find out he was *Englisch* and she'd be devastated. Caleb couldn't hurt her like that, especially not after how Baker betrayed her trust. Then it occurred to Caleb he was betraying Rose's trust himself—the difference was that she didn't know about it.

And he'd do whatever he could to ensure she never found out, but that didn't mean keeping his distance from her again. *Today is August 6, which means I have a month left to spend with Rose and I'm going to make the most of it!* Unfortunately, he also only had a month left to search for the coins, which had kept him so busy he wasn't able to chat with Rose nearly as often as he wanted. Either he was busy searching the woods or making his way along the rocks on the shoreline near the cabins, or she was consumed by picking berries and rolling piecrusts.

"But tomorrow's *Suundaag*," he said aloud as he

tapped the icon next to Ryan's name on his cell phone. "Which means I can go canoeing with her…"

When his brother's voice mail came on, Caleb disconnected, waited a few minutes and tried again, to no avail. *Where could he be?* Caleb envisioned Ryan being taken into custody, and he immediately began to pray for peace for himself and for his brother, wherever he was and whatever was happening to him. Not five minutes later, Caleb received a text saying, Sorry, can't talk now. Everything's OK. Can u call me tomorrow after church?

Sure. 2 EST, he texted back, perplexed but relieved Ryan was okay. Caleb pulled the Bible off the top of the dresser. Reading it had become his nightly practice, and it was such a source of wisdom and comfort he was glad he hadn't brought any other books with him to Serenity Ridge.

It was past midnight when he turned off the lamp, but Caleb couldn't turn off his thoughts; once again, they were mostly of Rose. *Ach! I won't be able to go canoeing with her tomorrow until after I call Ryan!* The delay would set him back only a half hour or so, but even thirty minutes felt like a big loss when he considered how quickly summer was drawing to a close. *At least I'll get to ride home alone with her,* he comforted himself before rolling over and finally dozing off to sleep.

On the way to church the following morning, Hope piped up from the back of the buggy, "We figure we ought to tell you this now, Rose and Caleb, before you hear it from someone else at *kurrich*. Last night at the carnival, a group of us bumped into Oliver Graham and his friends again."

Although most Amish considered the carnival too worldly to attend, Caleb was aware it was a popular gathering place for Amish teens during their *rumspringa*. "Did he bother you?" he asked.

"Well, he didn't *do* anything. But his *onkel* is a detective and Oliver overheard him talking on the phone last weekend at their *familye* reunion. Oliver said the law enforcement agencies are closing in on the thief, and when they find him, *Mamm* and *Daed* will be arrested for aiding and abetting a criminal."

"That's *lecherich*!" Rose and Caleb exclaimed in unison.

Charity added, "He said we have limited time to decide whether we're more afraid of what the criminal will do if we turn him in or what a prosecutor will do if we conceal evidence."

"Conceal evidence?" Rose scoffed. "What evidence?"

"According to Oliver, the stolen coins are hidden somewhere on our property and we know where they are but we're using our religion as an excuse not to get involved."

Caleb was incensed but Rose actually chuckled. "That's *narrish*!"

"*Jah*, but not as *narrish* as Oliver's friend, Clint Dale, telling everyone when he was hunting near our property last week he saw *Mamm* carrying a shovel through the woods," Charity ranted. "He said she was probably moving the coins to a new hiding place so the thief could pick them up without being intercepted at our *haus* by the police."

"I told him *Mamm* couldn't possibly have done that because *Mamm* and *Daed* haven't even been home for over a month." Hope sounded smug about proving Clint wrong, but Caleb inwardly moaned, realizing she'd essentially announced the women were staying alone in the house.

Charity harrumphed. "You'd have thought that would have shut them—I mean stopped them from saying anything else. But Oliver suggested *Mamm* and *Daed* probably fled to Canada because they want to avoid the court system, just like the Amish avoid paying taxes."

"But we *do* pay taxes!" Rose said, referring to the fact they essentially paid the same taxes as the *Englisch* except for Medicare, Social Security and self-and unemployment taxes, since the Amish didn't collect those benefits. "That goes to show Oliver doesn't have any idea what he's talking about."

Caleb broke in, "Regardless, I think it's time I have a talk with Oliver's *onkel*."

"The detective? Why? Because of some ludicrous stories a couple *buwe* concocted to antagonize the *meed*?" Rose's voice was high-pitched and wary. "You know that isn't our way."

"Not usually, *neh*, but this isn't a *familye* matter or an issue between members of our *kurrich* that can be resolved with help from the bishop or deacon," Caleb reasoned. "This is about our safety. If there's a chance a criminal might return to the camp for stolen goods, we should be kept informed. Also, it's possible law enforcement could send a police officer to keep watch on the camp for our protection."

"*Gott* is protecting us!" Rose sputtered. "We don't need any more police presence at the camp. *Ant* Nancy said it was very disruptive the first time. We heard rumors similar to this last month and nothing came of them."

Caleb figured it was better not to argue on the way to church; better not to *argue* at all, especially since he didn't want to do anything to jeopardize spending an afternoon alone with Rose. He didn't reply, and the girls' conversation turned to the topic of the fish fry and canoe race coming up at the end of the month.

"How many *leit* do you think will *kumme* from Unity?" Hope asked Charity.

Charity's reply was barely audible, but Caleb thought she said, "What you really want to know is whether Gideon's cousin from Unity is coming, isn't it?" Her question was followed by giggling and whispering that kept up until they arrived at church.

The deacon's sermons usually captivated Caleb's attention—he particularly appreciated hearing portions of the Bible read in German—but today he was engrossed in thinking about what Oliver had told Charity and Hope. Caleb couldn't fathom any detective worth his salt discussing an ongoing investigation, but he *could* imagine Oliver being sneaky enough to eavesdrop on his uncle.

Yet how much of what Oliver said was an accurate representation of what he had possibly overheard and how much was fabricated? From other comments the teen had made to the twins, it was clear to Caleb he resented the Amish. But did that necessarily invalidate his remarks about law enforcement closing in on the thief? Or about the thief returning to the camp? Most of Oliver's claims were outlandish, but a few had an element of plausibility. It was kind of like what he said about the Amish not paying taxes—he was partly wrong, yet partly right. Caleb stewed. Was he partly right about the situation with the coin thief, too?

As the twins expected, other parents had been told about the rumors, and while Caleb was eating lunch with the men after the worship service, Miriam Lapp's father said, "We heard a young *bu* has been taunting Charity and Hope about their *eldre*, saying they're linked to that matter the FBI was investigating this spring."

"*Jah*, my *suh* told me the same thing last night," Gideon Eicher's father commented. "Such a shame to torment the twins like that, especially when their *daed* is so sick."

Caleb was glad the subject was out in the open. Now he could solicit the men's advice about whether or not he ought to talk to Oliver's uncle. "What do you think I should do about it?" he asked.

"Remind them to avoid the *bu*. To walk in the other direction if they see him coming. It takes two to argue."

Caleb hadn't meant what should he do about the girls interacting with Oliver—he meant what should he do if what Oliver said was true.

Abram seemed to have caught the gist of Caleb's

question. "Are you concerned there might actually be a criminal returning to the camp?"

Caleb tried to sound nonchalant. "It has crossed my mind, *jah*."

"Have you seen anyone suspicious on the property, or has anything out of the ordinary happened?"

Caleb racked his memory. Twigs snapping in the woods. A canoe floating away. An open drawer... Each of these occurrences could have a logical explanation, and he'd seem foolish if he told the other men about them. "*Neh*, not really," he admitted.

"Then I don't think you ought to do anything at this time except pray. Let's do that now." Caleb and the deacon bowed their heads, as did the other men at the table. "Lord, we ask Your protection for Charity, Hope, Rose and Caleb. Protect them from fear, as well as from danger. Give them strength to respond with grace to those who might wish to trouble them. We ask for healing for Sol, too. *Denki*, Lord for being our very present help in trouble. Amen."

Abram clapped Caleb's shoulder, adding, "I'm glad you're staying at the camp—I know Sol feels better you're there, too. And I think it's wise to be vigilant. We'll stop by from time to time to check in, but if there's anything you need before then, let us know."

Caleb appreciated the support and vote of confidence. He was also comforted because instead of suggesting Caleb lacked faith or was overreacting, Abram recommended remaining vigilant. But Caleb realized it was Abram's prayer, above all, that had given him a sense of real peace.

When he returned home and called his brother, Caleb heard a woman giggling in the background, along with Liam's laughter. *Who could* that *be?* "It sounds like you have company."

"No, not company. Sheryl's here. We just got back from church and we're getting ready to eat lunch. We, uh, camped out together last night—all three of us, in a tent in the backyard. That's why I didn't pick up. I forgot all about our scheduled call and left my phone in the house. I happened to notice it vibrating when I went inside to use the bathroom."

Caleb was happy Ryan and Sheryl seemed to have found some common ground so Liam wouldn't have to listen to their incessant arguing. He told Ryan the latest news and asked if his brother had heard similar rumors.

"No, no one has updated me about anything recently, so as far as I know, the investigation is still open. Waiting is agony. Thank the Lord I have Liam and Sheryl to distract me," Ryan said, which surprised Caleb. He didn't think going through a divorce was considered a welcome distraction. His brother hedged, "You don't suppose it's possible that…"

"That what?"

"That Nancy and Sol really do know more than they've been letting on?"

"No!" Caleb barked. There were many questionable possibilities in his mind, but Nancy and Sol's truthfulness was not one of them. He lowered his voice to repeat, "No. Absolutely not. The Amish might not actively seek out the police for matters they can resolve on their own, but they're law-abiding citizens. More important, they obey God's law, which means if they were questioned, they wouldn't lie—especially not to protect a criminal. I'm as sure about that as I am about…about the fact *you're* not the thief!"

"Okay, okay, I hear you. I'm sorry. I didn't mean to question their integrity, I only wanted to rule that possibility out," Ryan apologized.

"That's the problem. How can you and I rule anything out—or in? What do we really have to go on? A cryptic, anonymous note? Something a teenage kid said? Conjecture?" Caleb usually tried to put a positive spin on the situation in order to buoy his brother's hope, but right now he was having difficulty keeping his own perspective afloat. Summer was wrapping up and Caleb felt he was no closer to discovering anything worthwhile than when he'd first arrived.

"Maybe you *should* go have a chat with that detective. Get a sense of what's what. Find out if you're in any jeopardy. It's possible the police want to surveil the camp but out of respect for the Amish, they're not."

"I can't," Caleb said, remembering how aghast Rose had been at the idea. "It's not the Amish way and I'd draw attention to myself. I can't blow my cover now." *I can't* ever *blow my cover.*

"Hey, listen, as much as I'd love for you to find the coins, I don't want you to take any unnecessary chances." Ryan's voice cracked. "I'd rather go to prison than have anything happen to you, Caleb."

Startled by the intensity of his brother's sentiment, Caleb made light of his concerns, which had been his concerns, too, until the deacon prayed for him. "What could possibly happen? For all we know, the note you got was a ploy to distract everyone while the thief was taking off for Mexico. And while he was on his road trip, he probably spent the coins in every vending machine between Chicago and Cancún!" When Ryan didn't laugh, Caleb grew serious again. "Even if what Oliver Graham told the girls about the thief coming back is true, there's nothing to suggest he plans to harm anyone. The heist was a white-collar crime. The thief is greedy, not violent."

"The prospect of losing a million dollars' worth of stolen property can turn a greedy person into a violent one pretty quickly," Ryan countered.

"If that's the case, I'm sure the police are on top of it. The FBI is on top of it. It's likely they're already surveilling the camp. Like you said, they're just not telling us about it because we're Amish and they know it violates our principles."

Ryan chuckled. "*We're* Amish?"

"What?"

"You said *we're* Amish and it violates *our* principles," Ryan echoed. "You do know you're still… What do the Amish call us? *Englisch*, right?"

Sometimes, I wish I weren't, Caleb thought. *I wish I could stay here forever because, even in the midst of all this chaos, I feel more tranquil and at home now than I have since…since I lived with the Amish in Pennsylvania.* "Yeah, the Amish would consider us *Englischers.*"

"Speaking of *Englisch*—or actually, of German—the other day I received the mail you had forwarded from your home. You got a big envelope from the university."

"That's probably my teaching contract for the year. I've got to sign it before the semester begins. Could you put it in a plain envelope and send it to me here? I don't want anyone to see the university's return address."

"Then you're definitely staying in Maine longer? You really don't have to—especially if you think you're at risk."

"I know that. But I want to." *Not just because of the hunt for the coins, either.*

"A couple weeks ago you were concerned about the dangers of staying there and now you're insisting you won't leave. What changed?"

"God is sovereign, so what do I have to fear?" Caleb said, paraphrasing Rose. "But promise you'll do one thing."

"Whatever you need."

"Pray for me—for all of us here."

"I already have been praying, but I'll keep it up."

"Denki," Caleb said. Then, realizing he'd spoken in Amish, he clarified, "That means *thank you* in *Deitsch.*"

"Bitte schön," Ryan replied.

"That's *you're welcome* in German, not in *Deitsch*, but it's not bad for an *Englischer*," Caleb told him, and their call ended with both of them laughing.

For once, instead of Hope and Charity running off to Miriam Lapp's house after church, Miriam had accompanied the twins back to the camp. Rose was relieved; considering the conversation they'd had with Oliver Graham, she preferred that Hope and Charity not hang out where they might bump into him. Not because she gave what Oliver had said any weight, but because it had resulted in Charity and Hope being upset—and it had almost resulted in an argument between Rose and Caleb, too.

The girls were in the kitchen gathering snacks, including the blueberry muffins left over from last night's supper, to take with them canoeing. Rose managed to sneak one for herself and she ambled out onto the porch with it, thinking about Caleb. He had seemed a lot more relaxed on the way home than on the way to *kurrich*. She wondered what he was up to right now.

She'd barely sat down when he sauntered up the path and settled into the other glider. "Hi, Ro—oh, muffins! Have you got any more of those?"

"You can have this one." She handed him her muffin. "I don't know why I took it—I'm not the least bit *hungerich*."

"Do you have to be *hungerich* to eat a *blohbier* muffin?" Caleb's grin outshone his eyes. Or maybe it was that his eyes illuminated his grin.

"I'll get you a glass of *millich*." As she was inside pouring it, Rose heard the cell phone ring, but she didn't take business calls on the Sabbath. When she returned to the porch, the muffin was gone and Caleb was brushing crumbs off his lap. Rose extended the glass to him before taking her seat again.

He accepted the milk, then immediately set it aside and leaned forward, resting his forearms against his knees. "Listen, Rose, there's something I need to speak to you about, and I'd like you to hear me out before you say *neh*."

Her heartbeat rattled. For the briefest moment she wondered if he was going to ask to court her. How would she answer? "Go on," she replied.

"I'm sorry I suggested we should go to the police. After talking to Abram and praying about it, I realized I was letting my concern—my *fear* that something might happen to you or to the twins—get the best of me. So, I want you to know I have no intention of contacting Oliver Graham's *onkel*."

Rose's ears and cheeks stung; how silly she'd been to imagine he'd ask to be her suitor. Yet how sweet it was to hear him express concern for her and the girls. "*Denki*. I appreciate that." She smiled, though Caleb's forehead was riddled with lines.

"But I still think it's important to exercise caution. So, I'd like to suggest you and the *meed* consider not going off canoeing or hiking on your own. I think there should always be at least two people together."

"Is this your indirect way of asking me to go hiking with you?" Rose quipped. There it was—she *knew* she could spark a smile across Caleb's lips again.

"I *do* hope you'll *kumme* hiking with me this afternoon, *jah*, but I also hope you'll agree not to go into the woods or canoeing alone."

"Okay, sure," she said, nodding. Once again she could hear the cell phone in the background; she should have silenced the volume when she was inside getting milk. "I'll tell Charity and Hope not to wander off alone, either—although the two of them are usually inseparable anyway."

"Wow." Caleb leaned back in his chair. "I didn't think you'd agree so easily."

"Oh, I'm still not concerned we're in any danger, and I don't want us to lose our wits again, but this seems to mean a lot to you, so pairing up instead of going out alone is a small concession for me to make," she explained.

"*Denki.* It *does* mean a lot to me." Caleb's eyes gleamed as he added, "It means so much that if you said *neh* I was prepared to cash in the favor you owe me! I'm glad I didn't have to."

Rose tittered. "Well, don't wait too long—that favor expires when we head our separate ways in four weeks." At the thought of summer ending, Rose was gripped with apprehension. Not merely because she was still over five hundred dollars short of her financial goal, but also because she was going to miss this place. These people. Hope and Charity and Caleb. *Especially Caleb.*

"I actually already have something in mind—" Caleb said, but he was interrupted by Hope charging through the screen door in tears, Charity on her heels and Miriam wringing her hands behind both of them.

"That was *Mamm* on the phone," Hope sobbed. "*Daed*'s health has taken a turn for the worse. She wants us to *kumme* join her in Ohio as soon as we can."

Chapter Nine

Rose leaped to her feet and enveloped both of the twins in her arms. She wanted to tell them everything was going to be all right, their father was going to be fine—or maybe she wanted someone to say that to *her*—but she knew she couldn't give them false hope, so she just held on to them. After a few moments, the girls pulled away and Hope wiped her eyes. "I'll help you pack, but let's pray first, okay?" Rose asked.

She extended a hand, palm up, to Hope on one side and to Caleb on the other. Caleb reached for Charity's hand, and she reached for Miriam's, and Miriam completed the circle by taking Hope's opposite hand. They bowed their heads and shut their eyes. Too distraught to pray aloud herself, Rose squeezed Caleb's fingers and whispered, "Could you?"

"Our Lord *Gott*, we *kumme* to you with troubled hearts," Caleb began somberly. Hope caught her breath, and Rose feared the young woman would break into tears again as Caleb continued, "We're concerned about

Sol's health, yet we know You're the great physician, the One who can heal all our illnesses and forgive all our sins. We don't know what Your sovereign will is for Sol's life, but our prayer is that You'd make him well again."

As Caleb asked *Gott* to give Charity and Hope a safe and trouble-free trip, Rose cherished the feeling of his warm hand engulfing hers. She had the same sense of being able to trust him to accompany her on this dark journey that she'd had when he led her down the path from Paradise Point on the Fourth of July.

After he finished praying, Miriam said, "*Kumme*, Hope and Charity. I'll help you with your suitcases."

The girls were following her into the house when Charity said, "We have to tell Ivy and Arleta we won't be able to mind the *kinner* this week. They'll need to know soon so they can find someone else to help."

"I'll go tell them," Caleb offered. "I can arrange for a van driver to pick you up in the morning, too."

"What about you?" Hope asked Rose. "How will you manage by yourself?"

"I'm not by myself. I have Eleanor and Caleb," Rose assured her, even though she had the same misgivings about how she'd keep up with everything at the camp.

"I'd love to help you serve breakfast and clean up in the mornings," Miriam volunteered. "It will give me a break from taking care of my *breider*."

"Oh, but I was going to ask if you'd watch Ivy's *kinner* in my place," Charity suggested.

"No way! I'd rather watch my *breider*!" Miriam's expression of dismay momentarily caused the twins to giggle. "I'll ask my *mamm* to help find a *maedel* to care for Ivy's *kinner*."

"Don't fret about those details now. We'll work things out later so no one is left short staffed," Rose told them.

But as she lay in bed that evening, she struggled to create a plan for keeping up with the responsibilities of running the camp and harvesting the produce, while also making pies and jam for her own profit. Amity Speicher, a newlywed and the district's schoolteacher, might be available to cover one of the girls' mother's-helper jobs—until school began again anyway. Maybe Mildred Schwartz could give a hand to the other mother? As for making pies, Rose thought, *Helen said she'd be flexible if something came up and I couldn't bake*... But she quickly rejected the idea of canceling Helen's standing pie order. It was a reliable source of extra income, and Rose didn't want to let the *Englischer* down. She'd just have to rise even earlier or go to bed even later than she'd already been doing.

Rose pulled the sheet to her chin and rolled over. But instead of slumbering, she watched the shadows of pine branches dancing on the wall until she couldn't keep her eyes open any longer. Nearby, a loon wailed plaintively. *I know exactly how you feel*, she thought, and drifted off to sleep.

Not long after Caleb had taken Miriam home and informed Ivy and Arleta that Hope and Charity were going to Ohio to be with their parents, a series of storms bowled across the lake, and even now gusts of wind clapped choppy waves against the rocks outside his window. But that wasn't what was keeping him awake; Caleb was anguished over Sol's health and bothered by the idea of Rose staying in the house completely alone.

Since he couldn't sleep anyway, he got out of bed and took the Bible off the dresser top to continue reading where he'd left off. As he flipped the leather cover open, he came across the photo of Liam. Caleb recalled how he'd told his nephew he'd come back to Chicago and go camping with him as soon as possible. That felt like a lifetime ago and he wondered how many teeth Liam had lost since then. He tucked the photo away and exchanged the Bible for a sheet of paper and a pen.

"Sol," he wrote. *"I'm sorry you've been so ill. I will continue praying for you daily."*

> *Things are going well here at the camp. The beans, broccoli and cucumbers are flourishing. The potatoes were infested with aphids earlier in the season, but the mums and zinnias have attracted enough ladybugs to remedy that situation.*
>
> *Please greet Nancy for me and let her know Rose, Charity and Hope have kept everyone happy and well-fed. One guest even sent a thank-you note saying he gained seven pounds while his family was here—but it was worth it. (I could say the same thing myself!)*
>
> *I reeled in a couple four-pound trout a few weeks ago, but the twins told me you've caught*

fish twice that size. You'll have to show me what I'm doing wrong when you return at the end of August.

Caleb reread the letter before signing it, and then he uttered another prayer for Sol's health and went back to bed. He woke extra early to collect eggs and milk the cow so Hope and Charity wouldn't have to—he wanted them to get as much sleep as they could before their journey. Since a van driver wasn't available to travel such a long distance at short notice, Charity and Hope had to take the bus, which involved several transfers and nearly sixteen hours on the road, and Caleb knew from experience how grueling the trip would be.

As he deposited eggs into a basket he'd found in the barn, Caleb chuckled to himself, recalling the first morning at the camp when he left the coop door open and the chickens escaped. *At least my boots are broken in now, so I don't have blisters anymore.*

"*Guder mariye*, Caleb." Rose's quiet voice broke through his thoughts.

Turning, Caleb did a double take. Although Amish women sometimes wore their hair down at home in the morning or evening, he'd never seen Rose without hers fastened into a bun and covered with a kerchief or prayer *kapp*. Now her loose tresses softly framed her face and poured past her shoulders in a dark velvety torrent. Caleb couldn't think straight.

"For once I'm wearing a head covering and you aren't," he blurted out.

"*What?*" Rose's mouth puckered with the word.

"I—I—I..."

Rose tossed her head back and laughed, her hair rippling as she moved. "I think someone needs more sleep. You shouldn't be out here collecting *oier* anyway."

"It's okay. I won't break them. I'm using a basket." Caleb held it up.

"I didn't mean that. I meant I would have done it," she said, coming to his side and reaching into the nesting box. He extended the basket so she could place the egg inside. He might have been quicker picking berries than she was, but her slender hands were more deft when it came to plucking the eggs from the bed of pine shavings. "I was a real shrew to you that first morning, wasn't I?" she reminisced woefully.

"*Neh*, not a shrew. Just a little briary," he teased.

"Briary?" She stopped gathering eggs to narrow her eyes at him.

"*Jah*, you know, like a briar." He took her hand and turned it over to point to where her wrists were embedded with raspberry prickles.

"Oh." She didn't move. Caleb knew he ought to release her fingers now that he'd shown her what he meant, but the best he could do was to loosen his grip. Sadness eclipsed her face. "You're right. I really can get under a person's skin, can't I?"

Jah, but not in the way you're thinking. Caleb cleared his throat. "You can't help it—it's all in your name. But a rose is beautiful, too."

As Rose swiftly withdrew her hand to reach into the nesting box again, Caleb thought, *Uh-oh, I shouldn't have said that.* No matter how much he meant it.

* * *

Rose wondered whether she should thank Caleb for the compliment. *He didn't actually say* I'm *beautiful—he said a* rose *is beautiful.* He couldn't have been flirting with her, could he? Not here, standing beside the chicken coop first thing in the morning, with her eyes puffy and her hair wild.

Not knowing how else to respond, Rose replied earnestly, "I'm glad you gave me a second chance to prove I'm not always briary. *Lots* of second chances. Your friendship is important to me. Especially now when everything is so—so..." She was overcome with an urge to weep, but she held it in and fastened the coop door shut. "I can take the basket now."

Caleb allowed her to grasp the handle but he didn't let go of his side. When she gave it a tug, he tugged back until she met his eyes. "I'll help you with whatever you need, Rose," he said. "Picking *hembeer* and *blohbier*, checking guests in and out, or—or buying a pair of earplugs so you don't have to listen to Eleanor prattle while you're preparing meals."

Rose chortled. "I don't mind her babbling while we work, as long as her hands are moving as quickly as her mouth is."

Caleb released the basket handle. "Have you thought about how you're going to make extra pies and jam while the *meed* are away?"

"I have a couple ideas. Right now, the most important thing on my mind is making breakfast and sending Hope and Charity off to Ohio."

"Mine, too—after I *millich* the *kuh*." Caleb agreed

to come to the dining hall when he was finished. Since the girls were leaving so early, this morning Rose was preparing breakfast for the four of them before making it for the guests.

They ate quickly and then hurried to the barn together. Rose hugged Charity and Hope, and gave them a canvas bag filled with cards for Nancy and Sol, half a dozen jars of blueberry jam to share with their relatives in Ohio and enough snacks to last the girls all the way across the country and back. As she watched the buggy pull away, Rose allowed the tears she'd been fighting all morning to stream freely down her face. *Dear* Gott, *if it's Your will to take Sol home, please at least allow Charity and Hope to get there in time to say goodbye first.*

After praying, Rose sobbed even harder, primarily because she feared for Sol's health, but also because she'd miss her cousins in the coming weeks. Soon she'd have to leave the lake and Serenity Ridge behind; she'd have to bid farewell to Caleb, too. It was enough to make her want to bawl like a baby for the rest of the day, which of course she couldn't. She had guests to serve. Rose blotted her face with her sleeve and smoothed her apron, but as she shuffled back to the dining hall, a few stray tears cooled her cheeks.

"Good morning," a guest greeted her in a hushed voice on the path near cabin four. He carried a fishing pole and his two young children hopped alongside him, one with a pail and the other with a net. They waved happily at Rose.

Glancing up, the man's wife waved, too. "Such a lovely day, isn't it?" she trilled.

"It is, *jah*." Rose forced a smile even though there was nothing lovely about the day. Still, the good thing about having such a long to-do list was that it left no room for wallowing, and by the time Miriam arrived, Rose's eyes were dry and her smile was sincere.

Miriam proved to be every bit as capable and diligent as Charity and Hope. As she punched down the dough for bread, she told Rose she and her mother had visited several houses in the district after Caleb brought her home the previous afternoon. Together they'd arranged coverage for Hope and Charity's babysitting roles.

"Maria Mast can help you and Eleanor prepare and serve supper from Monday through Friday. I'm sorry to say I couldn't get anyone to help with lunch, though."

"*Denki, denki, denki* to you and your *mamm* for recruiting people to help!" Rose sang out. "As for lunch, I just set out bread and cheese, fruit, dessert and paper plates. It's the easiest thing I do all day."

Caleb stopped in later for a second cup of coffee and he seemed almost as happy as Rose was when she told him about the new staff arrangements. "That's what I love about the Amish—everyone's so community-minded."

His comment struck Rose as peculiar. *Community-minded* was how *Englischers* described the Amish in newspaper articles or library books Rose had read, but it wasn't a term she'd ever heard an Amish person use. Serving one another was at the core of their Christian beliefs; it was an expectation, not something to boast about. "Aren't people *community-minded* in your district in Wisconsin?"

* * *

Caleb's face felt inflamed. He lifted the cup to his mouth and took a swig to buy time before answering. "*Jah*, they are. I just meant… I meant…" He faltered. "I guess I was trying to say I appreciate the settlement here. The *leit* are especially helpful."

His answer seemed to satisfy Rose. "Speaking of helpful *leit*, is your offer to help with whatever I need still valid?" she asked.

"Absolutely." Caleb took another swallow of coffee; his mouth was so dry.

"Since today is *Muundaag,* I need to deposit the rent. But I noticed the *hembeer* are close to going bad on the north end of the field, so they should be picked this morning—"

"No problem, I'll take care of them. You said the north end, right?"

"*Jah*, but I thought I'd pick the *hembeer* and you could deposit the money."

Caleb balked. "You want me to go to the bank?" Rose didn't even allow the twins to take the rent to the bank.

"*Jah*. Helen is coming soon and I need to talk to her about what kind of pies she wants this week. But if you'd rather not—"

"*Neh*. I'd like to go." Caleb couldn't help teasing, "Are you sure you trust me with all that cash? I might stash it in my *hut* for safekeeping and it could blow away…"

Instead of the smile he'd hoped to evoke, a frown tarnished Rose's expression. "Of course I trust you with the cash. I'd trust you with my *life*, Caleb."

"Denki," he murmured, setting his hat low on his head so she couldn't see his eyes. Caleb couldn't imagine any woman ever saying something that meant as much to him as what Rose had just said and it nearly moved him to tears. Whether that was because he was overcome with joy or overwhelmed with guilt, he couldn't tell for certain.

Rose took an instant liking to Maria Mast. Known for being an excellent cook, she was good-humored, candid and energetic. And, while she didn't initiate idle chitchat herself, she seemed unfazed by Eleanor's incessant jabbering.

"Maria got married last December, didn't you, Maria?" Eleanor addressed both Rose and Maria simultaneously.

"That's right." Maria carried a large bowl of broccoli florets and a colander to the sink.

Now Eleanor turned to Rose, marveling, "She was a first-time bride. She'd never been married and widowed before then."

Recognizing Eleanor was making a thinly veiled reference to Maria being single until she was in her thirties, Rose ignored the younger woman's remark. "Please take the plates into the dining hall, Eleanor," she requested brusquely.

Eleanor scuffed over to the cupboard and removed the plates in twos. "Your husband is from Indiana, isn't he, Maria?"

"Jah," said Maria as she dumped the florets into the colander and turned on the faucet. "I met Otto when he

came to Serenity Ridge to visit Levi Swarey, his departed sister's husband. But you were at our *hochzich* and you know this already. Why are you asking me about it now?"

"For Rose's benefit," Eleanor said bluntly, and Rose guffawed at her nerve.

"What would benefit me more is if you'd take those plates into the dining hall."

Eleanor dallied, carefully aligning the patterns as she stacked the tray with dishes. "Did you and Otto have a long-distance courtship, Maria?"

"*Jah*. For a short time, when he returned to Indiana for a few months before moving here permanently."

"That's what I think Rose and Caleb should do once they leave Serenity Ridge. They could continue their court—"

"Eleanor!" Rose was mortified.

Eleanor leaned in Maria's direction and whispered loudly, "She pretends they're not a couple, but they really are."

"That's not true! You know what Scripture says about talebearers," Rose warned, deliberately using a term from the Bible to prick Eleanor's conscience. It didn't work.

"I'm not trying to be a talebearer. I'm trying to point out that there's still hope for you, Rose. If Maria could get married when she was over thirty, there's no reason—"

"Eleanor—the plates!" Rose's voice had a daunting edge to it, so Eleanor finally picked up the tray and retreated from the kitchen. "I'm sorry about that, Maria. Eleanor can be…indiscreet at times."

Maria just laughed. "It's nothing I didn't hear often enough before I got married—sometimes from my own *familye*. They thought I should have married the first suitor to court me. My sister-in-law kept saying I wouldn't be able to have *bobblin* if I didn't hurry up and get married—and that was when I was in my mid-twenties!" Maria patted her burgeoning belly. "But I'm so glad I waited until I met Otto."

Rose had never spoken with anyone except her sisters and mother about marriage, and even they wouldn't have been as forthright as Maria was being about the subject. There was something about her confidence that inspired Rose to confide, "I was planning to get married in Pennsylvania in the upcoming wedding season, but we…we called it off."

Maria turned off the faucet and shook excess water from the colander. "Do you miss having him as your suitor?"

"Neh," Rose answered after a thoughtful pause.

Nodding, Maria wiped her hands on her apron. *"Gut.* As I told my sister-in-law each time I broke up with a suitor, I'd rather stay single my entire life than marry a man whose absence didn't splinter my heart to pieces."

"So would I," Rose agreed.

In the days following the girls' departure, Caleb timed his work in the fields to coincide with Rose's berry picking so he could give her a hand if she needed it—and to his delight, she always needed it. Sometimes they sang as they worked, sometimes they joked and once they prayed aloud for Sol. But Caleb treasured their conversations most of all; Rose truly was like a flower, opening up to him more and more beautifully beneath the summer sun.

On Friday afternoon, she even told him about her recent correspondence with Baker, saying she thought she'd finally made it clear to him they had no future together. This news made Caleb happier than he had a right to be; after all, it wasn't as if *he* and Rose had a future together, either. His heart did a little jig all the same.

"Getting through to my *mamm* might be even more difficult than getting through to Baker. She keeps pressuring me to reconsider a courtship with him," Rose grumbled. "That's one of the reasons I'm not looking forward to going home."

"What are the other reasons?"

"Well, if I earn enough money for the lease—which isn't guaranteed—I'll have to spend most of my time at the café."

Caleb was incredulous. "But running the café is your goal, isn't it?"

"*Jah*, of course it is. But I'll miss working outside, the way I do here. I'll miss the people, too."

"Anyone in particular? Someone whose name begins with the letter *C*, for instance?" Caleb was blatantly joking, but he also wanted her to express she'd miss him so he could say it back to her.

"You mean Charity? *Jah*, I'll definitely miss her. And Hope, Nancy and Sol, as well as Abram, Jaala and

Eleanor." Rose was teasing, too, counting on her fingers as she named the people she saw most often. "I'll miss Helen, too."

"Aren't you forgetting someone?"

"*Ach*, you're right!" Rose smacked her forehead. "Henry. Of course I'll miss Henry, but we're going to write to each other every day, so that will ease my loneliness."

Caleb rolled his eyes the way Rose sometimes did, feigning aggravation. "You're hilarious, you know that?"

"Am I? I thought I was *briary.*"

"You're hilarious *and* briary."

Rose chucked a blueberry at him but it sailed over his shoulder. "Oops. Guess I *missed you*, Caleb…" She giggled at her own wit. "There. I said it. Are you *hallich* now?"

"Delighted." He tossed a handful of blueberries in her direction but not a single one hit her. "Looks like I missed you more, Rose."

She gave him a saucy smirk. "*Jah*, I know."

Caleb grinned and they resumed picking berries again. He supposed he should have felt guilty for flirting with her when he knew nothing could come of it, but he rationalized it was all in good fun. *Besides, she's flirting with me, too.*

Later, as they were eating supper, Rose mentioned she'd forgotten to collect the money jar and put the leftover produce away, so Caleb offered to do it for her. When he reached the roadside stand he was alarmed to find the shelves toppled, vegetables and fruit strewn into the road, and broken jars littering the grass. His first thought was a car had accidentally crashed into the small building, but he didn't see any structural damage; nor were there skid marks on the pavement.

Then he noticed Rose's sign, still upright, was thickly splotched with raspberry jam. A big pink blob obscured her name, so instead of reading Rose's Pies the sign now said S Pies. *Spies.* Caleb caught his breath and examined the markings closer. The wide circular smears reminded him of Liam's finger paintings. This was no random accident; it was a message from the thief. It *had* to be. But did it mean the thief believed the Petersheims were spying on him? Was it meant to intimidate them, to keep them quiet?

His mind buzzing, Caleb collected as many shards of glass as he could and set them in one end of the wagon. There was no salvaging the rest of the produce, so he heaped the squished berries and badly bruised vegetables into the wagon and added the money jar to his haul, too. After setting the shelves upright he tucked the defaced sign beneath his arm and carted the whole mess to the barn. Later he'd recycle the glass and chop up the produce for compost; for now, he filled a bucket and grabbed rags, a broom and a flashlight, and returned to the stand. By the time he had finished cleaning the mess, Maria's and Eleanor's buggies were gone, which meant he could discuss the matter with Rose in private.

As usual, he found her in the dining hall preparing ingredients for making pies and bread the next morning. Caleb hesitated, carefully weighing his words before he spoke. He regretted having to deliver such distressing news when Rose was already burdened, and he hoped she wouldn't fall apart. But when he told her what happened, she just clucked her tongue and shook her head. "I spent so much time making that jam and putting up the produce. I can't believe someone thinks it's funny to ruin it all. What a waste."

"I'm afraid it's not meant to be funny," Caleb said. "I think it's meant to frighten us. It's possible Oliver was right about a criminal being in the area."

Pouring flour into a measuring cup, Rose disagreed, "*Neh.* It's only someone playing a prank—probably the same kids who did this before."

"This happened before?" Caleb struggled to keep his voice down. "When?"

"I don't know, a couple weeks ago."

"Why didn't you tell me?" he yelped.

"Because I didn't want you to overreact, the way you're doing now," Rose said calmly, tapping the bottom of the flour sack. "I don't like what they did any more than you do, but it's not as if someone got hurt or something was stolen. Last time, they even paid for the pie they destroyed."

Caleb was astounded by Rose's naivete. "That's because their intention wasn't to steal money—it was to threaten us. Don't you see? Listen, I know I said I wouldn't go to the police, but now we have no choice—"

"*Absatz!*" Rose slammed the measuring cup on the counter and flour flew up in a puff. "It was *my* pie and *my* jam that was destroyed. This is *my ant* and *onkel*'s business, and they wouldn't want the police snooping around here. If you can't respect their wishes—especially when my *onkel* is... When he's...he's *dying*—then maybe you should leave!" Rose fled the room.

Caleb exhaled loudly and rubbed his fingertips hard against his forehead. He never expected Rose would suggest he should leave, and at the moment he was tempted to do just that. But he couldn't abandon her now, when he was more suspicious than ever the thief was in the area. For that same reason, he couldn't abandon his search for the coins. Yet Rose's vehement objection showed Caleb that contacting the police was absolutely out of the question. Which left him with only one option.

He tipped his head to each side to crack his neck before joining Rose in the darkened dining hall. She was sitting at a table, dabbing her eyes with a napkin. He sat on the bench beside her, facing the opposite direction, toward the lake. "You're right. I overreacted. I'm sorry."

Rose sniffed, as if she didn't quite believe him. Or maybe he just thought she didn't quite believe him because he didn't quite mean it. What he *could* say with conviction was, "I have no intention of disrespecting Nancy and Sol's wishes."

"You won't go to the police?" Rose clarified.

"I won't go to the police," he echoed. Bumping his shoulder against hers, he added, "Even though I wholeheartedly believe anyone who'd waste your pie or jam should be locked up in jail."

Rose snickered. "I'm sorry. I overreacted, too. I'm just so—"

She didn't have to complete her sentence for him to know what she meant. She was burdened. About her uncle. Her business. The guests in the cabins. "I know. But it's going to be okay," he said as much to himself as to her.

For a fleeting moment, she rested her head against his shoulder, and it was all he could do not to press his ear against her head, too. Then she was swinging her legs over the bench and standing up. "I'd better get back to work," she said.

When he returned to his cabin, Caleb considered calling his brother to tell him about Rose's sign, but he decided the news might unnerve him and then Ryan would try to convince Caleb to call the police or to leave Serenity Ridge right away. *I'd better just keep my mouth shut and my eyes open. And from now on, I'll need to stay even closer to Rose.* Which might have been the one good thing to come from someone vandalizing the produce stand.

Chapter Ten

"You have a new sign," Helen observed when she picked up her order on Saturday morning. "Did the pie-throwing vandals wreak havoc again?"

"*Jah*. This time they knocked over the shelves and broke a lot of jars, too, so watch your step. Caleb tried to pick up all the glass, but I've found a few more pieces."

"They ought to be held accountable for what they did!" Helen exclaimed. "Or are you going to justify it by telling me they paid for everything they ruined?"

"*Neh*, not this time." Rose had no idea how she'd make up for the loss. She felt so anxious about the un-expected financial setback that for the first time in her life she seriously considered making the jam on the Sabbath. *I would prepare a supper if I didn't have enough leftovers—what's so different about making jam?* Of course, she knew the difference—supper was a neces-sity, whereas making jam for financial gain wasn't. Still, the temptation plagued her as she paced the porch Sunday morning, waiting for Caleb, Abram and Jaala to come for worship.

Upon their arrival, Abram and Jaala announced they wouldn't be staying for lunch the way they usually did. Aquilla King, a widow, had caught the bug that was making the rounds, so they were going to her house to minister to her.

"You look fatigued, Rose," Jaala noticed. "Are you coming down with something, too?"

"*Neh*. I'm just worn-out with all there is to do around here."

"It's a blessing to have Maria and Miriam helping you, isn't it? I remember how grateful Nancy was after you agreed to fill in for her so she could travel to Ohio," Jaala commented.

Rose's face burned; she shouldn't have complained about work, especially because she'd received so much help with it. She was barely able to meet Abram's eyes when he asked if she'd heard from Nancy lately. "*Jah*. She called on Thursday and said Sol is still fighting hard."

"Let's give thanks for that," Abram suggested, and everyone bowed their heads in prayer.

The next thing Rose knew, Jaala was gently nudging her arm. Rose sat upright with a start. Had the men seen her sleeping? She was utterly humiliated by the possibility. As it was, she couldn't imagine what Jaala thought about her.

But when it came time for Jaala and Abram to leave, the older woman embraced Rose. There was no condemnation in her voice as she whispered, "You must get more rest, dear."

The four of them walked out to the porch, where Abram asked Caleb, "Have there been any problems here this week?"

Rose didn't want news of the vandalism getting back to Nancy and the twins, but if Caleb told the deacon no, he'd be lying. She held her breath, waiting for his reply.

"Nothing we can't manage." Caleb's answer was evasive but true, and Rose could have hugged him for it.

"I'll bring lunch out here," she said after Jaala and Abram left. She ducked into the bathroom to wash her hands and caught her reflection in the mirror. Her prayer *kapp* was askew and there were dark semicircles beneath her eyes. *I do look fatigued*, she thought. A nap would do her good—but so would spending the afternoon outdoors with Caleb. She went to suggest they pack a picnic and go canoeing instead of eating lunch on the porch.

"That sounds *wunderbaar*. I was going to suggest it myself, but you seemed tired."

"Why? Because I fell asleep during prayer?"

"Did you? I didn't notice—not until you started snoring anyway."

"I did not!" Rose protested as a tall, stocky *Englisch* man and a skinny *Englisch* teenage boy suddenly came around the corner. She didn't remember them checking in on Saturday.

"Hello," the man said as they climbed the stairs. "Are you the property owners?"

* * *

The stranger addressed both Caleb and Rose but he was looking straight at Caleb. *"Jah,"* he answered. Then he clarified, "We're managing the camp."

"My name's Leland Perry. I understand your family experienced something upsetting recently." As the man spoke, the scrawny teenager slouched behind him, picking his thumbnail.

"What?" Caleb was confused. *How did an* Englischer *hear about Sol?*

"Your produce stand was vandalized, wasn't it?"

Caleb's mind spun. Had the man seen the damage in passing? Or was it possible he was an FBI agent or a detective who'd been staking out the property? Then who was the kid?

"Yes," Rose answered succinctly. The *Englisch* word sounded peculiar coming from her.

The man nudged the teenager forward. "Oliver has something to tell you."

The boy's brown hair flopped over his eyes and his hands were jammed into his pockets. Without looking up, he mumbled, "I ruined your pies and knocked the shelves over. Sorry."

That was when it dawned on Caleb that this kid was Oliver *Graham.* The boy who'd been harassing Hope and Charity. Caleb briefly considered telling the little punk if he ever bothered the twins or touched Rose's property again, Caleb would knock *him* over. Instead, he prayed, *Please,* Gott, *help me to show mercy.*

"If you tell us what the ruined items cost, my nephew will compensate you," Leland said.

Your nephew? The man standing before him was Oliver Graham's uncle—the detective. With every fiber of his being, Caleb wanted to pull him aside and grill him about whether anything Oliver had told the girls was true. *I gave Rose my word I wouldn't go to the police—I didn't say I wouldn't talk to them if they came to me.* But Caleb knew that was a weak argument and he couldn't arouse Leland's suspicion by asking questions an Amish man wouldn't ask.

Rose stepped closer to Oliver. "I appreciate your apology and I forgive you. I need to review my bookkeeping. Would you and your uncle like a piece of pie while you're waiting?"

Oliver drew his chin back in surprise, but Leland answered, "Thank you, but we're having lunch soon." He turned to Caleb as Rose went into the house. "Oliver said he didn't break any shelves, but you and your wife must have had to clean up a big mess."

Caleb nodded; there was no point telling the detective he wasn't married to Rose.

"Oliver's parents own cottages on Black Bear Lake so he knows how busy the summer season is. Since you spent your valuable time cleaning up after him, he can spend his vacation time helping you with a project here at the camp."

Great! He can clean the stable, harvest potatoes and then mow the lawn by the barn—with a manual push mower. Maybe then he'll have more respect for the Amish. "Repaying Rose will be compensation enough," Caleb answered, as Rose came outside and handed Oliver a slip of paper. He pulled a fistful of money from his pocket and paid her.

"Denki," she said, the only word she'd spoken to him in *Deitsch*.

"It won't happen again, will it, Oliver?" Leland prompted his nephew.

"Uh-uh," Oliver muttered.

"Sure is tranquil around here," his uncle said, surveying the lake before the pair tramped down the steps. "Enjoy your afternoon."

As Caleb watched them disappear around the house, it occurred to him that Leland hadn't said how he'd discovered Oliver was the vandal. *With a detective for an uncle, he probably doesn't get away with much. Although, someone else might have seen him and told his parents...* Then it occurred to Caleb that Rose might think *he'd* reported the vandalism to the police after all.

Before she had a chance to question him about it, Caleb defended himself. "I don't know who told the detective about the produce stand, but it wasn't me."

Rose looked startled. "I know it wasn't. You said you wouldn't go to the police and I believe you."

There it was again. Rose's trust made Caleb feel a hundred feet tall and yet like a complete phony at the same time.

"I don't know *how* Oliver's *onkel* figured out he was the vandal, but I'm glad he did," Rose told him. "Now I won't have to cover the loss for the ruined produce, and you can rest assured that this has nothing to do with any stolen coins."

But that doesn't mean we don't have to be vigilant.

The coin thief might still be out there. Caleb didn't want to argue the point, so he said nothing.

"The best part of this is now Oliver can have a clear conscience," Rose added cheerfully. "Baker told me it was terrible knowing he'd done something wrong and could be found out at any minute. He said he wouldn't wish that kind of guilt on anyone."

I know what he meant, Caleb thought. *But sometimes, it's a necessary burden to bear.*

"I'll go change my clothes and stick lunch in the cooler. Meet you by the water, okay?" Rose suggested.

"Are you sure you won't be too tired?"

"Not if you do all the paddling." Rose was teasing, but when they reached the beach, one of the canoes was gone and two guests were setting out in the other one, which meant Rose and Caleb had to use a rowboat. Caleb ended up rowing after all.

"Where to?" he asked. "Paradise Point?"

"That's where that young couple is headed. If it's okay with you, I'd like to go somewhere away from guests. Someplace quiet."

"That leaves the islands or Relaxation Rock."

Or Kissing Cove. The unbidden thought caused Rose to blush. "Relaxation Rock, please."

They were quiet until they reached the other shore, where they climbed the rock and chatted as they enjoyed their picnic. Afterward, Rose reclined on the quilt they'd spread on the flat surface as Caleb devoured a second piece of pie. The sun on her face and the sound of the lake splashing against the sand had a lulling effect and

Rose didn't think about her uncle's illness, the guests or earning extra income. Her worries floated away effortlessly, like a leaf on water...

When Rose woke, she bolted upright, embarrassed that Caleb had seen her fall asleep twice in the same day. But he wasn't beside her. She shielded her eyes and scanned the shoreline—he was clambering over the rocks a hundred yards from her. When he noticed her waving, he cupped his hands to his mouth and called, "I'll be right back!"

Rose scooted down the rock on her bottom and waded into the lake up to her shins. "Hunting for a buried treasure?" she asked when Caleb came up beside her. For some reason, the question made him stutter.

"*N-neh.* You were sleeping and, and—"

"Was I snoring again?" she asked teasingly.

"*Neh.* But you were drooling."

Rose nudged him hard enough that he stumbled sideways in the water, catching his balance only by grabbing on to her forearm.

"If I take a dunk, you're going to take one, too!" He tugged her arm playfully, drawing her into deeper water, but she was utterly serious as she pleaded with him.

"*Neh*, please don't pull me out any farther. I don't know how to swim."

Caleb immediately released his grip. "You don't know how to swim?" He sounded astonished.

Rose figured fewer Amish people *could* swim than couldn't. "Don't make fun."

"I'm not making fun. I'm just amazed that you can't

swim, yet you have no fear of drown—of being out on the lake."

Rose shrugged. "I never said I have no fear of falling in. But I wear a life vest and I trust *Gott* to keep me safe."

Once again, Caleb was surprised by how Rose demonstrated her faith. He used to think she was reckless—foolish, even—for not being more cautious. But more and more he appreciated how she blended good sense, courage and trust in God's sovereignty. He was still going to watch out for her—that was why he made sure he could see her from where he'd been combing the shoreline—but he realized he might enjoy the rest of his summer more if he worried less.

Rose suggested it was time to go. Apparently, a few of this week's guests had special dietary needs and were preparing their own meals. Rose wanted to be available if they had questions about where to find things in the kitchen. Reluctantly Caleb brought the quilt and cooler down from the rock and loaded them into the rowboat. "Can we circle back the opposite way?"

"You're the captain," she said, giving him a sharp salute.

They took seats facing each other, their knees almost touching. As Caleb rowed, Rose dipped her fingers in the lake and then flicked them dry. Caleb had never noticed the freckles across her nose—or maybe they'd only come out today. When she glanced up and caught him studying her, Caleb smiled and fixed his eyes on a distant hill behind her.

"Two more weeks until the fish fry and canoe race," she reminded him as they approached Kissing Cove.

"And three more weeks until the end of the summer."

"Are you eager to get back to the *kinner*?"

"What *kinner*?"

"The *scholars*. The *kinner* you teach, remember them?"

"Oh!" Caleb pulled so hard on the oars he slipped forward and his knees tapped against Rose's. He stopped rowing but didn't slide back in the seat. His voice was husky when he said, "To be honest, I'm not looking forward to going back to *schul* yet. I don't want summer to end." *I don't want this* moment *to end.*

Rose's golden eyes held his gaze as she leaned slightly—almost imperceptibly—closer to him and nodded as if to show she understood. Or to show she felt the same way. *One kiss. Would it be so wrong for us to share a single kiss?* Caleb knew he couldn't cross that line, but neither could he pull away. He couldn't *look* away. He couldn't even blink. *Help me, Lord*, he desperately prayed. *I don't want to do anything to hurt Rose, but—*

At that second, two people emerged from the woods about fifty feet from where Caleb and Rose drifted in the rowboat. Caleb gestured toward them with his chin. "Looks like we have company."

Rose bounced abruptly backward in her seat and raised her hand, calling out a greeting. The man and woman looked right at Caleb and Rose, but instead of returning the greeting, they spun around, practically diving back into the woods.

"Was that *Eleanor*?"

"She looked tall enough to be," Caleb replied, hoping he was wrong. He could only imagine the rumors she'd spread about him and Rose sitting so close in the rowboat.

"I wonder why she didn't wave back to me."

"Maybe she was embarrassed to be caught in Kissing Cove with a man." The words were out of Caleb's mouth before he realized how hypocritical they sounded.

The irony apparently flustered Rose, too, because after slapping a mosquito on her shoulder, she said, "I really ought to get back to prepare supper for the guests. Can we cut across the lake instead of circling back in a loop?"

"Sure," Caleb agreed without pointing out today was the Sabbath and the guests had to fix their meals themselves.

Those two catnaps she'd stolen during the day must have refreshed Rose because on Sunday evening she lay awake until almost midnight without so much as yawning. She couldn't stop thinking about how Caleb had almost kissed her—*again!*—that afternoon in the rowboat. This time, she was as sure of it as she was of her own name.

Of course, in the end he *hadn't* acted on his desire, and Rose sensed it wasn't merely because they weren't courting. She even doubted it was the interruption by the couple coming out of the woods. Something else was holding him back from openly expressing his romantic feelings for her, and Rose figured it had to be he thought a long-distance courtship was too impractical. *Considering I'm about to make a long-term business investment and we live almost a thousand miles from each other, he's probably right*, Rose tried to convince herself.

She glanced at the glowing hands of the little clock on her nightstand. It was ten past twelve; one more day of her summer with Caleb was over. She closed her eyes—not to sleep, but to keep herself from crying.

On Monday when Helen arrived to pick up the pies, she surprised Rose by saying, "I heard you were very gracious when Oliver confessed he'd vandalized your produce stand."

Rose squinted at the woman. "How did you know about that? Were you the one who—"

Helen shrugged. "Those of us in Serenity Ridge's hospitality biz are pretty tight. We look out for each other. I might have mentioned what happened to your produce stand to Carol Graham, Oliver's mother. Seems Oliver tracked in raspberries on his shoes and stained their carpet twice this summer. Carol's husband is out of town, so she asked for her brother's help in handling the situation."

Rose giggled. "My *mamm* could always tell where my brothers had been by what they tracked into the house, too."

Helen tapped the side of her nose. "They call it woman's intuition, but a little observation can go a long way."

"Well, I appreciate your observation and your help. If there's something I can do to return the favor, please let me know."

"Can you stay here year-round and bake dessert for the inn?" Helen asked, causing Rose to chuckle. "Don't laugh—I'm serious. Several people posted comments about your pies online and now the guests ask what's for dessert the moment they arrive. I know you have family and work commitments in Pennsylvania, but I wish you could stay here permanently."

Rose wished it, too. In fact, it was almost all she thought about as the days slipped away. The closer the end of the week drew, the more Rose resented having to work to meet her financial goal. On Friday, as she began measuring ingredients for the next day's baking projects, Rose thought she'd gladly forfeit the café lease for an evening of canoeing or relaxing on the porch with Caleb, instead of having to wait until *Suundaag*.

The cell phone rang, interrupting Rose's moping. *Does someone honestly think we'll have a vacancy this late in the season?* But when she glanced at the display screen, she recognized the Ohio area code. Nancy and the twins wouldn't call on the business phone unless there was an emergency. Her hand shaking, Rose picked up the phone. "*Ant* Nancy?"

"*Jah.* It's me, Rose. I had to call right away to tell you—" A single sob cut Nancy's sentence short.

"It's about *Onkel* Sol, isn't it?" Rose didn't want either of them to have to say the word *died*.

"*Jah.*" Now it sounded as if Nancy was coughing— or laughing. Was she hysterical? Rose hoped the twins were with her. "The *dokder* said he's turned a corner! My Sol is going to be okay."

Rose gasped. "Praise *Gott*! Oh, praise *Gott*!" she

declared, laughing and crying at once, just as Nancy had been doing.

Her aunt gave her more details about Sol's recovery, saying he still had a long way to go and they wouldn't make it back to Serenity Ridge until after Labor Day. Then Rose briefly chatted with Hope and Charity. Afterward, she put away the flour and measuring cups and raced down the path to Caleb's cabin to tell him the good news and invite him up to the porch to celebrate with another piece of pie.

"I like the drawing Liam made for me," Caleb told Ryan when he called him on Saturday evening. He was looking at it as they spoke. It was a picture of two people in an SUV with camping gear and a canoe fastened to the roof rack. Liam had written "Uncle Caleb" and drawn an arrow to the man in the driver's seat, and had labeled the passenger Me.

"Tell him I can't wait to see him."

"Won't be long now. So, any news to report this week?"

"I'm afraid not." When he wasn't taking care of the grounds, cabins and gardens or helping Rose harvest berries and produce, Caleb had been re-searching the woods near the camp in an attempt to uncover something he'd missed earlier in the summer. On Thursday, since it was raining anyway, he'd even broken the staff rules and set out in the canoe after supper to hike the trails near Paradise Point, the one parcel of land he hadn't thoroughly explored yet. But the side trails were poorly marked and he'd spent as much time trying to get his bearings as he did looking for the coins. "I'm sorry I don't have more to show for my efforts, Ryan."

"Are you kidding? Regardless of the outcome, I can't thank you enough for all you've done. It means the world to me, although I understand why you might feel like you've wasted your summer."

"No. This summer has been..." Caleb couldn't say it had been the best summer of his life, knowing it had been the worst summer his brother had ever had. "Summer's not over yet. I'm going to keep searching. And re-searching."

"If you don't find the coins, you don't find them." Ryan sounded uncharacteristically nonchalant. "Either way, it's going to be okay."

Is he in denial? Doesn't he realize he could still go to prison and lose Liam? "How can you be so calm all of a sudden?"

"I guess because I've finally given the situation to God. He's sovereign and I have to trust His plan for me in all of this."

Caleb chuckled. "Rose often says something similar to that."

"Too bad she's Amish. A woman with faith like that is a treasure," Ryan remarked offhandedly. "Anyway, I'd better get Liam ready for bed. Enjoy the rest of your weekend."

"I will." *Just as soon as Rose and I get time alone together.*

Because Nancy and the girls wouldn't be back in time for the fish fry, a group of women, including Miriam, Jaala, Maria, Eleanor and Eleanor's mother, agreed to help Rose organize the event. They were meeting at Miriam's home, since it was centrally located, and Rose had left the camp in Eleanor's buggy right after the women finished doing the supper dishes.

Since Miriam's parents were visiting a sick relative in Unity, Miriam was left in charge of her five younger brothers. Rose offered to spend the night and help her take them to church in the morning. Caleb understood she was reciprocating the help Miriam and her mother had given her, but he still was disappointed. Riding to church with Rose was one of his favorite things to do and now he'd have to go alone. "Guess I better get used to it," he muttered to himself.

As grateful as she was for her neighbors and friends' help planning the fish fry menu and organizing the logistics during Nancy's absence, Rose found herself wishing they'd stop talking about every last detail. She wanted to go to bed. Not that she imagined she'd get much sleep at Miriam's house—her brothers had eaten such large servings of the spice cake Jaala brought they were bound to be awake for hours—but she wanted Sunday to arrive so she could go canoeing with Caleb. It was nearly nine o'clock when they finally wrapped up the meeting. It took the women an additional forty-five minutes to get out the door.

Which turned out to be fifteen minutes less than it took Rose and Miriam to get Miriam's brothers out the door the following morning. *Now I see why Miriam prefers to work in the dining hall over watching the* buwe,

Rose thought as the six of them raced across the lawn to take their seats before church began.

After tying a handkerchief into the shape of a rabbit to keep Miriam's youngest brother occupied during the sermon, Rose scanned the room until she located Caleb. He was at the end of the row to her right, sandwiched between Eleanor and Henry. Rose smiled when she noticed he was fidgeting. Was that because he felt trapped, or because he was as anxious for church to end as she was? Rose immediately repented of her irreverent thoughts, but she still wished she could trade places with Eleanor.

After lunch, Rose sneaked away from the kitchen before all the dishes had been dried and put away. She skittered outside to where Caleb was chatting with Henry and Isaiah Gerhart beneath a maple tree. After greeting both men, Rose pointed to a sinister bank of clouds in the western sky. "Looks like a storm is coming. You know how nervous thunder makes the *gaul*, Caleb. We ought to get going." In case Caleb didn't get the hint Rose wanted to leave, she added, "I left all the windows in the dining hall open, too. If we hurry, I can close them before the rain comes in."

"See? Rose agrees with me about the rain. You can't go out on the lake now," Henry said to Caleb. Then he explained to Rose, "I invited him to *kumme* play horseshoes with a group of us men but he said he's going canoeing."

"Ah, well, the rain hasn't actually started yet," Rose backpedaled. As if on cue, a crack of thunder echoed across the valley and raindrops spattered the maple leaves overhead.

"C'mon, Caleb. You can ride with me," Henry offered. "Isaiah can bring the others."

Maybe Rose and Caleb couldn't go canoeing, but they could play a board game or do a jigsaw puzzle on the porch. Feeling as if she and Henry were in a tug-of-war over Caleb, Rose smiled victoriously and asked, "You do know that people get just as wet playing horse-shoes in the rain as they do canoeing in the rain, don't you, Henry?"

"*Jah.* True," Henry said thoughtfully. "But if it's raining, *schmaert* people will play horseshoes in the barn. Only a *dummkopf* would try to paddle a canoe in one."

Isaiah cracked up and, to Rose's chagrin, Caleb's lips twitched, too. "Suit yourselves," she said, her cheeks hot. As she turned on her heel to leave, Caleb frowned and mouthed the words *I'm sorry.* It was a small consolation, but at least it showed he regretted not being able to spend the afternoon with her.

On the way home she considered stopping at the phone shanty to call her parents, but she decided against it. Rose was already sad about going home in a few weeks. If her mother tried to push a courtship with Baker on her again, Rose didn't know if she'd be able to hold her tongue—or fight back her tears.

By the time she unhitched the horse and put the buggy in the barn, the squall had already blown over. She wiped rainwater from the dining hall windowsills, and then returned to the main house and slumped into the armchair in the gathering room. *Maybe if I take a nap, when I open my eyes again it will be to see Caleb coming around the side of the* haus.

What she woke to was the sound of the window shade flapping against the panes. Rose glanced at the clock on the bookshelf; it was already four twenty! Caleb must be home by now, she thought as a rumble shook the house. Half a minute later, a torrential downpour pelted the roof and trees and ground. No, it was *hail* Rose saw bouncing off the porch steps. A sequence of flashes lit the air, followed instantly by a deafening crack. *I guess it's a* gut *thing we didn't go canoeing after all*, she admitted to herself.

That didn't mean she wanted to be stuck alone in the house for the rest of the evening. So when the precipitation turned back to rain, and the lightning and thunder subsided, Rose dashed to the cabin to see if Caleb had returned yet. The door was closed, but he didn't answer it when she knocked. Rose noticed rain was blowing sideways through the screen of the big picture window, so she stepped inside to close it. Once she'd unhooked the glass frame from the overhead beams, she swung it carefully forward on its hinge and clicked it shut. Then she retrieved a towel from the bathroom.

While she was mopping up the puddle, Rose noticed a couple of papers the wind must have blown to the floor. She picked them up carefully and as she laid them flat on the dresser to dry, she couldn't help glancing at them. One was a photo of a little boy in *Englisch* clothing and the other was a child's drawing of two figures in a car. They were labeled Me and Uncle Caleb. Caleb was the one driving.

Rose staggered backward and collapsed into the armchair. *There must be a logical explanation for this. There has to be.* She was breathing in tight, rapid gasps, and her heart thrummed audibly. No, that wasn't her heart. Rose listened closer and realized the dresser drawer was vibrating. She opened it and pushed aside a pair of socks to locate Caleb's phone. Rose didn't think twice about reading the text from Ryan, which said: Forgot to tell u last nite u got more mail from univ. Should I send it 2U ASAP? Hope u r taking a Sabbath from yr research. Talk 2U soon. Rose slammed the dresser shut.

Her ears were ringing so hard she didn't know Caleb had come through the door until he asked, "What are you doing in here?"

Rose seized the photo from the dresser top and waved it in front of Caleb's face. "Who is this?" she screeched.

"That's my nephew, Liam. I've told you about him," Caleb replied matter-of-factly. Gently, he took the picture from her fingers and set it on the dresser before slowly turning to face her again. He needed a moment to think of what to say next, but Rose fired another question at him.

"Is he *Englisch*?"

Caleb nodded dumbly. He'd never seen Rose's eyes blaze like that before.

"Are you?"

Caleb sucked in his breath and his eyes welled. He couldn't buy any more time. It was over. He was going to have to say it, the one word that would change everything between them. *"Jah."*

The look on Rose's face could have curdled milk. "Don't you dare speak *Deitsch* to me," she snarled and started for the door. Caleb stepped sideways, blocking her path.

"Rose, please. You don't understand," he implored.

"I understand perfectly. You're not the man I thought you were." She held her stomach and stared off to the side as if the sight of him was making her sick. "I expect you to pack your bags and leave by tomorrow morning or I'll have Abram over here faster than you can take off your *hut*," she threatened, and he didn't doubt she would. He still didn't budge.

"Please, Rose, just give me a chance—"

"No," she refused in *Englisch*, shoving past him.

He reached over her shoulder to press his palm against the door, holding it shut. Yes, he'd deceived Rose, which was undeniable, but she'd forgiven Baker. She'd forgiven Oliver. Yet she wouldn't demonstrate even a smidgen of grace toward Caleb, despite all he'd done for her. Despite everything they'd shared. "If you don't let me explain, then *you're* not the woman I thought you were," he said.

"Let me out of here. *Now*," she demanded, so he dropped his hand. As she stepped through the door, she sneered, "Goodbye, Caleb—or whoever you are."

Which made Caleb so furious if he'd had a pie right then he would have smashed it against the wall.

Chapter Eleven

Rose stomped up to the house, but instead of going inside she paced the porch, nearly as angry with herself as she was with Caleb. That big deceitful liar had been using her the whole time! This was just like what Baker had done. No. It was *worse* than what Baker had done because Baker only lied about money; Caleb lied about who he *was*.

Rose should have seen the evidence that had been right beneath her nose. Caleb's peculiar mannerisms and accent. The way he avoided certain questions and topics. His extensive knowledge of *Englisch* ways. He must have thought he was so clever, tricking her—tricking *all* the Amish people in Serenity Ridge—into believing he was Amish. They'd welcomed him into their homes and church. Into their *lives*. Had he no conscience whatsoever? What was it he hoped to gain by "researching" their community—a promotion at a university? Caleb hadn't struck Rose as someone who was motivated by wealth or prestige, the way some *Englischers* seemed to be. But then, she'd gotten everything else about him wrong, too.

The rain was letting up, but Rose's fury wasn't, so she strode down the driveway, thinking she should have shoved Caleb into the water when she'd had the opportunity at Relaxation Rock. She reached the end of the dirt road and turned onto the country highway, walking until her dress was soaked through with mist and sweat. Stickier, hotter and angrier than when she started out, she returned to the house and flopped onto the sofa in the gathering room. Rose would have preferred to sit on the porch, but she didn't want to risk seeing Caleb or him seeing her.

I won't have to worry about that after tomorrow, she thought. A new worry took root. What was she going to say when people asked where he was? Despite her threat to go to the deacon if Caleb didn't leave, Rose had no intention of telling the *leit* he was an *Englischer.* She couldn't bear the humiliation of admitting she'd been fooled, and she wanted to spare their feelings, too. She'd have to say he left because of a personal crisis, and leave it at that.

And what would she do for a groundskeeper until Labor Day? Even if Rose had the skill to manage the basic upkeep and make urgent repairs to the cabins, she didn't have the time. She was more determined now than ever to meet her financial goal, and every spare second would be devoted to baking pies and making jam. *I'm not going to let Caleb's behavior destroy my business the way Baker's did.* She decided she'd ask Abram if he'd put out the word she needed help.

As Rose went into the kitchen to make a sandwich, she thought she saw a flash of blue outside the window, but when she looked again nothing was there. *That's Caleb's influence on me.* She snickered. *Turns out he was the only intruder who'd ever been prowling around the property!*

Too steamed to stay cooped up in the little cabin, Caleb figured that, since it was his last day at the camp, he'd search the trails at Paradise Point, for what little good it would do. He'd come to believe the note was a complete ruse, but at least hiking would give him something to do besides stare out his window, stewing. As he climbed the steep incline, he remembered the day he'd suggested racing blindfolded and Rose had gotten so upset when the canoe cracked. He also recalled how peaceful he'd felt watching the fireworks display with her on the Fourth of July. Now she was infuriated with him again. It was as if their relationship had come full circle. He couldn't wait to get out of the loop and go home!

But as he stood at the crest of Paradise Point surveying the wet, green hills and lush valley below, Caleb reflected on the community he'd found in Serenity Ridge. Rose wasn't the only person he'd grown fond of here. What right did she have to push him out? Caleb had an obligation to Sol, and he wasn't going to let Rose stop him from fulfilling it. Not without a fight. So, when he returned to the cabin, instead of packing he decided to take a shower.

He was taking clean clothes from the drawer when

he noticed his cell phone was on top of his socks instead of beneath them. It didn't take much to figure out Rose must have read his texts, including the new one from Ryan that said, Hope u r taking a Sabbath from yr research. Caleb plunked himself into the armchair. *Rose probably thinks I'm here to conduct an anthropology experiment,* he brooded. It was one more reason he wanted the chance to explain.

After a few minutes of ruminating, he called his brother and asked him to read aloud the letter from the university. As Caleb suspected, it was a reminder to return his teaching contract or risk losing his fall course load. "Yeah, I guess I'd better take care of that," Caleb admitted.

"Before you go, I have to tell you about something Sheryl and I decided," Ryan said. "We've been praying a lot, and this afternoon we talked to our pastor and officially decided to stop the divorce proceedings."

Caleb was floored. "Are you serious?"

"Yeah. We finally realized it's time to stop fighting with each other and start fighting *for* our marriage." Ryan told him how they'd been going to counseling. They were still working on some issues, but he was moving home the following weekend. "Liam's overjoyed, of course."

Caleb expressed his happiness about the news, too, but after hanging up, he felt so low he crawled into bed even though it was barely dusk. Instead of water against the shore, all he could hear were the sounds of happy families laughing and chatting as they returned from wherever they'd spent the afternoon together. And because it reminded him of what he'd never had, he pulled a pillow over his head and turned toward the wall.

In the morning, Caleb rose extra early to milk the cow and complete his other chores as usual. He brought the milk to the house and knocked on the door, but Rose wouldn't open it until he left, so he set the pail down and went to the dining hall to wait for her inside the kitchen.

She flinched when she saw him leaning against the sink, but as she twirled to exit the room, he announced, "I have something to say, and I'll follow you around all day if I have to until you listen to me."

Rose stopped in her tracks; instead of facing him, she pulled a bowl from the cupboard. "Go ahead, but you're wasting your breath."

Caleb plunged ahead. "I admit I lied to you about who I was. I lied to everyone here. And on one hand, I'm very, very sorry."

"One hand?" Rose mocked, cracking an egg into a mixing bowl.

"*Jah*—yes, I'm sorry because it was ungodly and deceptive, and I can't even imagine how hurt and angry you must be, but…" Caleb poured out his whole story, speaking as quickly as he could. He expected Rose to meet his eyes or ask him a question or to otherwise show some sign she was listening, but her profile was impassive as she continued baking. By the time he was done, he'd confessed every lie, fib and evasive answer he'd ever told her. He ended by saying, "I know it's asking a lot for you to forgive me, Rose, but I'm begging you to try to understand. You have to believe me when I say I didn't do it to hurt you—I did it to help my brother. And my nephew."

"I understand perfectly." She picked up a wooden spoon and dipped it in the bowl. "Now, please leave the camp."

Rose's abrupt response hurt, but Caleb was prepared for it. *"Neh."*

Rose stopped stirring. "If you leave now, I won't tell anyone about your...*identity*. If you don't leave, I'll go straight to Abram. Everyone in the community will find out. You might not care what the *leit* think of you, but eventually gossip will spread to the *Englischers*. The police will find out you're an impostor, and that won't reflect well on your brother."

Caleb was undeterred. "I committed to working here until the day after Labor Day, and that's what I want to do. And since you owe me a favor, you're going to let me stay."

"I'll do no such—"

"You gave me your word, Rose."

She snorted. "And you think I'll keep my word just because I'm Amish?"

"Neh. Because your *onkel* is ill and there's a community event coming up. And because I still want to help *you* meet your goal—"

"Liar!" Rose shrieked, spinning to face him. "You want to stay so you can look for some stupid ancient coins that can't even be used for currency anymore!"

Caleb couldn't blame Rose for distrusting him, but he winced at being called a liar. *"Neh.* I've given up looking for the coins. I want to stay *in spite* of knowing I'm not going to find them."

Rose turned her back to him again. She was stirring frenziedly. Finally she allowed, "If you stay, you are to remain out of my sight. I will not eat with you. I will not talk to you. And you aren't ever to discuss your... your *identity* with anyone else here. Agreed?"

It's as if I'm under the Bann *and I'm not even Amish.* "Agreed," Caleb said.

On Tuesday, the second evening Caleb didn't show for supper, Eleanor came into the kitchen where Rose was drying the last dish and inquired, "Caleb's not really still outside harvesting potatoes, is he? You two had a lovers' quarrel?"

"Stop saying such things," Rose warned her through gritted teeth. "Or I'll tell everyone you were alone with a man in the woods near Kissing Cove the other day."

"I was *not*," Eleanor protested adamantly before scuttling into the dining hall to help Maria wipe down the tables.

Rose didn't know what, when or where Caleb was eating, but she was glad he kept his word and didn't come to the dining hall at mealtime and avoided her throughout the day, too. She was mostly glad anyway. As the week wore on, there were short-lived moments when her acrimony toward him softened enough so that some small part of her hoped he'd approach her again. She hoped he'd say he was playing a joke that went too far and he really was Amish after all. It was the same kind of wishful thinking that made her long to turn back time to when she still believed he wanted to kiss her...

Then she'd be disgusted with herself for entertaining the thought and even more disgusted with Caleb for toying with her emotions. With God's grace and a lot of prayer, she'd eventually forgive him for that, and for the other ways he'd betrayed her trust. Meanwhile she poured her energy into earning the three hundred dollars she still needed for the lease, while also serving guests at the camp.

The week seemed to last a month but finally Saturday arrived: August 27, the day of the fish fry and canoe race. As Rose waited for Helen to pick up her order near the produce stand, she remembered Jaala suggesting Rose and Caleb should pair up for the canoe race. *I hope she doesn't say anything to him about that this afternoon*, Rose fretted.

"I won't see you again before you leave, but Sally will be here on Monday morning to collect the order," Helen said after they'd put the pies in her trunk. Rose had forgotten Helen and her husband were going to Europe for three weeks. The *Englischer* gave Rose a small envelope, as well as a hug, and Rose waved until Helen's car disappeared around the bend. Then she hustled back to help Miriam and Eleanor check guests out and clean the cottages.

It seemed the last *Englisch* family had just driven away when the first Amish families rolled up the dirt road. There was a flurry of activity as the women brought food into the dining hall and the men set up charcoal grills outdoors. Because the Unity settlement was also invited, Rose didn't know half of the people in attendance, and she tried to guess which young boy Hope had expressed interest in. *It's too bad the twins can't be here. They were really looking forward to this*, she was thinking as Jaala approached.

"Are you going to join the canoe race?" she asked, just as Rose feared she would. "The last teams to race are taking their places now."

"*Neh*. I need to help fry the fish." The men who were participating in the tournament had been on the lake since the wee hours of the morning and they were starting to come back now. It was their responsibility to clean what they caught and then the women would prepare the fish for frying.

"You've been making meals for guests all summer— let someone else do it for a change. Go join the *schpass*."

Rose didn't want to take part in the race, for fear she'd see Caleb. Since this was a relay, he was helping transport participants to their designated locations on the lake. She figured as long as she stayed near the dining hall they wouldn't cross paths. But Henry had overheard Rose's conversation with Jaala, and he pestered Rose to be his partner until she finally relented.

The teams consisted of four members, with one female and one male racing together in each canoe. Five canoes raced at a time, for a total of twenty participants in the race, and teams wore matching colored arm bands to identify themselves.

The race began at Relaxation Rock. From there, the teams paddled past Kissing Cove and in between the two islands. When they reached the shoreline near the trailhead for Paradise Point, the first pairs of partners would get out and hand off their canoes to their team-mates. The second pairs then raced back to the camp, leaving the first group behind to be picked up later.

Isaiah Gerhart used the rowboat to transport Henry and Rose to the area of shoreline below Paradise Point. While they were waiting for Abram to bring the last pair of racers over from the camp, Rose sat on a fallen log beside Henry. Maria and Otto, as well as Levi and Sadie Swarey, were also racing and the four of them perched on the edge of the embankment, dangling their bare feet into the lake. Another young couple Rose didn't recognize—they were likely from Unity—stood off to the side in the shade without talking to anyone else.

"Here comes the fifth team," Maria said, pointing to the water. To Rose's discomfort, Isaiah was ferrying Eleanor and Caleb across the lake.

Once Eleanor came ashore, she taunted Henry and Rose, "I know we can beat at least *one* team here, can't we, Caleb?"

We'll see about that. Irritated, Rose walked over to speak to the couple standing by themselves. Pointing to the small cooler the man gripped in his hand, she re-marked lightly, "You brought your own supper? Your team won't take *that* long to get here, will they?"

She'd only been joking, but the man frowned with-out answering and the blonde woman with him averted her gaze. Rose realized there was something about her that seemed familiar. Rose was about to ask if she was related to someone in Serenity Ridge or if she'd visited their church when Eleanor began to clap and shout.

"Here they *kumme!* I see yellow—that's our team, Caleb!"

"Ours is right behind them. Quick, Rose, get over here." Henry beckoned.

As she and the couple from Unity joined the others on the edge of the embankment, the men began hollering and whistling at the incoming canoes.

Eleanor cupped her hands over her mouth and shouted, "Go, go, go!"

The woman from Unity copied her and the two of them elbowed their way in front of Rose as they vied for position nearest the water. They were both even taller than she was, so Rose had to stand on her tiptoes to see how her teammates were faring. As she peeked over the blonde woman's shoulder, Rose's eyes registered something odd before her mind could process what she was seeing. There was a tiny hole in the woman's ear, as if from a piercing. *I shouldn't judge*, she scolded herself. *I did things on my* rumspringa *I regret now, too.*

There was a commotion as Caleb and Eleanor's teammates got out of the canoe and Caleb and Eleanor got in. Rose and Henry's teammates arrived right behind them, and the blonde woman and her partner's crew came next. Rose's skirt got soaked to her knees as she helped her teammates out of the canoe, but she didn't care. She was so intent on beating Caleb and Eleanor she looped her life vest around her neck but didn't take time to buckle it. "Go, Henry, go!" she urged as she picked up her paddle.

Henry must have wanted to defeat his sister as much as Rose wanted to defeat Caleb, because he paddled with a ferocity Rose didn't know he possessed. Ten strokes later they were within two canoe lengths of catching up.

"We're gaining on them!" Rose exclaimed. Suddenly their canoe was jolted from behind to the right and Rose had to grab on to the side with her free hand to keep her balance. As she and Henry lost momentum, the blonde woman and her partner pulled ahead of them.

"Oops, sorry," the woman said, grinning facetiously as her canoe overtook Rose and Henry's.

Her brilliant smile reminded Rose of diamonds and suddenly she realized why her ears were pierced: she was Julia, the woman who'd requested a tour of the waterfront earlier that season. All at once, everything clicked. *The coins! The cooler! Paradise Point!* Rose's reflexes kicked in and she leaped to her feet.

"Caleb!" she screamed. Eleanor kept paddling, but Caleb gave Rose a backward glance.

"Stop them!" Rose bellowed, frantically waving her paddle as Julia and her partner headed in the direction of Relaxation Rock instead of toward the camp. "They've got the coins. They're going to—"

Before she could complete the thought, Rose toppled sideways, shattering the surface of the water like glass.

Even over his shoulder, Caleb had noticed Rose's life vest wasn't fastened around her chest, but before he could warn her to sit down, she foundered. In one swift motion, he stood, twisted around and discarded his own vest before hurtling himself off the back of the canoe. Caleb cut through the water as if his arms and legs were fins, and he didn't come up for air until he was within twenty feet of Rose. She was thrashing violently with one arm, and with the other she clung to the life vest, which was bunched up beneath her ears. Henry must have dropped his paddle because he was using his arms like oars to row toward Rose. Caleb reached her first.

"Relax. Let the vest do the work," he said. He gripped her by the arm to stop her from flailing. "Here, let's get this buckled—"

It took some wrestling with the straps, but once the vest was properly secured around her torso, Caleb pulled Rose back toward land. By then, the other racing teams had arrived and a couple men waded into the lake up to their chests so they could usher Rose and Caleb the rest of the way in. Eleanor must have fished Henry's paddle out of the water for him because the brother and sister pulled to shore in their canoes a minute later.

"I know you wanted to distract us but jumping overboard was a *lappich* thing to do just to win a race," Eleanor joked, clearly oblivious to what Rose had yelled about the coins.

Caleb waited for Henry to pipe up, but he must not have heard, either, because he busied himself with squeezing water from his pant cuffs without saying a word. *Must have been the shouting from shore drowned out Rose's voice, or else it was because she was facing away from him...*

"I guess I got overly excited," Rose said. "Sorry I frightened everyone."

Was she protecting herself from getting involved, or protecting him from the public humiliation of having his identity exposed? Either way, Caleb was grateful Rose didn't say anything else.

"I think you frightened Caleb the most," Sadie Swarey commented. "He's shaking."

Her husband replied, "He's probably cold. We should get back to the camp so Rose and Caleb can change their clothes."

"There's not enough room for all of us to go at once," Maria pointed out. "I wonder why that other couple took off for Relaxation Rock."

"They weren't from Serenity Ridge so they probably got mixed-up about where they were supposed to go," Rose said, further confirming she had no intention of disclosing Caleb's secret. "They'll *kumme* back when they realize their mistake."

Caleb knew as well as she did if they really were the thieves, the couple wouldn't come back. Most likely, they'd already abandoned the canoe and run through the woods to where they had a car waiting on the main road. By the time Caleb returned to the camp they'd probably be halfway to Canada. While it grieved him to know they were getting away, there was virtually nothing he could do to stop them now, short of involving law enforcement agencies. But the very idea of them disrupting the Amish community's celebration or bringing Rose into the station to tell them what she knew made his stomach turn. Caleb had promised her he wouldn't go to the police and he was going to honor his word. He owed Rose that much; he owed all the *leit* of Serenity Ridge that much.

Gott, please don't let the thieves get away, Caleb

prayed simply as Levi ferried him and two other passengers back to the camp. He made the same silent request throughout the evening, which passed in a blur. And after everyone left and he retired to his cabin, Caleb knelt beside his bed and asked again, *Please don't let them get away.*

While he was praying, someone knocked on the door and he opened his eyes, expecting to see a straggler from the fish fry, but it was Rose.

He'd barely stepped outside before she asked, "Did you hear what I shouted before I fell in?"

He nodded. "You told me to stop them. You said they had the coins."

Rose threw her hands in the air. "Then why didn't you go after them? After everything you went through to come here—and after everything *I* went through because you came—you threw it all away? That was just plain *dumm*! You should have chased them, Caleb. Then at least all of your…your *deception* wouldn't have been for nothing!"

In the pause following Rose's tirade, Caleb thought about Ryan saying he and Sheryl had decided to stop fighting each other and start fighting for their marriage. Caleb and Rose weren't married, but they'd had a friendship—a close relationship—that was worth fighting for, too. "I came back because of you, Rose. I was afraid you'd drown." He mustered his courage and added, "I couldn't imagine anything worse."

Rose's lips parted in disbelief. She shook her head. "I had my life vest. I would have been fine."

"It wasn't fastened, so I couldn't be sure of that."

She let her arms go limp at her sides. "Well, *denki* for pulling me to shore."

"*Denki* for trying to help me stop the thieves. You didn't have to do that, either."

"I didn't think it would be fair to your brother if they got away just because I was mad at you." Rose smiled weakly before asking, "Have you called the police?"

"*Neh.* I'm not going to, either."

Rose looked at him askance. "If you expect *me* to go to them—"

"I don't expect you to. I'd *appreciate* it if you went— and so would Ryan—but I respect your decision not to and I trust *Gott* will work the situation out," he told her. "But will you at least tell *me* why you believe they were the thieves?"

A smug smile played at Rose's lips. She described how she'd noticed the woman's ears were pierced and then recognized her as being Julia, posing as an Amish woman. How she'd realized it was likely the same woman they'd seen with a man near Kissing Cove, and the same woman Oliver's friend told the twins he'd spotted in the woods near the camp carrying a shovel. "What else would she be searching and digging for except the coins?"

Caleb was skeptical. "But what makes you think she found them today?"

"The man with her was carrying a cooler."

"It might have been their supper."

"Not likely. They wouldn't have taken off so fast in the other direction if all they were hiding was a ham sandwich." They both chuckled and then Rose said,

"Besides, when you consider the Bible verse on the note your brother received, it makes perfect sense the coins were buried at Paradise Point."

"What do you mean?"

"'Lay up for yourselves treasures in heaven,'" Rose quoted the first part of Matthew 6:20. "*Paradise* is another name for heaven. *Paradise* Point… Get it?"

"Wow. I never made that connection." Caleb still had a lot of unanswered questions, especially about who'd sent the note to his brother, but now he was absolutely convinced Rose was right; Julia and her partner had definitely made off with the coins. "Hey, do you think they were the ones who pushed our canoe in the water on the Fourth of July?"

"*Neh.* The waves carried it off."

"Waves? The waves weren't big enough—" Caleb objected before he realized she was teasing him, almost like old times.

Rose sighed. "This was a long day, so I'll let you get some sleep now."

Caleb was tempted to ask if he could accompany her to church one last time but that would be like asking her to pretend she didn't know he was *Englisch.* "Good night," he said instead. "I'll see you…around."

When the full realization of what Caleb had sacrificed for her sank in, Rose pressed her face into her pillow to muffle her sobbing. It wasn't only that he'd let the thieves go in order to pull her from the water that made her weep; it was the hundreds of ways he'd helped her and demonstrated kindness and affection all summer.

The thought of being without Caleb in her life was, as Maria had put it, splintering Rose's heart to pieces, and she cried herself to sleep.

The next morning, as she was preparing for church, she found the card Helen had given her on the desk in the hall. She opened it to read: *"Rose, here's a small token of appreciation for making this the sweetest season the inn has ever experienced. Remember my offer— I'm sure our guests would relish your apple, pumpkin and mincemeat pies, too!"* Helen had enclosed five hundred dollars in cash, which was over two hundred dollars more than what Rose needed for the lease, and she was simultaneously filled with gratitude for the gift and grief about returning to Pennsylvania.

As she tucked the money away, a man called her name through the screen door. It was Henry, and his round face was more serious than she'd ever seen it. After she joined him on the porch, he said, "There's something that's been weighing on my heart lately and I can hardly bear it any longer. I need you to listen carefully before you tell me *neh*."

Ach! Is he going to ask to court me? "Okay, I'll try."

"This spring I, uh… I was hunting by Paradise Point and I saw something—someone. I saw two people, a man and a woman, and they were digging—"

Rose gasped. So he *had* heard what she'd yelled about the coins yesterday, even though afterward he'd feigned ignorance. "You know about the thieves, don't you?"

"Jah." He hung his head. "After Eleanor told me about the FBI interviews, I did some research at the

library. I felt so bad when I read about the man from the museum being suspended from his job. I wanted to speak up, but I was afraid—I'd already been in trouble with the game warden for hunting after hours. I rationalized that since the FBI didn't question me directly, I didn't need to report what I saw. But I felt so guilty I sent an anonymous note, a clue. I was constantly worried about you and the twins. I kept trying to return to the Point to see if the coins were there. I figured once they were gone, I wouldn't have to worry anymore."

"Oh! So *that's* why you kept hanging around. I thought it was because…"

"Because I *liked* you? Eleanor may have told you that, but frankly, Rose, you're kind of old for me," he said, which made her giggle. "Besides, I thought Caleb was secretly courting you—until yesterday when you called out to him on the lake, I didn't know he was connected to the coins. He has the same name as the man from the museum—Miller. It's a common name, but… are they related? Is he… Is Caleb *Englisch*?"

Rose nodded, confirming Henry's guess. After the summer she'd had, she was only mildly surprised by what Henry had confided. "I hope you feel better now that you've gotten that off your chest." *I also hope I can convince you not to tell the* leit *that Caleb isn't Amish.* Rose wanted to protect his identity, at least until he left Serenity Ridge.

"A little," he said. "But I think it's time I talk to the law enforcement agencies… And I think, uh—"

"*Jah*, of course. I'll go, too." It was easy for Rose to complete his thought; she'd been thinking the same thing all morning. "You do understand we might get in trouble with the law for not coming forward sooner, right?"

"*Gott* is sovereign. We'll ask for Him to work everything out to His glory and our *gut*."

They agreed to go to the police station together after church. Rose couldn't wait to tell Caleb herself.

Caleb stared out the window, astounded. He'd just gotten off the phone with Ryan, who'd called to report the FBI had apprehended "Julia" and her partner on the other side of Relaxation Rock. Apparently, the agency had been biding its time to catch the two thieves red-handed so prosecutors wouldn't have to rely on the testimonies of reluctant Amish witnesses in court.

"Was she someone you knew at work?"

"Nope. She posed as a temporary cleaning lady. She didn't have a key card but apparently she used mine. That's why the agents thought I was involved. Supposedly she's known to be quite the master of disguise."

I'm not, Caleb thought mournfully after he ended the call with his brother. He was watching sunlight dance on the water, imagining Rose heading to church alone in the buggy, when she appeared at his door. Before he could even cross the tiny room to open it, she was telling him Henry was the person who had sent the anonymous note and that they both intended to go to the police. Caleb shook his head in protest, but Rose insisted.

"It's my turn to help you and your *familye* the way you've helped me and mine."

"That's very thoughtful, but it's not necess—"

"I *want* to do it, Caleb. I should have gone yesterday. I'm so sorry I didn't." Her eyes welled with contrition.

"*Neh*, I mean it's not necessary to do. They caught the thieves on the other side of the lake. Ryan's name has been cleared."

"That's *wunderbaar!*" Rose exclaimed and promptly burst into tears. At first Caleb thought she was over-wrought with relief, but when she covered her face with her arm and cried so hard she gasped, it seemed the most natural thing in the world for Caleb to draw her to his chest.

"Rose? What is it?"

"*Gott* forgive me but I can't stand the thought of being without you in my life," she wailed, holding on to him as tightly as she'd clung to the life vest the day before. Or maybe he was the one clinging to her.

"Does that mean you've forgiven me?"

Rose dropped her arms and took two steps back. In the moment before she answered, Caleb wondered whether she could hear his heart imploding. Then she looked him in the eye and said the one word that would change everything between them.

"*Jah.*"

Epilogue

After the wedding service, Abram and Jaala wished Rose and Caleb blessings in their marriage. "I probably shouldn't say this because I don't want to embarrass him," Abram confided, "but I knew Caleb's secrets from the start."

"You knew he was *Englisch*?" Rose wondered why the deacon hadn't warned her.

"*Neh*. I knew he cared deeply for you and the girls. I knew what a hard worker he was and that he desired a stronger relationship with *Gott*."

"He hasn't changed much since then," Rose said, squeezing her husband's hand. "Except for becoming Amish, I mean."

"And I hardly ever forget when to take my *hut* off or put it on anymore," Caleb joked.

After Abram and Jaala went to the dessert table, Nancy and Sol approached. "You're looking strong," Rose said to her uncle.

"Selling you and Caleb the camp was one of the best

decisions we ever made. My health is better, I'm closer to the clinic and Nancy is *hallich* to be living near her sisters again. Even the *meed* have adjusted well, especially because they get to *kumme* back here and help you during the summers."

When Nancy and Sol excused themselves, Liam came over and announced, "I like this *hochzich*, Ant Rose. And your *haus.*"

"*Denki,*" she said. "Who taught you to speak *Deitsch*?"

"*Onkel* Caleb."

"Your accent is even better than his was when he first came here."

Liam looked at Rose with big eyes. "Will people think I'm Amish, too?"

"*Neh,*" Caleb told his nephew. "We'll make sure they know from the start you're *Englisch*. We don't want to trick anyone, do we?"

"*Neh*, but I still need to learn more words so I can talk to the other kids when I come here to go camping in the spring."

"I know someone who can help you with that," Caleb said. He touched Rose's elbow. "I'll be right back. I'm going to introduce him to David and Elizabeth Swarey."

Meanwhile, Rose's mother sidled up beside her. "Such a beautiful smile you're wearing," she said, cupping her daughter's chin in her hand.

"*Denki, Mamm,*" she said. *It's the smile of a woman who has no regrets...*

* * * * *

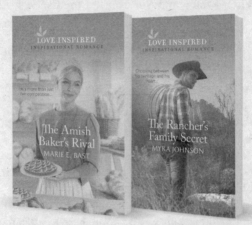

SPECIAL EXCERPT FROM

❧

LOVE INSPIRED
INSPIRATIONAL ROMANCE

*To heal from a past tragedy, Emily Carver and
service dog Lady have devoted themselves to teaching
children—including new school handyman
Dev McCarthy's troubled son. But Landon reminds
her too much of her own mistakes. Can Emily possibly
risk her heart again?*

Read on for a sneak peek at
Her Easter Prayer *by Lee Tobin McClain,
part of the* K-9 Companions *series!*

She leaned back, watching him.

Curiosity about this man who could make the best of
a difficult childhood—and who actually owned a garlic
press—flashed through her, warm and intense. She didn't
want to be nosy, shouldn't be. His childhood wasn't her
business, and she ought to be polite and drop the subject.

But this man and his son tugged at her. The more she
learned about them, the more she felt for them. And maybe
part of it was to do with Landon, with his being the same age
her son would have been, but that wasn't all of it. They were
a fascinating pair. They'd come through some challenges,
Dev with his childhood and both of them with a divorce,
and yet they were still positive. She really wanted to know
how, what their secret was. "Did you grow up in the Denver
area or all over?"

"Denver and the farm country around it." He slid the
bread into the oven. "How about you?"

"Just a few towns over on the other side of the mountain." Indeed, she'd spent most of her life, including her married life, in this part of the state.

He didn't volunteer any more information about himself and Landon, so she didn't press. Instead, she leaned down and showed Landon Lady's favorite spot to be scratched, right behind the ears. Now that they weren't working anymore, he was talkative and happy, asking her a million questions about the dog.

It was hard to leave the kitchen, cozy and warm, infused with the fragrances of garlic and tomato and bread. Her quiet home and the can of soup she'd likely heat up for dinner both seemed lonely after being here. But she had her own life and couldn't mooch off theirs. "I'd better let you men get on with your dinner," she said and started gathering up her books.

"You want to stay?" Dev asked.

The question, hanging in the air, ignited danger flares in her mind.

The answer was obvious: yes, she did want to stay. But an Unwise! Unwise! warning message seemed to flash in her head.

Spending even more time with Dev and Landon was no way to keep the distance she knew she had to keep. As appealing as this pair was, she couldn't risk getting closer. Her heart might not survive the wrenching away that would have to happen, sooner rather than later.

Don't miss
Her Easter Prayer *by Lee Tobin McClain,*
available April 2022 wherever
Love Inspired books and ebooks are sold.

LoveInspired.com

LIEXP0222

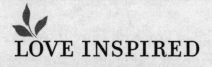

LOVE INSPIRED

Stories to uplift and inspire

Fall in love with Love Inspired—
inspirational and uplifting stories of faith
and hope. Find strength and comfort in
the bonds of friendship and community.
Revel in the warmth of possibility and the
promise of new beginnings.

Sign up for the Love Inspired newsletter
at **LoveInspired.com** to be the first
to find out about upcoming titles,
special promotions and exclusive content.

CONNECT WITH US AT:

 Facebook.com/LoveInspiredBooks

Twitter.com/LoveInspiredBks